DEE

THE DIARY OF A MERCHANT SHIP AND HER CREW
during
The Battle of the Atlantic
1942

A.C.Gyles
Copyright © 1998

Fiction

```
Lest we forget the two out of
  every three merchant seamen
who during the first years of war
       never made port
```

A POD BOOK

Published by P.O.D. Publishing
145 Springdale Road, Corfe Mullen, Dorset
England

On behalf of

COPYRIGHT © Tony Gyles 1998

All rights reserved. No part of this publication may be reproduced, stored in a retrieval system or transmitted in any form or by any means, electronic, photocopying, recording or otherwise, without the permission of the copyright holder.

ISBN: 0 953 1737 1 2

This book was designed by P.O.D. Publishers on behalf of the copyright holder and produced and printed in the UK by:

The Basingstoke Press
Hampshire, England

DEEP THEIR GRAVE

Born in 1925 Tony Gyles was educated at Bristol Grammar and Chard. He preferred sport to learning and dodged his final exams by going to sea in April 1942 as a saloon-boy.

Originally destined for Dartmouth, poor eyesight diverted him instead to an M.N. radio college in 1943 after which he volunteered for Navy duty, ending up in the P.O.'s mess as a radar mechanic.

After demob and another spell in college he took up civil flying as radio officer/navigator finding himself in Kenya in 1947. In 1949 he obtained a coastal mate's ticket and went fishing for a couple of years, until joining the Kenya Police. He served with distinction during the war against the Mau Mau.

In 1961, unable to afford the sea passage for his wife and family of five children, he took them and their dog on the round trip to Britain by road, via the Sahara, repeating the journey when they finally left Kenya in 1963.

After 'messing about' in the pub and hotel trade he returned to the sea in 1972, obtaining a Master's ticket in 1976 and rising to Mate with a German company before joining the Fremantle Port Authority in Australia as tanker safety officer.

Tony built his own house 'out in the sticks' at a place called Jarrahdale where he competes in combined driving and scurry events with his Caspian pony - and spends his leisure time writing, with the help of his wife of 51 years. His incredibly full and varied life has equipped him well to write with conviction about the subjects he knows best.

PROLOGUE

In previous wars bringing up supplies to the front was done with baggage trains pulled by horses. Although the Germans made much use of horses in World War II, for the Allies it was the merchant ship which became the hub of the war wheel. Without them the war would have been lost before it had really started, and indeed there was a time in late 1942 when Britain was on the brink of starvation both for food and materials and in danger therefore of defeat.

Whilst air and land battles and major naval engagements were much in the news, little was mentioned of the daily struggle which went on with such ferocity over the lifeline of the seas.

On land and in the air 18 was the lowest age for combat, but at sea, both in the Royal and Merchant Navies, boys as young as 15 could be found. In both these fleets these boys accepted the wildest perils of the sea and faced death or mutilation alongside men of every age, some old enough to be their grandfathers.

In June 1942, at a far greater rate then either ships or crew could be replaced, the enemy sank one merchant ship every four hours. Come what may ships and their crews had to sail, for if they did not, in the words of Prime Minister Winston Churchill, "Then truly, Europe would be plunged into the abyss of a new dark age."

This is the story of one of those ships and the crew who sailed in her. It is the story of their life at sea and ashore, of their perils and laughter, of their drunkenness and sobriety during the dark and savage days when men and boys went down to the sea in ships and fought and died and endured. Days which, in that frightful year, came to be known as `The Battle of the Atlantic'.

Although convoy WS 25 probably did sail for African ports sometime in nineteen forty two it is not the convoy of this story and the names of the characters, ships and their escorts are fictitious.

In memory of the following ships:

M.T. NARAGANZA
lost with all hands 1942.

M.T. ROBERT F. HAND
lost with all hands 1942.

M.V. ARDENVOA
lost 1942, Cabin-boy missing.

There but for the grace of God.....

DEEP THEIR GRAVE

They that go down to the sea in ships,
that do business in great waters;
These see the works of the Lord,
and His wonders of the deep.
PSALM 107
verse 23, 24

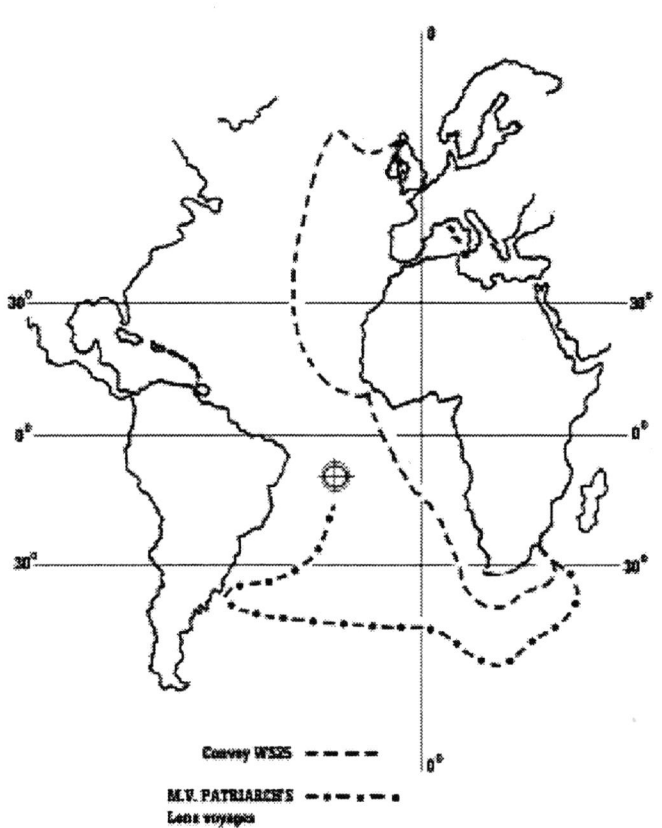

VII

CHAPTER ONE
AUGUST 1942
SOUTH ATLANTIC

The sky was rapidly becoming lighter. He lay stiff and uncomfortable fore-and-aft along the hard slatted seats which topped the 'boat's floatation tanks, his eyes level with the top rivet of the after knee, on the last but one thwart. Now once again the rivet began its upward journey.

During the last seven days he'd studied, and would never forget as long as he lived, every battered rivet just visible under the coats of grey paint. In between talking with the others and asking questions of old Father Neptune, studying those rivets had helped to pass the time.

Soon one of the others would tell him it was his turn to take the tiller and search the endless expanse of water with its horizon they never seemed to reach. At their present rate it would be weeks before they reached land, but there just might be that tiny speck which would grow larger and take the form of a ship to rescue them from the edge of eternity. Only then would he stop counting. Meanwhile the boat was rolling on the slight swell, the starboard side rising into the air, seeming to touch a lonely puff of cloud far above them, before once again rolling slowly back the other way - for the ninetieth time since he'd woken.

He rolled his eyes to look at the others; not a difficult task since the lifeboat was only twenty one feet long. He wondered whether he looked as much of a ruffian as they did with their creased and grimy clothes. The salt air had matted the nurse's hair into rat's tails, which she'd attempted to tie in a ponytail with a piece of her belt. His hair was still relatively tidy for, like all the stewards, he kept a comb in his pocket. The quartermaster, reverently referred to as Father Neptune, and second officer were luckier, they still had their caps which protected their hair and faces. But the second officer had on a pair of shorts, unlike the other three who had been in long trousers when they took to the boats, and his thighs were badly sunburned and blistered, as were the cheeks and noses of the nurse and the boy.

Ninety one! There was no wind so the sails were not hoisted to prevent unnecessary wear. Each time the lifeboat rolled the halyards would slap against the mast with a sort of `shuss-pah' sound. There'd been no wind since yesterday morning so three of them had to row while the other steered. The nurse said they should rest for ten minutes each hour. She also made them cut a strip from their clothing to wrap around their hands to try to reduce the blistering.

The saloon-boy had learnt to row at Weymouth one summer holiday and only last summer had taken a girl friend out in a skiff at Saltford. He thought he was quite good at it but when he'd taken up the lifeboat oar and shipped it in the crutch that first time it seemed ten times as heavy as anything he had handled before. Now, after each stint, it felt as if his arms had been separated from their sockets, added to a sore backside and numerous other aches.

Now he was remembering: how they had watched the raider pick up the rest of the Patriarch's crew from the 'boats around the sinking launch, seemingly unaware of the accident-boat's stealthy departure towards the approaching dusk.

When darkness had overtaken them the second officer stopped the motor whilst he and the quartermaster decided on the course to be taken come daylight. It was in the first light of dawn that the rowing had started.

"Best keep what little diesel we 'ave for when we sights a ship or nears the shore," Mister Baines, the gravelly voiced quartermaster had declared. Despite the presence of the second officer he seemed to have taken command of the tiny boat. "I think we oughter row back over the way we came last night 'case Jerry left someone behind like. Anyways that be the way we want t'go so, young Dick, get that oar out and you too Mr.McTavish. You take the tiller here Miss and I'll do a bit of rowing me-self". And so they had rowed back several miles until they came to the four empty lifeboats.

They went alongside each in turn taking from them the rations and whatever Mr.Baines thought might be useful to augment their own scanty supplies. By the time they left the last one and scoured the floating debris from the launch a light breeze had sprung up. They hoisted the heavy red canvas sails and headed westwards. Not long afterwards they came across a vast amount of flotsam from the ship which had, only yesterday, been their home. They searched in vain for their captain until, with heavy hearts, they left that melancholy bit of ocean and sailed in the direction of South America.

Richard Wentle, the saloon-boy, had listened the previous night as the second officer and quartermaster discussed their predicament. Both had agreed that the South East Equatorial current would bear them westwards. From the last sun-line bearing, coupled with the midday altitude the Second had known their position to within a couple of miles. He reckoned that there were about 750 of them to go to the nearest land, Brazil.

The nurse had been puzzled as to how, with no instruments other than the boat's compass and his watch, the Patriarch's navigating officer would know where they were. Now, after a week of noting the time when the sun was due north, giving them a vague idea of their longitude, they could only guess at how far they had come.

The first twenty four hours in the 'boat had passed without too much hardship for Richard Wentle, apart from suffering acute embarrassment at having to use a baler as a piss-pot in front of the others, particularly the girl. It was all very well doing it up in the bows but noises still carried. Also during that first day the hunger had not been too bad for, as usual, he had eaten well the previous lunch time. Now, rationed to a dipper of water morning and night and a biscuit, Horlicks tablet and a spoonful of condensed milk twice a day, he suffered continuous hunger pangs. On the second day he had been seasick. The motion of the small boat was totally different from that of the big ship and now he felt continuous nausea.

The only saving grace for not having enough to eat was that the makeshift piss-pot was hardly used. Since his bum was very sore he thanked God for that small mercy. Toilet rolls did not feature in lifeboat emergency supplies and seawater was not a good substitute. The ever present smell of the rime of salt on the gun'les didn't help either.

To keep their minds off their predicament they each took turns to speak on any subject for fifteen minutes. At some stage it had come up in conversation that he had studied some Shakespeare and appeared in a school play as Mark Anthony. Consequently he'd had to quote as much as he could remember, closing his eyes, trying to imagine himself back at school. Now, with chapped lips and diminished saliva it was becoming increasingly difficult to talk. Apart from keeping his brain active his schooling seemed of little use to him in his present plight.

Now on this morning of the eighth day his youthful quest for glory 'doing his bit for King and Country' was fast waning. Back aboard the ship he had held the old quartermaster in awe for the days he had spent in sail. Now he had a nagging feeling, and he felt guilty about it, almost disloyal in fact, that perhaps, just perhaps, those 'old tea clipper' skills might not be enough to get them through.

The shortage of rations and fresh water worried him more than the fact that there was less than an inch of wooden plank between him and the bottom of the sea a couple of thousand fathoms below. Would they starve to death and their bodies go putrid before the sun bleached their bones? There had only been three days when the wind had blown enough to fill the sails. How would the old man get them home if the wind didn't blow?

His whole body ached. Were it not for his soft and bulky life jacket, acting as a cushion by day and a pillow at night, things would have been a damn sight worse. He would have given anything to be back on board and scrubbing the deck of the office flat or even enduring a bollocking from Mr.Akker. Yesterday he'd got a bollocking from

Mr.McTavish when he lost his balance going up fo'ard and fallen across the officer. The others called him `Dick' but not McTavish who called him by his surname. Yesterday he'd called him an `oaf', which had drawn an admonishment from Baines. "Steady Mr.McTavish, the lad couldn't help it." He had observed that over the last couple of days the second officer had become more malevolent towards the saloon-boy.

Dick remembered Harry London saying that the Second had changed since last trip. He gave up counting and closed his eyes, thinking back to that day three months ago, which now seemed more like three years, when he had jumped at the chance of joining his late ship. Here in the South Atlantic the sun would soon be blistering their tender flesh but that day back in England had been so different.

* * *

SPRING 1942
BRISTOL

The rain started again, not decent rain with drops that showed the power of their fall, but that fine English mist which floated underneath an umbrella or down the inside of an oilskin collar, making a person feel miserable. The taxi headlights, already diminished by the blackout shields, were almost useless. Forced to use this back street because of the military convoy leaving the docks, the old and battered Austin lurched and bumped as the driver tried to avoid rubble as yet uncleared from the last air-raid.

Apart for a chink of light from a glass-less window covered with cardboard, everything was either a shiny grey in the headlights' diffused beam or pitch black. Every now and then the darker mass of the terraced houses on either side gave way to a lighter blackness where a bomb had torn a house asunder. Except for that chink of light there was no sign of life. The people had either fled or been evacuated or were, at ten o'clock at night, already in their Anderson shelters, damp and cold and enveloped in the misery of war.

For the umpteenth time on the six mile trip to Avonmouth docks the driver coughed and wheezed, almost losing control of the vehicle.

"Sorry Guv," he croaked. "Got a bit of gas on the Somme in the last lot." Indeed, as he sat huddled over the steering wheel in a worn overcoat, scarf wrapped tightly around his neck, cloth cap pulled down to his eyes and long bushy moustache, he looked every bit an `Old Contemptible'.

The man in the darkness of the back seat who had, up till now, responded with a non-committal grunt, said, "I was lucky, no gas on Gallipoli, just caught a couple of bullets".

"So you was in the last lot as well, Sir"? Why the driver had said `Sir' he was not sure but there was something about his passenger that carried the air of authority. He had caught a glimpse of the man and a boy when they had left the pub's private door and used a torch to cross the pavement to his cab. The man was tall and perhaps in his early forties. He had an educated voice and sounded as if he was used to issuing orders, the way he had said "Avonmouth docks please". Now his reply sounded more subdued.

"Oh yes, very much so".

The driver had to concentrate to make a right turn, but a few yards further on a khaki clad figure wearing the red cap of the Military Police loomed out of the murk and held up a large gauntlet covered hand. Behind him they could see the hooded lights of army trucks, gear boxes grinding as the drivers increased speed as if in haste to quit this dismal place.

"Sorry Mate, you'll 'ave to wait a bit. A few more to come yet. Sod this bloody rain." He turned on his heel and went back the few paces to the junction of the main road, his poncho-cape glistening in the dim headlights.

The man in the back of the taxi gave an involuntary shudder. The sight of the MP and the trucks had brought back dark memories, reminding him of why he was here with his son beside him. Soon to make that farewell which thousands of other fathers had done before him. As his father had done in 1914 when he, the platoon commander and his brother, Bert, his second in command, had embarked at the end of their leave.

His thoughts strayed back further, to when the battalion had been newly formed and for six months he had been lulled into a false sense of security. The training had not been too onerous and he had enjoyed learning the art of warfare. As billeting officer he had made sure that he and Bert were in the right place down in Weston and since he played the piano tolerably well he was much in demand at parties. Yes, they'd had a pretty good time while other divisions were sent to the slaughter house of Flanders. Then had come the long march down to Salisbury Plain, the endless rows of tents and soaking rain making life intolerable. Embarkation leave had come as a relief and the warmth of family and home lulled their senses. On their last day the family had arranged a farewell party. To drown their fears the brothers had drunk too much, but that had been the way of things then.

His father had never been to war but he knew of the mounting casualties and the statistics that reckoned the life expectancy of subalterns at no more than three weeks. On that day long ago, on Templemeads station, amidst the hubbub of sniffling children and crying wives to the back ground of shouted orders and the hissing of steam escaping from the engine, had his father feared that this would be the last he would see of his sons?

Neither father nor sons had known that on rejoining their regiment they would be issued with tropical kit, which meant only one thing; they were going to fight Abdul the Turk not the Germans!

Now it was his son who was off to war, not clad in khaki but in civilian clothes with only a small lapel badge of silver with the letters M N to show what he was about. Out there on the Atlantic, would the Germans make the lad's first taste of action as horrific as his had been?

Not for a single day since had he been able to forget that day that began as he and his men had climbed down from the deck of the troopship into the barge, or the disgusting smell as they neared the beach. The midshipman in charge of the barge had remarked that it was caused by the rotting bodies of the dead as they lay between the trenches. Nothing in their training or at the officers' briefing earlier that afternoon had prepared them for that smell, or what was to follow three days later when he had given the order to fix bayonets. This was no parade ground exercise. There would be no sacks to bayonet, only real men, like themselves. How he'd prayed that he would not let his men down as the hands of his watch under its silver guard had crawled round to the time when that order had to be given; and the fear had threatened to overwhelm him.

The three days they had waited in the lower trenches of ANZAC Cove with the occasional whine of a shell followed by a heavy crump as it exploded over the beach, and further away in the distance the rattle of a machine gun or crack of a rifle, had not prepared them for that first terrifying battle. Would his son Richard be as terrified as he had been? And would they, after the last farewell in a few moments, ever see each other again?

"Ok, you can go." The M.P's gruff voice brought him back to the present. Waving the taxi on the soldier mounted his motorbike and disappeared into the night.

"About bloody time too," wheezed the taxi driver, recovering from another bout of coughing.

The taxi was again stopped by a dockyard policeman at the dock gates. The rain also chose that moment to stop, allowing the passengers to alight and remain dry.

Richard's father pulled something from his pocket and handed it to his son: "This brought me luck in the last war. I pray it'll do the same for you in this one." It was his silver watch guard.

"Gosh Dad, that's wizard. Thanks a million! I'll fix it on as soon as I get aboard." Putting it in his pocket he held his hand out in a farewell gesture to his father, who clasped it in a grip of iron and with his other arm drew his son to him, silent tears running down his cheeks.

"Goodbye son, and keep your head down!" He tried to sound flippant but on the last word his voice cracked and with a sob he turned back to the waiting taxi. Inside he drew his hip flask from a pocket and took a large swig then silently handed it to the driver.

"Yes lad?" queried the policeman as Richard, having put on his Burberry and picked up his case, advanced the few paces to the custodian of the Dock Gate.

"I'm joining the Patriarch, Sir."

"Your pass then? You can't go inside without some identification. For all I know you might be a German spy with a bomb in that there case!"

"Oh, yes, of course. Sorry". The lump in his throat was the same he felt each time he went back to boarding school. The reality of war was yet to come. He took his newly acquired seaman's discharge book from his coat pocket and produced the ship's boarding pass given to him earlier that afternoon.

"O.K, off you go then and have a good trip." The constable's voice was paternal but inwardly he was sad for he had seen too many pass through his gate never to return.

"Thanks, I hope I will. It's my first you know". The boy's voice was in complete contrast to that of the older man, almost flippant for there was none of the fear that his father had felt for him. He was still too young and, despite the air-raids, yet to see death close at hand. As he walked briskly through the gates and into his new world he suddenly felt his youthful exuberance lifting his spirits.

Earlier that afternoon he'd received a telephone call from the shipping master telling him that a pier-head jump had come up and if he still wanted a ship to get to the office at once. Now, two hours later it all seemed so different. The wharf had been teeming with soldiers in a seemingly endless line, marching single file into the ship through a gun-port, breaking ranks every so often to allow the wharfies shouldering crates and boxes of stores aboard.

He'd had quite a job to push his way through the throng towards the main gangway. Once on the ship, and what a thrill he'd felt as he stepped onto the deck for the first time, an officer had detailed a crew member to take him to the chief steward's office.

The chief steward was a small dumpy middle aged man, bald, with metal rimmed glasses and a bad temper. He was not at all impressed that the new saloon-boy had not brought his gear aboard with him. He was even less impressed when he discovered that the boy had never been to sea. Richard was left in no doubt as to how he felt about shipping masters who sent useless people aboard on sailing day! At which point the lad thought that his seagoing career was about to end before it had even started.

"Well the second 'll just have to put up with having to bloody well train you." Grudgingly the Chief Steward had written out a chit to the shipping master to `sign this fellow on'. He then hit the roof again when Richard told him it would take three hours after he'd signed on at the shipping office to get home, collect his gear and get back aboard. But he had managed it, with the help of his father's friend who'd conjured up the taxi which had brought him back to the docks after a quick meal at home.

Now, as he walked towards the ship that was to be his home for an indefinite time he could not make up his mind who presented the greatest threat: The Germans or the Chief Steward. He paused to look up at the huge flared bow towering above him. 'Patriarch'. The embossed name, covered in grey paint to hide it from distant eyes, was momentarily visible in the feeble glow of a lorry's headlights.

"Patriarch!" He said the name out loud, savoring it, his excitement rising. To get a better look he turned and scrambled across the couplings of a stationary line of railway coal trucks, then up onto the back of a lorry which stood by the cavernous doors of a warehouse. From his higher perch he could see over the trucks and heads of the people around the ship and get a better look at her. Young and impressionable his heart swelled with pride and he felt the blood race in his veins.

To the uninitiated the ship looked like any other ship. She had two funnels, two masts, a row of lifeboats and was painted a drab grey. But to those who knew her she was an individual. Although she was one of three sisters all built in the same yard, her soul was different from the others. From the plate on the stern which wept in a following sea no matter how tight the rivets were hammered, to the number one donkey engine which never started first time. To the quartermaster on the wheel there were those two degrees of rudder which made her steer differently from her sisters, and for the night watchman on his lonely rounds, that creak in the engineers' accommodation. It was these little things which gave her her soul.

She lay, dark and solid, held fast to the quay by massive ropes and steel-wire cables, towering over the boy on the dock side, the trucks of her masts lost from view in the damp blackness of the night. In front and behind her, squeezed in stem to stern along the narrow confines of the dock so that their masts and derricks formed grotesque patterns, lay other ships but these held no interest for his eager eyes. Unlike 'his' ship the others showed little signs of life in the feeble light.

"What bist thee doing oop theer, thee yoong booger!" a voice hailed angrily, "Seeing what thee can pinch? Git 'ta 'ell out o'it afore I clouts thee one!"

Rudely the boy's thoughts were shattered. Like a scalded cat, he jumped from the lorry and dodged a kick from the irate driver. He scrambled over the railway trucks' couplings again and was almost back under the crane when he tripped over a wire and fell heavily into a puddle of oily water. Dripping, he got to his feet and ruefully rubbed a sore knee. Behind him he heard the sound of laughter.

"That'll teach thee!"

"Go to blazes!" he retorted, careful not to raise his voice enough for the lorry driver to hear.

He brushed himself down as best he could and wiped his hands on a handkerchief. What an ass he'd made of himself, he thought, deciding he'd better get aboard before he fell into the dock! He picked up his case and took a few steps towards the edge of the quay, drawing back in fear as he looked down into the black void between ship and shore, suddenly feeling unsure of himself.

Only a few minutes ago he had confidently taken leave of his father feeling very much an adult. Now in this place which smelt of wet concrete, diesel oil and a myriad of other things he could not identify but which made up the smell of docks all over the world, he was assailed by loneliness and indecision. He was not sure which of the two gangways he should use to get aboard, the short brow into the side of the ship or the long one up to the deck?

The problem was solved for him. The brow cleared of men and a crane swung it back onto the quay. He heard a loud clang as the steel gun-port door swung shut. Someone shouted near him and the railway trucks jolted into movement adding to the noise and the seeming chaos, but as inexperienced as he was he knew that the sailing of such a ship could not be a quiet and serene affair. All the noise and movement had a purpose and he was a part of it, a very small, almost infinitesimal one, but definitely a part of it.

He squared his shoulders and advanced to the foot of the gangway. An officer in a bridge coat stood looking at a damp sheaf of papers attached to a clipboard. He was about to ask the officer what he should do when he was brushed aside by an army sergeant whose shoulder flash bore the letters DEMS in the blue and red colours of the artillery. The soldier mounted the gangway at a run.

Someone swore and a voice said; "Well so long mate, must get aboard now."

The boy felt a surge of panic lest someone should haul this gangway up and leave him behind. He edged nearer to the officer who took no notice of him. He coughed, uncertain whether he dare interrupt someone who wore a wavy strip on his epaulettes.

"Er, excuse me, Sir, but could you tell me where I might find the chief steward please?"

"In his bloody cabin and probably pissed out of his tiny little mind. Who are you anyway?"

"The new saloon-boy, Sir."

"About bloody time. Well see the quartermaster at the head of the gangway. Uh, that's the lot then," the third radio operator muttered and made a tick on the crew list attached to his clipboard. The twenty year old sparks was about to embark on his third voyage on the Patriarch and felt that gangway officer was a responsibility that should have fallen to someone else.

At the top of the gangway Senior Quartermaster Jim Baines leant on the ship's rail and watched the activities at the foot of the gangway. He did not like the third radio officer. He had no idea what he was like at his job in the radio shack but he talked like he thought he was God's great gift to women and any crew member who did not wear gold braid was treated by him with disdain. Baines, who was old enough to be the spark's grandfather, reckoned he would look down his nose on someone once too often and end up in the gutter.

"Evening Jim, here we go again then," the DEMS sergeant said at the head of the gangway.

"Sure thing Bill. Let's hope all goes well." Baines and the sergeant had developed a friendship born out of mutual respect and similar ages. The sergeant, being too old for active service with the artillery in which he had served in the last war, was a volunteer and looked after the ship's armaments.

It seemed a long hard climb up the gangway and by the time Richard stepped onto the deck he was sweating despite the cool night air. He paused, feeling disappointed that the deck felt no different from the shore, and for the second time in a few minutes he was pushed roughly to one side.

"Get that bloody case out of my way!" the officer in the bridge coat barked.

A large callused hand pulled the offending article to one side and a not unkind voice asked, "Are y' the new saloon-boy?"

Richard turned to see a man clad in wet oilskins and a sailors hat. His face was in shadow but somehow the boy knew that here, at last, was someone prepared to help him.

"Yes Sir. I was told to report to the chief steward, can you tell me where I might find him?"

"Oh indeed but if I were y' I wouldn't disturb 'im. Go and report to the second steward. He should be somewhere around the gun-port flat; through the first door there an' down three flights of stairs. An' don't call quartermasters Sir, save that for the gold braid. Right, cut along now."

"Thanks quartermaster, thanks a lot," he replied gratefully, dragging his suitcase towards the door indicated. Moving aside the heavy black-out curtain he failed to lift his foot high enough over the wash-sill and promptly cracked his shin, Damn!

Can I do nothing right, he cursed silently, trying to ignore the pain.

He found himself in a large square with walls paneled in a light coloured wood and formed to look like a shop window and office doors. The name above the first door read 'Purser'. On the for'ard wall was a twelve foot painting of the ship in all its peacetime splendour. Black hull with white upper-works, buff funnels and masts. She was depicted moving across a blue-green sea with a foaming bow wave and, unlike so many artists' impressions of ships, this one really looked alive. A low sun reflected on the varnished accident boat as it hung from its davits fifty feet above the water.

"Oh gosh!" he exclaimed, awed by the beauty of the painting.

"And what might a dirty tramp like you be doing in the first class accommodation?"

Turning in alarm he saw that the voice belonged to a jovial looking man of medium height, black hair slicked back with what he presumed was a liberal dose of Brylcream. He bore one broad gold zigzag stripe on his arm and stood eyeing the boy with his hands on his hips.

"Please Sir, I'm looking for the second steward. Can you tell me where I can find him?"

"Well you can stop looking. And since you don't seem to know what this means." He tapped the zigzag gold braid on his left arm "You must obviously be the new saloon-boy. And what the hell happened to you?" He sniffed. "You don't smell drunk but you certainly look it!" The twinkle in his eyes belied the gruff voice.

"I fell over, Sir," he replied lamely, looking down at his nearly new and previously spotless raincoat, now bearing an oily stain.

"So it seems. Well report yourself. What's your name and where's your book? There's no time to waste in this ship!" The Second Steward's manner of speech was staccato but the saloon-boy sensed that here was a man whose bark was worse than his bite. Nevertheless, he braced himself as he had been taught on the school parade ground.

"Wentle, Richard Wentle, Sir." He pulled out his book which the second steward flipped through casually.

Mr. Boyd eyed Wentle keenly. Ten years experience had taught him that there was more to be gained by studying a face than reading the stereotype remarks in a discharge book.

"Never been to sea! Trust the bloody Pool Office to do this to me on sailing day. How the blazes am I to train you with half an hour's notice? Answer me that boy!"

"I don't know, Sir but I'm sure that I can pick up the job pretty fast."

"Pick up the job? Haven't you even been to sea-school?"

"No Sir," he replied with less assurance.

"Proper Greenhorn 'aint he?"

For the first time Wentle became aware of a youth standing behind the second steward. He looked surprisingly like Wentle. Both were about five foot nine and lightly built with fair wavy hair and fresh boyish faces. Wentle, however, wore glasses which the other did not. Mr Boyd noticed the similarity of appearance but reckoned their backgrounds were poles apart with one being the product of a council school and the other probably at least grammar.

"That'll do from you Perkins. Go and tell the gangway quartermaster that I've finished down in the gun-port flat." He turned back to Wentle. "Not been to sea school even. I think you're in for a bit of a shock and it makes it all the more difficult for me."

"Sir, I'm sure I can learn. I won't let you down."

"Lor' listen to 'im. 'e'll 'ave us all in tears!" chimed in Perkins as he disappeared through the black-out curtain.

"What experience have you Wentle, at scrubbing decks or polishing brass? Have you ever waited at table and how old are you?" the questions came thick and fast.

"Well Sir, I used to be a fag once at school and had to keep the prefects' study clean. I'm almost seventeen." He somehow felt that this experience was not quite what the second steward had in mind. Indeed that worthy grinned at the comparison. From the boy's cultured voice he would have expected to see him up on the bridge as an apprentice not as a would-be assistant steward. The boy was obviously keen and would no doubt make the grade. Anyway at this late hour there were no options.

"All right, Wentle, Perkins'll show you to the boy's peak. You'll be called at six in the morning. Turn to in your oldest clothes because you'll start by scrubbing out in the First Class Saloon, which'll be your normal place of work. Mr. Akker, the saloon steward, will tell you what to do and will be your immediate boss." Giving the now returned Perkins his orders he disappeared down an alleyway.

"What's his name?" Wentle asked as the two youths started down a wide stair case.

"Boyd and he thinks himself God Almighty. Come on Green'orn get that fat arse of yours moving quicker 'cause I need to get me 'ead down."

At the bottom of the stairway was a dining saloon, now bare and deserted. Perkins led them through an equally deserted serving pantry and into the galley, where they were greeted by a pimply faced youth with ginger hair.

"Whatch'er Tiger, 'ows things?"

"Fucking dandy Ginger, just dandy. Secundus 'as me playing nursemaid to a bloody green'orn what goes by the name of Wentle. What the 'ell you doing 'ere at this time anyway?"

"Bloody chef reckoned the place wasn't clean enough an' 'ad me hauled out me wanker pit! What's 'e then," nodding at Wentle "something the cat spewed up?" Ginger made as if to swab the deck again but sent the new saloon-boy crashing against the big black baker's oven with the mop between his legs. "Don't 'ave any sea legs do 'e Tiger." He subsided into roars of laughter.

Wentle picked himself up for the second time that evening, holding his rising anger in check. This was not the time to give as good as he got. Instead he lamely followed after his guide who had disappeared through a black-out curtain into a short passage leading to the well-deck.

"What's your name old man?" Wentle had yet to learn that Perkins resented his presence aboard the Patriarch. He felt a little sick from the ache in his shoulder and his shin still hurt. Loneliness and home sickness were taking a hold of him in this new world which smelled so different from his home and where everyone seemed so unfriendly.

"Actually, old man," replied Perkins mimicking Wentle. "If your nanny had washed your ears properly you'd have heard Secundus call me Perkins." Lapsing back into his normal speech he added.. "To you I'm the captain's tiger, which means 'is steward and that makes me bloody important, 'an don't you fucking forget it neither!"

They passed in silence across the well-deck, under the bridge housing and past number two hatch before pushing aside another black-out curtain and into the dimly lit fo'c'sle.

"Seamen's smoke room," Perkins muttered as they went by a large room in which half a dozen men were smoking and talking. "The small cabins 'ere are fer the quartermasters, bosun 'an such like 'an the larger ones 'round the gallery are the seamens' peaks or, for the ignorant likes of you, cabins. We goes down these stairs 'ere." Which he did by taking both feet off the deck and sliding down with his hands on the guardrail. "And arrives on the catering crew's deck which is where we lives."

Wentle followed holding on to the rail with one hand and bumping his case down a step at a time. They were now in an open flat which Wentle realized must be the top of a hold. To get out they had either to go back up the two narrow stairways, or up an iron ladder welded to the for'ard bulkhead leading to a small hatchway. At the for'ard end of the flat was a short passage which terminated in a steel door clipped shut and padlocked. A nameplate read `No 1 Hold'.

He caught up with the tiger who had stopped at the doorway of a large cabin at the for'ard end of the gallery on the port side.

"Mates," he announced to the occupants. "Allow me to hinterduce 'is Lordship the Toff." He made a mock bow. "An' a right Charlie if ever there was one. Straight from 'is ma's tits 'e is, an' 'es all yours." He turned on his heel, lifted one hip and farted loudly. "An' that's what I thinks of 'im!" he added as he left.

Richard Wentle surveyed his cabin mates to be and the place in which he would spend his sleeping hours and off-duty time. There were two rows of double tiered metal bunks, four athwartships and two along the far side of the cabin under a porthole. Each bunk was fitted with a mattress and bed linen. The only bright thing in the room was the blue of the company's crest embossed on the cover. Bolted against the bulkhead to his left were six small lockers. There were no tables or chairs simply because there was no room for them. In fact Wentle reckoned that there was hardly room to dress if they all got out of their bunks at the same time. His heart sank. This minute and bleak place, home to six boys, was painted a dirty off-white and smelled of stale bodies, cigarette smoke and the tiger's pungent fart.

A podgy looking lad with greasy skin and a plaster on his neck, returned the saloon-boy's gaze from the lower bunk under the porthole. From the bunk in front of the door two other youths took in the newcomer. They, like their podgy companion, were dark skinned but their eyes did not hold the same hostility to their new shipmate that those of the tiger had done.

"Hello, my name is Richard Wentle," he started awkwardly. "As the tiger said I'm a bit of a greenhorn, I expect that you chaps have done dozens of trips?"

The podgy one answered first. "Porky Bates, pantry-boy. Three trips."

"Bert 'itchcock, also pantry-boy," said the younger of the other two, "From Liverpool and wish to God we was there now!"

"Harry London officers mess-boy. Done two trips aboard here. There are a couple of other pantry-boys, Ginger is finishing the clean up and Balls-itch is having a piss, he's always scratching 'imself hence the name. Here, dump that bloody great case of yours on the bunk while you get your gear stowed." The last lad stood up and Wentle saw that he was a small five foot nothing and desperately thin. His face, although not lined, had a haggard look, almost as if he was an old man.

"Your bunk'll be the top one under the porthole and this'll be your locker. Come on Bert, move over so's Dick can stow 'is gear."

Thus Richard Wentle, Seamen's Discharge book, or to give it its correct name, Continuous Certificate of Discharge, number R243568, moved into the boy's peak of the M.V.Patriarch and went to war.

CHAPTER 2

Whilst Richard Wentle stowed his gear in the boy's peak, almost at the bottom of the ship and, but for the fore peak and cable locker, right in the bows, Captain Ronald `The Padre' Spencer, D.S.C. sat in his cabin high up under the bridge.

As master of the M.V.Patriarch his quarters were spacious and comfortably furnished. A sheathing of deep red mahogany paneling covered the steel bulkheads whilst the ceiling was done in a white material to avoid the condensation which would plague those who had top bunks in the crew's quarters. There was the obligatory picture of his ship and one of the King and Queen on the after bulkhead. Since he was expected to have the occasional important passenger for coffee or drinks there was a long settee under the for'ard windows as well as two armchairs, with a coffee table in between. Fitted to the starboard wall was a mahogany desk upon which stood two photographs, one of his wife and the other of his son in the uniform of a midshipman in the Royal Naval Reserve. Their leaves had never coincided and it was now over two years since father and son had seen each other. Midshipman Spencer was presently serving in a flower class corvette somewhere in the North Atlantic.

On the port side of the day cabin was the captain's bedroom with bathroom opening off it. The bedroom was about the same size as the catering staff's boys' peak; luxury indeed but he had known what cramped conditions were like. As a midshipman in the navy he had slung his hammock in the gunroom of the old battleship Irresistible.

The Irresistible had gone down in the Battle of the Narrows in March 1915 and with it his record of service, which would have shown that he was entitled to promotion to sub-lieutenant. Rescued unharmed along with almost all the crew he had then become one of many midshipmen who were put in charge of the pinnaces, barges and other small craft which ferried the troops ashore for the Gallipoli landings in April of that year. As spring became summer the heat intensified and with it, if the wind was in the wrong direction, that awful smell! He recalled a night when one of the soldiers had said that it smelled just like a slaughter-house only worse.

Spencer had spoken briefly to the soldier's officer, having noticed as they boarded his pinnace that the badge on the back of his cap indicating they were from his home county. Had he been at the dock gates half an hour ago it is doubtful that he would have recognised the same officer bidding an emotional farewell to his son, now part of his crew.

The end of the Gallipoli campaign had seen Spencer belatedly promoted to sub-lieutenant, but, most importantly, with seniority back dated. He was sent to the Dover patrol base to serve in the new small torpedo boats. A Distinguished Service Cross, for rescuing the crew of a sister-ship off Ostend and the capture of a German M.T.B, was not sufficient to bring him to the particular notice of `Their Lordships of the Admiralty' when naval funds were axed. With no one to speak for him he, along with many others, was honourably discharged from `His Most Britannic Majesty's Royal Navy'. His services were no longer required. Luckily he had obtained a berth as fourth officer on a newly built passenger ship. He had been with the company ever since, despite the depression when many an officer had been forced to sail as a seaman.

The Captain had no idea that a new saloon-boy had just joined the ship. He was far too busy on sailing day with visits to the senior naval officer for routing orders; discussions with the chief engineer about bunkers and all tied in with the chief officer's calculations of their deadweight, draft and stability. Each head of department had his own problems to solve, and earlier in the day the second steward had been presented with a serious one. The captain's steward had been sent to a shore hospital by the ship's doctor. The normal custom was to promote the saloon-boy, if he was of the right age and competence, and sign on another boy. That way there was less dislocation amongst the stewards who would be more than upset at the loss of tips! Naturally the captain had been advised of the change but Mr.Boyd was worried that Perkins was not the right man for the job. Time would tell.

Crew changes were left to heads of departments and as long as there were enough men aboard for the ship to function properly that was, at this moment, all that interested the captain. Later in the voyage the purser would bring their books to him for his signature and since he rarely left the bridge in war time, most would remain only a name and rank or rating.

Chief Officer Charles Boulton was the antithesis of his captain in looks. Two years older than Spencer he was of medium height with grey hair, bushy eyebrows and a little overweight. Spencer, on the other hand, was six foot one, still quite handsome and sported an immaculately trimmed goatee beard. The two men had been together for the past two years and had forged a deep respect for each other. It had become their custom when Boulton reported that all was ready for sailing to partake, according to the time of day, either coffee, tea or, as now, cocoa and discuss any last minute items that may have cropped up. Having received the report that all departments were correctly manned with every one now aboard and that the ship was ready for sea, Spencer asked the Chief Officer what he thought of the new trooping staff.

"The colonel seems a typical `Blimp' to me and the Adjutant not much better. Thank goodness the sergeant major and staff sergeant seem to be on the ball otherwise I feel our good purser would have much reduced gin time!" Both men grinned at this last remark for as his name implied, Ted Good, was good at his job but did have a tremendous capacity for pink gins.

"Yes I'm inclined to agree with you. Not that I've seen much of them, just over the usual drink when Ted brought them up to be introduced yesterday morning. Still, we have to remember they've both come out of retirement and volunteered for the job so I suppose we mustn't be too hard on them." He paused to drink the last of his cocoa. "There is one thing I wish to mention Charles. I recommended last trip that you get your own command and while I was in the agent's office this afternoon I spoke on the blower with Baltimore. He confirmed that you'll have your own ship next time around. Congratulations!" He stood up and offered a hand to his chief officer. "Now I think we should adopt the horizontal position for the next couple of hours."

Down in the lower and 'tween decks of the ship's number four and five holds, and in the peace-time first and second class cabins, a thousand troops were settling in and trying to sleep in conditions far more cramped than the boys peak.

Normally the Patriarch would be carrying some fifteen thousand tons of frozen meat and up to two hundred passengers from South America. Then, hopefully, back-loading general cargo and more passengers. Now, with her freezing pipes removed and stored in number one hold, the hapless soldiers became human cargo. The officers were not as badly off situated on A deck with six to a cabin originally meant for two. But at least they had bunks, as did the sergeants and a few lucky corporals who were cramped four to a cabin in the second class, a deck lower down.

The rest of the troops, with their kit bags and bits and pieces, made the best of things in the holds. Here they were to sleep in tiers of three temporary bunks or hammocks slung from stanchions specially erected for the purpose. It was questionable as to who would be more comfortable, those in the bunks with their straw filled mattresses, commonly known as a `donkey's breakfast', or those in the swaying hammocks? With only one blanket, their battle-dress and greatcoats, they were at first cold and then, as the mass of bodies heated the air, became too warm despite the wind chutes specially rigged to give some fresh air. Holds designed for frozen meat were not normally ventilated.

If a soldier needed the toilet he had to climb the ladders to the after well-deck and queue. If he wanted to wash he would again have to queue at the double line of steel wash-basins stretched across the after end of each hold.

As the voyage lengthened and the weather allowed, as many as possible would eventually sleep above decks, avoiding conditions which quickly degenerated into something akin to a

Glasgow slum. It would take time before seasickness was no longer a problem and self preservation, together with some discipline, improved their lot.

The duty engineers went about their job of preparing the huge diesel motors for sea. Lube oil had to be heated and starting air-bottles topped up. The boilers and generators had to be checked to make sure they were functioning properly. Up on deck the watch had changed. The second sparks smoked a cigarette by the gangway while the quartermaster went to check the moorings. In the passenger accommodation the lamp-trimmer, now acting as the night watchman, showed the army regimental police how to find their way around. The hustle and bustle on the dockside ceased, leaving the ship to slumber uneasily before returning to war.

* * *

"Captain it's three thirty. Here's yer tea." The quartermaster had knocked loudly before entering the day cabin, placing the tea cup on the desk by the bible. "The rain 'as cleared but still some cloud about." Each quartermaster knew the drill with which to wake the ship's master. Tea made in the small pantry just across the passageway and served piping hot with milk but no sugar. "Captain, Sir are you awake?"

"Right-oh QM I'm with you." Spencer swung quickly out of bed, a practice he had adopted many years ago after once falling asleep again, which earned him the biggest roasting he had ever received from the mate he was supposed to have relieved a quarter of an hour earlier.

He doused his face in cold water, took a sip of tea then dressed. At night he favoured a warm white polo-necked pullover knitted for him by his wife, rather than collar and tie, and allowed his officers to do the same. Now, seated at his desk, he sipped again at his tea and opened the bible at the book mark.

Spencer was known throughout the company's fleet as `The Padre' and, indeed, he would have made an excellent chaplain. He was compassionate and understood his fellow man, and he never tried to force his beliefs on others. Now, as was his custom at the start of each voyage, he read his bible. At least, he had it open, for he knew by heart the words which were printed on the page before him.

> They that go down to the sea in ships
> that do business in great waters;
> These see the works of the Lord, and
> his wonders in the deep.
> For He commandeth, and raiseth up the
> stormy wind, which lifteth up the waves
> thereof.
> They mount up to the Heavens, they go down
> again to the depths;
> Their soul is melted because of trouble.
> And He bringeth them out of their distress.

> He maketh the storm a calm so that the
> waves thereof are still.
> Then they are glad because they be quiet; so
> He bringeth them unto their desired haven.
>   (PSALM 107, verses 23 to 30)

"Amen!" he said out loud and carefully closed the bible. He replaced the book at the back of the desk and finished his tea. Crossing to the settee, he picked up his greatcoat from where he had dropped it earlier, a habit that annoyed his wife intensely. Meticulous in most things he had the habit of never hanging up a coat. Before donning the coat he knotted a silk scarf around his neck and, satisfied that it showed just the right amount above the coat collar, reached for his gold braided cap. That on correctly, not too jauntily like Third Officer Giles, but just enough angle so that he did not appear too staid, he was ready. Stepping over the low wash-sill, the captain pulled on leather gloves as he walked the few paces along the passageway and out onto the small bit of deck which was his special preserve. Only personnel going or coming from the bridge were allowed across it. Directly below was the accident boat deck and navigating officers' accommodation and above, the bridge. An oilskin clad sailor on some errand stood respectfully aside as Spencer appeared from the doorway. Sniffing the damp night air the captain mounted the short ladder to the bridge.

"Good morning, Sir. Engine room telegraphs and steering tested. The pilot is waiting." Young Giles, gay and debonair as always even at this hour, reported the bridge ready for sea with a genuine smile of welcome for his captain. Spencer had never been able to surprise him on these occasions. The third officer's voice and mannerisms were those of a man lucky enough to have been brought up in a family home and educated where money was not in short supply.

"Thank you Mr.Giles." The captain's voice was surprisingly soft for such a big man.

"Sir, the glass is steady and the met report is fair apart from occasional drizzle and with the possibility of a gale late tomorrow."

The two officers left the open wing of the bridge and passed into the wheel-house, where a single small red light reflected feebly on the polished brass of the compass binnacle and engine room telegraphs. All deck lights, other than one on the fo'c'sle and another right aft on the poop deck, had also been turned off to preserve night vision.

Behind the wheel flexing arthritic fingers, stood old Jim Baines. Slightly built but despite his age still erect. He was by far the best quartermaster in the company. His hands were calloused from years of hard work in the old sailing ships and yet, on the wheel, they had the gentle touch of a woman. In dirty weather Baines could feel the ship better than anyone and Spencer had long since got used to the old fellow's way of talking to the ship as she laboured in a gale. They had sailed together on many a long voyage.

"Evening Baines. Every thing all right?"

"Aye Captain. The old girl's aquivering to be gone."

Spencer was not sure he liked his ship being referred to as an old girl. After all, she was only eight years old, but he knew that the quartermaster meant it affectionately. If young Jones the apprentice, had called her an old girl Spencer would have issued a blistering rocket. Fine seamen like Jim Baines were allowed a certain degree of latitude.

"Good. It won't be long now." Seeing the pilot come in from the starboard wing of the bridge he added. "Good evening to you Pilot. Nice to see you again." He stretched out a hand in greeting.

In peace time his company's trade was with the London docks. When the Blitz started and a meat ship from another company was sunk alongside the wharf, followed by damage to a sister-ship to the Patriarch, they were re-routed to either Liverpool or Avonmouth.

This Welshman from Penarth was the company's preferred pilot for the Bristol Channel. He was short in stature so that on some ships he had to stand on tip-toe to see over the wind dodger. He always turned up in bowler hat and shabby raincoat with a referee's whistle on a piece of string round his neck, an appearance that belied his capabilities. At times he seemed to cut corners too finely but in reality he was taking advantage of every little current and back eddy with uncanny skill.

"Good morning to you, Captain. Not too good a night but at least it'll keep Jerry at home, look you." Spencer liked the singsong intonation of the true Welshman.

"Yes indeed. Will you have your usual before we go?"

"That I will and thank you". The pilot passed through a black out curtain at the back of the bridge and into the chart room where the fourth officer, knowing the routine, was waiting with a flask of hot cocoa.

The captain went out onto the port bridge wing and into the little shelter which protruded a couple of feet over the ship's side. He looked both ways along the dock. Groups of two or three dockers stood around the mooring bollards ready to let go the lines. There were small knots of other people around whose job it was to see the ship off; customs officers, the agent, army and navy types and miscellaneous hangers-on whose jobs nobody on the Patriarch could quite fathom. They stood there under the dim dock lights wishing that the ship would sail so that they could all go home to their beds. Satisfied that all was ready Spencer crossed to the other wing. In the greater blackness of the Patriarch's shadow, two tugs were passing up their heavy tow ropes. All was ready and the captain returned to the comparative warmth of the wheel-house.

"Single up fore and aft to breast ropes." Spencer's order was clear and firm. Giles repeated it back to make sure he had heard correctly and then moved to the bridge 'phone. In a matter of seconds the fo'c'sle and poop became hives of activity. The mates lifted their megaphones and yelled at the dockers to let go all but the two breast ropes. With not even enough wind to shift the damp mist, the tugs would have no difficulty in getting the ship away. One by one the ropes and hawsers splashed into the placid water, sending out unseen ripples as they were dragged by the anchor winch gypsies back to the ship. Seamen cursed as they struggled with the wet moorings which, once aboard, were sent down into the bo'sun's store out of harm's way for the long voyage ahead. In the eyes of the ship the chief officer made sure that everything went according to plan whilst aft the second officer, Malcom McTavish, did likewise. Nothing could be left to chance.

Looking out over the black waters of the dock Spencer watched the screened navigation lights of the two tugs as they moved forward, ready to take the strain. It was a scene he had witnessed innumerable times before and yet it never failed to enthrall him. Sailing time, like docking time, had its own special feeling for him. Romantic thoughts of the ports to be visited, diminished only by sadness at leaving his family.

Before, there had always been the challenge of the elements. Now there was much greater danger from a more deadly enemy. He was acutely aware of the responsibility resting on his shoulders; one that he gladly accepted and prayed to God that he would successfully discharge for the eventual safety of his ship and the people in her.

Down on the well deck an ordinary seaman coiling a heaving line paused to watch the dark figure of his captain up above. There, to him at least, was the almost holy figure of `The Captain', Cursed by disgruntled seamen or affectionately called `The Old Man' when things went right; a man whose authority was only marginally short of God's.

The captain heard the bridge 'phone ring and went back to the wheel-house. "Singled up fore and aft, Sir."

"Thank you Mr.Giles." Then to the pilot who had just joined them, "She's all yours Pilot." Spencer stood behind the captain's chair as the pilot started to give his orders. There was little for a captain to do at such a moment for, as the third officer was just writing in the log, `Ship proceeded under Master's orders, Pilot's advice'. The master who disregarded the pilot's advice was a foolish one indeed.

The pilot moved out on to the starboard wing and blew hard on his whistle then, letting it fall on its string, raised his megaphone. "Let go all! O.K Bert, Charlie, take her off now," he called first to the mates at the ends of the ship and then to the tug skippers.

In the logbook the third officer entered the time and the words `All Gone'. Save for the short time they would spend in the lock the vessel had severed all connection with the land and would be an entity on its own, devoid of outside help. A thing alive and throbbing as long as the great engines below kept up their rhythmic turning.

Richard Wentle, saloon-boy and, save for the pantry-boys, considered to be the lowest form of life aboard, had been sleeping fitfully when the noise of the windlass hauling in the ropes vibrated downwards to the boy's peak and woke him. He was suddenly wide awake, realising that the ship must be about to sail. Carefully avoiding waking the others he left his bunk, donned his Burberry and, despite the fact that he would be called for work in only two hours, made his way above decks. Not for all the tea in China would he have missed this momentous occasion in his short life.

Out by number two hatch he felt the deck quiver as the tugs took the strain. In the comparative quiet of the night he could hear the orders being given from the bridge. He was going to sea at last and his heart beat faster. Level with his head, and only a few yards off, he could see the mast-head lights of a tug. He could hear the vibrating throb of the powerful engine and the hissing of the water as her propeller bit into it. Slowly the ship slewed out into the blackness of the dock. The small gap of dark, dirty water between vessel and wharf grew slowly bigger until, at last, the shore was no longer visible.

The previously placid waters of the dock were now a churning, seething mass of foam under the tremendous driving power of the tugs as they moved the big ship. One of them, after an order from the bridge, recovered its tow-rope and hurried around the Patriarch's stern. There she put padded nose against her big sister and pushed until the Patriarch was in line with the darker blackness of the lock.

To the fascinated Wentle the tugs seemed to fuss around like a couple of terriers but with far less noise, bar an occasional toot on their sirens in answer to the pilot's whistle.

The engine-room telegraph rang shrilly and the ship's two screws gave a few turns, enough to move the Patriarch for the first time under her own steam. So gently did she fetch into the lock that the dockers with their large fenders were hardly required. The lock gates closed behind her and since the tide was right, it only required a few minutes of draining before the far gates opened and the river mouth and then the open sea lay before them.

Once again the tugs took over; one pulling, the other with just enough weight on the tow aft to stop the stern swinging. Once clear of the lock the Patriarch's own engines became alive. There were more shouts and blasts on the pilot's whistle and the tugs were let go. Hauling in their tow-ropes they disappear back into the lock.

Forgetting his cold hands and chattering teeth Wentle watched in fascination as the lock wall slowly slid away from them in the darkness. A darkness in which an occasional pin-point of coloured light flashed its message to those on the bridge.

Under the Patriarch's stern the sea boiled as her own engines gave her impetus. The long journey and whatever it may hold for them had begun.

Chief Officer Boulton, as was the custom in the Merchant Navy, looked after the fo'c'sle when leaving or entering harbour. Now, as he went about securing the fo'c'sle for sea, he thought that this custom was not always a good idea. If he was to go master himself next trip he would have liked to have been up on the bridge, brushing up on the things that would look so different than from here in the bows. He would have to speak with the captain about it but in the meanwhile he had a job to do. In peace time the mate would normally remain on the fo'c'sle for a while `just in case' but in the wide mouth of the river and channels it was unlikely that the anchor would have to be let go, and he had a more pressing job to see to. He shone his torch around the wet deck in one final check.

"All right Bo'sun this lot seems okay so let's get the boats swung out." He led the way down on to the well-deck and towards the main accommodation decks, then up the three companion stairways to the long boat deck.

In times of war, when ships could sink in minutes or less, it was essential to have the lifeboats swung out and ready for instant embarkation. Now, at a quarter to five in the morning, with just the faintest glimmer of dawn to the east, all the seamen not engaged with immediate watch keeping duties set about the lengthy task of making all ready. Of course there were those who felt that the job could be left until the forenoon watch and one who had just banged his thumb with a gripe hook said so in no uncertain terms.

"Bugger the fucking thing, why the 'ell can't we leave the bastards where they are 'til we can see prop'ly. We shan't see no bloody U-boats up 'ere."

"Listen you flaming idiot!" rejoined the bo'sun's mate who was just as tired and miserable as the seaman. "When I came in 'ere last trip the Mongol City 'it a bleeding mine right in front of us and went down in ten minutes flat. If you thinks you can flamin' well swim in these currents off Portishead you're a bigger idiot than I thought. Now fer fuck's sake stop bitching and get that bloody gripe properly secured. At this rate we'll be missing breakfast!"

Both men were right in their statements for with the protective minefield that had been laid from the north Devon coast across to Ireland, the U-boats were now leaving the Bristol Channel to the

Luftwaffe, who obliged by dropping the new acoustic mines.

The magnetic mines laid in the first year of the war had been effectively countered by the degaussing of ships thanks to a Lt.J.Ouvry R.N who had disarmed a mine that had been left high and dry in the Thames Estuary. A fine example of one man saving the lives of many but now several ships routed to the ports of Bristol, Cardiff or Newport had fallen victims to this new acoustic mine.

One by one the chief and second officers checked that each boat was properly swung out and secured and then sent the men below to catch up on their missed sleep. Soon the damp decks were deserted and silent, only on the bridge was there movement.

"Port five.... meet her." The pilot issued his orders calmly, showing none of the considerable strain under which he laboured. There were now no lights in the wheel house save for those on the binnacle, gyro repeater, engine telegraphs and rudder indicator, all of which were dimmed right down. Lookouts and officers alike screwed up their eyes as they peered out into the greyness searching for the minute flashing lights of the buoys and thankful that at last the rain showers seemed to have stopped.

As each buoy was sighted the third officer plotted the ship's position on the chart whilst the fourth kept his gaze on the echo sounder. Between the reports on the buoys and depth of water under her keel the pilot kept the big ship in the fairway. He knew the courses to steer between the buoys by heart and after years of experience judged the rate of flow of the currents based on the time of high water. It was team work but the final decisions were those of the pilot. A miscalculation here, a wrong reckoning there and the Patriarch would be fast aground on a mud bank on a falling tide, revealed by the dawn for all to see and to ridicule the man who put her there. A twelve hour delay waiting for the next tide to re-float her could mean missing the convoy. A battalion of soldiers not arriving at their port of disembarkation at the right time could have disastrous consequences. Just as the mine disposal expert had saved many lives so could a careless pilot loose just as many!

"Steady as she goes!"

"Steady as she goes, Sir," echoed the quartermaster.

Abaft the chart room in the warmth of the radio-room, the third radio officer checked his gear. He pulled down a large knife switch to put power onto the sets. Like the copper pipe connecting the transmitters to the aerial bulkhead it was highly polished. The flick of a switch on each transmitter and receiver brought various meters to life and a crackle from two receivers. Throwing the aerial switches to dummy load he adjusted and then tested the transmitters. With the dummy load glowing he tried the Morse keys and, satisfied that all was working correctly, switched back to the main aerials. Next he drew forward the log book and made the entries showing all was well and the time the station was opened. Sitting down he put on a set of earphones and drew a clean signal pad forward to where the Morse key was screwed to the table and made sure there were two sharp pencils ready.

This was a lonely job but his were the ears of the ship. His quick deciphering of a message could mean the difference between life and death for many a seaman. Taking down a grubby paper-back western from a side shelf he swung his feet up on the desk and opened the novel at a turned down page … `the rustlers galloped off with the sheriff in hot pursuit.' And so he read as he kept a listening watch, his ears alert for the sound of morse code coming through the ether.

In the engine-room, as on the bridge and in the radio-room, there were those for whom sleep was not possible. The junior second engineer accepted a cigarette from his watch mate, the fifth, and then started off on his rounds. Those heavy oil engines, each twenty feet high, had to have their quota of oil and grease if they were to keep turning for the next couple of weeks. It was not unknown for a greaser to fall asleep on watch, particularly after returning so recently from a run ashore and drunk that extra pint to make up for the months before they would be able, once more and God willing, to enter the warmth of an English pub.

CHAPTER THREE

"May I have your attention please!" The ship's loudspeakers shattered the relative peace of the early spring day, disturbing half a dozen seagulls taking a rest on the muzzle of the aft four inch gun. They took to the air in screeching disgust. It was nine twenty and as the Patriarch had been at sea for almost four and a half hours, now was the time for her passengers to be made to realise the realities of the war at sea. Even those amongst the troops who had survived the miracle of Dunkirk and made the journey back to Blighty would find the forthcoming journey rather different. On that trip from France to England it had been a case of anywhere on any boat, but now all must know where they had to go if it became necessary to abandon this ship.

The voice of the elderly bespectacled chief radio officer was clear and concise despite his boredom from having had to make the same announcement time and again since the Patriarch started trooping over two years ago. He continued; "In ten minutes the ship's alarm bells will ring for boat stations. When this happens all troops will muster at their allotted stations. You will now all report to your messes where your boat stations will be explained to you by your officers. Thank you." With a click the speakers were switched off and for a moment there was a hush throughout the ship. Then down on the troop decks the men resumed their animated conversations. They had just finished eating their baked beans on bread washed down with tepid tea and now they were being chased once more by unseen authority.

"Shan't travel this line no more," said one wit. "Always chivvying ya abaht they are. Don't give ya no time ta henjoy tha cruise!"

"Don't worry cock, you won't get a chance to if we stops a torpedo when we're down 'ere," came the rejoinder from one who saw the more practical side of their situation.

Exactly ten minutes later the bells rang out with their shrill clanging. Despite the earlier warning there was more than one man who nearly jumped out of his skin. For those in the crew who had been through it all before it was a horrible sound. It twisted the gut almost to the point of vomiting as once again the thoughts of sleepless nights, anxious hours of waiting and the ever present possibility of a watery grave became paramount. Occasionally there were those who suddenly cracked and could take the strain no more but, as in all the services, they were in a minority.

The Patriarch was now steering west by north at seventeen knots. A grey ship whose decks slowly became covered in khaki and, here and there, patches of airforce blue as the men came up from below.

The rain of the previous evening had cleared and a watery sun shone weakly down on them from between scudding clouds. Small waves were broken by the wind in a smother of white, portended a rough change in the weather. From the mizzen gaff a new red ensign fluttered in the wind relieving an otherwise somber scene. Far out on the starboard beam the blue hills of Wales showed their tops.

The pilot had been dropped at Barry Roads and the crew had taken up their normal coastal watch-keeping. The chief officer, unshaven and almost sleepless, had the ship under his control. Behind the wheel a quartermaster moved his jaws rhythmically as he chewed a piece of gum. The second quartermaster of the watch and a seaman were on look-out on either wing whilst the captain sat in his chair in the wheelhouse. In the chartroom the senior apprentice, Dai Jones, made an entry on the chart and saw how near and yet so far he was from his home near Ogmoor.

In the bowels of the ship the chief engineer was on the plate and sent all who could be spared to their boat stations far above. Routine was establishing itself.

The decks, the boat deck at the top, the promenade and main were now all crowded with waiting lines of soldiers clad in cumbersome cork life-jackets. To most the term `boat station' was a misnomer, `raft' would have been more to the point, for although the Patriarch had been fitted with eight extra boats and many rafts, there were still not enough to go round. If the ship had to be abandoned quite a few would have to take a ducking.

To the crew, some of whom had not sailed on the ship before, this was the first opportunity to look around at their shipmates. The saloon-boy, Richard Wentle, stood with five other crew members out in front of the thirty five soldiers who had been detailed to the second starboard lifeboat. The purser, a florid, grey haired man, whose uniform looked as if it had seen better days, polished his glasses. Satisfied that he could see clearly, he pulled a piece of paper from his pocket and read out a list of names given him by the chief officer. One by one the crew answered and as they did so, Baines the quartermaster, in a rasping voice, detailed their jobs in the boat.

"Brown, bow-man and first oar, Macmasters, second oar. O'Toole, third...." and so it went on until Wentle found his job was to put the bung in. Next the purser and the second radio officer, the other officer assigned to the boat, together with Baines went round the waiting soldiers and made sure that each one knew how his life-jacket should be worn. Finally the old quartermaster gave them all some very pertinent advice.

"If for some reason y' can't get in the boat and 'ave to jump for it, make sure y' crosses y'r arms over the front of the life-jacket like this. If y' don't then the cork will up and smack y' in the face when y' 'its the water. Like as not it'll break y'r ruddy neck as well!" Subdued mutterings met this remark and continued whilst the men waited to be dismissed, which was not until the chief officer and trooping commandant had been round each boat station and then reported back to the captain, who in turn addressed everyone through the loudspeaker system.

"Gentlemen this is the captain. Now I want you to listen carefully to what I have to say, for how you act on it may have a profound effect, not only on your own life, but also on those of your shipmates. Each day for the next five or six or until I'm satisfied that things are being done correctly, the ship's bells will sound boat stations at half past nine in the forenoon watch. This means that you must fall in where you are now so please ensure that you fully understand how to get there. At any other time that the alarms go it will be for real so move quickly and in an orderly fashion. If you try rushing it nobody will get anywhere." He paused to let his words sink in. "I am now going to sound `Action Stations' which will only concern the crew or those of you who have been specially detailed. This would normally be sounded before boat stations but, of course, I can not guarantee that". He nodded to the chief officer who pressed the red alarm button with a short and then a long blast. As the sound died away the captain spoke again .

"There is one more signal which I pray to God you will never hear and that is for abandon ship. It is a series of short blasts on the ship's siren; should that be sounded you will carry out the orders of the ship's and your own officers." He paused for a moment to let his words sink in. "Well there you have it! You now know what boat and action stations sound like. I hope that we shall not have to sound off too often but, if we do, remember what I have told you and we shall stay on top. Thank you. You may now fall out."

"Funny sod 'aint he," remarked a soldier behind Wentle. " 'alf a mile of ruddy water under us and 'e 'opes we'll stay on top. Better bleeding well 'ad or me missus 'ill miss 'er allotment!"

Boat stations fell out amidst a buzz of conversation as the men made their way from the boat deck, the normal preserve of officers. Wentle hesitated. He knew that he should report back to the saloon right away but he decided that a wigging from his direct boss would be worth the answer to his dilemma. He advanced to where Quartermaster Baines stood by the davit winch.

"Excuse me Quartermaster but could you help me please? You see I think I know what a bung is but not where to find it in the boat. I could hardly show my ignorance in front of the troops but the truth is this is my first ship."

"It must have been y' who come aboard while I was on gangway watch last night. Y' looks a bit cleaner now. What 'ad 'appened to y' lad?" This time Wentle could see the smile on the old salt's face. The eyes were so deep set that they were almost invisible after years of peering across the oceans, screwed up against the glare in the tropics and the salt spray of rough seas.

"Well Sir, I tripped over and went face first into a dirty puddle. Rather messed up my coat too." Wentle felt that here was someone at last that he could talk to without feeling ashamed of his ignorance aboard.

"That's all right, we all fall over sometimes. I remembers once years ago, when I was about y'r age, I was deck-boy on the barque Tallion, pretty as any she were too. We were bound round the 'orn, took us three weeks to make it too, but that's another story. Anyways, after we was round the 'orn and 'eading for Pernambuco we're caulking a bit of the poop deck and the chippy 'e was keeping the tar warm up for'ard so the bosun sends me there for another pot. On the way back to the poop the bosun yells at me to get a move on so I did but I was right careless. Someone didn't belay a rope proper and I goes flat on me face with the tar all over the deck! Blimey what a ruddy mess, y' should 'ave seen it. It took me a watch to clean it up an' another to holystone the boards back proper looking like. I never spilt tar again to this very day!" He finished with a chuckle. "Well now, let's 'ave a look for this bung."

Baines clambered into the centre of the boat, steadying himself on a life line. Wentle observed how the veins stood out on the back of the old man's hand. With his silver hair and lined, weather beaten face, Wentle reckoned that the quartermaster must be very old indeed. As he followed Baines into the boat, stepping across the small gap between boat and ship, he saw the white rushing water sixty feet below. It looked a long way down and he hoped that the boat's falls were in good order! Level with the after thwart the QM pointed to a conical piece of wood secured with a lanyard.

"Well there it is lad. All tied on with string. If we kept it in the boat 'ud fill with rain water an' we can't keep the boat cover on 'cause it 'ud take too long to remove if we were in trouble. So we 'as to leave the bung out and it's the one thing y' mustn't forget if we 'as to use the boat or a lot of people'll get their feet wet!"

"Yes sir. I can see they would!" he replied, warming to this friendly old man of the sea. "You been to sea a long time, Sir?"

"Aye, long enough to have shipped before the mast when even y'r dad was still flying the yellow duster! Aye it's been a long time but a good time. All through the last war and now this one but I'm getting tired of all these sinkings; too many fine ships going to the bottom, an' men too." Pensively the sailor's eyes wandered out to sea, the new saloon-boy crouched on the thwart alongside him. Boy and man of two very different generations drawn together by a common bond, the sea and their present peril. One dreaming of what was to come and the other of what had been. Times had changed and with them the ships but the sea remained the same. An exacting and stern taskmaster but one who gave just reward to those who were faithful to it.

A gull screeched past and brought the boy back to the present with a jolt. He stood up. "I must be getting below Sir. I'm late. Good bye." He climbed back inboard as Baines replied.

"Aye, cut along now but come back and ask if there is anything y' want to know. And", he emphasised the word, "as I told y' last night, don't call me Sir. Tisn't proper!"

"No Sir, I mean Quartermaster. Thank you very much." Wentle crossed the deck and into the first-class lounge then descended the main stairway, still very much in a whirl in his new surroundings.

Excitement had caused him to sleep only fitfully and because the forced draft was not working the peak was very stuffy. Once he had tried to open the porthole to get some fresh air but had been bawled out by one of the others who had been awake.

"Want to sink the fuckin' ship mate? If someone comes in and switches on the bleeding light it'll show fer miles. Ain't you never been in no air-raid?" Porky Bates had, of course, been quite right!

It seemed like he had just fallen into a deep sleep when the night watchman had stuck his head in the peak and yelled for them to get a move on. Having paid a brief visit to the bathroom before turning in the night before Wentle thought that it might be prudent to get there quickly. There were only six wash basins, a couple of showers and two small baths between a peace time complement of some fifty catering staff! On this voyage there was another problem; there was only sea water in the taps and his soap would not lather. With so many troops on board the fresh water was only turned on for a limited period each day. He was learning quickly that life outside school and his comfortable home was not going to be easy. Clad in blue trousers and patrol jacket he had found his way to the saloon and reported to the saloon steward.

Mr.Akker was a large corpulent man in his forties with a voice like a fog horn. By the time he had explained to Wentle what his duties were and how to go about them nobody in the saloon was left in any doubt of his lowly opinion of the new saloon-boy.

Given a mop, scrubbing brush, bucket and bar of soap Wentle wondered, as he filled the bucket from a tap in the pantry, if he had made a mistake in persuading his father to let him come to sea in this way? First, on hands and knees, he scrubbed clean his allotted area from the picture of the ship to the purser's office, and part of it twice because Mr.Akker had not been satisfied. Next he had to scrub the area around the captain's table in the saloon which he managed to get right first time. Then there was the big brass frame around the window by the table to be polished, which again was achieved first time. Polishing the brass buttons and webbing buckles of his uniform back in the school cadets had given him useful experience. He thought of his ex-school fellows who, at half past six in the morning would still be lingering in their comfortable beds, but Mr Akker's roar brought him quickly back to the present.

"Whilst at sea Wentle, the captain has all his meals up on the bridge or in his cabin. That means that his tiger has to wait on him up there so you'll have to look after his table down here!" Akker continued: "Watch Lewis there and lay the table as he does, your cutlery is there in your dumb waiter. Now look smart about it! And when you've done that get for'ard and shift into clean gear and make sure that your white coat isn't creased to buggery. God help me." The orders came one after the other like a roaring torrent, but that was Akker's way. Make any newcomer fully aware that he, and no one else, was the petty officer in charge of the saloon. Once they had the idea firmly in their minds and there was no danger that they might start muscling in on his tips then he could ease off a bit.

Cleaned up, Wentle was back in the saloon to serve breakfast, his white jacket neatly creased, thanks to a tip Lewis had passed him. For a small consideration, generally a pound a trip for boys, the laundry man would wash and iron his jackets. On hearing that the boy had only one coat hanger with him, he also said that the carpenter was a decent fellow and could probably find some wire with which to make some.

Then Akker was back again. Tea to be served in individual pots accompanied by hot water; cocoa or chocolate to be mixed and served likewise but coffee to be poured from two pots, one milk the other coffee and poured simultaneously according to the officer's wish. The ingredients? "There boy, staring you in the face right by the hot water urn. God help me." All this ten minutes before the first sitting, during which he kept a very close eye on Wentle as he served his first meal.

"To start with boy you don't walk in there with only one plate in each hand, you should be able to carry five! Like this." He picked up two empty plates and held them in his left hand then balanced a third on his wrist and picked up a further two in his right hand. "Put the first couple on the dumb waiter and then pass the others around. Don't forget the mate always has tea so don't waste time asking what he wants and do that top button up properly. God help me!"

At the end of the sitting Mr.Akker was quite pleased with the new boy, although he did not tell him so. Only one plate of porridge dropped on the deck, the doctor getting kippers when he had asked for poached eggs and the trooping colonel calling the lad a dolt because he did not know what `half and half' coffee was! He, Bullhorn Akker, as he was sometimes known but never in his hearing, should be able to make something of the youngster.

By the time the second sitting, comprising warrant officers and senior sergeants, was over there was quite an improvement. Wentle found the N.C.Os far more easygoing and, indeed, slightly embarrassed at receiving such service, while joking good humouredly at his shortcomings. True the menu they received was considerably less than the officers', which did make things easier.

It was a quarter past nine before the stewards were able to snatch a hasty meal themselves. Since they had no mess-room they ate where they worked, which meant that they got their food directly from the first class galley, often including leftovers; a distinct advantage over the rest of the crew. Apart from the fact that all the milk came from tins, there did not seem to be much in the way of rationing. Being a passenger ship the Patriarch had copious storerooms and generally victualled in South America for the round trip.

There had hardly been time to give the dirty dishes to the pantry boys for washing up when the alarm bells sounded. Boat stations! With a sudden sinking feeling in his stomach Wentle had realised that he did not know where his station was and that he did not even have a life-jacket. Fortunately Lewis again came to his rescue, finding a spare jacket in a locker. He also knew where the saloon-boy's station was.

With the ebb tide under her the Patriarch made good time down the Bristol Channel so that by midday she had Swansea abeam. The weather deteriorated as she held steadily to her course until the wind had increased to a sou'westerly force seven. This made life uncomfortable for all those aboard who had still to find their sea-legs.

Bill Howell, the DEMS sergeant, ordered the canvas covers put over the four inch gun aft and had the twin Lewis machine guns on the poop deck dismounted as the spray started to come aboard. Up on the boat deck the soldiers detailed to man their Bren guns in the anti-aircraft mode had difficulty keeping their feet. Not that it mattered much as, unlike ships on the east coast run, the chance of being strafed by enemy planes was not great, but it could happen and it gave a few of them something to do.

Those aboard who were lucky enough not to be troubled by sea-sickness took little notice of the ship's motion, other than to adjust their walk. Wentle was amazed to see a steward leave the pantry with a tray balanced on one hand just above his shoulder, compensating for the ship's roll by leaning ten degrees first to one side and then the other. Wentle felt that he would wait until after lunch before trying that!

The meal was served without mishap and before the motion grew too bad. He discovered that the number of N.C.Os were fewer than the trooping staff's paper work showed so he had no second sitting. Consequently the captain's table was used exclusively by the senior ship's officers, the trooping colonel and his aide.

Akker had kept a close eye on his new steward and given him a hand now and then. After his own meal he was told to take an hour off before coming back to the saloon to help with afternoon teas. With his kapok life-jacket over his white coat Wentle kept warm despite the wind as he lingered on the well deck. He watched the bow waves fan out, meeting the waves coming in from the south west, forming spirals of spray which were immediately caught up by the wind and blown off so that the sunlight, when it appeared from between the wind driven clouds, caused the droplets to sparkle. As the sunlight came and went so the sea changed from grey to green and back again. After a while he went down to the peak and climbed up on his bunk.

Had he stayed in the fresh air and on his feet, he might not have succumbed to sea-sickness but the air in the boy's peak was pretty foul. The engineers had still not fixed the forced draught and Harry London smoking a Woodbine added to the fug. Very soon, as Wentle's balance became affected, the rivets on the deck-head started to move far more vigorously than was attributable to the movement of the ship. He closed his eyes only to find streaks of light remained, and the queasiness in his stomach was worse. It was then that he realised he was about to be sick!

He almost fell off the bunk in his effort to get down to the deck and grab for the bucket under the lower bunk. Kneeling on the deck he threw up!

Nausea made the cabin swim before his eyes and his muscles cramped as he retched time and again, much to the amusement of Ginger.

"Look at our new shipmate fellers! 'e never should 'ave left 'is muvver, poor wee feller!" he crowed, picking at his nose.

"Oh shut up Ginger," retorted Harry, "You spewed your ring up last trip too!"

Richard Wentle finally stopped retching and slumped onto Porky Bates's bunk still clutching the bucket of stinking vomit. He thought of making some suitable rejoinder such as how Nelson was always sick, but he could not summon up enough energy. Instead he wondered why he had ever wanted to come to sea!

After about ten minutes he managed to stagger over to the heads and get rid of the contents of the bucket. There the air was just as fetid and soon he was clutching the lavatory pan for support as he started retching again, trying to catch a breath between the muscle contractions even though there was nothing left to come up. As the spasms subsided he realised that he would be better up on deck. After swilling the bucket under the salt-water tap he returned to the peak and collected his life-jacket. As he put it on he wondered what he would have done if the ship been torpedoed whilst he was being sick; he was sure that he would never have made his boat station!

Half an hour later he lurched his way back to the saloon, his stomach empty and with a head that felt as if it was about to burst. Mr.Boyd, the second steward, arrived at the same time and seeing the boy's condition ordered him to take an apple from the pantry, eat it immediately and stay out on deck until he felt better!

As the Patriarch proceeded westwards the low pressure system causing the gale moved across northern France in the opposite direction so that the wind backed and decreased. Having cleared the Pembrokeshire coast in daylight course was altered to the north west until the chief officer took over the watch at twenty hundred hours. He and young Jones were able to get a good running fix from The Smalls lighthouse despite its reduced war time power. Altering course once more they steamed north by east up the Irish Sea with the ship rolling gently.

When the necessary entries had been made in the logbook, detailing those on watch, the ship's position, course and weather, the two officers joined the look-outs on the open bridge wings. With the ship now in darkness and no navigation lights showing, there was the ever present possibility of a collision with other similarly blacked out vessels. With complete trust in his second-in-command the captain lay down in the pilot's cabin situated just behind the radio-room. Fully clothed with a blanket over him he closed his eyes and hoped he would not be woken by that urgent cry of `Captain to the bridge!'

There was no emergency call for the captain during the night but, as he had written in his night order book, he was called at four in the morning and was present when the next position was plotted on the chart off the Calf of Man. From here he gave the third officer permission to make the final course alteration which would take them the last forty odd miles to Belfast Lough and their convoy. At five thirty he had his new steward called and told him to lay out his best uniform and that he would take breakfast on the bridge at six thirty.

In the presence of his captain and the other officers on the bridge Perkins was far from the brash, coarse mouthed youth that he affected to be when with the boys below decks, or with the other catering staff in the saloon. Had the second steward seen him going about his duties and cooking the captain's breakfast in the small pantry under the bridge he would have been pleasantly surprised.

When Mew Island came abeam, in keeping with the routing orders given him by the Senior Naval Officer back in Avonmouth, Spencer ordered speed reduced to eight knots. Shortly afterwards they were challenged by a motor gunboat which came tearing up to them with creaming bow wave shining in the morning sunlight.

People who were up and about on the shore gave the drab, grey ship with her decks still wet from the morning washdown no more than a glance for she was just another ship joining another convoy. That she could, like any other ship, be about to die in the forthcoming convoy never entered their minds.

The skipper of the M.G.B shouted up the bearings required for their anchor place amid the conglomeration of vessels which were already in the Lough and bade them follow him through the swept channel and open boom gate. With the gunboat's motors throttled right back and a further reduction of speed aboard the Patriarch they glided almost soundlessly through the water, now looking like quicksilver as it caught the sun.

Spencer knew how difficult it was for the small vessel ahead to go so slowly; designed like a Jack Russell Terrier to move in at high speed, hit their target and then retreat as quickly as they came. He likened his ship to a lumbering Saint Bernard by comparison and he wondered where the minesweeper was which had met them on previous visits.

"Coming up to the bearing now Sir." Third Officer Giles was leaning over the azimuth mirror intently sighting along it to the headland nearby and then swinging it to the large bell buoy off the port bow.

"Stop engines. Stand by to anchor Mr. Strickland". Spencer gave his warning to the fourth officer. "Steady as you go Quartermaster".

Strickland repeated the order down the telephone to the fo'c'sle where the chief officer already had the port anchor cleared and eased out of the hawse pipe.

"On the bearing now, Sir"

"Let go the anchor. Slow astern both."

The second quartermaster again grasped the polished engine room telegraphs and moved both handles to the required position. When the shore started to move in the opposite direction showing that they had stern way on Spencer ordered "Stop both."

On the fo'c'sle the heavy anchor chain roared out of its locker in a cloud of rusty dust. As each shackle mark appeared so a seaman rang the bell; once, twice and then three times.

"Hold on," shouted Boulton above the din raising a clenched fist to the carpenter on the winch. He looked over the bow to make sure that the cable was streamed ahead; satisfied he turned towards the bridge and with raised arms and crossed wrists showed that the ship had got her anchor. At the same time a seaman ran up a black ball on the forestay halyard to show all and sundry that the Patriarch was now anchored.

"Finished with engines Mr.Giles if you please". The engine telegraphs clanged again and the engine vibrations died away leaving the ship strangely quiet. Fourth Officer Strickland went down to the main deck to supervise the lowering of the gangway.

The captain went below to shower and change into his shore going uniform for he knew that it would not be long before a naval launch arrived to take him into Bangor for the convoy briefing.

In the accommodation and holds the troops sorted themselves out and then queued by messes for their breakfast. The second class lounge and saloon had been partially combined to form one large mess room that was, even so, nowhere near big enough so that the troops spilled out onto the decks to eat their food. Cooked for them by their own army cooks they were not as fortunate as the few who dined in the first class saloon.

Apprentice Jones, now on anchor watch with the chief officer, reported the approach of the naval launch and, as instructed, blew heartily down the voice pipe which connected the bridge to the captain's bedroom. He blew so hard that the whistle, stuck in the mouth-piece the other end, jumped out of its socket and twisted and turned before coming to rest at the end of its chain.

Spencer who was writing up the master's log at the desk got up and crossed to the voice pipe. "That must be you Jones blowing out the whistle as usual. One day you'll break its chain!"

"Yes Sir. Sorry Sir, but better to wake you than you sleep on. Naval launch approaching Sir."

"Jones I was not asleep! Ask the chief officer to meet me at the gangway and warn Mr.McTavish he's coming ashore with me today: And Jones, how does the weather look now? You know I want you to report that each time I'm called."

"Yes. Right Sir. Sorry. It's getting quite warm and I don't think it will rain today, Sir."

"Thank you. Then I shall not need a coat." Going back to the desk the captain took hold of a short lanyard which was attached to his briefcase and tied the free end to his wrist with a clove hitch. Last year he had nearly lost the case between ship and launch. Although it did not contain the crown jewels, as some wag had gibed, it did contain the Western Approaches Convoy and Merchant Navy Signals Instructions which would undoubtedly be referred to at the forthcoming conference and were, therefore, at the moment worth more than a king's ransom.

Having handed over the ship to Boulton's care, for there was much for the chief officer to attend to while he went to the convoy captain's conference, Spencer watched as the launch came nearer. The sailors in the bows and stern stood up with their boat hooks at chest level. When the watching troops realized that the launch's crew was female a chorus of wolf whistles rent the air.

As if she had been handling the boat all her life the Wren P.O coxswain eased back the throttle and went astern so that the craft swung broadside to the gangway and exactly in position. As one the two boat-hooks flashed out and hooked on, one to the gangway and the other to a rope positioned for the purpose.

Accompanied by his second officer Spencer stepped aboard the launch. Although as a civilian he was not entitled to a salute the coxswain did so out of respect. Then, noticing the ribbon of his D.S.C., added a chirpy "Good morning, Sir," discreetly watching the rather good looking captain join the other officers already in the small midships cabin. He would be quite a catch she thought, giving the order to `shove off.' Once again the two boat hooks came to rest at chest level.

"Cor, wish I could be right where that boat'ook is" exclaimed a soldier whilst one of the older men called. "Well done Lass. You show 'em how it should be done," and the cox'n acknowledged the compliment with a small smile.

The captain was away for four hours finding out where their position in the convoy would be, which was the Convoy Commodore's ship, the mean courses to be steered and where their destination was, plus sundry other vital bits of information. During that time the chief engineer and chief officer were not idle. Two barges came alongside, one with bunker fuel and the other fresh water so that when she sailed the Patriarch would have full tanks and maximum range. Boat stations were mustered and the DEMS sergeant took the opportunity to exercise the Bren gun crews as well as his own men on their Lewis guns aft. All on board were glad of the few hours at anchor to sort themselves out.

Wentle used the time between laying up for lunch and serving it to explore the long corridor that led from the galley down aft. It led past the linen room and laundry, then into the engineer's accommodation with its saloon, greasers' mess and galley; on by the second class galley and finally out into the after well deck containing number four hatch. Passing under the after-castle accommodation, with its hospital and cabin for the doctor's assistant, until he was right aft under the four inch gun platform. Weaving his way through the troops on deck he felt quite important having ducked under the rope from which hung a notice saying `Crew Only. Out of bounds to Troops.' Here, by the ensign staff, he was momentarily quite alone and as the vessel was at anchor the red ensign of the merchant marine flapped lazily above him.

The Belfast Lough seemed full of shipping. He counted at least twenty large merchantmen, which seemed a lot but then this was the first gathering of ships he had seen since before the war when his father had taken him down to Portsmouth for Navy Week. It was, in fact, going to be a small but fast convoy bound for West and South Africa.

That so many ships could be brought together in one spot and all with the right cargo for the same place, impressed Wentle. The organisation behind it must be terrific. Troops and their equipment from one direction, tanks and rations from another and each to their allotted ship. The escorts to be found and fuelled; courses to be arranged and codes to be decided; captains to be briefed and crews to be signed on so that the merchant ships could sail. He wondered who it was who said, `Let there be a convoy to...' and started it all off so that he, Richard Wentle, just out of school, should be sailing in one of those ships. It made him feel very humble for all he had to do was scrub a bit of deck each morning and clean some silver! It was the people on the bridge, in the engine or radio-rooms that really mattered and he envied them.

   Boulton, still suffering from a lack of sleep from sailing night but relieved that McTavish had taken over the watch, joined his captain in the spacious sunlit cabin for afternoon tea and doughnuts. Rolled in cinnamon with little sweetening the doughnuts were specially made to the Captain's liking. On the coffee table was a large buff envelope labeled OHMS and bearing the ships name, her call sign letters and her number in the convoy, No; 18. They sipped their tea eyeing the envelope, one knowing its contents and the other wondering into what dangers it would lead them tomorrow.

CHAPTER FOUR

Tomorrow came at 0500 hours. Hands necessary to raise the anchor and sail the ship were called. They quickly drank cups of tea before hurrying to their respective stations ready to proceed to sea. Precisely at 0530 hours, when there was just enough light to read it, a signal was run up on the Convoy Commodore's ship. She was a twenty thousand ton liner anchored at the seaward end of the Lough nearest to the boom. Acting on the signal the twenty vessels of the convoy started to heave in their anchors, disturbing the ubiquitous seagulls, who rose up screaming in protest at their sleep being disturbed. The cables made a steady clank, clank, clank as they passed over the gypsies and then clattered down into the cable locker after the stinking seabed mud had been hosed off, plopping back into the water in large lumps.

The boom defence vessel hauled back the gate and two coal burning trawlers, converted to coastal mine sweepers and belching black smoke, steamed through the open boom and began to stream their paravanes. Although the channel had been swept yesterday the convoy ships and their cargoes were far too precious for any chances to be taken. One of the mines sown for the protection of the Lough might have come adrift in the night with fatal results.

Behind them, at a suitable distance so that the noise of the paravanes would not swamp its listening device, an asdic trawler searched for any possible lurking U-boat. The lesson learned from one Gunther Prien, commanding U-47 who, in only the second month of the war, managed the impossible by sinking the Royal Oak inside the impregnable Scapa Flow, taking seven hundred and eighty six of her crew to a watery grave! In war the impossible must be considered possible.

The three trawlers were crewed by fishermen who, although on Merchant Navy pay, were now part of the Royal Naval Reserve having been signed on T124X articles. They were supposed to wear proper navy uniform and act in a disciplined manner but they were men who knew what it was like to fish the cold waters of the Orkney and Shetland Isles. And who, when they thought the Danish authorities were not looking, were not averse to a bit of poaching off the distant Faeroes. They knew how, with a bit of luck, to survive the vilest of storms and to deal with the insidious black ice which could so quickly capsize their small craft. They understood the discipline of the sea but could not tolerate what they saw as the `bullshit' of the regular navy. They lived hard and they drank hard so that when the base Regulating Petty officer had tried to smarten them up he was told simply to `fuck off or he would land in the dock.' The man, a product of years in the navy and doing everything `by the book', had nearly had an apoplectic fit and promptly put in for a transfer!

To skippers used to towing otter-boards with nets between them, towing paravanes was child's play. The commissioned gunner nominally in charge of the small flotilla was quite happy to leave things as they were for there was nothing he could teach these men. As for the two asdic operators who were `hostilities only', they happily accepted the well meant gibes about being `Bull and Brasso' boys and hoped that they had been forgotten by the drafting office.

As the grey of dawn changed to daylight the previously slumbering ships slowly, and in some cases it seemed too slowly, became alive as their anchors came home into the hawse pipes and all was secured for the forth-coming voyage. Now was the time when the masters showed their worth as ship handlers and for many it was a very trying moment. Usually, when at close quarters with other vessels, they had a pilot aboard who handled their ship for them. Now they were on their own and some felt that the eyes of their peers were boring into the back of their necks.

Because of the ebb tide, all the ships were facing the wrong direction and must be turned short around.

"Wheel amidships. Half ahead port, slow astern starboard." Since his days as a motor-gun-boat skipper with the Dover patrol Spencer had always enjoyed ship handling and now, on his bridge high above the placid waters of the Lough, as the rising sun heralded that rare occasion a perfect spring day, he felt relaxed and confident.

"Starboard fifteen. Stop starboard...Slow ahead both...Meet her."

Baines, out of his normal eight to twelve watch, echoed the orders to the man on the wheel. "Meet her." and then as he read the gyro compass "Ship's head zero six five Sir." Spencer needed his best quartermaster on the wheel at a time like this. God forbid that they should collide with another ship.

"Steady as she goes....stop both. We're overhauling our position. Mr.Strickland let me know if that one to starboard alters the bearing....Ah,Charles," as the mate appeared on the bridge, "I could do with your eyes on the port side for me."

"Steerage way off her, Sir."

"Thank you Baines. Slow ahead both."

And so it went as they inched their way towards their slot in the procession of ships which, once in open waters, formed up on either side of the commodore. When the first line of five was complete the second was formed and then the third and fourth. Finally they advanced to the north east, a phalanx of steel ships, each doing its best to keep two cables distance from its neighbours.

When he was satisfied that each ship was in its allotted position the commodore ordered an increase of speed to eight knots. They were now far enough out into the North Channel to come round on to the course which would clear the Maidens and take them safely between Rathlin Island and the Mull of Kintyre, thence to the Atlantic.

The two mine-sweepers recovered their paravanes and, together with the asdic trawler, disappeared towards the Firth of Clyde leaving the sea ahead clear.

For the vessels in the first line the change of course a hundred degrees to port was relatively simple for there was no one to bump into. But if they were to keep their line abreast there were speed adjustments to be made. Those on the inside of the turn had to slow a little and the others speed up so that the columns came round in an arc.

This first alteration of course was a major test as to whether the convoy instructions had been understood and written up correctly on the blackboards which now hung in the front of every ship's bridge. It was also a test of the liaison between masters and engineers for broad engine room telegraph commands of `dead slow, slow, half or full' did not cover this sort of manouvre. It had to be done by engine revolutions for the required speed. If an engineer did his sums wrong a collision was likely! For a newly promoted master in his first convoy this was a very anxious time.

As the convoy completed the turn, and with only one very narrow near miss, the commodore, a retired admiral, breathed a sigh of relief. He had been one of those naval officers who doubted the capability of merchant navy captains to carry out complicated maneuvers when steaming in close formation. Now, after eight convoys as commodore, he had completely revised his opinion. Perhaps they would not be able to handle a flotilla of destroyers steaming at thirty two knots but in peace time they spent far more time at sea than their opposite numbers in the Senior Service and therefore became consummate seaman.

"Escort group in sight red one o, Sir." The commodore had been facing aft watching the vessels come into position but now swung round at the report from his yeoman petty officer, raising his glasses. There, hull down, was the unmistakable mast and bridge of a destroyer clearing Rathlin Island.

"Aircraft bearing red four five." Immediately the leading signalman took up the Aldis lamp and challenged it. All on the bridge knew that it should be their air cover from the Coastal Command base the other side of Londonderry, but nevertheless.... A light blinked back at them...."Correct recognition, Sir."

"Thank you Yeoman." The Admiral breathed another sigh of relief. It was all starting to come together. Their escort was about to join them and they had a `friendly bird' above them. "Make to all ships. Increase to fourteen knots."

When the Patriarch cleared the headland a whisper of a breeze came off the shore bringing with it the scent of fresh earth and new grass. From a coppice of tall trees came the harsh cacophony of rooks calling to each other. Here and there the rising sun caught the drops of morning dew adding speckled silver to the lush green of the grass. In one field a herd of black and white cows, content after their early browsing, ambled towards a milking shed ready to give their morning quota. Except for the ships it was a scene of tranquillity and peace untouched by the vileness of war.

With the chief officer once again officer-of-the-watch Ronald Spencer had a brief moment to take in the beauty of the shoreline and thought of his wife at their country home in Essex. Inevitably he wondered, as always when they quit the land for the last time, if he would be lucky enough to see her once more. He knew that many in the convoy would never return to their homes again for, if they survived the sea passage, there was the ultimate desert battle waiting for them.

Some would die instantly, without any conscious knowledge of being blown to pieces. Others would die screaming from the intolerable pain of their wounds. There would be those who did not make a sound, but the look in their eyes would reveal the fear of what lay beyond their last shuddering breath, determined to go with dignity if that was to be their lot.

"Jesus Christ, Jones, keep your bloody eye on the commodore! What's that signal?" Boulton spoke sharply for this was not an easy time for those on the bridge.

The second quartermaster called out the flag hoist and Jones, at seventeen in his last year of apprenticeship, scanned the blackboard where the major signals were written up for quick reference. "Increase speed to fourteen knots, Sir."

The Patriarch's new saloon-boy felt the ship's vibration alter as the speed increased and longed to be out on deck to see what was happening. Serving breakfast had been easy. The chief engineer was down in the engine room making sure that all went as it should do in his noisy domain. This left only the two army officers, the purser and the doctor to be served. The conversation was subdued and they did not linger at the table so that he was able to lay for lunch, take a quick breakfast himself before being dismissed. Akker said that it was unlikely there would be boat stations while the convoy was forming up.

Donning his life jacket he made his way for'ard to number two hatch and looked up at the fo'c'sle head, wondering if he was allowed up there? "To hell with it, they can only roast me," he muttered and climbed the ladder.

On that most for'ard of all decks he found himself totally alone amongst the winches and derricks required to work number one hatch, skirting around the massive anchor winch as he walked towards the eyes of the ship. A strong breeze ruffled his hair and flapped the untied tapes of his life jacket as he gazed around taking in his first sight of a fully formed convoy.

Ahead there were two ships which seemed smaller than his own whilst those in the next column appeared to be larger and those in the centre larger still. One had three funnels and, it seemed, an endless row of lifeboats. Although no one vessel was like another they were all painted a uniform grey and had a small hoist of signal flags. A white bow wave left a frothing wake on the blue sea behind each vessel.

Wentle had brought two books aboard in his gear, a small but thick black volume of `Brown's Merchant Ships' and another `Basic Marine Engineering'. The former listed all the major shipping companies with their funnel markings, silhouettes and particulars of all their ships. Tomorrow he would try to identify the other ships in the convoy. Now, as he watched a destroyer take up station, he wished that he had also brought his copy of Jane's Fighting Ships.

Looking aft he could see that the last ship in the centre column was an armed merchant cruiser not unlike the famous Jervis Bay which had defended her convoy against the pocket-battleship Admiral Scheer in November of nineteen forty.

He had read the story of how, hopelessly out gunned, all aboard had known that it was suicide to take on the might of the Admiral Scheer, but for an hour she held the German battleship at bay whilst the ships in her convoy scattered. Eventually, blazing from stem to stern, she was sent to the bottom. In that one hour of glory she had saved thirty two of the thirty seven vessels in her convoy for, after they had scattered, the Scheer had only been able to catch five. Because her position had now been compromised she gave up the chase and ran for home. A number of the Jervis Bay crew had been on T124X articles being part of the peacetime crew.

In this convoy, WS 25, the Patriarch was the third vessel in the port line. Wentle noted that the last vessel in the line between them and the A.M.C was a large ocean going tug, flying the Dutch ensign. On the other side of the A.M.C was a Cam ship with her single fighter on its catapult fixed for'ard of the mast, over number one hatch. Four destroyers, one at each corner of the convoy, looked like the ones the Americans had lent Britain, old and battered with four funnels. The one almost out of sight but weaving back and forth ahead of the convoy seemed to be more modern. Above, in the clear blue sky, a second Avro Anson joined the first. Aircraft recognition learnt in the school cadets was of use after all! The sight of the destroyers and aircraft made Wentle feel very safe, how could any U-Boat get near them with such a strong escort?

Had Admiral Noble, at Derby House back in Liverpool, known that a cabin boy in convoy WS 25 felt `safe' he would no doubt have been most gratified. It was the Admiral's job as Commander-in-Chief Western Approaches, together with his staff, to find those escorts from their bases in Londonderry, Liverpool and Greenock; a job that at times seemed almost impossible.

In the large underground operations room, where one wall was covered by a map of the Atlantic from the east coast of America and as far east as Archangel in Russia, a Wren climbed a set of steps and placed a card with WS 25 on it between Rathlin Island and the Mull of Kintyre. She also placed another showing the escort group number, then, at the bottom of the map, several other cards noting the fact that the convoy had an A.M.C and a CAM ship and was at the moment covered by two coastal command aircraft. One card headed `destination' bore the word Freetown.

The Admiralty, from their Intelligence Centre at Bletchley, and the ships of the convoy, once they were attacked and could therefore break radio silence, provided the information which enabled operations to show all the ships at sea between America and Britain on that gigantic map. The known position of the enemy was also marked. Through interpolation the admiral and his staff could decide which way to route the convoys and advise the escort commanders of U-boat activity. At least that was the theory but, out there on the broad Atlantic, there were many imponderables to make a mockery of theoretical plans.

The last convoy routed for the Cape and carrying much needed reinforcements for North Africa had been told to steam north west for a day then southwards to pass east of the Azores before eventually turning in towards Freetown. That convoy, presently only three days from Capetown, had so far not lost a ship and so the planners in Derby House decided to route WS 25 on the same base course. However, when the convoy was on the same latitude as Land's End the first imponderable occurred.

"The glass is falling David, it's dropped two millibars in the last hour". The fourth officer was making the hourly entry into the logbook and made his comment to the third, a gangling ginger haired youth who was still troubled by acne. Roy Strickland's last trip had been his final one as an apprentice. He was now acting fourth until he could sit for his second mate's certificate. In war time it was difficult to be in the right place at the right time to take an exam. It was even more difficult to study, though he had heard that, as officers were in short supply, examiners were being more lenient than they would have been in peace time.

"That doesn't surprise me Roy, the swell's definitely increased and the clouds are getting thicker and lower. What do you reckon the wind is now, force six?"

"Yep, about that. Shall I call the Old Man or wait 'till he comes back?"

"Wait. My guess is that he's only gone for a leak so doubt if he'll be long."

The master of the Patriarch when coasting to join a convoy, liked to have his chief officer at hand during the morning hours but now the two junior officers were back on their normal watch, the eight to twelve. By custom it was a watch when it was easiest for a master to keep an eye on his less experienced watch-keepers.

He also liked to have old Jim Baines on their watch. A man of such vast experience was often worth more than an officer still 'wet behind the ears'. Baines also knew when to make a suggestion in a way that it could not be ignored and yet not cause offence.

"Yes Mr.Giles, y're right Sir. I reckon it's time we sent the A.B down for oil-skins. Me rheumatics is beginning to make trouble an' that's a sure sign of a blow."

The two young officers looked at each other and grinned. Father Neptune, as they affectionately called the quartermaster, was invariably right and the A.B had already left the bridge without waiting to be told. Baines' word was good enough for him.

By the time the watch was changed at midday the sky was totally obscured by clouds so that no sights were possible and only the dead reckoning run from the morning star position could be plotted on the ocean chart. The seas had risen to some fifteen feet and the wind was blowing the tops off in long streams of froth. The barometer was now reading nine nine six and still falling.

Spencer had passed the word to all heads of departments and the trooping colonel that they were in for a big blow and that all loose gear should be securely stowed and lashed where possible. The bosun and carpenter had supervised the striking of the wind chutes to the holds before they were blown to shreds. Next they double lashed the ladders. With little air circulation the squalor of their first day at sea soon returned to the troops below but it could not be helped. It was either that or have tons of water sloshing down on them.

When the watch changed Baines eased himself down the ladders and made his way to the duty mess alongside the crew's galley. In weather like this the two cooks had made a stew in half full saucepans and told everyone to help themselves from the galley. The steward in the officer's saloon did likewise, for it was hopeless trying to lay a table even if the fiddles were up. Mess-boy London had poured a cup of water over the table cloth to reduce the sliding effect.

Baines took down his mug, which was suitably adorned with a picture of Neptune, half filled it and then wedged himself in the corner between table and bulkhead. Nearby a seaman, between noisily sucking at his mug, complained at the ship's motion. Baines said nothing but wondered how the man would have reacted had he been with him down off the Horn in the old days of sail. He'd have known then what real hardship was!

In the first class saloon things were no better. The chef and his aides had managed to prepare a roast lunch; the vegetables in the pantry bain-marie were fairly safe but the butcher was having a hard time trying to keep the large joint in one place long enough to carve it! Not that he had to carve very much for seasickness was already starting to take its toll.

Wentle, following the advice of Lewis who looked after the chief engineer's table, also used a cup of water on the table cloth, much to the amazement of the trooping colonel who had come down a few minutes early for his lunch. He showed no signs of being troubled by the ship's movement. Silver service was out of the question so the pantry-men dished up whatever was required.

Lunch over, Wentle did not feel at his brightest but Lewis warned him that if he went for'ard to hang on to the life-lines which had now been rigged across the well decks. However the lad thought that he would be better off where he was and munched a piece of dry bread when the saloon was clear of the few diners. Heavy spray was now continually coming aboard and unless he had to there seemed no point in getting wet.

Soon after one o'clock the commodore signaled a cessation of the zigzag. It was becoming increasingly difficult to handle the ships. With the wind out of the west and the convoy's mean course almost due south all vessels had now started to roll heavily.

Depending on how the mates had been able to stow the cargoes in the holds some vessels rolled comfortably while others rolled too fast and whipped from side to side threatening to snap their masts.

The small fast cargo ships carrying the troop's equipment were mostly over their peace time loading marks and bordered on instability. If the mates ran water into the double bottoms to minimise the possibility of capsizing they would enhance the stress problems. As one mate put it to his captain "We're between the devil and the deep and it looks like the deep might win!" With great difficulty in keeping the Aldis lamp trained on the bridge of the commodore's liner he told the ex-admiral that his ship was going to fall out of line and heave to.

An hour later the commodore had no alternative but to order all ships to scatter and then heave-to and fend for themselves. The wind was now of such force that rain was being blown almost horizontally so that it became difficult to separate wave top from rain. The wave height had also doubled.

In the restricted visibility flag hoists were useless and so the message had to be passed from ship to ship and down each column. For the convoy to heave-to en-mass would present yet another danger. Some ships, particularly those larger liners in the middle, would drift at a different rate from the more deeply laden smaller vessels offering less wind resistance. It would therefore be necessary to give each vessel more sea room, hence the order to `scatter' with the outside lines in the convoy turning first whilst the others continued their advance until they too could turn.

On receipt of the order to scatter the Patriarch's captain ordered the tannoy to be used to warn all aboard that the vessel would be turning through ninety degrees and to hang on tight. Tom Bentley, the apprentice on watch with the second officer, had great difficulty in reading the `scatter' message for, even in calm weather, lamp signaling was not his best aptitude. Fortunately the chief radio officer was on the bridge and lent a hand with the onward transmission to the vessel astern of them.

Spencer looked around his bridge. McTavish and young Bentley, a quartermaster on the wheel and the stand-by A.B. Out on the wings the second quartermaster and another A.B. kept a look-out as best they could. There too was old Baines, off watch but hearing the warning on the tannoy he knew that he would be needed. All were clad in oil-skins and sou'westers some of which were too good a fit to leave room for life-jackets, several of which lay in a heap in a corner of the dull and damp wheel-house.

Turning to the quartermaster on the wheel the captain said: "Kingsley, would you please hand over to Mr.Baines but stay close and watch every move he makes, then you will know for next time." And then to the apprentice. "Bentley, close the chart room door or you'll have charts everywhere. When you've done that open and hook back the starboard one so that I've clear access. Malcolm, engine telegraph please but first warn them we are going to manoeuvre."

With both wing doors now open the wind and rain howled through the wheel-house with such force that Spencer, waiting for the right moment as the Patriarch rolled, had to lean against it. He took the few steps to the door where he held on tight whilst looking up wind at the seas bearing down on them.

"Slow ahead both." Already his eyes were smarting from the force of the rain and spray. "On this next one Baines. Two short on the whistle Second." This was the signal that a ship was turning to port, not that the ship astern would hear but it was the correct procedure.

The Patriarch rolled to port and then rose up as the wave passed under them until she started to roll the other way. "Port twenty. Half ahead starboard." With the extra thrust from the starboard propeller the bow started to swing and slowly climbed into the back of the wave before it outran her and the next one began lifting the stern, but still the turn continued.

"Slow ahead starboard." With the sea astern the danger of broaching had been avoided.

"Midships!" But Baines was watching the swinging bows against the waves ahead and had already passed through amidships and put on five degrees of starboard wheel to check the swing.

Spencer came back into the wheel-house. With the wind astern he no longer had to shout above its racket. "All right Baines she's all yours, just keep her running. Second, time us to run two miles, say at six knots. Bentley, let me know when we lose sight of the convoy."

After twenty minutes they turned the ship once more and with engines at dead slow rode the rest of the storm out. Keeping almost head to sea and taking the waves on the shoulder of the bow was a much easier movement than rolling their guts out, even if the bows were rising some forty feet into the air and then sliding down the back of the wave as it lifted the stern upwards.

Spencer had the bosun send up two extra hands to supplement the look-outs and then had each relieved every half hour. Nevertheless by the end of their four hours on watch all of them were cold and wet through with stinging eyes despite the fact that at the end of their stint outside they had been sent below for a hot drink and sandwich. Only when the chief officer took over did Spencer leave the bridge and stretch out in the pilot's cabin. In the radio room next door the second sparks had the volume turned well down for the rain and spray were causing so much static on the aerials that the receivers were almost useless save for the strongest signals.

If the crews of the merchant ships thought that they had it rough it was nothing compared to the men on the escort destroyers. Their ships were built long and slender for speed. Without the buoyancy of the merchantmen's bluff bows a wave first tossed them high into the air and then, as it passed the tipping centre, they would crash down into the trough, burying their stems deep into the next sea, making the ship shudder from stem to stern as if she were made of jelly. Sleep became impossible. As they struggled to rise from the trough fifty tons of water would cascade down the fo'c'sle, crashing past the guns and smash like a clap of thunder against the bridge-housing, to be followed by the crest of the next wave breaking upon them.

The men on their open bridges could only duck as the crest hit them and then hope that they would not see another ship in the brief moment they had to look around in the driving rain and spume before the next wave pounded them. There was not a lot they could do about it for to come anything but a few degrees off the charging seas would have meant almost certainly being laid on their beam-ends and inevitable destruction.

During the height of the storm it was impossible to change the watch. Climbing the bridge ladder would have been dangerous even for the most agile monkey with a good tail to aid his hands and feet. Full bladders added to their misery. Relaxing the muscles needed to do the necessary fought with those that were tense trying to hang on. With half frozen fingers they would struggle with their fly buttons and if they did manage it they could only piss where they stood.

Below decks some water had inevitably found its way in and slopped from fore and aft and side to side taking bits of uniform, books and various other items with it. The sailors were in a worse mess than the soldiers on the liners and they deserved every farthing of the six pence a day `hard layers allowance' which it was their privilege to receive for serving in such vessels!

Storms that come up as quickly as the one which hit WS 25 generally blow themselves out just as rapidly and so it was with this one. By daylight the wind had dropped to a mere force eight gale and veered round to the north causing a nasty cross sea, but at least the cloud was lifting and the rain easing.

With visibility at about two miles Jones logged the fact that from the Patriarch's bridge an escort destroyer was just visible on the port beam. Fine on the starboard bow was the rescue tug also at the limit of visibility but at times disappearing from sight in the troughs of the seas. Astern, at about a mile and a half, ghost like in the murk, the big three funnel liner. Boulton, wedged in a corner of the wheel-house sipping cocoa, realised that she must have drifted past them very close. Far too close for comfort in fact and he was glad he had not seen her do so.

A light started to wink at them from the destroyer and this time Jones was on the ball. "Interrogative Sir."

"Give them our number then."

Jones had to repeat it twice before it was acknowledged for the movement of the destroyer was still rather like that of a rodeo bull just released from its pen! Then, with difficulty, came a second message.

"Can you close me?" only Jones read it as "Clothe me," and asked his chief officer what on earth the navy meant by that? Whether it was the apprentice's fault or the signalman the other end was not known but in that sea it was easy to send an extra dash and dot. Then came "Where are we?".

Boulton disappeared into the chart room for a moment and came back with his dead reckoning position on a piece of paper and told Jones to send. "My guess 49°.20'30"N 25°.30'W. What is yours?"

It was highly unlikely, with no sights taken for twenty four hours and the weather endured while hove to, that any of the ships would come up with the same answer. In such cases the destroyer captain would generally take a mean of all the positions given and pin the tail on the donkey, so to speak.

Spencer, called back to the bridge by his chief officer, took in the situation and gave the O.K to close the destroyer. Slowly Boulton eased the Patriarch to port until he was four cables from the escort which, with the seas that were running, he considered close enough. By the time the liner astern had come up to them and the tug dropped back and positioned herself on its other side, the wind had dropped further and visibility had improved considerably.

At convoy conferences, for the very reason that had now befallen WS 25, all captains were given certain co-ordinates through which their convoy was to sail. So it was that these few ships, at a considerably reduced speed, now set course for the next latitude and longitude in their orders and hoped that others would join them on the way.

By the time Wentle served lunch, silver service being still impossible, the sun was trying to break through. When it did the sea turned to green only to be etched with white where the wind still tore the tops off the waves. The bosun and carpenter gathered their men together and, with the aid of the few soldiers who had now found their sea legs, struggled with the wind chutes and sent much needed fresh air into the holds. There N.C.Os formed working parties and started the clean up.

At eleven fifty five, just as watches were about to change, the escort destroyer's radar picked up an aircraft coming in from the east and went to action stations. On the Patriarch's bridge it was a quartermaster who noticed the navy guns being trained upwards and around to the east before seeing the signal hoist run up to her yard. He called the attention of the fourth officer to it. Also hearing, and then looking for himself, Spencer ordered action stations to be sounded.

Down aft in the DEMS quarters, a large square cabin built around the four inch gun burette, the corporal was just about to dish up their first reasonable meal since the height of the storm when the alarm bells went off. Concentrating on what he was doing the bells made him jump so badly that the contents of the saucepan landed on the deck. "Christ Almighty!" he gasped and stood transfixed for a brief moment before dropping the saucepan to the deck and jumping for the steel ladder which led to a booby hatch and thence onto the gun platform.

In the toilet, just off the cabin, Sergeant Bill Howell was literally caught with his pants down. The movement of the ship was now such that he reckoned the water slopping around in the toilet pan would no longer wash his backside. He had just sat on the seat when the bells sounded. `Bloody Hell!' He would be the last at stations instead of first and when the reason got around it would be the day's joke among the gunners!

Leaving the door swinging, he struggled to pull his trousers up and move at the same time. At that moment the ship rolled shooting him through the bathroom door back into the cabin, to land at the feet of the last two men by the ladder, his bare buttocks pointed uppermost!

"'Struth Sarge!" exclaimed the one who had cushioned his fall, "no time for screwing now!" and disappeared up the ladder leaving Howell struggling with his belt and his dignity.

No sooner had the cover and tampon been removed from the four inch, and the Lewis guns almost secured on their mountings, than they were told to stand down. The destroyer's armament was being trained fore and aft, its IFF set having identified the aircraft as friendly. It was their air escort from a coastal command base in Cornwall come to look after them. Not that a U-boat could possibly fire a torpedo until the swell had abated a lot more. Nevertheless it was a comforting sight when the big Sunderland flying boat dropped down to a couple of hundred feet and, flying round them, waggled its wings in greeting.

This would be the last day that WS 25 would be in range of friendly shore based aircraft but, for at least one more, they could still be found by the enemy Focke-Wulf Kondors operating from their base near Bordeaux.

For the rest of the day the weather continued to improve and one by one, or two by two, the convoy slowly reformed. As dusk was gathering the last vessel to rejoin became visible to the east. It was the one which had dropped out of line first, and it was thanks to the vigilance of the Sunderland's crew she did so before nightfall. The aircraft had sighted her miles away to the north east and given her the rough course to close the convoy. Now, with duty done and darkness almost upon them the flying boat signalled the commodore.

"Sorry but must go now. Bye bye and good luck." Once more he dropped down, waggled his wings and was off on the long flight home.

The night passed without incident and while some men slept the sleep of exhaustion others went once more to their watches with red eyes and tired minds. The merchant crews had suffered no injuries. Most knew how to give and take with their ship's movements but the wild gyrations of the destroyers had caused a broken leg, several dislocations and cracked ribs. Fortunately each escort carried a doctor who did whatever he could to ease the aches and pains.

Amongst the troops those who had been unable to keep their feet now gave the army doctors practice in setting broken limbs.

Breakfast came and went but now the saloon was full of sunlight and totally different from the empty and forlorn place of yesterday. During the storm Wentle had remained, except for a visit to the heads down the alleyway, in the saloon. There was no way that he was going to go below to the fo'c'sle. He had noted that he was not the only steward to do so.

Yesterday it had been impossible to carry out the normal routine of keeping the place clean but this morning Akker made sure that everything was back to its pristine correctness. Once again shipboard routine was establishing itself come what may.

CHAPTER FIVE

Since the storm had upset all but basic watch-keeping routine Spencer and Boulton decided that the troops should be reminded what boat stations meant. So after a mid-morning muster, the trooping commandant and the chief officer, who by rights should have been asleep in his cabin, were almost at the end of their inspection when the alarm bells sounded for action stations. The sparks urgent voice came over the loudspeaker system. "This is not a practice. I repeat this is not a practice. Enemy aircraft in sight. Enemy aircraft in sight. Except for gunners all troops remain at boat stations!"

"Mein Gott. Ein Flotta! Helmut, sehen sie an?" and the pilot of the Kondor swung her a little to port and tilted the nose down. The plane came through another puff of white cloud and there, far ahead, were small white steaks on the sea with a pin-prick of dark at their south'ard end.
"Klaus, unser Stellung. Schnell, schnell!"
Aboard the German aircraft there was great excitement. They were a new crew and until now had not made a sighting although this was their fifth flight out into the Atlantic. No longer would they have to endure the jibes in the mess about them being blind or losing their way, instead they would be stood beers all round!
Hastily the navigator checked their position and made out the sighting report. Within four minutes

the radio operator was in contact with their base back in France.

Down on the boat deck of the Patriarch Wentle heard the loudspeaker's message with some excitement. Like most on board he had been through many air raids. When home from school he had been a police messenger and as such had been out and about and seen the day-time dog fights high over Bristol or, at night, listened to the unsynchronized motors of the German bombers and the whistle of their bombs. But, unlike his mother who drove ambulances in Portsmouth, he had so far been spared the sight of the seriously injured or mutilated dead. Also, unlike others in the crew, he did not realize what the enemy aircraft now portended.

On the Escort Leader of Group Three, H.M.S Whistler, Commander Nicholls knew only too well what damn bad luck this was for the convoy. A few miles either way and the Kondor might not have seen them. He knew that the plane would be signaling their course and composition direct to Doenitz's H.Q. in Lorient. It would continue to circle the convoy and send out homing signals to any U-boat in the area.

There was only one thing that he, as escort commander, could do and that was to launch their one and only Hurricane fighter from the CAM ship. While it was being readied he ordered a few rounds to be fired at the intruder to keep it at least out of bombing range and hopefully distract the crew's attention from the activity on the CAM ship.

Wentle saw the CAM ship drop slightly astern and turn so that she was head to wind and the Hurricane was pointing into it. Almost immediately there was a puff of steam as the catapult shot the fighter forward and clear of the ship. It was momentarily lost from sight as it dipped towards the sea before climbing sharply with its engine roaring. Now banking, the pilot headed in the direction of the black balls of anti-aircraft fire and started a steeper climb before disappearing into a cloud.

There was no way that the large and much slower German plane could get away from its adversary even if they had seen it. The first they knew of their danger was when the fighter dropped down on them and raked them from wing tip to wing tip leaving their inner port engine on fire and their navigator dead.

Climbing and banking the Hurricane came around and put a burst along the length of the fuselage. The Kondor went into a side-slip, its wing tip clipping that of the fighter which had come in perilously close to make sure of the kill.

Squadron Leader Hythe-Foxworthy D.F.C was a product of Cranwell and a regular air force officer. As a newly commissioned pilot in 1937 he had been lucky to be posted to number 111 squadron which had been the first to be issued with the new Hurricane fighters. By the fall of France he was a flight commander and, having managed to extricate what remained of his flight to England, had fought high, and mostly out of sight, above the beaches of Dunkirk. Having ditched in the Channel, been rescued and landed at Dover, he was one of several in R.A.F uniform who had been unfairly booed and cursed by a number of Dunkirk survivors who wanted to know where the R.A.F had been while they were being strafed on the beaches.

He had also been `One of the Few'. Again shot down, but this time over Kent and unhurt. Later he suffered badly burned hands when he pulled one of his pilots out of a flaming aircraft after a pancake landing. He was grounded after his scarred hands went into spasm during a landing approach and he nearly wrote both himself and his aircraft off. This had also occurred in the air but he had managed to hide the fact. Unfortunately for Hythe-Foxworthy the group captain had seen his botched landing and wanted to know why such an experienced pilot had made `such a cock-up'.

Where there's a will there's a way and when volunteers for `CAM ship' pilots were called for Hythe-Foxworthy had managed to persuade the station M.O that a CAM ship pilot did not have to land his plane again, he just baled out! It was highly unlikely that pilots in these aircraft would be in the air for more than a quarter of an hour anyway! All the arguments in support of the view that he should be an instructor or a ground controller were not enough to keep him on the ground.

Now, finding himself suddenly upside down some ten thousand feet above the sea, those disfigured hands were vital to his survival as he fought his totally unbalanced aircraft. Pulling the joy-stick back and to his right with both hands he pushed with all his weight on the rudder-bar with his right foot and, miraculously, the plane flipped the right way up before going into a controlled dive.

The Kondor pilot had no such control over his plane as it spiraled down with its port wing ablaze. Before it reached the sea it blew up, its debris almost enveloping the three parachutes which had opened only moments before.

At five thousand feet Squadron Leader Hythe-Foxworthy decided it was time he also took to his parachute but he had a problem. The canopy to the cockpit slid back without trouble but as soon as he took the pressure off the rudder bar and joy-stick the Hurricane's damaged wing forced it to fall away. There was no way that he was going to be able to climb out of the cockpit and jump in a proper orderly fashion, as he had done over Kent.

Releasing his safety harness he stood up still holding the 'stick over, then, as the plane started to roll, let go and hoped that the force of gravity would throw him clear.

Back in the convoy the troops lining the decks had given a ragged cheer when the Hurricane started to climb away from them and then watched in silence as the fight began. Some of them had been at Dunkirk, remembering their anger at the way the R.A.F had appeared to let them down, unable to see the dog fights above the clouds. Now they felt sympathy for the lone pilot as they witnessed the collision; cheering with a mighty roar at the sight of his parachute opening.

All that remained was for the pilot to be picked up by the rescue tug, which also retrieved the three Germans from their ducking.

No more than ten minutes had elapsed from the time he was catapulted off to landing in the water. It took twice as long before he was sipping a rum and being rubbed down by a sick-berth attendant on the tug. He felt immeasurably pleased that the M.O who had declared him fit to fly was now vindicated and that, as a `CAM pilot' he had justified his existence. A feeling that was re-enforced when a message was handed to him from the commodore which read simply: `Thank you Sir.'

The voice of the Patriarch's captain stilled the buzz of conversation amongst the troops. "Gentlemen, for those of you who could not see the action just fought on our behalf the score is one Kondor down and one Hurricane pilot wet but safe. There also appears to be the possibility of three prisoners. However, I would warn you that the German was very busy with his radio when he was downed so it's quite possible that some of his under-water friends may well be paying us a visit shortly. Please make sure that you have your life belts with you at all times. You may now go for your belated lunch."

Ship's standing orders were that when action or non practice boat stations were sounded all galley stoves or appliances, whether oil fired or electric, were to be doused. For the troops eating aft the re-heating of their lunch did not make much difference either way to the quality, but in the first class galley the chief baker had a lot to say about Jerries who caused him to spoil one of the captain's favourite sweets!

On the destroyer Whistler, Commander Nicholls had more on his mind than a belated luncheon. Baring a miracle, enemy H.Q now knew that they had a fat target with its exact position and course, assuming that the Kondor's navigator knew his job.

The Admiralty had so far not sent them any base course changes so it was, again, to be assumed that all was clear ahead of them. He had to decide, as escort commander, whether to keep straight on or alter course to east or west, which might take them from the frying pan into the fire? Whatever his decision it was going to be based on nothing more than intuition.

Nicholls decided to keep straight on for now and since their position had already been compromised he advised the Admiralty of the happenings of the last half hour and his decision.

Wentle was sitting on number three hatch gazing at the other ships sailing on a now placid sea. The seething grey and white water of three days ago had given way to a deep blue and instead of the hurricane force wind there was now only enough to occasionally ruffle his hair. He wondered how things could change so dramatically, and whether he had done the right thing to come to sea like this.

When he left school at the end of his last term he had been a prefect and had won his swimming and hockey colours. He had been vice-captain of the school hockey eleven and also played in the cricket and rugger first teams. This term he would have been house captain, for the present incumbent was leaving to become a midshipman Royal Naval Volunteer Reserve under the Y scheme. Should he have stayed on until he had passed the school certificate exam and then done likewise?

The work he had to do as the saloon-boy was not too onerous and with his education he was capable of more complex activities. Then there was the cultural shock. He could not understand why his cabin mates, not so much Harry London but certainly the others, swore every second sentence. At school an occasional `bloody' might be used but only from the seniors. If he used `damn' within the hearing of his mother he was liable to be scolded. `Bloody swine or bastard' was the height of bad language he'd heard used, but here on the Patriarch epithets such as 'fuck' 'cunt' and 'bastard' were in constant use. He had understood from conversations in the prefect's common room after the school holidays, that to engage in the action of the first was most pleasurable, the second was the most beautiful and softest place on a girl. And you only ended up with the last if you didn't use a french letter. For the life of him he could not understand why it was necessary to describe it in such a denigrating fashion?

Then there was the dramatic change in his financial status. He had just come from the purser's office after being berated by the assistant purser, someone who until this morning he did not even know existed, for not turning in his discharge book. Something else he did not know he should do. While he was in the office he asked what his pay would be and was astounded to be told that it was two pounds ten shillings a week plus another two pounds ten danger money! At school his pocket money had been two shillings and six pence every Friday and during the holidays, if he helped his father in the pub, he generally managed to pick up an extra quid. But now, five pounds a week!

He remembered the naval captain, who had come to the school to explain about the Y scheme, telling them that a midshipman's pay was seven shillings a day, so in that respect he was jolly well better off. Lewis had also told him that it was usual for the saloon-boy to earn an extra ten shillings a week from other stewards if, during the afternoons when he was just sitting in the saloon keeping an eye on things, he laid up their tables for dinner. Perhaps after all... but his musings were brought to an abrupt end by the raucous clatter of the alarm bells.

Convoy WS 25 received a new routing some two hours after the Kondor had been shot down. The sighting report from the Kondor had been sent and acknowledged in plain language. When the Admiralty received Nicholls' report, their own and Bletchley's monitoring stations had already picked up the Kondor's transmission. They could do what the Germans would expect them to do, tell WS 25 to change course and sail east until darkness overtook them and then turn south again. Although Admiralty knew (thanks to Bletchley and the code breaking `Enigma') that there were some U-boats to the west of WS 25 they did not know about U-37.

U-37 should have been a hundred miles farther to the west with the rest of her pack but she had been delayed by trouble with the fuel pump on the port diesel motor. This had reduced her speed to seven knots which now found her in a position several miles ahead and out to the east of the convoy.

The lone submarine had not been detected because the seaplane from the A.M.C, which had been flying since dawn as the convoy's only air cover, had been hoisted back aboard for refueling. There was also a problem with one of its magnetos.

Had she been airborne she would undoubtedly have seen U-37 and forced it to dive.

The U-boat's final piece of luck was that the destroyer Warbler, which was patrolling ahead and to port of the convoy, was having intermittent trouble with both her asdic and radar equipment caused by the pounding she had received during the storm. The electrical artificer and the radar mechanic had just found the fault in a fractured power cable when the first torpedo struck.

Lieutnant Lille, in temporary command of U-37, had been lying on his bunk in a foul mood because of the engine problems when a look-out reported something on the horizon just for'ard of the beam. The officer of the watch confirmed the sighting and ordered a crash dive, which brought Lille to the control room in a hurry. Back up to periscope depth he now searched the horizon to the north. Sure enough there were the masts and funnels of what might be a destroyer. He ordered a depth of twenty metres then stopped both motors. With negative buoyancy they lay in wait until the vessel came closer.

Five minutes elapsed, which seemed an eternity to all aboard, and then another quick look. Down periscope. His ill temper left him for what he had seen was a convoy conveniently altering its course slightly to starboard, giving him a better firing angle. Better still, the destroyer was no longer heading straight for them.

Getting under way he changed course so that he would close the convoy from behind the destroyer. Another five minutes and up attack periscope. Perfect, start the plot!...

The mate on watch on the Bellevue, an ex banana boat, was a different type to those on any of the liners in the convoy. He had neither been to sea school nor been an apprentice but had advanced from the fo'c'sle. The bastard son of a tea planter in Siam he had been endowed with some of the brains of his father and the astuteness of his Chinese mother. Unlike his half brother, who had been born the right side of the blanket and therefore sent to England for his education, Martin Ziang had attended the local village school.

His father either could not or would not admit to his existence but did pass over small sums of cash from time to time to his mistress. Realising that her son had academic potential she purchased advanced schoolbooks for him but, in an obtuse way, this only served to heighten his jealousy of his half brother which festered and grew into a hatred of his father.

At the age of fifteen he made the local headman's daughter pregnant. Since she was a year younger he felt it would be wise to disappear, but first he would need money. He waited until his father had collected the plantation wages and coolly stole the lot.

He went south to Bangkok and from there worked a passage to Hong Kong. He spoke Cantonese fluently and it was easy to rob a brothel owner before moving quickly on. Looking much older than he was he found a vacant berth in an English ship as a seaman but first, lest some bastard robbed him, he opened an account with the Bank of Hong Kong.

Two years later, having learned parrot fashion to take sights, he was back in Hong Kong and decided that it was time he had a `ticket'. By `borrowing' the mate's license for a couple of days he soon had an excellently forged one of his own. Then he met up with a captain who owned a small tramp steamer and whose mate had mysteriously disappeared overboard. Since Martin, as he now called himself, spoke the language of the coolie crew and the ship traded only in the Far East the job was his.

Over the next twelve years the master, mate and chief engineer of the Marigold prospered. The cargoes the ship carried just paid her way but it was other nefarious dealings which brought the real profits.

By early nineteen forty the Marigold was falling to pieces through old age. The cost of a replacement did not appear viable whilst, for men who had spent their lives in the Far East, there was an atmosphere about the area which did not feel right. The Japanese were not to be trusted and business was declining so the three decided to go their separate ways, taking with them their not inconsiderable savings.

In London Martin met a widow and as there was some mutual physical, plus for him financial, attraction they got married. Settling in her country house it took less than a year for her to become disenchanted with some of his gross ways. He too was fed up with her constant nagging about how a country gentleman should behave. He stormed out of the house one day and made enquiries about going back to sea. His `ticket' was given only a cursory glance. `Would he take a pier head jump as third mate?'

Now here he was on the Bellevue, a hard case used to making very quick decisions to keep out of jail or stay alive.

"Torpedoes on the port bow," screamed the lookout. "Coming straight at us!" He stood transfixed as the white lines sped towards them.

With one movement Martin, who had been standing near the man on the wheel, barged him out of the way and started to spin the wheel to port faster than he had ever turned one before. This was his first active experience of the war at sea but his instinct for survival, honed to a fine pitch in the China Sea, took over.

Slowly the bows of the Bellevue began to swing and with the rudder hard over, the ship started to heel as the momentum of the turn took effect. Mesmerised, the lookout watched as the torpedoes came nearer and then were lost from sight under the swinging bow. There was a tremendous clang as one hit the ship at a combined speed of over fifty knots followed by several lesser ones as the unexploded missile bounced down the ship's side. It took about five seconds for the lookout to realize that he had not died, then he pissed in his pants. He knew, like everyone else aboard, that number one hold contained many tons of ammunition!

On the Patriarch her fourth officer was leaning on the wind dodger of the starboard bridge wing when the vessel ahead of them started to swing to port. Seeing the torpedo tracks appear from in front of the Bellevue heading for the next line of ships he shouted a warning to those in the wheelhouse

David Giles, mate of the watch, heard Stickland's warning and dived for the alarm bells. Down on number three hatch Wentle was galvanized into action and raced for the emergency ladder leading to the boat deck. When he was almost at the top there was an explosion nearby followed by another a moment later.

Panting from his climb he was the first of the crew to arrive by his lifeboat followed shortly by two seaman. Then came the purser followed two minutes later by the second radio officer who had been woken from a deep sleep and arrived unshaven and in shirt sleeves.

Doing up the tapes of his life jacket Wentle caught sight of the liner Alcavia in the line to starboard and abreast of the Bellevue. Like all the vessels she was rolling gently and the torpedoes had struck when the ship had been on the end of her roll to port. As she leaned over to starboard a gaping hole became visible around which the plates were blackened and twisted. From that black hole some of the sea water which had gone into it now spewed out and with it came debris and bodies.

The second torpedo had hit further aft dislodging the port plumber block and causing the propeller shaft to fracture. With its load suddenly removed the port turbine started to race in a manner that its governor was powerless to stop. It began to disintegrate. Flying steel killed a greaser outright and cut electric cables, causing fires which quickly spread and severed the emergency stop from the control plate to the starboard turbine. In the few moments it took for an engineer to swing a valve by hand the Alcavia came near to taking the Patriarch to the bottom of the sea with her.

For those on watch on the Patriarch, on the bridge, in the radio-room or down in the engine-room, there was no such thing as boat stations for it was they who had the ship under their direct control. For the engineers and greasers the noise of the two explosions was far different from those who heard it above decks. The sound waves hit the side of the ship like claps of thunder and vibrated back and forth vying sickeningly with the normal engine room noises. They knew it meant `some poor bastard had copped it' and fairly near at that.

In the radio-room the chief joined his junior. It was standard emergency procedure for two operators to be present. On the bridge the captain told his junior mate that he had taken the ship under his control. He watched the stricken Alcavia veer to port under the thrust of her now single propeller. Despite the ten degrees of opposite helm, which was all her quartermaster could apply before the steering jammed, she continued to come round on a course which should take her between the Bellevue and the Patriarch.

The Alcavia's captain knew from the feel of the ship under his feet that she was mortally wounded and rang down to stop engines. The engineer down on the plate also knew and opened all the steam escape valves before a wall of fire engulfed him. As the dying vessel turned so she heeled, exposing more of her mortal wounds as more sea rushed into her belly.

Soldiers running from their cabins to the stairways leading upwards were swept from their feet as a tidal wave tore through the alleyways demolishing weakened bulkheads and cabin doors as if they were matchwood.

As the water advanced so the air pressure before it grew until it was a howling gale when it reached doors leading to wider spaces. Here and there men clawed and punched friends in their frenzy to get away from the grasping hand of death.

On land these soldiers would have stood firm in the face of an advancing enemy but the sea was foreign to them and their fear of it dominated their actions. As the engine room became an inferno and the fire spread the generators failed. The lights went out adding to the panic and confusion. Then the deck tilted sharply to port as momentum came off the vessel and they could no longer stand.

Gradually the cries of rage and fear from below were silenced as the water levels rose and the ship's list increased. Trapped in their steel coffin they started the long journey down into the depths.

Above decks the roar of high pressure steam escaping through the funnel vents meant men had to shout to make themselves heard as they slipped, fell or jumped into the sea.

The bridge crew of the Patriarch had all seen ships sunk and men die but each time it happened they felt it more deeply. Now they all turned towards their captain waiting to be told what to do for they also knew that the Alcavia presented a threat to them. A threat seemingly made worse by the continuous scream of escaping steam coming to them across the short stretch of water as if this alone would be their Armageddon.

Spencer turned to look at the Bellevue. She seemed to be stopping her swing to port and might well be in the way if he took the Patriarch away from the convoy, a logical evasive action which would give them plenty of sea room. In the few seconds it took him to decide what to do the third officer had already moved to the engine telegraph.

"Emergency full ahead Giles!" The extra flow of water around the rudder would make it more effective. The brass indicator went to full astern and then back to full ahead on a pre-arranged signal with the chief engineer.

The chief, who had just arrived on the plate, took hold of the black knobs of the throttles and pushed them past the note stuck on the board which read `17 knots' and right up to their stops. Immediately the revolution counter on each motor started to climb.

The mean speed of the convoy had been set for fourteen knots but every ship had to be able to steam faster than that to keep pace with zigzag requirements. The Patriarch could do a comfortable seventeen but the chief knew he could push his motors past that in an emergency. If the `Padre' wanted to get the hell out of wherever they were so be it!

The Chief and his duty engineer watched the temperature gauges as the previously adjusted governors allowed the revolutions to creep up past the maker's recommendations.

"Starboard twenty!" Spencer kept his eye on the swinging Alcavia.... "Midships." That should keep them clear of her stern provided she held her present speed. If he took his ship too far to starboard they would be in grave danger of colliding with the ship astern of the torpedoed liner.

"Stickland, keep your eyes on the Bellevue." With engines now gathering revolutions the extra vibration could be felt on the bridge as their speed started to increase.

The Alcavia! Was her bearing still changing or was it wishful thinking?

"The Bellevue is swinging back into line Sir,"

"Thank you." Spencer acknowledged the report without taking his eyes off the ship crossing so close ahead of them. "Oh no!" he groaned, observing that the bearing was now constant as the Alcavia seemed almost to stop in her tracks, slewed farther to port and then, with all eyes riveted on her, she capsized right in front of the Patriarch. Collision seemed unavoidable.

"Hard a'starboard!" Spencer's voice had gone up an octave, and then almost in a whisper. "Dear God please no." It seemed an age before the Patriarch's bow started to swing but he dared not let it go too far.

"Midships....Port ten." If ever there was a time that he needed his skill in ship handling it was now.

"Midships, and for God's sake keep her steady man!" The stress was beginning to tell. There was just room for them to clear the hull, which was now on its side. But right across their path was a trail of debris and amongst it a thousand men!

"Stop both, in the name of God, Giles stop both!" He almost sobbed the last words. Half a cable to go; fifty yards; twenty five and then they were gliding through the flotsam.

On the Patriarch there was not a sound except for the hum of the machinery far below and they all clearly heard the cries of those in the water. The propeller shafts were no longer connected to the engines but inertia continued to turn those large slicing blades right through the trail of debris.

Aft, at the last boat station, the DEMS corporal muttered "Gawd 'struth," to nobody in particular as, looking aft, there appeared in the ship's wake a bloody trail of bodies.

"Port ten. Half ahead both...meet her." There was a tremor in Spencer's voice as he issued his orders. He had no time to dwell on what had happened beneath his ship for he must get steerage way back on her lest they collide with the vessel now only a hundred yards to starboard. He felt sick and young Giles saw the haggard look on his captain's face as the fourth mate reported.

"Bellevue back in line Sir."

The Patriarch was now steaming between the two lines of ships but level with the Bellevue. All she would have to do to get back into line was to slow a little and come to port. After the last five horrifying minutes that would be simple but Spencer's hands were shaking so badly he had to grip the handrail tightly lest they should be seen.

"Charles!" Without turning his head he spoke to the chief officer whom he knew would, by now, be somewhere on the bridge. "Would you please take over for me and get her back in line. Mr.Strickland, tell the chief sparks to pipe for the trooping adjutant to come and see me. I am going below for a moment."

Down in his day cabin Spencer looked at his shaking hands then strode quickly to his bathroom and vomited into the lavatory. Recovering himself he waited several minutes before the adjutant arrived, listened to the captain's request, and then departed to find one of the army padres to come and say Mass for him. Not since that night off Ostend when they had boarded the German gunboat and he had killed with a cutlass had he felt so wretched.

Down on the boat deck someone had told the crew to get into the lifeboat. Wentle was sitting astride the after thwart watching the stricken Alcavia as she fell out of line and curved round to pass ahead of them. How could this be happening? They had five destroyers, to say nothing of an A.M.C to look after them? He'd been told that because of their speed and strong escorts it was unusual for troop convoys to loose ships yet here was one making a terrible noise and disgorging bodies; it just did not make sense! Then there was his own ship, it seemed to be all over the place with the vibration increasing as he had never felt it before only to suddenly die away and everything become quiet.

He felt a thump in his side and heard a gruff voice say. "For fuck's sake put the bloody bung in!"

The bung! Oh hell, he had forgotten all about it. As he was about to place it in position he saw through the hole the sea below and in it the heads of several men and heard their cries for help. At that moment he became very, very frightened. He might have been one of those in the water and indeed it could still happen to him! In that instant, with death so close at hand, he became a man and going to sea became a very serious business.

The radar and asdic sets on the destroyer Warbler slowly came to life as their power was restored and the asdic operator reported a contact at red O six O, range two thousand yards. Advising the escort commander and the French destroyer Villeneuve, which was guarding the flank of the convoy, of her intentions she swung around to the attack. U-37 turned away from the convoy diving deep and for the next two hours played cat and mouse with her adversaries until, considerably damaged, she outwitted them and made off to her base at La Pallise. (U-37 survived the war and was scuttled in May 1945)

The ship astern of the Patriarch followed in her tracks but had time to avoid the survivors of the Alcavia. The rescue tug Nieu Zee now came up to the edge of the pitiful mass and began to take aboard the living. Those who could climbed the cargo nets to her decks but every now and then one of her crew would dive overboard to help those who could not. Soon her accommodation and decks were crammed to capacity and very carefully she backed away promising she would be back soon. Then, at twenty knots, she chased after the convoy to transfer her sodden passengers to the A.M.C. making room for those she had left behind.

The spotter seaplane became airborne just before the Nieu Zee caught up with the convoy. Transferring the survivors was a lengthy task requiring both vessels to reduce speed. This would, of course, make them an easier target should there be any more U-boats around.

Commander Nicholls brought the Whistler down to the two vessels and on learning that there could well be another two loads of survivors to pick up knew he had a problem.

Each time the tug returned to the area of the sinking she would have further to go and further still to come back. Now they had the aircraft again he decided that both ships should go back with one of the destroyers to carry out continuous asdic sweeps around them while the seaplane circled above. It was a bold decision because it would leave the rest of the convoy exposed but there were perhaps a thousand men back there in the water.

He cursed the fact that the sixth destroyer, which started with them, had turned back only a few hours after they had cleared the Northern Channel. She had been due a refit but her chief thought that they would be able to put in one more trip. Unfortunately he had been wrong. She had developed major engine trouble simply through overwork.

Nicholls swung the Whistler around and at thirty knots ran up the port side of the convoy until he was within radio range on the `talk between ships' set and then gave the Villeneuve orders to come back to the convoy.

The escort commander's W/T office reported that they had not picked up any transmissions from the enemy so it appeared that it was unlikely the convoy's position had been compromised. Commander Nicholls decided not to break radio silence and held their present southerly course.

Fortunately for the Alcavia's survivors the water was fairly warm but when the tug disappeared after the convoy many started to lose hope. Some had only been carrying life-belts which had been torn from their grip as the ship capsized and they now struggled to find something to hang onto and stay afloat. With the almost instant heeling to port there had been no time to lower any lifeboats although a few life rafts had been freed and now dotted the sea amongst the struggling men and debris.

Bubbles of oil came to the surface as a ruptured fuel tank began to leak, and then, to add to the swimmer's horror several bodies suddenly shot up out of the water, falling back with loud plops where they bobbed around in a macabre dance. The dead men had been freed from the vortex of the sinking liner and the buoyancy of their life belts had shot them to the surface.

One of the ship's officers shouted that everyone who could swim should get clear of the debris and then stick together in groups to make it easier to be picked up. "It worked for me last time I was in this mess so why not now?"

Slowly men took up the challenge until the quick were separated from the dead. When the three ships were sighted by the men in the water it was mid-afternoon and the pick-up went much faster. The destroyer slipped her two whalers, which went to the aid of those who had been separated from the main groups.

When evening turned into night the captain of the Nieu Zee called for complete quiet but no more cries could be heard, just the lapping of the sea against the hull.

The navy whalers investigated three pin pricks of red from the lights carried on the shoulders of the merchant crews life-jackets. One sailor was unconscious with his leg almost torn off and he was taken aboard, but the others were dead. Since there was no time or room to do otherwise, they were left where they were.

With heavy hearts the last of the survivors were transferred to the A.M.C; a total of one thousand two hundred and twenty one men out of the three thousand souls who had been aboard the Alcavia.

This was one of the worst losses of life from a merchant ship sinking and, as when the Queen

Mary had cut one of her escorts in two, was kept from the press and radio.

The evening of the Alcavia's loss was uneventful except that none of the troops in the convoy went anywhere in their ships without their lifebelts. Most of the merchant seamen had adopted this practice a long time ago. Their lifebelts were their best friend. At times its bulk could be a damn nuisance and finding the best place to put it while you worked could be a problem. The engineers and greasers left theirs in the flats outside the steel doors that lead down to the bowels of the ship. It was far too hot to wear them and the ladders too steep to come up in a hurry using only one hand if they carried them. The DEMS gunners had been issued with the navy blow-up type which were worn permanently around the waist. The engineers would have been better off in some ways with this kind, however, in a lifeboat the kapok ones were warmer and helped to fend off exposure.

In the saloon there was a cupboard under the stairs which housed brooms and cleaning gear and was most convenient for the stowage of stewards' life-jackets. Wentle was lucky. Next to his table were half a dozen coat hooks used by the ship's officers for their caps and coats when dining in the saloon. Now the top item on each was a blue life-jacket and no one objected to the saloon-boy adding his.

Since the convoy was down around thirty degrees of latitude the day had been quite warm and now the evening was mild.

Harry London and Wentle were in the boy's peak having finished their jobs and their evening meal. Harry had suggested that they take their mattresses up onto number two hatch and sleep there. It was, he said, done by most of the stewards once the weather was right. It was both pleasant and that much nearer to the lifeboats! It meant that they would have to be a bit quicker when turning-to in the morning since their bedding could not be left out during the day, but it would be worth it.

Together they struggled up the stairs clutching their mattresses and a blanket and secured a place on the hatch. The canvas over the heavy wooden hatch covers was still quite warm from the day's sun and after the earlier storm, was very clean although covered with a fine coat of salt.

Dusk was approaching and Quartermaster Baines had just finished his last pipe before going on watch when he observed the two boys on the hatch. He went back into the fo'c'sle, re-emerging a minute later with a heavy seaman's jersey.

"Here lad, take this. It'll get colder during the night and a sweater like this can be a godsend if we gets unlucky and has to take to the boats. Like young 'Arry 'ere, I knows!"

"Thanks Quartermaster, thanks a lot. Jolly decent of you." Wentle took the sweater and changed it for his patrol jacket and then, using the soft life-jacket as a pillow, lay back on the blanket.

Perkins, the captain's tiger, had been lounging by the bulwarks with the officer's steward and seen the old quartermaster's kindly act. Why he disliked Wentle he did not really know. Perhaps Wentle reminded him of the boy who lived up in the manor and with whom he'd had innumerable fights. After which his father, when he found out, had given him the belt and administered the usual rebuke about `they being the labourers on the farm should know their place in the world. There were them that were born with luck on their side and them that weren't and, anyway, the squire treats us right fairly.'

At the sea-school he had attended the system rightly taught the boys to respect and obey their officers. To give Perkins his due, he did try. The third officer for instance was obviously of the class that lived in the Manor but he did not look down his nose at Perkins like the junior radio officer who was definitely not `top drawer'. But there was nothing Perkins could do to influence who was made an officer. But now here was one of the so called `officer class' down in the fo'c'sle and he bitterly resented the fact.

When Baines disappeared in the direction of the bridge, Perkins again mimicked the saloon-boy saying to no one in particular. "I say you chaps, look at the Toff all dolled up. Proper pansy 'aint he. Reckon old Baines is after his ring, what?"

"Knock it off Tiger," said the officer's steward and turned away in disgust. Everyone aboard liked Father Neptune.

Wentle said nothing although inwardly he boiled. He had thought it damned nice of the old Q.M to look after him like that. People like Perkins just had no decency at all.

Realizing that his jibe had fallen flat the tiger decided that he needed to save face. Climbing on to the hatch he walked towards his own bed roll but at the last moment side stepped to where his pet aversion lay and made as if to trip over the outstretched legs. "Oops, sorry old chap!" he said, kicking Wentle's ankle.

This was more than Wentle could take. Quick as a flash he rolled over onto his knees and launched himself at his adversary. As he had learned on the rugby field his shoulder slammed into Perkins' thigh, sliding his arms around and down the legs, bringing his target crashing onto the hatch, winding him. Before the tiger could recover the saloon-boy was astride him, settling his knees into the other's arm muscles. Perkins cried out in pain. With one hand holding a wrist hard down the other caught a little finger and bent it backwards in a move that was definitely not learnt on the rugger field and which brought forth a scream of invective.

"You fucking bastard y're breaking my bloody finger, let go fer fuck's sake!"

Wentle did so and grasped the wrist instead but at the same time screwed his knees once more into the biceps. He was gratified by a further cry from Perkins and "I'll fucking murder you if you don't let me up."

"Not damn likely chum," replied Wentle through clenched teeth, exerting all his strength to hold the older youth down. "You can stay there until you learn some manners!"

At this point a voice from up on the bridge called out wanting to know what was going on down there.

"O.K Sir, I'll deal with it." The bosun, whose cabin was the first in the port entrance to the fo'c'sle, had appeared on the scene and now growled at the two. "You'd better stop right there or I'll 'ave you both logged, you stupid bastards! 'aven't we enough on our plates without you idiots fighting!"

Wentle got up and, not sure to whom the voice of authority belonged said, "Sorry Sir, but he pushed me just a bit too far."

The bosun had so far had no reason to speak with the saloon-boy. Under normal circumstances catering staff were nothing to do with him, but he'd heard on the ship's grapevine that the new lad had an unusual accent for such a rating.

"You're new to the sea they tell me so you'd better learn pretty quick that I don't allow no fighting aboard any ship I'm bosun of! Got it?" then, recognising the tiger, continued. "As for you Perkins, if you want to stay the old man's tiger you'd best mend yo'r ways bloody quick!"

Again the voice from above wanted to know what was happening.

"It's all right, Sir, I've settled it." Adding a muttered "bloody nipper" so that only those close to him could hear. He'd recognised young Strickland's voice. "You need to keep your mouth shut 'an all. Down 'ere is my kingdom."

Baines, who was port lookout and alongside the fourth officer, said. "Best leave it to the bosun, Sir," and seeing the captain emerge from the wheelhouse, "begging you're pardon captain."

Spencer, having only partially heard what was going on, merely said, "Quite so Baines, quite so. A nice evening Q.M. Let us hope that it stays peaceful."

The enemy did not find the convoy again and the night passed without incident, but for Wentle his sleep was far from peaceful. Twice he woke in a sweat hearing the cries of those men in the water. It seemed that he lay there for hours just looking up at the stars and listening to the sigh of the wind as it felt its way around the ship. Occasionally he heard faint voices from the bridge.

"Right you lot. Get y'r 'ands off y'r pricks and move!" This voice was right in his ear and belonged to the night-watchman. Wentle opened his eyes to find that it was daylight and time for the daily drudgery to begin.

CHAPTER SIX

As each meal went by Wentle became more proficient at his job so that Akker had only occasionally to either help or bail him out. He decided that despite the thundering voice he liked the saloon steward for the man did seem to be fair. At breakfast times he and their immediate boss, Mr.Boyd, appeared just to stand around keeping an eye on everything. But for lunch and dinner Akker became the wine steward and Wentle admired the way he moved around so quickly with his tray held above the shoulder never seeming to spill a drop!

Wentle also noted how many times Akker's hand went from his tray to his pocket and decided that he must be making quite a bit from tips. Even though the junior army officers would be earning far less than any of the stewards they felt that in such surroundings they were beholden to leave some change on the trays. Wentle learned later that giving change in small denominations usually ensured that at least something was left. Naturally Akker and, in the evenings his carefully chosen helper, ensured that the barman was properly looked after.

So it was that tips formed a very important part of the catering staff's life and the system was quite rigid. If a passenger wanted to sit at a different table then that was up to the second steward to arrange; a special meal or diet was also his prerogative but the tips would be shared with the appropriate member of the galley staff. The chief steward? Well his was the job of ordering all the stores required to feed every one aboard and the ships' chandlers ashore naturally wanted to ensure that they got the order and not the opposition down the road. And so it went on; the cabin stewards looked after the linen keeper and the laundry man.

`Gobbledeguts', as the chief steward was irreverently known in the boy's peak, was very aptly named although perhaps `Humpty Dumpty' would have been more descriptive. He was shaped just like an egg. His bald head and pouched face with its steel rimmed glasses disappeared into his body almost without a neck. From there on the body rapidly became larger until his uniform jacket stuck out over a protruding belly and hung like a skirt.

The chief was finding that after nearly twenty years the inactive and well fed life aboard ship had its disadvantages. Moving around in the narrow confines of his office and store-rooms was difficult enough but when it was necessary to wear a life-jacket as well it became almost impossible. Climbing the stairs in a hurry to get to boat stations made him puff and pant and he was invariably the last to arrive; when he did he was only too pleased to leave everything to the overbearing third sparks. Perhaps it was time for him to think about going ashore but, like Scrooge, he did like to count his growing bank balance each leave!

Unable to take his afternoon nap because of dyspepsia, the root cause of his bad temper, he was passing through the saloon to his office for some Milk of Magnesia when he caught sight of Wentle.

"Boy, what's your name? I've forgotten." This was the first time since the interview before signing-on that he had spoken to his saloon-boy and he would not have bothered now if it were not for the grapevine. Here was a chance to vent his spleen on someone.

"Wentle, Sir."

"Well Mr.Bloody Wentle, I hear you were in a fight last night and I don't like my staff doing that, particularly a whipper-snapper like you. Getting too big for your boots already are you? Just you watch it! Why aren't you cleaning silver or something instead of sitting there reading?" He picked up the book in a podgy hand. "Good God, Engineering. You're a fool. Make a damn sight more money in catering than you ever will down below!" and he stomped off to his office.

The officers' saloon and lounge ran across the width of the bridge housing with windows facing for'ard. At one end was a large dining table with its attendant dumb-waiter, at the other were armchairs and a long settee. It was home to the navigating and radio officers, the assistant purser and the apprentices.

While Wentle was reading down in the first class saloon Dai Jones was spending a compulsory two hours wrestling with his books on celestial navigation. Having just looked up the answer at the back of the book and found that he was wrong he exclaimed. "Damn and blast I just can't seem to do the bloody thing!"

To which the assistant purser remarked, "No doubt you would if it had a skirt on," as he turned the page of an Esquire magazine. "Now shut up Dai, you distract me."

"Oh get stuffed Bill, it's all right for those who don't have a job to do!"

It was true that whilst the ship had troops aboard rather than passengers the `Ass Pee', as he was nicknamed or after a few drinks, `Donkey's Piss', had little to do. What work he did do was mostly the purser's who was delighted to side shift his work in the name of `experience' to his junior. It left him plenty of time to spend with his drinking partner the doctor.

One of the second officer's duties was acting as `schoolmaster' to the two apprentices. In peacetime it could easily be fitted into the ship's routine but now the rigors of wartime watch-keeping, particularly when in convoy, placed a considerable added strain on everyone. Until this trip McTavish had done his best to help the two youngsters with their studies but since he came back from leave neither seemed to be able to do anything right. Tom Bentley, who stood watch with the second, had told Dai that time and again he was being balled out for next to nothing so no doubt, thought Dai, he would get a bollocking for this afternoon's work. He wished he knew what was making the second such a grouch.

When the Patriarch had docked at the end of last trip Malcom McTavish had, as normal, been on the second leave roster. He did the mate's job whilst Boulton was on leave and then went off himself thus enabling the loading to be carried out by the chief officer. The chief had been very surprised when the second had come back two days early. Every day of leave was precious.

McTavish had changed considerably. He was moody and kept to himself, performing his duties correctly but almost zombie-like. Boulton learned from him that his wife had been killed in an air raid in Edinburgh and that his family was looking after their two year old daughter but then McTavish had clammed up.

Boulton tried to imagine what the grief from losing a wife would be like. Would it be the same for him as for the much younger, and relatively newly wed Scot? He had been married for twenty years and the children more or less grown up, would that make a difference?

The facts as told to him by McTavish were correct but the second had not told of the circumstances that had brought his wife to Edinburgh on the night the Germans had chosen for a quick hit and run raid on the ancient city.

*   *   *   *

Second Officer McTavish walked from the bus stop and turned into the road in which his house stood. Being quite warm for the time of year he slung his greatcoat over a shoulder and with his case in one hand and a heavy food parcel in the other quickened his pace at the sight of his home. The strain of the past three months at sea, which had left him looking tired and worn out, started to leave him and he began to feel more like the lively and cultured man his wife had married.

Like any other serviceman he thought now of the woman he loved and what it would be like to be with her in a bed which did not move and to sleep by her side undisturbed by alarm bells. To feel the warmth of her body next to his and after their passions were spent how her inner strength would slowly seep into him returning some of the joy of living. He knew it would take several days for his body to become accustomed to not having to get up at midnight to take over the watch and that in all probability that first night's sleep would stretch well into tomorrow.

Now he could see his house clearly. It was a semi-detached, typical of the mid thirties architecture with a front bay window capped with black painted gable roof. The walls were a white pebble dash finish and when the roses along the bottom came into bloom later in the year the whole effect would be quite pleasing and, he mused, in ten more years the mortgage would be paid off.

Four more houses to pass; he thought now of the thrill of that first kiss, the smell of his wife's scent and how he would carry his small daughter on his shoulders around the garden and hear her shrill cries of pleasure. For two weeks perhaps it would all help to keep his mind off the unpleasantness of war.

He had sent Eileen a telegram informing her of his time of arrival and then caught a bus to Templemeads station. From Bristol the train had been packed and he had sat on his case in the corridor. But after changing trains at Crewe, where he bought a cup of lukewarm tea and a piece of stale slab cake, he was lucky enough to obtain a corner seat for the rest of the tedious journey across northern England and into Scotland. Now, two hours late, he was finally home, and the fact that the sun was actually shining surely augered well for his leave.

Elated he opened the front gate; he really must fix that squeak this leave; into the small but tidy garden, seeing as he did so, the bay window curtain move. Before he reached the front door it was opened by his sister, Maureen and little Fiona rushed out to greet him, clinging to his legs sobbing. Seeing the expression on his sister's face turned his leave to purgatory.

Two days previously Eileen had asked Maureen if she would baby sit while she went into Edinburgh to visit an old friend and do some shopping, and would it be all right if she stayed the night?

Yesterday evening a policeman had called to check if this was the home of an Eileen McTavish. On learning that it was, he regretted he had to tell Maureen that Eileen and a soldier with her had been killed in an air raid.

Apparently they had been staying in a small hotel when the building next door had suffered a direct hit. The adjoining wall had collapsed killing a number of the hotel occupants. The woman in one of them had been identified from her ration book and the man from his pay book. He was one Captain Stuart of the `Green Howards'. The War Office was, of course, being advised but that would take time. In the meanwhile the constable wondered if Maureen knew him and if he lived locally?

While Maureen went to the local call box to 'phone their mother, her brother, dazed and numbed by the news, had wandered upstairs where in their bedroom he found the note. It read simply that Malcolm's wife had met another man. She was very sorry but they were in love and hoped eventually to get married. He was on embarkation leave after which they would be going down to Aldershot where his regiment was stationed until he went abroad. She knew she was doing wrong but could not help herself and apologised to everyone for the pain she knew this would cause. If Fiona could stay with Granny she would come back up in a couple of weeks and do whatever the family wanted her to do.

As the days passed the numbness gradually eased and Malcom came to accept that his wife was gone. But it would take a lot longer before he would accept that the world with all its perversities had still to go on its daily way. At night little Fiona woke crying for her mother who, she had been told, was now in heaven.

The contents of the note had been kept from the rest of the family and Maureen sworn to secrecy, but after a further ten days the hurt was undiminished and he decided that he would be better off with something to occupy his mind. The house and family had too many memories. So it was that he returned early to his ship.

As usual on her last day alongside, whilst the Patriarch took her troops aboard, the second officer was busy starting up and checking the gyro compass, dealing with chart corrections and laying off their course to Belfast. – given to him in strict confidence. There were numerous other duties which were the lot of the officer responsible for the ship's navigation and he therefore had no idea who the troops slowly winding their way up the brow and into the gunport flat were.

On that first boat stations in the Bristol Channel all the soldiers and airmen wore great coats, but subsequently he saw that some shoulder flashes bore the insignia `Green Howards'. A thought had started to nag him and eventually he knew that he had to find out if this was that 'rotten sod's' battalion and possibly something about the man. No doubt it was stupid of him not to let sleeping dogs lie but in such situations it was impossible to always be rational.

Coming off watch he looked at Jones' work, showed the apprentice where he had gone wrong, gave him a bollocking for being bloody careless and then made his way aft to the ship's office flat. In the area which Wentle scrubbed daily he found the trooping staff sergeant working on a programme for a forthcoming ship's concert and enquired the best way to find out if a friend, a captain, in the `Green Howards' was aboard?

Yes, the sergeant could go through the list for the third regiment of the `G.H' but it would probably be quicker if he spoke direct to their adjutant who would know the captain personally. He had no idea where the adjutant was at the moment but if the second officer would come back in the morning about ten he should be in the office.

The evening and night passed without incident as the convoy made its way south. As the latitude decreased so the weather became warmer and most of the troops shifted into tropical shorts and shirts.

McTavish had put a notice on his cabin door to be called at half nine. Normally he would sleep until about ten, take a shower and then make himself a cup of tea for he did not take breakfast while watch-keeping, sleep was more important.

Once more at the trooping office, he was greeted by a young captain who enquired how he could be of assistance.

"I was wondering if there is a Captain Stuart with you? I met him once and thought that as his regiment was aboard perhaps he might be?"

"Well, unfortunately old man, poor old Stewee has bought it!" He touched the second officer's arm and nodded in the direction of the corridor where they would be out of earshot of the other soldiers in the office. "He was two days overdue his leave and we thought he'd gone AWOL, then just before we came aboard this old tub we got a message to say that he'd copped it in some hotel in Edinburgh." He paused to light a cigarette, which irritated McTavish. "Since he lived in the city he must have been up to his usual pastime of screwing some guy's wife! He used to say there was more thrill in married women, half the fun was in not getting caught but he did once. He was knocking off the company commander's wife which really was a bit too near the bone; you know the old adage `don't shit on your own doorstep'! He had a hell of a job getting out of that one but officers were, 'still are for that matter, in short supply so a quick transfer to this battalion and Bob's your uncle! Quite a character was old Stewee, known as the `Rake of the Regiment'. Bloody shame really. He used to keep us in hoots of laughter in the mess with stories of his escapades. Even if you only believed half what he said he still must have scored more times than the rest of us put together." He paused to take a long drag of his cigarette. "Say, Second, why don't you come and have a G an T before lunch? It's a regimental tradition with us just like you navy chaps with your Pink Gins. The fellows will be pleased to meet you and you could hear a few of good old Stewee's tales. What do you say?"

"Thanks but no, I don't drink at sea and anyway at midday I have to drive this Old Tub as you call her". How he had been able to stay outwardly unmoved by this eulogy of Stuart he did not know but by the time he arrived in the solitude of his cabin he was seething. Rage at finding out what sort of man his wife had left him for. Rage at the vision of the man inside Eileen. Shaking uncontrollably with eyes blurred and totally beside himself he slammed his fist into the photo of woman and child which hung on the bulkhead.

The hurt in his hand and the voice of the officer's steward, who happened to be passing, slowly brought McTavish back to sanity. His hand was a mess, in two places he could see the bone of the knuckle.

The steward, on hearing the breaking of glass had opened the cabin door. "Why you've cut your hand, Sir. It looks quite nasty" and then noticing the Second's face. "You look like a ghost. I think you'd best get down to the Doc right away Mr.McTavish, Sir, I'll come with you but best put something over those knuckles." He fished a handkerchief out of a drawer.

By the time the two men reached the hospital flat where the doctor held court, the rage had left the Second and only the pain remained. He felt totally numb inside but otherwise rational.

Brightman, the hospital assistant, slid a glass out of sight when he saw who his visitor was.

"Where's the Quack chum? Mr.McTavish has had an accident and I think he'll need a few stitches."

Brightman took a quick look at the injury and gave McTavish a piece of gauze to hold on it before tearing off to the first class lounge in search of his boss. Hargraves, who was waiting for the purser to arrive before ordering his first pre-lunch drink, was annoyed to be called away because some damn fool officer couldn't look after himself properly. He was somewhat mollified when Brightman pointed out that it was one of their own officers and not a soldier who needed attention.

Since there were two army medical officers aboard the ship's doctor did not have a great deal to do although, as they worked from his surgery, he had to be there just in case. He longed for the return of the pre-war days when there were lady passengers who needed his attention and with whom he could indulge his passion for dancing. He was knotting the last stitch when a voice blared out making McTavish jump and the gut tore through the edge of the wound.

"Patriarch. Captain to the bridge please!"

Spencer had been in the chartroom. When he heard Commander Nicholls' voice on the Whistler's loud hailer he went out onto the starboard wing. Watching the speed fall off the destroyer as she came up from astern, he tried to think what his ship might have done wrong to bring it to the personal attention of the escort commander.

When the two vessels were level bridge to bridge an officer stepped up onto the warship's wing grating and, raising a megaphone.

"Morning father and a happy birthday!"

Good God, John! A suddenly elated Spencer raised his own megaphone. "John what a surprise. I thought you were still in the Violet. And thank you for the good wishes, I'd forgotten all about it. How long have you been in Whistler?"

"Day before we sailed to look after you lot. Transferred on promotion!" Spencer's son raised a finger to the epaulette on his shoulder. Since the two ships were only twenty five yards apart Spencer could clearly see the interwoven lace a of sub-lieutenant of the R.N.R. "When my captain heard you were master of the Patriarch he kindly arranged this little visit. How was mother when you left?"

"Fine, John fine. And thank you Commander Nicholls, this has made my day." He saw the commander wave a hand in acknowledgement and then his voice came over the loud hailer once again but this time the volume was lower.

"My pleasure Captain. When the boys from Freetown arrive tomorrow we'll be leaving you so have a good trip. I'll keep an eye on this young man for you." With his free hand he good humouredly pushed John's cap down over his eyes. "Bye for now". The loud speaker went dead and as father and son waved goodbye to each other the destroyer gathered speed on her way to the head of the convoy.

When the escort commander had driven from Londonderry to Belfast for the convoy conference he had no idea that the subbie who had joined his ship the previous evening was the son of one of the captains. That the subbie was R.N.R was very pleasing for it meant that he would be a competent watch officer and a good navigator, particularly as this one had done three years at H.M.S Conway before coming into the Navy. After a course on torpedoes and mines at H.M.S Vernon followed by gunnery at Whale Island he would be a welcome addition to any warship. It was a pity, Nicholls thought, that he had not been able to come alongside the Patriarch sooner but with one escort short it just could not be done while they were in a known U-boat area.

On the Patriarch Spencer was delighted at having been able to see and speak with his son, but sorry that it was for such a short time. That they had been so close to each other for the last six days seemed unreal; and now the boy was in destroyers which, after motor-gun-boats, were about the best!

The arrival on the bridge of the second officer to take the midday sights broke the captain's train of thought. "What on earth have you done to your hand, Malcolm?" he enquired catching sight of the bandage.

"A bit of an accident, Sir but nothing to worry about". McTavish was now reasonably in control of himself. The outburst in his cabin had released much of the mental anguish of the last fortnight.

"Can you use a sextant properly?"

"I believe so, Sir."

The midday meridian altitude sight was the quickest and simplest sight of all to work out and the result combined with the dawn star fix, and a mid-morning sun position line gave them an accurate latitude and longitude. While the second and third officers used their sextants and the fourth marked the time Spencer thought again of his son.

Tomorrow, all being well, their present escorts would be relieved and, despite having refueled from the A.M.C during the last couple of days, they would be off to the Azores for further replenishment and provisions. With full bunker tanks they would then, more than likely, head back north to take over escort duties on a homeward bound convoy. The U.S. or Canadian Navy would bring a convoy from Halifax half way to the U.K. and then the R.N. would take over. On such duties John would at least be more comfortable in a destroyer than the much smaller corvette and, possibly, safer.

The captain waited on the bridge until his second officer had finished plotting their position on the ocean chart and taken over the watch before going to his cabin for lunch. Something worried him about McTavish so he decided to do without his usual afternoon siesta in the pilot's cabin and find various excuses to go out onto the bridge. But first that lunch.

As the weather was fine Perkins had been asked to bring up a menu from the first class saloon and from it Spencer had chosen one of his favourite dishes, steak and kidney pie. Served up properly in a heated silver entree dish it should arrive hot without having to be re-heated, and thereby possibly spoilt, in his pantry.

The convoy was still far enough to the north for the sun to be streaming into the day cabin. That and the inner warmth from speaking with his son gave him a feeling close to contentment and, he had to admit, a little envious of John being in a destroyer. At heart he was still a navy man.

When war seemed inevitable the Navy had found Spencer and wanted him back but with the years away from the service and at forty three it would probably have meant a shore job, at least at the beginning while ships were in such drastically short supply. That was the last thing he wanted. Fortunately his company had prevailed against Their Lordship's request, pointing out that he was far more useful as one of their captains in a ship whose cargoes were of vital importance, rather than driving a desk ashore or possibly teaching navigation.

Spencer had never liked having a steward standing behind him watching his every move as he ate his food so he rang the little bell for his tiger who was in the tiny pantry across the alleyway.

"Perkins please tell the chef that was, as usual, excellent. I'll have the pears now." Perkins disappeared towards the pantry. Before he could return, the quiet of the cabin was disturbed by clanging alarm bells sounding action stations.

In one movement the captain pushed back his chair, grabbed his lifebelt and strode for the door snatching his cap off the hook as he went out.

In the first class saloon the alarm sounded as the chief officer was about to take coffee. He too, rose rapidly from the table, but in reaching for his lifebelt and cap he caused Wentle to spill coffee over the table cloth and into the lap of the trooping commandant. As with all the other officers aboard the colonel was clad in tropical shorts and the coffee was piping hot. With a roar of pain he jumped up, knocking the purser's arm and causing his brandy to fly into the face of the doctor, who exclaimed "Damn and blast this bloody war!" The chief engineer, sitting at the end of the table, was out of harm's way and laughed heartily as he left the table and made for his life-jacket on the wall hooks. `Sometimes' he thought, `the war had its lighter moments' and rapidly made his way to the engine-room.

"What the devil has happened here, Wentle?" Akker had been on the other side of the saloon serving drinks but seemed to have flown across to the saloon-boy's table. When he saw the colonel open his fly and dab at his genitals with a serviette the saloon steward had to turn away to hide the smile on his face. Mr.Boyd also came over to see what was up.

"It really wasn't my fault, Sir," stammered Wentle. "The chief officer almost knocked me over."

The doctor chimed in. "Yes, don't blame the boy. It wasn't his fault," and then, "Colonel, you'd better come along to the surgery and I'll give you something to put on that lot or you might never be able to use it again!"

Unfortunately the colonel did not see the funny side, while the purser, who did not have an action station, demanded another brandy and to "Bloody well put it on the colonel's bar chit!"

The Patriarch's standing orders stated that the officer of the watch was to sound action stations whenever the enemy was reported. Spencer's reason for this was twofold; it made sure that those below decks were aware that things could hot up at any moment and secondly the DEMS gunners might just be lucky enough to get a shot at a U-boat on the surface. Now as he arrived on the bridge the apprentice and an A.B were getting a Hotchkiss machine gun out of its locker.

McTavish greeted him. "The Villeneuve has run up the `Contact' signal, Sir." He pointed to where the destroyer was tearing off to the east with several flag hoists at her yard arms. Farther out still their faithful old seaplane was almost standing on its wing tip while it circled low over a smoke float it had dropped in the sea a few minutes before.

As the Villeneuve neared the spot the 'plane gained height and resumed a greater circle around the convoy. Through their binoculars they watched as the destroyer slackened speed and then slipped its whaler. From its signal yards flags were hauled down and others run up and at the same time a light started flashing a Morse signal to the Commodore's liner.

"Take it down, Bentley" snapped the second officer as he read the letters. "Might as well know what's happening."

The `contact' the plane had made was not a U-boat but a large area of wreckage of some hapless victim of one. As the Villeneuve came back into its position on the flank of the convoy, its whaler pulled slowly through the depressing area of debris. After quarter of an hour it became a tiny speck on the horizon and its crew began to feel very alone. The sea stank of oil, which had mostly been on fire and now floated in black lumps almost like coke. Amongst it they found a partially burned raft on which were five charred corpses. That they had once been men was almost beyond credibility.

"Mon Dieu," muttered the cox'n as he made the sign of the cross then, finding no sign of life anywhere, ordered his men to pull in the direction of the disappearing convoy and sent up a red Very-light flare. Once again the dead were left untouched. Nothing could be done for them, what mattered were the living.

Those who'd had their lunch disturbed by having to go to action stations now returned and finished their meals. There was more than one grumble about why action stations always seemed to spoil a meal, but when the reason for the latest interruption got around the ships most were thankful that it had not been them out there on the raft.

The following afternoon two V and W class destroyers with four corvettes took over guardianship of the convoy and Commander Nicholls and his group bade WS 25 farewell. There was no more than a force five wind blowing so the passing of the convoy's documentation went smoothly. A waterproof canvas bag was sent between the escort leaders using heaving lines.

With a destroyer ahead and astern and a corvette on each corner the convoy continued untroubled, sighting the African coast three days later.

A day out from Freetown they welcomed the sight of an R.A.F Hudson bomber, which made sure the waters ahead of them were clear of the enemy. Since the day of the escort change the old seaplane had been unable to fly. Catapulting off was no problem but the sea had turned rough and recovery would have been. Even if it survived landing without having a float torn off or going nose first into an unexpectedly large wave, hooking back onto the crane for hoisting aboard would have been difficult enough.

Meanwhile, on the Patriarch's bridge, watch followed watch as it did for those in the radio and engine-rooms. For the catering department the daily task continued of seeing that everyone was fed. The chef and the chief steward had their morning sessions to work out forthcoming menus whilst fortifying themselves in the appropriate manner. That done the chef would then have another tipple with the chief baker and the butcher in the cubbyhole that passed as his office.

Wentle was amazed at the amount apparently drunk by the people over him, but he had to admit that despite it they did seem to get the job done, but then he, Wentle, had never had more than cider to drink despite his father being a publican.

He had been informed that mail would be collected upon reaching Freetown, so after quickly laying up the tables, at which he had become quite adept, he wrote to his father and girl friend. He realized that there was not much he could put in the letters because of the censor. He would liked to have described the various people around him but as the censoring was done on board he would have to be doubly careful of what he wrote. He did feel that his father would laugh at the `coffee over the colonel' incident but left it out of the letter to his girl. He was not sure she would appreciate mention of the area upon which the coffee had landed and that was half the joke. If the conversation of his cabin mates was anything to go by Mary was a bit of a prude.

Akker, come to make sure all was ready for afternoon tea, brought their impending arrival on the shores of Africa into reality by giving him the first of a daily Quinine tablet. "If you don't take it boy you'll get malaria as sure as you're standing here. Now let's have a look at these tea tables. God help me."

In peace time, afternoon tea would have been served up in the lounge for those who wanted it but now it was put out on the four middle tables, which had yet to be laid up for dinner, and taken by the army officers mostly standing up. If the ship was rolling it meant quite a bit of extra sweeping up for Wentle after tea was over.

*   *   *

Africa! Wentle was bitterly disappointed to find that there would be no shore leave for any of the crews.

As Akker put it. "Can't have you people catching a full house from a bit of Black Velvet!"

The truth was that Freetown would be totally unable to cope with the number of troops in the convoy. There would be virtually nothing for them to do except to catch V.D. Better everyone stay on board and sweat it out while the ships were replenished with water, bunker fuel and some fresh provisions. And sweat it out they did!

Watching the film `Saunders of the River' and several of Frank Buck's `Bring Them Back Alive' series on the capture of zoo animals had given Wentle no idea that humidity was such a part of daily life in tropical Africa. The jungle had looked exciting up there on the screen but now that they were at anchor close to the north shore, where the greenery came down almost to the water's edge, perhaps it was not all easy adventure for the mosquitoes were most unfriendly.

The assistant stewards waiting on tables were still wearing the same heavy blue trousers and white coats with which they had started the trip. Only the officers and Akker were allowed, in deference to their rank, to change into full white uniforms. The result was that they all perspired heavily and only donned their coats a few minutes before each meal. Wearing them all the time meant that they quickly became saturated down the back. This continual sweating gave Wentle a new problem.

A couple of days before their arrival in Freetown he had noticed a pink rash on his thighs around his pubic hairs. Not knowing what form V.D. actually took he immediately thought that somehow his cabin mates had given it to him. According to their boasts they all, except for Harry, had a prostitute whenever ashore. Now with the extra sweating the rash turned a vivid red.

On the second day at anchor Wentle, who had been too embarrassed to see the doctor, now summoned up enough courage to ask his friend Harry what he thought. The mess-boy immediately burst out laughing.

"Bloody Hell, Dick that's not the clap, it's dhobi rash! It's caused by the salt water and soap! When you wash your gear in salt water you've got to rinse it well with fresh and make sure you get all the soap out. Now nick off and see old Brightman down in the hospital and he'll give you Gentian Violet which'll turn it from red to blue then you'll look like the fairy on the Christmas-tree!"

*   *   *

Safe behind the anti-submarine boom and far from enemy bombers there was at least one bonus for all concerned. Portholes and windows could remain open at night and all ships were a blaze of light. A sight, which after nearly three years of blackout, Wentle had almost forgotten.

By day the water-barges went from ship to ship whilst bunker needs were taken care of by two ocean going tankers, with the assistance of tugs. A third remained at anchor and one by one the escorts visited her. Rumour had it that four tankers had left Venezuela, the unlucky one disappearing in a gigantic ball of flame. There were no survivors. (In the Caribbean and along the north coast of

South America almost a hundred ships had been sunk in the first six months of 1942.)

Lunch aboard the Patriarch on the second day was a boisterous affair at the table where the four R.A.F officers, in charge of the airmen bound for the Empire Flying School in Rhodesia, ate their meals. They had asked permission through the trooping commandant for the pilot of the CAM ship Hurricane to take lunch with them. When he came down the saloon stairs he was given a standing ovation in appreciation for shooting down the Kondor. When one of the four R.A.F types discovered that he had helped to teach Hythe-Foxworthy to fly at Cranwell there was cause for more celebration.

Akker had a busy and very profitable lunch hour looking after the `fly-boys' as he called them. When the launch from the A.M.C came to fetch the squadron leader the pilot took his second ducking of the trip. Missing his footing at the bottom of the gangway he disappeared into the murky waters and surfaced considerably more sober than before he fell in!

Convoy WS 25 should have left Freetown at first light on the third day but just after dinner the previous evening a signal came from the commodore's ship for all captains to report aboard forthwith. Strickland was ordered to clear away the starboard accident boat and with an A.B. and a junior engineer, who got even more sweaty trying to start the engine, move her to the gangway.

The commodore's cabin was a spacious suite which would normally have cost its occupants a considerable amount to hire. The admiral explained that sailing would be delayed for at least twenty four hours as an enemy raider had been reported in the area. Part of Force H from Gibraltar was on its way south to look after them. On no account was the convoy to sail without the covering squadron! In the meanwhile all ships were to remain on two hours sailing notice.

Back aboard his own ship Spencer sent for the chief officer and engineer, both of whom had been about to turn in. He told them of the orders over a coffee, since he had already had several whiskies with the Admiral, who had asked him to stay behind when he noticed Spencer's D.S.C. ribbon. He wanted to know what his R.N. connections had been.

At least the delay meant that the watch keepers would get an extra night's sleep. In situations like this Spencer reduced the bridge anchor watch to one officer, one Q.M. and an A.B. thus giving every one a chance for much needed extra sleep. He was himself grateful for another night in his own bed, able to lie down without all his clothes on. He wrote in his night order book that one man was to keep his eyes on the commodore's liner at all times and that he was to be called should sailing orders be received.

CHAPTER SEVEN

At 1000 hours on their fourth day in Freetown WS 25 sailed from the safety of the estuary with its festering heat for the cooler air of the South Atlantic Ocean. As chaperons they still had their two destroyers and four corvettes but these were augmented by two Dutch warships, a cruiser and a destroyer, which were on their way to join the small Dutch flotilla operating in Australian waters. The A.M.C remained at anchor.

Lunch had finished and those who could were taking their ease on deck watching what seemed to be another convoy coming towards them from the north. McTavish, who was back to normal as far as his duties were concerned, studied them through his binoculars and reported to his captain that they appeared to be warships.

"Damn it, I do believe there is a battleship amongst them, Sir! To what do we owe their presence I wonder?"

"That's the battle cruiser Nelson and her escorts. Couldn't tell you before but the reason we stayed in harbour was because we had to wait for that lot to come and hold our hand. It seems there's a Jerry raider around." Spencer stopped to fill his pipe, which was the only luxury he occasionally allowed himself on the bridge and, of course, only during daylight hours. Since he spent an average of sixteen hours a day there it was little enough. It was a luxury that troubled his conscience for he did not allow others to smoke on duty, fearing that it could prove a distraction. At the very moment a lookout ducked his head to light up could be the moment when a periscope made its brief appearance.

The warships rapidly closed the convoy, taking up station five miles out on the starboard beam. There they looked very formidable and reassuring. McTavish remarked to the quartermaster that. "I'd like to see the Deutchland or whoever is around come and have a crack at us while we have those boys with us."

"Aye Sir, so would I for if that be the Nelson then it'd give my young brother a chance to use that gun of 'is. Last I 'eard from 'im 'e was in one of them bloody great turrets."

"Oh, indeed. Then I hope he can shoot straight, Powell."

"I reckons the Navy will 'ave taught 'im that all right. They be pretty bright really, 'though I can't say as 'ow I'd like to wear me uniform all the while 'specially ashore an' put up with all that bull. Still 'e likes it. 'e's a regular too."

"Takes all kinds to make the world go round, Powell. It's nearly time for another zigzag." He went into the wheelhouse to consult the blackboard and then phoned the engine-room.

Down in the engine-room the junior second answered, "O.K. Malcolm, when you say, speed down to thirteen knots for four minutes." He wiped his hands on a piece of cotton waste which, together with the humble oil can, were as important to the well being of the ship as were the navigator's parallel rulers and dividers, or the pencil and message pad in the radio-room.

"Shut up, Eddie! There's something coming in on five hundred metres!" The junior sparks had been whiling away his off watch time by twiddling the tuning knob of the stand-by receiver and at that moment the cabin was filled with the strains of a Strauss waltz, all be-it mixed with considerable static. Reluctantly he did as the second told him and turned the volume right down then bent over his colleague to listen intently.....

`Dee dah dee..dee dah dee.. dee dah dee..dee dah dee' R R R, the SOS signal to be used when a ship was being attacked by a surface raider. Dah dee dee..dee, DE meaning from. MVHL QTH 0325N 2543W...then started a series of precisely timed dashes meant to activate the automatic alarm receiver of any ship whose operators might not be listening out. The 3rd R/O took the two paces necessary to reach their own equipment and turned it off before its bells started to ring. He need not have bothered for the faint and harsh note of the distant spark transmitter ceased.

"Eddie, keep listening while I let the bridge know!" The second got up but before leaving the cabin thumbed through a thick book which contained the call signs of hundreds of vessels....."MVHL, Maldive Castle," he said and scribbled the name on the message form bearing the tragic message.

"Hello Mike. Lost some volts or something?" As he greeted the sparks McTavish saw the serious look on the face coming towards him and knew there was trouble.

"No Mac, something far more serious. The Maldive Castle has just sent out an S.O.S. saying she was being attacked." He handed the telegraph form over. "She sent her position and then broke off transmission. I thought that we should tell the escort in case they missed it?"

The navigating Officer took the form. "This position puts her a couple of hundred miles to the west of us. Poor bastards. Use the lamp would you Mike while I call the Old Man."

Aboard H.M.S Nelson the rear admiral commanding the squadron put down his cup of tea and crossed to where his navigating officer had spread out a chart.

"This is our position, Sir," and he pointed to a cross and a time at the end of a pencilled line showing their track since joining the convoy. "The Maldive Castle is here," indicating another cross with a large circle around it. "Distance off, Sir, is two hundred and twenty seven miles."

"Hmm!" The admiral rubbed his chin: "Sunset, Pilot? If we flew off the Walrus would she get there in daylight?"

"Questionable, Sir and recovery could be dodgy. We would have to show lights to get her back aboard."

"Hmm!" a very useful non-committal sound when in thought and the admiral used it often. "It could be what we're looking for Pilot, but if it isn't and we go on a wild goose chase and the convoy comes under attack while we are away....." He left the sentence unfinished. There was silence in the sea-cabin except for the sound of a bosun's mate piping `Hands To Tea.' A decision was required. One which only he could make.

Should he take his squadron to where the Maldive Castle was being attacked and hope that he would find there the pocket battleship for which they were searching? The position was quite a way from where intelligence thought the enemy could be. It might even be a surfaced U-boat using her guns. Perhaps the sparks had made a mistake in sending the position? His orders were to ensure the safety of the convoy, anything else was secondary.

He turned to his flag lieutenant. "Flags, tell Coles to take his chariot and investigate. If it is our quarry he's to shadow but not engage until we join him."

The decision was made. Shortly the destroyer Boadecia, fortunately refueled only that morning from the cruiser in the squadron, would leave her position and race off at thirty two knots to the aid of the merchantman. It would take her seven hours to run the distance down and the squadron a further eleven if they were required to assist.

Since the Boadecia would arrive in the middle of the night it might take her until daylight to find the wreckage and, if there were any, survivors. Dawn might come and find her under the guns of ..... it was all conjecture, time alone would give the answer. If it were the enemy the Boadecia would break radio silence to let them know. Meanwhile the convoy had to sail on.

The admiral called for another cup of tea, to replace the one that was now cold.

*   *   *

"Eternal Father strong to save,
Whose arm hath bound the restless wave.
Who bids the mighty ocean deep,
its own appointed limits keep.
Oh hear us when we pray to Thee
For those in peril on the Sea

Almost a thousand voices were raised in lusty song. Sunday had dawned fine and clear with the convoy on a mean course of sou'-west by south. Of the battle squadron there was no sign. The corvettes were out at each corner with the destroyer, her Dutch captain now the escort commander, sweeping out ahead. The cruiser was tucked safely in the middle line of the convoy behind the three funnel Empress of India. There was not a ripple to be seen on the slightly undulating blue sea, a perfect setting for the drumhead service being held on number four hatch aboard the Patriarch.

Private Jack Harper of the Royal Army Service Corps, stood at the after end of A deck looking down on the crowd of soldiers on the well-deck. If the service had been back in barracks in Blighty most of them would have done their damnedest not to attend. Now, a hundred miles or more from the shore, where there was no compulsion for anyone to attend, well over two thirds of the troops aboard crammed every available space overlooking and around the two padres conducting the service. In white robes, a flag covered table for an altar and their life-belts at their feet, the two `God Botherers' felt the presence of Him more than they had ever done back in their churches. The fact that those two churches were at opposite ends of the Christian spectrum was forgotten in their now common bond.

If the soldiers and airmen had been asked why they came so willingly to stand under the tropical sun to sing hymns to the accompaniment of an accordion, some would have said that they did not know; others that there was nothing else to do. Those with consciences may have answered that it was time they made amends with their Maker, for tomorrow might be too late. The majority would probably have admitted that they did not think of God much in normal times, but since these were far from normal times, they had come to pray for deliverance from the enemy.

The fact that the enemy, in many cases, also prayed to the same God was a point not lost on some, which made `belief' all the more difficult. If enemies had similar beliefs why were they fighting each other? For those who thought more deeply the futility of war became more apparent than ever.

The accordion struck up a note for the last verse of the well known hymn the words of which now seemed to take on a whole new meaning.

"O Trinity of Love and Power
Our Brethren shield in dangers hour.
From rock and tempest, fire and foe
protect them where so 'er they go.
Oh hear us when we cry to Thee
for those in peril on the sea."

Private Harper, a driver in the Royal Army Service Corps, was one of those who were there just to pass the time of day. He liked to think he had no use for God. Small in stature, with shaggy eyebrows and an unruly mop of hair, he was known by the name of `Twitcher'. At the orphanage where he had been brought up the other children had been unkind enough to nickname him after a nervous affliction in the right side of his face.

His mother had got rid of her illegitimate and unwanted offspring by the simple expedient of leaving him wrapped in a dirty blanket on the steps of a hospital soon after he was born. At the orphanage money was short and life was hard. Young Harper, a name given him at random by a nurse who happened to have a tin of Harpic in her hand when called by the matron, had had it tough, and tough he thought he was still having it. In fact his treatment in the army was no different from that of any other private soldier.

He had learnt about God at an early age but he did not take kindly to anything that was forced upon him; so religion was one of his 'hate' subjects.

Now he stood mouthing the words of the hymn learnt at the orphanage which, had he not been so full of self-pity, could have meant something to him as it did for so many there. Instead he left off singing and with a muted "What the 'ell 'as God ever done fer me!" turned and elbowed his way clear of the men around him.

He wandered a few yards for'ard with his mind enveloped in a black cloud. "Bloody people. Why should I be 'ere on this bloody ship? I never did nobody no wrong. I didn't want this war," he muttered to himself on one of his pet themes. "It's the bloody officers what made the war just so's they c'n boss poor sods like me around. Why should they 'ave everything and me bugger all. I'm just as good as they!" He found himself level with a stairway leading upwards to the boat-deck and on its railings was secured a notice which read OFFICERS ONLY in large red letters. He looked at it for a moment and then with a "Why the 'ell shouldn't I!" went up the stairs.

Owing to the church service there were only one or two people on the boat-deck and the comparatively clear space on that crowded troopship was a novelty to Harper. The planks of the deck shone almost white in the sunlight so that the dark lines of pitch between them stood out in stark relief. With the lifeboats swung out and lowered until their gun'ales were level with the deck, there was an unimpeded view of the endless sea.

Fascinated by the lack of rails between deck and boats Harper, with his life-belt held loosely in one hand and dragging on the deck, walked to the ship's side and stood near the bows of the after-most boat. Looking down the sixty feet to the water he became mesmerised by the bubbling white wake as the sea slid by the grey steel plates of the Patriarch's side. With his mind in a whirl of misfortune the soldier stood there for some time before a voice behind him said: "Anything wrong, soldier?"

The inquirer was a young captain who, being of the Jewish faith, had not gone to the service. Although he worshipped the same God he was not encouraged to do so in the ways of other faiths. He had watched Harper walk across the deck and sensed that something was not right. Harper, normally a nervous type was even more so in his present mood and in a place he was not supposed to be. Hearing the voice behind him he swung round and automatically took a pace backwards away from the officer. Instead of solid deck beneath his foot there was only air. For a brief moment he hung with his back across the bow of the boat before falling with a piercing scream down into the bubbling wake. The cork life-belt in his hand was torn from his grasp as he hit the water.

The sixty foot fall carried Harper deep down into the cool sea, down through the surface wave which was pushing outwards from the ship's side, down into the current which was going aft, to where the two big screws were slicing their way through the Atlantic.

"Man overboard! Man overboard!" yelled the captain, throwing a nearby life-ring over the side. Up on the bridge the starboard look-outs took up the cry and released the retaining pin on another life-ring to which a smoke-float was attached.

Third Officer Giles looked enquiringly at his captain who had risen from his chair.

"Steady as you go!" If the cry had been to port he would have put the wheel hard over and hoped that the stern would swing away from the man in the water. But to go to starboard with the next line in the convoy not far away was too risky just for the life of one man; with the Alcavia it had been different!

"The O flag Giles, that's all we can do. Q.M see to it please! Use the lamp Giles and let the rescue tug know in case they haven't noticed the smoke float. Mr. Strickland note the time then get down aft quickly and find out what happened!" Spencer was by now on the starboard bridge wing and watched as the vessel astern of them swung slightly to port and then back again so that she was able to take the smoke float on her starboard bow wave and let it go safely down her side.

A lookout on the tug was doing his job properly and reported the smoke float as it cleared the stern of the Patriarch. Even before the Aldis lamp had finished its click-clacking, she came hard to port and her speed dropped as she made for the smoke marker now clear of the last ship in the line. For half an hour she made widening circles around the life-ring before putting on speed and resuming her position in the convoy. Her signal lamp started to blink towards the Patriarch.

`SORRY...NO...SURVIVOR.'

And so Private `Twitcher' Harper became just another war statistic. His company commander had his clerk make the necessary entry in company records and was thankful that there were no relatives to which he would otherwise have had to write one of those letters saying `So sorry that your...'.

The trooping staff sergeant brought his records up to date by noting that there was one less person to feed.

The master of the M.V.Patriarch entered his log-book with the latitude and longitude of the incident, which gave Harper's grave a place on earth, while the only wreath was his life-belt. In a few days he would be forgotten as if he had never existed, just another tragedy of war.

Had Harper not died he would probably have been put forward, by those in his unit with sadistic minds, as a candidate for initiation by King Neptune when the convoy crossed the equator at three o'clock the next afternoon. In peace time the crossing-the-line ceremony was a fun affair indulged in by the passengers and presided over by the bosun.

This time the `King' was a burly sergeant and those to be initiated sundry junior subalterns whose names came readily to the mind of the Green Howard's regimental sergeant major.

The bosun provided the wig of rope yarn and the carpenter trident and crown. The engineers, together with the hospital assistant, mixed a heavy and pungent gunge for the shaving soap which was liberally applied anywhere that hair might grow!

After the not too gentle shave had been accomplished, a few minutes under the deck-wash hose left the initiates a bright shade of pink. To most it was all a bit of harmless good fun and helped to pass yet another afternoon at sea.

When the Boadecia rejoined the convoy after a fruitless search for the remnants of or survivors from the Maldive Castle or her attacker the general feeling was that the farther south the convoy went the less likely they were to come under attack. The weather in the doldrums gave them calm seas and warm nights and gradually tension relaxed.

A ship's concert was held and helped to relieve the growing boredom amongst the troops. For the first time Wentle was made aware that some opera music was worth listening to. Lewis had the typical Welsh ability to sing magnificently and silenced even the most sceptical in the audience with his rendering of `Vilia' from the `Merry Widow.'

A boxing tournament was held over several afternoons and it was suggested that Wentle might like to challenge Perkins to a bout in the ring but he felt that bygones were now bygones and more antagonism with the captain's tiger was not called for.

He saw little of Perkins who, because of his promotion, now slept in one of the assistant steward's peaks and tended to leave the boys alone. However Perkins was, indirectly, the cause of the saloon-boy's next misfortune.

It was ten minutes before dinner and Wentle had satisfied himself that all was ready when the second steward came over to him. "The tiger has got some bug or other and has been sent to his bunk so that means as soon as you're through here you're to take the captain's dinner up to the bridge. He's already ordered what he wants so all you have to do is to ask the chef for it. You will find a lay of cutlery and small table cloth in a drawer in the pantry opposite the captain's day cabin. You lay up on the desk. Have you been up on the bridge before?"

Wentle was dumfounded. He had to wait on the captain? Here in the saloon he felt that he was just about on top of the job, but the captain? In talking with Lewis he had discovered that in peacetime there would have been another steward in the saloon plus several cabin and a couple of deck stewards and that he, as saloon-boy would have been no more than the back-up for the saloon and Akker's general factotum.

"I asked you if you had been on the bridge before?"

"Sorry Sir, No I haven't. I didn't think I was allowed up there."

"Only on duty. Well nip up to the day-cabin now, lay the table and turn the heaters on for the bain-marie in the pantry but keep your eye on the time. Think you can cope?"

"Yes Sir, I'll manage."

"Can you tell me where the chef is please?" Wentle asked as he made his way into the stifling galley.

"In his den," replied the junior cook who did not quite catch the bead of sweat before it dropped into the saucepan over which he was working.

Knocking on the open door he asked the chef, "Please Mr.Mathews, Secundus has told me to report to you for the skipper's grub. Can you tell me what it is?"

The chef was having his after dinner tot with the chief baker and now with glass at his lips he spluttered, dribbling rum down the side of his mouth as far as the crevice between his two chins.

"What did you say? I presume, boy" and now his voice seemed to rumble from somewhere near his boots, "that you mean the CAPTAIN and his DINNER. We do not produce GRUB in this galley! Also the second steward is MISTER BOYD to you. Where do you think you are boy, on some ruddy little tramp steamer? Jesus Alf," he turned to his companion, "what's the Pool sending us these days?"

The chief baker rolled his eyes upwards and responded with "Buggered if I know Chef." Even in this cubby-hole of an office the status of rank had to be upheld in the presence of such a lowly personage as the saloon-boy. In the galley the Chef was lord and master and responsible only to the chief steward!

"Er, no Chef, Sorry Sir." Damn and blast it, always doing something wrong was Wentle's silent thought as both men fired rapid orders at him and bade him begone from their presence with mutterings about "God help the Old Man."

With loaded tray he departed for the bridge and the captain's pantry. With the hot dishes deposited in the bain-marie he climbed the ladder to the place which was the holiest of holies, where he became overawed by the presence of the people who were actually driving the ship.

An officer with one very thin gold stripe on his epaulettes, who looked not much older than Wentle, was talking into a telephone. Another with a slightly wider gold stripe stood by the man at the wheel looking at his watch. The captain in all his glory of four stripes was seated on a high chair, and by the far door stood old Baines who winked at him and put a finger to his lips. In the half light of dusk the atmosphere seemed to be charged with electricity. The saloon-boy, the lowest of the low aboard the ship, was now amongst the highest and stood transfixed in the doorway by what he was hearing and seeing. For a minute there was silence and then the third officer gave his order:

"Starboard five. Ring for seventeen knots." The quartermaster and then the fourth officer repeated back the order applicable to them, followed shortly by the quartermaster reporting:

"Five of port wheel on, Sir." The ships ahead of the Patriarch were already well into the swing to the new course of the zigzag and the Patriarch now followed suit, all on the orders of one man. The feeling of awe left Wentle and was replaced by one of extreme jealousy of that one man who was only, maybe, two or three years older than he. More than ever before Wentle knew that had it not been for the fact that he had been told his eyesight would deteriorate over the coming years, he should have been on a bridge like this.

More orders and minutes later the captain spoke in a voice full of authority and yet quite gentle, reminding Wentle of his late headmaster. With a smile towards the boy he said. "Yes steward, what can we do for you?"

Wentle found that the captain preferred to serve himself so that all went well until the sweet; a rice pudding specially made without sugar and creamed as only the chief baker could make it for his captain. There had been two in the oven and the chief baker had been explicit that it was the one on the right. Those had been the orders. Wentle had just sat down in the small pantry when the captain rang the bell for him and pointed out that he believed a mistake must have been made for this was a sweet rice pudding!

Nonplussed, Wentle apologised as he took away the miscreant pudding and the sweet bowl from in front of the captain. `Another balls up, God help me,' he thought, returning quickly to the galley, where he was met by an irate baker who told him his fortune in no uncertain fashion.

With the correct sweet on his tray Wentle left the galley with the aid of a kick from the baker, causing him to almost drop his tray when the boot landed. The kick from the side of the boot had not really hurt yet he felt as if he had received a couple of cuts with the cane from his house master for being caught making an apple pie bed. That had really hurt!

The meal over Wentle gathered up the dirty dishes and was about to step through the door when the captain's voice arrested him. "Lad, there appears to be half a boot imprint on the back of your white coat. Thank your lucky stars that the rope's end is not still in use; I can assure you that really hurts!"

A very deflated Wentle took up his tray and once again departed for the main galley but his troubles were not over. In the gathering dark and half way past number three hatch, he forgot the presence of a ring bolt in the deck. His tray went flying making a noise that he was sure must have been heard throughout the ship.

"Bloody stewards always making a row 'bout summat. You want to be careful mate or you'll be taking a turn over the side next!" exclaimed a passing seaman. Some one else said:

"Just the job! 'e'll frighten all the Jerries fer miles ahrunnd."

Totally crest-fallen Wentle started to recover the entree dishes and his tray. Because he had finally learnt how to carry the tray at shoulder height it had scattered its contents almost to the galley entrance. He expected Mr. Boyd to appear at any moment and tear him off a strip but instead Lewis was suddenly there helping to find the bits and pieces.

The fact that WS 25 was not bothered by the Jerries had, of course, nothing to do with Wentle having frightened them away. The entry of the United States into the war gave the U-boats easy pickings on the far side of the North Atlantic so why bother to go down south of the equator? It was not until the Americans realized what they were up against and got their act together that U-boats once again appeared in southern waters.

The Japanese also helped their allies by allowing the use of Penang in Malaya as a base for Admiral Doenitz's boats. From August 1942 to May 1943 the allies would lose 72 merchant ships around the South African coast but WS 25 would be safely at its journey's end before that onslaught happened.

So it was that, after a bad start, WS 25's luck now held. They left the doldrums and sailed into the south east trade winds and against the Benguela current. Gradually they entered the autumn of the southern hemisphere and changed back into warmer clothing.

On the Patriarch the final of the heavy weight boxing was held and the ship's pugilist, an A.B named Green, floored the army finalist in the third round.

Talk for the troops was of landing in Durban in a few days whilst for the crew it centred around what they would do during the four days the Patriarch expected to be alongside. Days which would be occupied by unloading and preparing for the two week run across the southern ocean to the Argentine. There was mention of a mail to be posted when they docked, so on the afternoon that Green was showing his boxing skills Wentle sat down to write home.

He still found it difficult to find a subject which he knew would not attract the censor's pen but there was one thing that had caught his attention. He wrote of how an Albatross, with a wing span that must have been all of six feet, followed the ship. He had first seen it two days ago gliding along just over the bow wave and watched it through the porthole by his bunk. For half an hour it hardly moved its wings, using the upward thrust of the wind off the wave. It seemed so free and effortless. He had read somewhere that these birds flew thousands of miles in their search for food before returning to their nesting place on two islands somewhere to the south of the African continent. He told his girl friend that it was the most beautiful thing he had seen since coming to sea and that it was folklore amongst seaman that such a bird carried the soul of a dead sailor. If he were to die then being an Albatross must be a wonderful thing indeed.

He wrote of his mistake with the captain's rice pudding and how stupid he had felt when he tripped over the ring-bolt. He had expected ridicule from the other stewards but instead they now seemed to accept him as one of them and part of the crew rather than a greenhorn and an interloper.

It was true that there were still times when he felt embarrassment with some of them because he could not speak or swear as they did. With Harry London and Lewis he felt more at ease for their ways seemed nearer to his own.

Lewis was, in fact, a university undergraduate who had once spent a vacation at sea. After failing an exam he had been called up, deciding that the merchant navy would be preferable to one of the armed services particularly since he espoused the idea of being a conscientious objector. Although he had already spent two days in a lifeboat he saw no reason to change his views and looked on the war as something abstract which did not affect his daily well being. He found that since joining the Patriarch, and this was his fourth trip, things were about as comfortable as they could be. He spoke tolerable Spanish and sang over the radio both in the Argentine and Uruguay and in consequence, along with his tips, was building up a nice little nest egg.

Harry London was a part war orphan. His parents had a small bakery in Battle, Sussex, and worked long hours in order to give their three boys, of which Harry was the eldest, a chance in life.

Very early in the war, when the Luftwaffe made their first excursions over southern England, one of their planes had strafed the road to Catsfield and it so happened Mr.London was delivering bread in his small van. Painted a bright red with the bakery name in gold it was a source of pride in the family. Washed and polished every Saturday afternoon it was meant to catch a customer's eye. Unfortunately it had also caught the eye of the German pilot.

Now Mrs.London and the fifteen year old second son were struggling to keep the business afloat. There had never been any expectations that the bakery would support the three boys and since he had a hankering to travel young Harry had found his own way to sea.

Harry would have liked to have become an apprentice but there was no way the family could find the indenture fee and then keep him for four years in uniform and, for the first year, pocket money; so young London became a cabin-cum-galley-boy in the best traditions of the sea.

His first ship had been twenty years old and conditions on it primitive. She was a coal burner engaged in bringing coal and coke down from Newcastle to London. The galley was infested with cockroaches and filthy when he had joined her at the Battersea Power Station wharf. Before the smoke belching collier had passed Shoeburyness Harry had been cuffed round the ears twice, had his backside booted once and been sworn at almost every other word by a drink sodden cook. He was almost glad when, off Great Yarmouth, she was bombed and sunk by a JU 88. Although she was in ballast she had taken half an hour to go down, time enough to get two lifeboats away. Towed into Great Yarmouth by a fishing boat none of the crew had even got their feet wet!

With his second ship he was not so lucky although he did spend two weeks in her before she, too, went to the bottom.

Outward bound to Salvador in Brazil and not in convoy she had been torpedoed in the area between the south going Guinea and the west going South Equatorial currents. The two rafts, for there had not been time to get the boats away, drifted first one way and then another on a mirror-like sea. Sitting only eighteen inches above the water the sun reflected back off the sea with an intensity that caused eyes to be screwed half closed throughout most of the daylight hours. At night they were first glad of the cool until, in the early hours, they began to shiver and eventually were once again thankful for the dawn.

Eleven men and a boy had taken to the rafts but on the first day one had died from the wounds caused by the exploding torpedo. On the second day another just did not wake up. Over the next four and a half weeks more bodies were pushed overboard until, when they were sighted from the passing M.V.Patriarch, only three remained alive, and they only just.

Early in the war some dockside workers had discovered that lifeboats and rafts contained emergency rations and that these, particularly the Horlicks tablets, were worth filching. The fact that such rations might mean the difference between life and death for some seaman did not seem to worry men who only had to endure an occasional bombing and spent most nights in their own beds. So it was that although the boat's rations, in their water-proof containers, had been checked before sailing the two rafts had been missed. There was a little water but all the survivors had to eat were a few hard ship's biscuits, almost impossible to swallow in dry mouths, supplemented with a very occasional raw flying fish.

With the continued exposure dehydration began to set in and they started to waste away. The sun soon blistered faces and any other exposed skin so that the loss of fluid through the blisters accelerated the dehydration. Painful sores developed on their buttocks and the backs of their legs from sitting on the hard damp wooden slats of the raft. As their body fluids grew less so their skin became parched and wrinkled, eyes became sunken in hollow dark sockets and the soles of their feet like tissue paper.

That is how they were when A.B.Green had sighted the tiny dark specs several miles away. The Patriarch had stopped to get the survivors aboard, the bosun swimming a few strokes to make fast a heaving line to draw the rafts alongside.

Careful nursing by the doctor and his assistant had brought the three survivors back from the brink of death. When the vessel docked at Avonmouth Harry London was just starting to walk again.

He realised that a ship like the Patriarch was a different ball game from the dirty old collier and he had asked about the possibilities, once he had recovered, of getting a berth on her.

Four months later Harry was back to normal health, except that many of the pockmarks from the blisters and the wrinkles around the eyes would not go away, when a telegram arrived at the bakery. Mr.Boyd had kept his promise and there was a berth as officer's mess-boy if he wanted it. A man in all but years, with a fortitude that might have been eschewed by men twice his age, Harry London went back to the war. The Germans had killed his father and he had seen shipmates die but he was damned if they were going to cower him into submission.

CHAPTER EIGHT

At exactly eleven thirty, just as final bets were being placed on the mileage run for the last twenty four hours, and Harry London had started serving the `seven bells' lunch for the officers going on watch at midday, trouble found the convoy again.

The previous morning the main part of the convoy had sailed into Cape Town leaving the Patriarch, Empress of India, the Bellevue and another fast cargo vessel the Potters Bank, heading for Durban. These four, together with the Dutch cruiser and destroyer, were steaming east by north with Cape St. Francis just visible on the port beam when there was an explosion on the cruiser.

They were in line abreast with the cruiser in the middle, the Patriarch was on her port beam with the Bellevue next. The other two flanked the cruiser to starboard. Just in case there might be a sub lurking somewhere, although no one thought it likely, the destroyer steamed ahead scanning with her radar and asdic. Neither of these instruments had given any sign of a contact so a mine seemed to be a reasonable assumption for the cruiser's plight; probably laid by a Japanese submarine.

The cruiser was holed right up by the bow so that daylight could be seen through her now twisted stem plates. Her captain immediately reduced speed to ensure that the for'ard water-tight bulkheads remained secure. He then signaled that they did not appear to be in any imminent danger of sinking and hoped to make Port Elizabeth but just in case he would have to take the destroyer with him.

Floating mines drifting with the currents were a problem. Either you saw them and altered course in time or you were unlucky. Some thought them preferable to U-boats, others were not sure.

Feeling decidedly naked without any escort the remaining merchantmen closed the gap left by the departing cruiser and continued to zigzag their way around the South African coast. All fervently hoped that the cruiser would alert the powers that be and at least some form of air cover would be given them, not that an aircraft would be of much use against mines. To add to their fears the barometer was dropping and white caps were appearing on the waves which would make it very difficult to see a mine, or a periscope. For those who had been in this sort of situation before it would be a psychological uplift to know that a friend was flying above them.

More than one of the `brown jobs', as some sailors called the soldiers, were heard to remark, "Bloody navy don't give a stuff going off and leaving us alone!" It was, of course, all a matter of priorities; cruisers were in very short supply.

Tea came and went and Wentle, thinking that after tomorrow he might at last get a run ashore in a foreign port, started to clear the tables with three other stewards. Mr. Akker kept an eye on things while taking a cup of tea himself. As far as Wentle was concerned this was one of the best times of the day for he was passionately fond of cakes and it was comparatively easy, when his boss was not looking, to take a couple for his own tea. Tables cleared he had just taken a bite from his second doughnut when a glass on the dumbwaiter shattered into a hundred pieces. Flabbergasted he stared with mouth open, but before he could comprehend what had happened the breath was knocked from his body and his ears felt as if they were being pushed inside his head. There was a roaring like a dozen express trains in a tunnel as the shock wave from a thousand tons of exploding ammunition hit the Patriarch.

The Bellevue had blown up!

"Come on Wentle, lets get the hell out of here." The stentorian voice of the saloon steward broke through the singing in the boy's ears. Suddenly the fear he had known when he'd heard the cries of the Alcavia's people in the water clutched at his vitals and his stomach tied itself in knots.

"Don't just stand there! For God's sake move!" Akker bellowed as he mounted the stairs to the upper decks.

The boy's reactions had been dulled by the magnitude of the explosion but now, as he saw the others leaving, he was seized by panic and cried out for them to wait lest he should be left on his own to be trapped below. He jumped the few paces to the pegs on the wall which should have held his life-jacket. It was not there; someone had taken it!

Almost choking with fright he turned and ran up the now deserted stairs. Reaching the landing where the stairways reversed direction he was suddenly flung from his feet to land in a heap against the paneled bulkhead.

The ship heeled viciously over to starboard, farther and farther she went. From the saloon came the crash of breaking crockery and sliding chairs. Still the Patriarch heeled creaking in every joint as she approached the point of no return. Desperately Wentle tried to rise but he seemed paralysed. Now he was going to die; this was the end. The ship was going to capsize and he would be trapped below. It wasn't fair, not on his first trip! Almost in tears he closed his eyes while the Patriarch struggled to survive.

The exploding Bellevue had caused a mountainous wave which had caught the Patriarch, steaming only two cable's length away, broadside on. All over the ship men were thrown from their feet by the violent and unexpected roll. On the bridge there was suddenly no one on the wheel, leaving it to spin freely. For what seemed an everlasting moment the ship hung at the point of live or die and then, as if she had made up her mind, started to come back up again and went with a mast breaking whip the other way. Men cursed and swore as they struggled to regain their feet.

As the force of the roll lessened Wentle heard a harsh voice above the creaks and groans and smashing crockery. A hand grasped his shoulder.

"For God's sake hurry!" It was Akker come back to look for him! He was no longer alone and suddenly his fear left him.

The ship was more or less back on an even keel by the time the two reached the boat deck amongst the crowd of jostling, pushing soldiers. Soldiers who, a few moments ago had been shouting and cursing, but were now awed into silence by the sight which met their eyes.

Where the Bellevue had been was a huge pall of black smoke rising hundreds of feet into the air so that it obscured the afternoon sun and cast their ship in deep shadow. From the sky bits and pieces of unidentifiable ship still fell to the sea, the white bubbles where they entered the water making a pebble-dash pattern between the small waves. Here and there on the decks of the Patriarch hot lumps of metal scorched the clean planking while one officer lay dead, his head split open disgorging his brains.

As the other vessels forged ahead the wind took the smoke to the west and a small part of the Bellevue's stern could be seen sliding beneath the waves.

Shattered by the force of the explosion and shaken by the fact that a six thousand ton cargo ship could cease to exist in a few seconds, the remains of the convoy sailed silently on. A sailor wrapped the dead officer's body in a piece of canvas and it was taken to the hospital where the army doctors took over. On the boat deck two more seamen fetched brushes and squeegees and someone turned a deck hose on. If not removed immediately the blood would stain the almost pristine planks and if that happened they would have to be holystoned or even replaced.

When the Bellevue exploded the Patriarch's captain had been in his chair talking to the chief officer. The vicious heel of the ship threw him to the deck cracking a wrist. The port look-out came rolling through the door and landed on top of him cursing as he did so. Jones lay unconscious by an engine telegraph with blood streaming from a gash in his forehead.

After what seemed an age the bridge-watch sorted themselves out; the quartermaster on the wheel brought the Patriarch back onto course and the alarm bells sounded for boat stations. Not that they were really needed for most men were already fighting their way to the upper decks.

Spencer told the mate to go around the vessel to see what the damage bill was while he took over the watch. The chief sparks was ordered to pipe for the doctor to come to the bridge while down in the engine-room a greaser cursed all Germans as he backed away from a fractured steam pipe nursing a badly scalded arm.

After half an hour at boat stations the catering staff were told to report back to their place of work. The first-class galley was a shambles. How the cooks had avoided getting hurt was nothing short of a miracle. Several large saucepans had spewed their contents over the deck along with all the different paraphernalia that the chef's department used to prepare the food. The chief steward decided that there was no way that the mess could be cleaned up and another hot meal made ready for two or three hours. Like it or not, whatever cold cuts and odds and ends there were would have to suffice for the evening meal.

In the saloon Wentle and the others started sweeping up a thousand pieces of crockery that, because the sea was still relatively calm, had not been secured in the dumbwaiters or had been on the tables already laid, and were now scattered all over the deck.

When the place was once more reasonably tidy it took some time to make a check on what was broken and for each steward to fetch replacements from the store two decks below. Like the troops still standing or squatting at their boat station the men in the saloon worked with a minimum of talk and all wore their life-jackets, Wentle having secured a spare one from under the stairs.

Back on the bridge the captain said to no one in particular "And then there were three!" thinking that with forty hours still to go, how many would eventually arrive? With his wrist in temporary splints and a sling he was in considerable pain but things could have been far worse. His ship had been well made and suffered no great damage although some of the troops had broken bones and, almost all, bruises. Young Jones, despite a cracking headache and five stitches under his bandage, insisted on coming back on watch. Definitely it could have been worse.

For the troops who were down in the holds it had been terrifying. First they were flung from their feet and then rolled in a heap rapidly to one side of the ship and then across to the other before they could regain their equilibrium. Those few who had been lying in their hammocks were the lucky ones. Gravity kept them in a horizontal plane while the ship gyrated around them. It was as if they were in a world apart from the cursing mob of bodies beneath them!

As for those on the Bellevue; one moment they had been alive and a split second later dead and there was nothing anyone in the other ships could do for them except enter the logbook and so note yet another casualty of war.

After sandwiches and cocoa Spencer lay down in the pilot's cabin for the last two hours of Charles Boulton's watch. He wondered about the next trip and if he would be able to trust his new chief officer as he did this one. He did not feel that the second officer was quite ready for promotion. The mechanics of the job, yes, but there was still something not quite right. Perhaps by the end of the year? He fell into a troubled sleep only to be woken, so it seemed, after a few minutes.

The two junior officers were taking over the watch. He listened to the handover, asked Jones how he felt and then climbed up on his chair. With two hands that used to be easy but now, with only one, he found it awkward. Dimly he could just make out the Empress of India with an occasional glimpse of the Potters Bank on her far side. He sent for his tiger and told him to find some hot food from somewhere. Even with the galleys closed down for the night a good tiger would find something.

For the next eight hours Spencer alternately paced the bridge, strained his eyes with the lookouts or checked that the officer of the watch executed the zigzags correctly. The three ships were still very vulnerable should there be a submarine ahead?

After they had recovered from the loss of the Bellevue, Spencer had exchanged signals with the captain of the Empress of India. Both thought that the sinking had been caused by another mine and decided that for the night at least the three vessels would remain together rather than each work up to maximum speed and go hell for leather and separately for Durban. All three felt, rightly or wrongly, that by staying together there was some mutual comfort. If there was no sign of air cover by the morning perhaps they would go their own ways?

The night passed without further incident and as breakfast was being taken they saw East London on the beam. From there came two seventy two foot harbour defence launches, spray flying back over their bridges as they corkscrewed their way through the swell towards the merchantmen. When they came nearer Spencer could see those on their bridges were clad in oilskins and was again reminded of his days in such craft all those years ago. Tiny ships, gallant ships, less than twice the length of the Patriarch's lifeboats, with decks wet and glistening in the morning sunlight as they thrashed their way out to their charges. As they closed the merchantmen a lamp flashed.

"Sorry we are so small but we will do our best. What is your mean speed?"

Spencer told his fourth officer to reply. "Size matters not if the spirit is willing. Fourteen." Small though they were the men in the remnants of the convoy were glad to see the launches with their White Ensigns streaming proudly in the breeze and their small guns pointing belligerently forward ready to do battle. But there was no battle as the ships worked their way to the north east.

By dinner time they passed Port St.Johns and then throughout the night they marked off their position by the lights of Margate, Port Shepstone and other towns until, at dawn, they were off Isipingo and in sight of their final goal.

Yet again a meal was disturbed but this time no one minded, breakfast could wait. Hands worked with a will to swing the lifeboats back in-board and sit them on their chocks. The seamen needed to moor the ship were then sent fore and aft ready for entering Durban Harbour.

The Empress of India followed one of the gun-boats through the boom defence with the Patriarch hard in her wake followed by the Potters Bank and the other gun-boat. Down to four knots they glided through the blue water and then stopped on request from a harbour control launch. To port a small group of people waved to them from the Bluff and were given a rousing cheer from the troops who packed the ship's rail and then, to Wentle's amazement, through the open saloon windows came the strident music of `Land of Hope and Glory'. It was a tune he had learned at school but now it was sung by a lone lady clad in white.

Durban's `White Lady', as Madam Perla Gibson was known, had made it her war effort to greet every troop convoy that came into the port

The last little escort, almost at the end of her fuel endurance, slid by and Spencer was able to shout a quick "Thanks for your company" to her skipper before his attention was required elsewhere.

A launch from the Port Health Authority hailed them to enquire if they had a doctor aboard and if so was he happy that no one had any form of contagious disease. If all was well "You may take down the quarantine flag, Captain".

As the stand-by quartermaster hauled down the yellow "Q" flag a Pilot launch came level with the bridge.

"Captain Spencer is it not?"

"It is indeed Pilot." Spencer winced as he forgot his damaged wrist and caught it against the wind dodger. "What can I do for you as you don't seem to be coming aboard?" The pilot ladder was hanging from the well-deck but the launch was making no attempt to go alongside it.

"We have a few problems Captain. Can you go alongside number two at Ocean Terminal without a pilot and tugs? It's the same berth you were at last time here. Port side to please."

"No problem, Pilot. Number two, port side to." During the mate's watch, Spencer had managed to have three hours sleep, shave, and eat a reasonable breakfast sandwich of bacon and fried egg up here on the bridge. Although he felt exhausted after the happenings of the last few days he knew that he was capable of this last manoeuvre. He went into the wheel-house and smiled an unspoken question at Baines who was behind the wheel and had heard the shouted conversation.

"Ready when y' are Captain"

"Right, let's go" and to the chief officer who was on the bridge "You're in luck Charles. No tugs! That gives us a little more to do," and then to the fourth officer who was by the engine-room telegraph, "Dead slow ahead both Mr. Strickland."

Slowly and with consummate precision the vessel approached her berth. Orders were given and obeyed whilst from the shore there were the sounds of a dockside coming to life. A train whistled, followed by the rattle of rail trucks moving off with a jerk, a crane squeaked as it traveled along its rails. The same smell that they had left behind at Avonmouth several weeks ago, except there was no rain, now assailed their nostrils. Clear of the wharf along the white painted dock wall was parked a row of army lorries and here and there small groups of men in khaki chatted and smoked while waiting for the men from overseas. Things were much as they had been back in Avonmouth except for one very big difference; here the sun was shining in a clear blue sky not pock-marked with barrage balloons, giving the overall impression that the war was a long way away.

"Steady as she goes. Stop both." Once again Spencer's long years at sea proved their worth. Although, in theory, docking was a simple exercise in the use of rudder and propellers, a slight miscalculation could result in damage to the wharf or a dent in the ship which in turn would mean pages and pages of reports to be written.

As the Patriarch manoeuvred so her propellers stirred up the mud from the harbour bottom discolouring the otherwise blue water.

McTavish, who had taken Boulton's place on the fo'c'sle, nodded to Able Seaman Green. With a swing of his brawny arm the seaman sent the heaving-line, with its heavy `Turks Head' knot at the end, snaking through the air to land at the feet of the waiting mooring-gang. Watching him McTavish thought that if Green played cricket he would hit the stumps from a boundary throw in, he was so powerful and accurate.

Quickly the line and its attendant thick manilla rope was hauled ashore and the eye passed over a bollard. Now the second officer lent over the rail and watched the back-spring then raised an arm in the air slowly gyrating his hand. In response the carpenter screwed in the clutch on the winch and started to heave the line tight. On the bridge two more orders were given and the ship's stern started to swing towards the dock side. Aft another heaving line shot through the air and then another mooring line was hauled ashore.

"Wheel amidships. Stop starboard." Jim Baines let go the wheel as soon as he had reported it amidships and stepped back a pace, his job now finished. He flexed his arthritic hands.

"Joe y'r turn with the ensign. I'll see to th' courtesy flag," he said to his offsider. Flag etiquette must be observed. At sea, when in sight of land or other ships, the ensign was flown from the gaff on the mizzen-mast but in port from the ensign staff right aft. Also when in port in a foreign country that nation's flag must be hoisted on the starboard yard-arm for'ard and it was the quartermaster's job to see it was done.

More and more ropes and hawsers left the ship's side and were hauled taught so that all were level. It was a sign of bad seamanship to have one line slacker than the rest. McTavish turned to the bridge and raised crossed wrists to show his captain that he was satisfied the ship was properly moored for'ard. A few minutes later David Giles reported by 'phone, for the extra lifeboats on the hospital deck obscured the view right aft, that he was happy with the moorings there.

'Finished with engines' had already been rung down to the waiting engineers and slowly the huge motors lost their rhythm and became silent, leaving the engineers still shouting their orders until their ears got used to the much lower noise level of the auxiliary power plants.

"Well, Mr.Baines that's that then," the captain said as the quartermaster pulled the South African flag from its pigeon hole.

"Aye Sir, I reckon the Old Girl 'as done us well. She can take a rest now. 'An begging y'r pardon Captain, I reckons y' could do with one y'rself. I'll find the tiger an' tell 'im to see y'r not disturbed for an hour or two. Mr.Boulton can carry the weight for y'," and he glared at the chief officer as if daring him to say otherwise but there was no need for the respect between the three men was mutual. Boulton had been up since a quarter to four and was tired but not as much as he knew his captain to be. He was beginning to realize what strain he would be under when he went captain of his own ship next trip.

"Thank you Mr.Baines I think I could, I think I could!" Spencer, eyes dark with fatigue, felt his reserves of strength ebbing now that they were at last safe for the time being. He walked slowly out to the port wing and looked along his ship. Down on the troop decks officers were giving their orders for disembarking to their N.C.O.s who passed them on with loud shouts and started chivvying the men to get a move on. For a moment Captain Spencer watched them. For five long weeks they had been part of his ship, cargo it was true but a live one, and for five weeks he had been responsible for their safety. A safety that he could not always guarantee but luck had been with him and here he was with his ship and her cargo safely in port. The first part of the voyage was now over. Soon the troops would be put ashore and no longer his responsibility. Like most captains he felt his ship to be a part of him just as he was part of her.

"Good luck lads," he said quietly before descending to his cabin. Locking the door behind him he threw his cap on the settee and picked up his bible. `Our Father which art in Heaven, hallowed be Thy name.....' and so he gave thanks for the safe deliverance of his ship and crew.

*   *   *

"Wentle! May I remind you that you are not on a pleasure cruise and that you are not a passenger!" The saloon steward placed his mouth close to Wentle's ear and almost purred the words. The youth was leaning on the well-deck rail watching the bustle on the quay. He jumped as Akker finished with a roar. "You're a member of the crew! Now bloody well get into the saloon and get that table laid or I'll have you logged. God help me!"

"Yes Mr.Akker, Sir," Wentle replied, not too worried about the reprimand for, since the evening before last, he had become aware that there was more to his boss than just his bark. In fact Wentle had been deeply moved when, after he had recovered from the shock of the Bellevue's sinking, the petty officer had come back down the stairs merely to help him and could have jeopardized his own life by doing so. It was becoming apparent to him that despite their coarse language and sometimes lurid stories, there was a lot of good in these men of the sea. He felt proud that he was being accepted as one of them.

For the first time since leaving Freetown all the navigating officers and the two apprentices were together taking a late breakfast in the now rock steady and relatively quiet officer's saloon, except for their chatter and the clatter of knives and forks.

Allowing for the fact that a ship earns most of her keep when ploughing the oceans it was nevertheless appreciated by her crew when she came to the end of a passage and the engine vibrations ceased. Now the unloading had to be started just as soon as the meal was finished, and who would be the unlucky ones who would have to stay aboard in the evening as Officer of the Deck?

The chief officer was dealing with the people who demanded to see the captain and could not be palmed off to one of the other heads of departments. When the captain surfaced the C.O. would catch up on his sleep; in the meanwhile Jones could go to his bunk while the others supervised the opening of the hatches as soon as the troops were clear of the decks.

The captain required that either himself, the first or the second mate should be on board during the night with one of the juniors as back-up. The sparks together with one quartermaster and an A.B would cover the gangway and moorings. How they arranged the times was up to them as long as the roster was posted on the notice board. Spencer realized only too well that the bridge team, more than any one else aboard, needed to catch up with sleep and get some sort of relaxation so, as with the anchor watch in Freetown, he `bent' the traditional watch keeping rules.

When the last of the army officers had left the first class saloon it became the stewards turn to have their breakfast. Akker spoke through a mouth overfilled with liver, splattering little pieces over the table cloth.

"Wentle boy, you want to leave the black velvet alone down here. The authorities take a dim view of white mixing with black so you could be in trouble with the law. Anyway, like as not, you'll end up with a full house if you poke your wick in one of them!"

"Full house? Oh yes, Mr. Akker of course, Sir. Would you pass me the salt please?" Since joining the Patriarch five weeks ago Wentle had learnt many new names and terms and quite a bit about life, but `full house' was a new one. He thought that it meant he would be likely to catch both gonorrhea and syphilis but no doubt Harry London, with whom he hoped to be going ashore this evening, would enlighten him.

Back in his cabin Malcom McTavish took a clean khaki shirt and old blue trousers from the drawer under his bunk. The black epaulettes he fixed on the shirt, with its two faded stripes of gold with a diamond between them, were somewhat tatty but they would do well enough to show the shore gangs that he was in authority. On deck the temperature was pleasant but down in the holds it would be warm and there was no sense in spoiling a white uniform. Suitably clad he brushed his fair tousled hair, which was beginning to grey at the temples, a fact which had only become apparent recently. He was too young for the cause to be anno domini so it must have been caused by the stress of the last two weeks!

The design of the Patriarch required the troops to be carried only in the two after holds, leaving the for'ard ones for their equipment. McTavish was keeping an eye on number three hold and the bosun on number two. Down in the 'tween decks a shore gang was pushing and heaving bundles and crates into position ready for the crane to sway them up and onto the wharf. Two seamen checked each lift to make sure that an accident would not occur.

With luck both the upper holds would be clear by the evening and tomorrow the lower holds opened up and cleared of the lorries which were down there.

"That sling hooked on O.K., Harvey?"

"Yes Mr.McTavish."

"O.K., heave her out then!" The second officer yelled up at the seaman on the well deck who signaled to the shore crane driver. As it was much quicker to use shore cranes the ship's derricks were all swung outboard of the vessel. He looked at his watch, time for the crew's `smoke-o'.

The second mate climbed up the iron ladder to the booby-hatch and out onto the deck. Sitting down on the pile of hatch covers he pulled off his gloves; his shirt was wet through and clung limply to his back. He pushed his cap to the back of his head and felt for his cigarettes, glad to be up in the fresh air. "Damn and blast it," he said out loud and got up to go to his cabin. Instead, seeing the bosun standing at the after end of number two hatch, he walked under the bridge castle towards him.

"Hello Bose, got a fag? Left mine in the cabin."

"Sure Second, help yourself." He handed over a packet of Players and turned back to watch a sling full of bundled blankets being swayed ashore.

"Steady up there!" he yelled as the crane driver swung his boom too fast and the cargo net started to gyrate. "Steady I say!" but his cry went unheeded. The net swung wide and outwards and caught the side of the bridge.

"Oh Christ. These bloody crane drivers!" the bosun swore as a corner of the net broke and started to spill its contents over the wharf.

The two men hurried to the other side of the ship to view the damage, just in time to see one of a group of army officers step backwards to avoid the last falling bundle only to trip and fall into the narrow gap between ship and wharf.

It was not unusual for drunken sailors to fall into the dock on their way back aboard but somehow they never seemed to hurt themselves. The army officer was less fortunate. As he fell his head caught the edge of a wooden sponson which kept the ship from rubbing against the wharf. The man rose to the surface and lay floating face down, a patch of red spreading on the back of his head.

A coloured dock worker and the other officers peered over the dockside at the man in the water. McTavish took one look, dropped cap and gloves to the deck, flipped his cigarette over the side and climbed on the ship's gun'ale. Carefully judging the narrow width of water he jumped feet first. The water was cool, dark and refreshing but he had no time to enjoy it. Breaking surface alongside the soldier he turned him over supporting him with one arm while he rested the other on the sponson. A moment later the end of a heaving line splashed in the water by them. The Second struggled to pass a bowline under the limp man's arms before willing hands hauled the inert body up the ship's side.

Someone dropped the pilot ladder and McTavish climbed back onboard. The soldier was laid out with the bosun kneeling by him and a group of sailors looking on.

"Bates, pull the corner of that tarpaulin here. You other two go an' get the stretcher from by my cabin an' look lively about it!"

Carefully the bosun covered the wet, khaki clad figure, then, seeing McTavish standing dripping by the bulwark said:

"Sorry Sir, but you was too late. Looks like 'e stove 'is 'ead in on the sponson poor sod." As he spoke the water trickling from under the tarpaulin became discoloured with blood. "That fuckin' crane driver ought t' be shot!" he finished vehemently.

At that moment a major, panting from running up the gangway, joined them. "How's the Adj?" and then realizing the body was covered, "Christ, he's not dead surely?"

" 'fraid so," McTavish answered, catching sight of the `Green Howards' flash on the major's battledress. Adjutant! God, this was the fellow who had been eulogising the prowess of his wife's lover. McTavish's stomach tied itself into knots at the memory.

Captain Spencer, in the privacy of his cabin, wiped his mouth on the spotless white linen napkin and rang the hand bell for his tiger.

"You may clear away now Perkins." Spencer felt deflated. His ship was no longer moving to the caress of the ocean; instead of the steady throb of engines it now reverberated to the sounds of unloading. Like most seagoing officers he did not like swarms of dockers crawling all over his ship. Of course they were very necessary but one was never quite sure what they were up to; indeed there were some middle east ports where it was necessary, around the accommodation, to keep fire hoses rigged and to have to use them on would be light fingered gentry!

At sea it was the ocean and you. Sometimes it was kind and benevolent but at others, like the storm of their first few days of this trip, a very hard task master but he would rather that than the paper work which being in port necessitated. Fortunately the trooping commandant said that the death of the Green Howard's adjutant would be dealt with by them so there was little to do on that score and what had to be done had already been taken care of by Boulton. Had it been peacetime such a happening would have meant reams and reams of reports! Both he and the colonel had commended McTavish for his prompt action.

Boulton was in his bunk and McTavish, having changed his clothes and eaten, was making sure all went according to plan with the discharge. The agent would be aboard shortly to advise the Patriach's captain when he was to visit the S.N.O. for orders for the next part of the voyage. Orders which he was sure would read: `You are required to take your ship without undue delay to the River Plate and there load a cargo for Great Britain.' It had been the same for the last six voyages and, no doubt, would be for the duration of hostilities; unless the ship became a statistic of the war.

For the next few days, the chief officer would be far busier since all cargo work and the readying of the ship was his direct responsibility. He, the captain, would, by comparison, be able to sit back for a while. Nevertheless he felt dejected because not until the voyage was over and he saw the sides of beef being swung out of the holds to an English dockside, could he justifiably consider his job well done.

Here in Durban the job was only a third completed with the longest part of the voyage still to come; then the captain's responsibilities would be even greater than before. Out there, alone and with thousands of miles of water to cross, there would be no convoy commodore to hold his hand and no senior officer escorts to tell him what to do. Instead the decisions would be his and his alone, for better or for worse. But for the moment there were minor decisions to be made, such as telling his tiger to arrange for him to take dinner in the saloon so that Perkins could have the rest of the day off and go ashore.

If the tiger was going ashore today, said Mr.Akker, then the saloon-boy could have time off after dinner was finished and tomorrow from after lunch. Box and cox was what the two would do for the time being.

CHAPTER NINE

"Last time I was 'ere", said Green "I lambasted two stokers from the Durban Castle; that were a scrap that were! Best I've 'ad fer years!"

"Yep, I remember that one Basher," replied another able seaman as they sat in the mess eating high tea. "That were the time you got a good shiner an' lost a tooth!"

"What if I did mate! I beat 'em fair and square didn't I? An' it were two to one too!" growled Green.

"Sure, sure no need ta get all 'et up abaht it mate! Where shall we go tonight then, the Bristol? Reckon we orter dip our wicks?"

As in the seamen's mess so it was in the engineers' saloon, the stokers' mess and up in the bridge saloon; all talk centred on going ashore. Some would make it the first night and probably wake in the morning with thick heads, while others would wonder if there would be a discharge from their pricks in ten days time. Each to his own designs. Some, like Brightman the doctor's assistant, would be lucky and have all the nights ashore. What the navigating officers needed most was a good sleep and after that they would see how they felt. For Third Officer David Giles the second evening would be his first run ashore.

The proverbial tall dark and handsome officer David Giles, at twenty two, was the answer to a maiden's prayer: had he been in films he would have held his own against Clark Gable. Now he stepped back a pace from the half mirror he had fixed to the back of his wardrobe door and admired himself, not out of conceit but he always liked to be correctly turned out. He was an ex-Conway boy and from a naval family, where manners and dress were always meticulous to the n'th degree. He was a good, if somewhat dashing, officer. As his friends said, without rancour, he would have made as good a pirate as Errol Flynn any day of the week! He was fortunate in as much as he had, thanks to a proud grandfather, a private income and was able to give the mess-steward a very generous tip to ensure that his uniform was always just right.

Like the day just gone, it was a warm evening so he decided that he would go ashore in long whites. The creases in the uniform were exactly right and the button-up collar of the jacket had just the correct amount of starch, not too much so that it made his neck sore, but enough to keep it from crumpling. The single stripe of gold braid with its diamond in the middle was the best quality that the well known service officers' outfitters Gieves could supply. The crown and anchor on his buttons were exactly up and down. Even the most bad tempered of naval commanders would not be able to find fault with his turnout today!

Locking his cabin door, for it was well known that dockies had a penchant for being light fingered, he made his way down to the main deck and jauntily strode along to the gangway where the chief radio officer was on watch.

"Off on the spree again, David? You want to watch it or one day you'll wear it away !" the older man jibed.

"Not likely Dave, it's made of India rubber! Be seeing you." And he bounded down the gangway.

Five minutes later the third officer threw a coin to a beggar who sat, huddled in filthy rags, at the dock gates; showed his pass to a policeman, then ignoring the Zulu rickshaw men and taxis, decided to walk up to the city centre. He started off along Shepstone Street at a brisk pace but soon realized that it was warmer than he thought. As he slowed down a large American car drew up alongside and its driver, a heavily built, bronzed man in his early sixties, wearing an expensive fawn Worsted suit called out: "Care for a lift young man?"

"Why, thank you Sir. That's most kind. It's a bit warmer for walking than I'd thought." The door opened and Giles climbed in.

"Where are you going?"

"Nowhere in particular. Probably have dinner and do a show or dance. Must make the best of one's first night ashore after five weeks on the jolly old briny."

"That's quite a while to be at sea." The driver spoke precise English with the accent of the Afrikaner but an inflection, like Giles, of one who has been well educated.

Giles, who had delighted in the study of England's naval history, replied "For these days I suppose it is. Nelson did two years without stepping ashore when he was in the Med. Dashed if I can see how they stood it for so long in those tough days. Have a cigarette, Sir?" The young officer pulled out his silver cigarette case and both men lit up.

"First night ashore? I didn't know we had a ship arrive today?"

"No, we came in yesterday but I was watch aboard and too damn tired anyway to go gallivanting!"

"Ah yes, the remains of a convoy. You had quite a tough time of things I hear." The car stopped at traffic lights and then went forward again. "What ship are you from?"

"Patriarch."

"A trooper, I believe?"

"That's right. At least, we troop outward bound and then nip smartly over to the River Plate for a cargo of meat before heading home. It all makes for a nice round trip."

"Yes, I suppose it does. Always wanted to travel myself when I was a youngster. Once went to Europe years ago but that's all." He paused to draw on his cigarette "Anyway, young man, is there not something about `careless talk costing lives' and so on? I might be a spy for all you know!" The driver finished with a laugh, blowing the horn as a native with a death wish dashed across the road in front of them without looking and was almost hit by the car.

Giles coloured slightly at the mild rebuke and replied: "Yes, you're right of course, Sir. Back in England, or over in the Argentine, I certainly would never talk like this to a stranger but down here? Surely there are no German spies!"

The car was nearing the centre of the city, "Tell me Mr...?"

"Giles, Sir. David Giles, Third Officer."

"Thank you. I wonder, Mr.Giles, if you might like to come home and take tea with us? I was late leaving the office so have not had mine yet. I know my wife will be only too pleased to meet you. We like to do our bit for you service lads when we can." He smiled benevolently at his young companion.

Giles had intended, after a meal, to go to a night club. He knew one that last trip had a particularly attractive hostess, but he rather liked this amiable old man. He put all thoughts of lechery from his mind, replying that he would be delighted and it really was a most kind offer.

"Not at all, not at all," beamed the older man. "We'll take the next turning to the right and go out along Marine Parade. I live about four miles out of town to the north. It's quite a pleasant drive,"

The big car swung around the next corner and weaved its way through the traffic, giving a wide berth to the rickshaw boys with their bobbing ostrich feather headgear. During the drive, Kruger, for that was the driver's name, kept up a running commentary on the city. Although Giles had been there several times before he now realized how little he knew about Durban.

Eventually the car turned into a graveled drive lined with alternate Flamboyant and Frangipani trees and came to rest in front of a large house. Spotlessly white, with red tiles and heavy timbered gables, it was of typical Cape Dutch design. Its air of cleanliness accentuated by brilliantly coloured flowers, amongst which Barberton Daisies predominated. David Giles had been brought up to appreciate good things and was delighted with what he saw.

"This is a lovely place you have, Sir," he remarked as he alighted from the car. "Absolutely magnificent! A tremendous lot of work must go into keeping those flower beds so beautiful!"

"Yes it is lovely isn'it. My Kaffirs do work hard. We've been here for thirty years now. Are you interested in gardening? If so I should be delighted to show you around after tea. Gardening is my hobby you know!"

They were welcomed on the stoep by a homely little lady who was obviously pleased to see her husband and his guest.

"Mother, this is Mr.Giles off one of the ships that came in yesterday. They had a pretty rough time of things so I thought he might like to have a cup of tea with us."

"Yes, yes, of course." She smiled warmly at David as he saluted automatically. "Do come in Mr.Giles. I'm always pleased to have someone to tea. It's all ready. We have it late because Mr. Kruger keeps such long hours at the office. I'll just tell the boy to bring another cup." Mrs.Kruger preceded the two men into the large hallway and then into a spacious and cool lounge.

"This is very kind of you, ma'am," Giles said as he seated himself on soft cushions in the bay window and, through its open section, caught the balmy scent of the myriads of flowers. In keeping with the outside of the house the room was spotlessly clean with symmetrically arranged heavy dark wood furniture.

Without having to be told, for he had seen the arrival of the guest, a black servant, wearing a long white robe and a red Fez, brought in another cup, saucer and plate of delicate china.

"Do you take milk Mr.Giles?"

"Yes please, ma'am." The war, the convoy and the long hours on the bridge seemed far away. In this idyllic and tranquil setting even the sea did not appear to exist. Everything was so absolutely right. Then just as he was about to sip his tea, Giles sensed that something had suddenly changed.

He looked up to see a girl of, perhaps, twenty, silhouetted against the french windows. She stood there for a moment with one hand resting on the door frame; quite the most exquisite girl he had ever seen. As she advanced into the room she moved with a supple grace, the red of her shorts and blouse bringing out the rich honey colour of her skin and accentuating the perfection of her body. As she greeted her parents her voice was as gentle as the sigh of a summer's evening breeze.

"Barbara, may I present Third Officer David Giles," her father said.

David stood up and bowed slightly, looking into soft brown eyes as he raised his head. Eyes which were kind and appealing, with a promise of something that was as yet intangible. For a brief moment the blood raced in his veins and he knew that here was a woman like none other he had ever met before.

"Your servant, ma'am," he mumbled as he took the outstretched hand in his.

During tea David Giles said and did the right things automatically but he felt awkward and ill at ease with the girl so close. He only got a grip on himself when she went to change and he and the old man went out into the garden in the evening twilight. There amongst the heavily scented white and yellow Frangipani he listened intently to all his host had to say.

Later the two ladies joined them for drinks under a blue Jacaranda tree in which were entwined innumerable fairy lights. The young officer found the conversation stimulating for they talked of many things from gardens to ships; London to Durban; yachts to motor cars, and on all subjects Mr.Kruger proved to be most knowledgeable. He talked briefly about his youth out on the veldt and Giles described his home in Dorset.

The twilight deepened into darkness and they had to be reminded twice by a servant that dinner was ready. David Giles was gradually becoming accustomed to the feelings which the girl aroused in him; feelings that were different from any he had experienced before.

When the meal was over his host suggested that David might like to go on a sight-seeing tour of Durban and, late though it was, he had to make another business call. He was sure his daughter would be pleased to drive David, a suggestion the young officer accepted with alacrity. The girl left the room and David overheard snatches of a telephone conversation she made as he sipped a Drambuie.

"No, I'm sorry Jerry. I know I should have 'phoned earlier but I just can't. It's one of Pa's sailor friends and you know what he's like if I don't take them out....No I can't help it....Tomorrow? I'll see, I'm not sure....all right. Bye for now."

Overhearing this made him feel embarrassed. After saying his goodbyes to her parents and as he opened the door of her car for her, he said: "Barbara. I'm awfully sorry if this has messed up your evening. I couldn't help overhearing your conversation on the 'phone. You could drop me off in town and then get hold of your date again?"

"What Jerry?" She laughed. "No thank you. You made a good excuse. He's such a bore!" then seeing David's expression, added hastily; "Oh, I'm sorry; I really didn't mean to be rude." As she got into the car she lightly touched his hand making him tingle all over.

In that fleeting touch something passed between them. The girl studied the car's dashboard while the young man walked around to the passenger's side and got in. Shakily he lit two cigarettes and handed one to her before she started the engine and they drove off towards Durban.

The car was the latest model MG open tourer and although Barbara handled it well David thought that she drove too fast. She talked, almost inconsequentially, about the town but it was not until they had drunk two whiskies at a beachfront hotel that the tension between them eased and they began to speak of their respective childhoods.

Despite the thousands of miles separating their two homes their early lives bore many similarities. David's childhood sprang vividly to mind as they sat on the veranda of Claridges Hotel watching the twinkling lights of the long boulevard reflected in the water of the bay. A sight spoiled by the vaguely discernible barbed wire on the sandy beach, supposedly there to stop any would be Japanese invaders.

He clearly remembered the long school holidays spent happily in the family's rambling country house at Studland. Summers when he spent hours sailing his dinghy around to Swanage if the weather was good. Cold wet winters when he and his sister read or played games before a roaring fire. Christmases when aunts and cousins had come from far and near to join the festivities, all presided over by a benevolent grandfather, or if the admiral happened to be at sea, David's father.

As he talked of these things to the girl beside him he was conscious for the first time since leaving the Conway, of a wave of homesickness of such magnitude that he again felt awkward and ill at ease and blushed in his embarrassment. Perhaps the war was at last getting to him, as it did to so many, that the love and warmth of a mother and family was needed to counter the insidious way in which it made men old before their time.

He tried to hide his feelings by calling for two more whiskies. He didn't normally drink just for the sake of drinking, or to get drunk, although there had been times when he had come `rolling home'! He now felt that he wanted to oust these other feelings with the heady sensation of drink.

He couldn't understand himself or the strange effect this girl was having on him. He would have had any other woman half way to bed by now. Only six weeks ago an earl's daughter had begged him to take her away for one last fling before he went back to sea. He couldn't understand his present reluctance with Barbara. He wanted this exquisite girl as he had never wanted any other and yet he was frightened to touch her.

The drinks were brought and they sat in silence for a minute or two, then Barbara asked:

"David, why did you go to sea?"

"Why did I go to sea?" He repeated the question gazing into his drink and moving the glass slightly so that the ice tinkled against the side. "I don't really know. It just happened. I remember my father saying one holiday `Time you decided what you're going to do with your life, my boy.' I don't think I had ever given it any serious thought before and I don't know that I did even then. I just replied; `Oh, go to sea, I suppose Sir.' I knew a bit about small boats and something about coastal sailing so it seemed the obvious thing to do. I suppose the fact that grandfather had been an admiral and father in the navy during the last war had some bearing on my decision. The more I thought about it the more it seemed the right thing to do. There was no war on at that time and it appeared to be a pretty good life. I went to the Conway, that's an officer's training ship, and finally to sea. By the time I obtained my second mate's ticket Munich was upon us and I only managed two trips before the war started." He paused to sip his drink.

"Now it's different. At times it's bloody awful, but after you've done a couple of trips and stood a watch something gets you which I can't define; it's something to do with the sea, the sky and God or whatever is up there? That might sound funny to you after all you must have heard about sailors getting drunk every night and spending their time in the nearest brothel, but it's true. The war apart, there's something out there which is so tremendously worthwhile having; there's a feeling you don't get ashore; it's as if you were close to God somehow! When you're up there on the bridge in the middle of the night with the ship directly under your control, it's different.

The stars, the sea, the very blackness of the night seem to speak to you; and if there's a storm and you come through it, when you see the first rays of the sun appearing in the clouds, you get a clean feeling right inside. It's...it's like listening to a peal of church bells reaching a crescendo!" The words had seemed to rush out and he paused to get his breath then, dropping his voice a little, continued.

"Now there's the war which, if anything, makes it more worth while. Not the sinkings and the killings. God, I feel sick every time the alarm bells go, but there's a tremendous spirit which the war has fostered between those who sail the ships. It doesn't matter if you're the cabin-boy, greaser or a mate. People have always talked of the brotherhood of the sea but now it's such a concrete thing that I could no more pack up and leave than I could fly! If only you could see a dawn out there on the Atlantic I'm sure you would know what I mean!" David Giles stopped talking and ran a finger round the collar of his white jacket. He realized he was perspiring heavily, despite the cool night air. He felt limp and exhausted and the effects of the drink had suddenly left him. He had said things to this girl that he had never said to any man or woman before. Things for which he would have been ridiculed in the saloon. He looked at the lovely face before him.

"I'm sorry. I must have lost my head to spout such trash."

"David." Her voice was infinitely gentle, "Promise me you won't ever say such words are trash again. The opposite is so true. Don't you see, what you've described is a way of life. A way meant by God. All those wonderful things you mention, the stars, the wind, the blackness of the night, all those are His and if you can appreciate them then you have found something that so few men can find, a reason for living!" For the second time that night she put her hand on his but this time she did not take it away and from its touch he experienced a feeling of such intensity the likes of which he had not thought possible. For a moment longer they sat, each with their own thoughts but both mystically in harmony. Neither one having the courage to give voice to their thoughts of mutual attraction so early in their acquaintance. Instead Giles finally broke the spell by saying.

"Don't you think it's time I took you home?"

She looked at her watch. It was past midnight. "Yes, I suppose you're right, though Pa doesn't seem to mind if I'm out late so long as he knows who I'm with. Mind you, he always wants to know where we've been and what we've talked about when I've been out with one of his sailor friends. He so interested in anything to do with ships." She got up. "Come on, I'll drive you to the docks. You can hardly see me home and then walk all the way back!" She laughed, a sound so effervescent that David's whole body tingled with sheer delight.

Together they left the hotel and walked to the MG. A girl blossoming into womanhood and a young officer who saluted meticulously when she dropped him off at the dock gates, having arranged to meet his lady the following evening. Wondering as she drove off why he had not kissed her as he would have kissed any other woman. He gave up trying to find a reason for his actions, woke up the beggar by the gate and gave the startled man a ten shilling note before returning to his slumbering ship. He returned the same officer in the same rig but different. No longer the flippant young man but one grown to maturity, with a new reason for living.

The following day was again unusually warm for a South African autumn, so David Giles once more donned a white uniform and checked his appearance in the mirror. There were two obvious bulges in the breast pockets into which he had pushed two packets of `Craven A 'cigarettes. No, that wouldn't do, he decided and reluctantly removed a packet from each. Two less for old man Kruger but it couldn't be helped, there was still the one in each of his trouser pockets. These `whites' were hardly the best rig in which to conceal `gifts' for folks ashore.

It was twenty to six and he should have been at the dock gates ten minutes ago but it couldn't be helped; there had been a problem in number four hold which had detained him.

At the gangway he ignored the ribald remark made by the uncouth junior sparks and hurried to the dock gate where he was dismayed to find no sign of Barbara. He checked with the policeman but no MG had been seen. Thinking that Barbara herself might be late he waited, pacing up and down, until half past six and then decided to take a taxi out to the house. But when the driver asked him where he wanted to go David realized he did not have an address. He hoped that he could remember the way!

The taxi deposited Giles in the driveway of the Kruger home, prevented from driving right up to the front door by the presence of four other cars beside the family's black Chevrolet. Three of the cars had `police' signs on their roof. Two uniformed constables were at the front door, one of whom put out a restraining hand when Giles went to enter. He wanted to know who he was and what he was doing there; then told David to wait on the stoep and disappeared inside. He returned a couple of minutes later.

"O.K mister, the Super will see you now. Go on in and take the first door on the right."

Giles went into the lounge where only yesterday he had had such a pleasant tea. Now there was no tea and no familiar faces. Two men in civilian clothes sat in the bay window, one wore grey flannels, blazer and a naval cravat the other slacks and an open sports jacket which just showed the butt of a revolver in an arm-pit holster. A sergeant and constable stood nearby whilst a third sat in an armchair writing in a note book. One and all eyed him with interest.

"Another sucker, Jan," said the civilian with the apparent naval connection.

"Name please!" rapped the other.

The lovely atmosphere of the room had disappeared. Now he had a feeling of foreboding, noticing that the three uniformed police also wore side arms. Giles began to bristle, answering curtly.

"I have already told your man outside and he told you! What the hell is going on? Has there been an accident or something. Miss Kruger was supposed to meet me at the dock gate an hour ago."

"No, there's been no accident. Why were you wanting to see Miss Kruger?"

"Well that's a bloody silly question!" Giles was now starting to get annoyed with this abrupt questioning. "If you must know I was damn well going to ask her to marry me!" Startled by his own words he wondered what had made him say them but suddenly he knew that it was the truth. "Anyway just who are you?"

"All right young man, no need to get het up. It's my job to ask questions. This gentleman is Lieutenant- Commander Piets of Naval Intelligence and I'm Superintendent van Deventer of Special Branch. Please take a seat and, by the look of your pockets you might sooth your nerves with a cigarette. Now, how long have you known Miss Kruger?"

David Giles sat down and lit a cigarette before answering, feeling foolish when he did. "Well, as a matter of fact I only met her yesterday. Mr Kruger offered me a lift and then gave me the hospitality of his house. Afterwards I went for a run around the town with his daughter. Look, for Pete's sake just what is all this about?"

"He seems genuine enough, Jan," the commander said. "Might as well tell him I suppose. He's obviously just the latest pick up."

"Mr.Giles," the superintendent continued in a less aggressive tone, his voice sounding infinitely weary. "We have reason to believe that Mr.Kruger is passing information about shipping to the enemy and that, as you will probably be aware, since he's a South African citizen, is treason! Tell me, did he pump you for news about the war at sea and in particular your recent convoy. I take it you're from one of the vessels that docked three days ago?"

David was flabbergasted! "B-but the idea is preposterous. The old man would never dream of such a thing! Oh... yes, I'm off the Patriarch."

"I'm sorry to disillusion you, Giles, but I can assure you that he did. We've been watching him and an accomplice, who operates a radio link to the German Consulate in Goa, for some while now. You are by no means the first officer to whom he has given a lift and then from whom, under cover of hospitality, gleaned a lot of useful information. It was all very ingenious, for who would suspect such a genial host of harbouring pro-Nazi sympathies. All the cross talk and simple questions put to you and the answers you gave helped to build up a picture of what happened in the convoys. The information that goes back to the German Admiralty is of immense value in ascertaining the truth of claims made by the U-boat skippers of having sunk this or that ship. Can you remember what you might have said about the specific losses in WS 25 and the future sailing of your ship?"

Incredulously David forced his mind back over the conversation of the previous evening. He remembered Barbara's telephone call...."one of Daddy's sailor friends"....she had said and then later..."Daddy does ask what we talk about and always takes a great interest in ships." He tried to think of any specific questions the old man had asked but of course there were none, everything had been in a round about way. He frowned as he thought and then said:

"We did talk about ships and the sea and the rate of sinkings. God, if what you say is true, then

I've been a raving lunatic! I told him that only two had gone down because the figure he quoted was too high and, as far as the sinkings were concerned, this had not been a bad trip really although one did not expect any losses in a troop convoy. We discussed how long the Allies could keep things up with the present rate of losses, my view being that we were on a knife edge." Giles drew long at his cigarette while trying to marshal his thoughts. "But I can't really believe that this is all true, it's too fantastic for words! Why would he do such a thing?"

The superintendent viciously stubbed out his cigarette, glared at the sailor and with raised voice almost shouted, "Damn you! Do you think I like this any more than you! I've known the Krugers for years so how do you think I feel?" He dropped his voice to a more conversational tone and continued; "Anyway, you told him that one troopship and a cargo vessel had gone down plus a cruiser damaged, for that was in the note he passed on to his radio operator. Why, you ask? The British troops killed his father and mother at the end of the Boer War and he has never forgiven them. Oh yes, there are quite a few that would not mind the Germans winning this war!" He pulled out a leather cigarette case and swore in Afrikaans when he found it empty. Automatically Giles pulled out one of the packets from his pocket and threw it to the superintendent, who having lit up continued.

"Since you were the final participant leading to Kruger's arrest I shall require a statement of facts as you've just told them. Might even require you to appear at his trial although the case has a forgone conclusion."

"What will happen to the old man?"

"With a war on treason is punishable by death. If he were a spy he would be shot. For this crime it will be the rope. And whatever we think, it is a crime."

"Dear God!" David muttered as the man from special branch continued.

"Mr.Giles, after this please do not think that everyone here who offers you a lift and hospitality is a potential spy! Far from it, they're ordinary honest people who are only too pleased to be of help to you. Only just watch what you say in future and remember that we have sent a lot of our chaps up north to fight in the desert."

Giles coloured at the rebuke and unhooked his collar which was almost choking him, then asked, "Where does Miss Kruger figure in all this? I just can't believe that she's mixed up in it!"

"No, as far as we can tell she has no idea of her father's sympathies. She knew about his parents being killed when he was a boy and that he was a bit sore about it but that's all. I think she was just a very useful, and very beautiful, piece of unknowing bait."

The superintendent's reply laid to rest a sudden gnawing fear which had arisen in David's mind. "Is there any chance of seeing her?"

"She's down at headquarters with her parents but both she and her mother are free to leave whenever they wish. We're only holding the old man. When are you sailing by the way?"

The young man had been shaken by the unexpected and almost adventure book story that had unfolded in the last half hour. Now he began to realise that he had to give evidence against a man who had shown him hospitality and kindness and was also the father of the girl he had fallen in love with. The whole thing had become unbelievable, a bad dream. Things of this sort did not happen in real life!

"Well?" the policeman repeated. "I asked you when you are sailing."

"Why the blazes should I tell you? You've just told me to be careful what I say," he snapped.

The superintendent grinned feebly as his words were flung back at him. The naval man broke in.

"He's off within forty-eight hours, well before anything can be arranged. I think that the answer must be a deposition before a magistrate. We can get that done this evening. The S.N.O. would never agree to the ship sailing without one of her navigating officers."

"Look here, do I have to make a statement? I admit that I have only known the Krugers a day but, damn it, it goes against the grain. However ridiculous it might seem to you, I just can't do it! Beside what the blazes would Barbara think of me? I meant what I said about wanting to marry her!"

The commander came back at him, almost snarling, "Look, I don't blame you for falling for the girl, she's a damn good looker, but good God man, what about your fellow shipmates? Think of the ones who have gone to the bottom because of Kruger's activities. Hell, for all we know, he could have been responsible for the Bellevue blowing up. A lot of people knew that not all the convoy had gone into Cape Town so perhaps he had time to summon his bloody friends. I've not always been in this damn desk job, I know what it's like to see men fried in burning oil."

David Giles, with all eyes in the room turned towards him, looked and felt uncomfortable. "Damn this bloody war!" he cried pushing back the chair and walking to the french windows where he threw his cigarette out onto the immaculate lawn. Why, oh why was this happening to him? In one breathless moment he had found a woman he wanted for his wife and now in another it seemed he was about to lose her. Then Piets spoke again.

"I'm afraid there's nothing you can do about it, Giles. You must know, apart from the moral aspect of the thing, your duty and all the rest. I have the power to order you to make a deposition and if you refuse you could be in all sorts of strife!"

David Giles turned slowly back towards his interrogator who had risen from his seat in the bay window and taken a couple of paces towards him.

"As it seems that I have no alternative then let's get it over with!"

"That's more like it, Giles. Forget the ruddy women, they're all the same when the lights are off! After all I'll warrant that you're not the first to get a leg over that girl and no doubt there'll be many mo..." The words were choked in his mouth as David Giles' fist crashed into his face sending him reeling backwards. It was not a scientific punch as Able Seaman Green would have landed, but a punch savagely thrown and intended to cause maximum pain. In an instant the two uniformed policemen seized the sailor from behind whilst the superintendent stood in front of his colleague to prevent him retaliating.

"You little sod! I'll get you for that! Charge the bastard with assault, Jan!"

"Shut up Bob, you deserved that. And you young man," he rounded on Giles, "Want to be more careful with your fist or you'll land in trouble! Sergeant Bekker take Mr.Giles down to the station and see about that deposition."

Still shaking with fury at the commander's words David Giles allowed himself to be led to one of the waiting police cars.

By the time they reached the police station Barbara and her mother had left to stay with relatives some forty miles inland. Only old man

Kruger remained and David could not have seen him even if he had wanted to. He was locked in a cell deep in the police station like any criminal, with an armed guard outside his door.

It took an hour and a half to find a magistrate who was free and another before the job was done. When David was finally told he could go, it was ten o'clock and, as much as he wanted to go and find Barbara, he dared not take the risk of going so far afield with his ship liable to sail sometime the next day. Anyway it was possibly not the best of ideas as the two ladies would be too distraught after the day's happenings to want to see him, particularly as they might look upon him as the catalyst for Kruger's arrest. Instead he got Sergeant Bekker to drive him back to the docks.

Once he was back aboard the Patriarch depression settled over him like a black cloud. He was told shore leave would end at midday tomorrow so there would definitely be no chance of going anywhere worthwhile. He could not even speak to Barbara since there was no 'phone where she had gone. In the familiar confines of his neat cabin the whole affair seemed totally unreal, but he knew the ache in his heart was real. Slowly he made himself realize that, incredible though it might seem, he had become entangled with a Nazi agent, and fallen in love with his daughter.

He thought vaguely what a story it would make when the war was over, except that he had sworn and signed a bit of paper acknowledging that he was now under the official secrets act. He was not allowed to say anything about the subject for the next thirty years!

Yesterday he had felt on top of the world and glad to be alive. Now he was in the depths of despair. How could he expect a girl to marry the man responsible for her father's arrest? It would be four months at least before the ship could possibly be back in Durban. He fumed at his helplessness.

At half past midnight, unable to sleep, he sat at his tiny desk and took out a sheet of writing paper. Under the embossed address of his home, `The Grange', Farm Lane, Studland, Dorset; he wrote M.V Patriarch, Durban and the date and time. For a moment or two he marshaled his thoughts before starting the letter:

My Dear Barbara,

When I arrived at your house this evening to find the police there I found it almost impossible to grasp what had happened. Despite all that I have been told I still pray that it is all one ghastly mistake. No matter what your father may have done, I want you to know that I hold no malice and I am sure that whatever he did he did with the courage of his convictions and as a very brave man knowing the consequence of such actions. Likewise I hope you will forgive me for playing, albeit unwittingly, a part in your father's arrest. I was also told that I had no option other than to make a statement which could well incriminate him.

By the time you receive this letter I shall be at sea again. If, when we return to Durban in a few months time, you refuse to see me I shall understand, although I pray that will not be the case. Whatever happens I shall always cherish the memory of the one evening we spent together.

   With affection,

   David Giles.

He read the letter through and then took a packet of fags from his pocket with the address where they were staying. Sergeant Bekker had explained that he was not allowed to disclose the family's whereabouts and then turned away to light a cigarette `accidentally' turning the occurrence book round so that Giles could quickly scribble the address on the cigarette packet. The envelope addressed, he returned to his bunk and lay brooding with hands behind his head until sleep finally overtook him just before dawn.

CHAPTER TEN

"Green, you feeling all right? 'as the pox caught up with you at last or summat?" The fo'c'sle party was mustered ready to cast off the lines from their berth at Ocean Terminal and the bosun running an eye over the waiting men had decided that Able Seaman Green needed chiding.

"What'cha mean Bose, there aint nothing wrong wiv me!"

"There must be 'cause you didn't 'ave to be bailed out'a jug this time ashore. No scraps! Now you gotta admit that 'aint like you!"

" 's right Bose 'cause we was too busy dippin' our wicks 'an when we'd finished it's true there was a couple a' blokes off the Empress whot made a rude remark about our ship like, but they was too pissed to fight so I lets 'em be."

At that moment the second officer climbed up the ladder and conversation lapsed. "Evening Bose. The pilot wants to single up to the back-spring so let's go." He walked to the eye of the ship, climbed on to the small platform and blew his whistle to attract the attention of the mooring gang. Raising his megaphone he started to issue orders which would, once more, send the Patriarch on her way to sea.

Down aft a still very subdued Third Officer Giles did likewise. On the bridge Chief Officer Boulton listened intently to all that was said between the captain and pilot. There would only be one more chance, when they sailed from the Argentine, before he would find himself on his own bridge and with all the responsibility the fourth stripe on his arm would bring.

So, after their short respite, the Patriarch and her crew went back to war. They sailed their ship out onto the cold wide ocean. A somewhat forlorn ship as, with no cargo in her, she rattled and groaned in places where she had not done so on the outward voyage. A lone ship under a moonless sky with its canopy of bright twinkling stars. It was difficult, with the city's lights bright on the receding shoreline, with full bellies and hangovers for some, to face the reality that there was a war and that death could be lurking in wait for them.

A bomber crew high above a German city with ack-ack shells throwing their plane about and the rattle of their machine guns as they fought off the enemy fighters, had little time to feel frightened or contemplate the prospect of death. Soldiers on the ground with the devastating noise of battle around them felt likewise. It was only when all was quiet that those men had time to think about such things. The merchant seaman, who rarely had the opportunity to defend himself, had little to break the solitude. He just sailed on and on across the oceans, doing what was at best a repetitive and at worst a boring job.

For hours, days and even weeks at a time those rattles, groans or the vibration of the engines became a monotonous part of his daily life. The bomber crews, when and if they returned, tried to forget the terror of their battle by living out the saying `eat, drink and be merry for tomorrow we die'. So too the merchant seamen tried to forget with talk of the whores they had left behind and those who waited for them at the next port, and how they would get drunk yet again. For all aboard the Patriarch, each in his own way during the next fourteen days of their solitary journey over four and a half thousand miles of ocean, there would be plenty of time for reflection.

For those on the bridge life would be a little easier without the constant risk of collision that being in convoy involved. Instead, apart from plotting their position and the perpetual zigzag, they would spend endless hours scanning the sea around them hoping against hope they would see nothing; the fear that they might keeping them ever vigilant.

For the engineers life would also be easier with the engine revolutions set for a constant seventeen knots. Hour after hour they would check their gauges and enter their logbook and hope that they would not have to ring the bridge to say that something was not as it should be.

For the catering staff in the first class saloon and its galley things would be very different. The cooks had no passengers to cook for, only the stewards, the four heads of departments and the two trooping officers who were aboard for the round trip. The pantry boys who had almost no dishes to wash and so filled in time scrubbing and cleaning, not only in the galley and pantry but down in the store rooms as well, were still able to spend more time in their bunks or playing cards.

As the Patriarch steamed to the west Wentle and Harry London leaned on the after rail of A deck outside the second class lounge or, as it had been more recently, the troops canteen and watched the lights of Durban twinkling astern. They were there because their daily tasks were finished and because they would be sleeping in the canteen for this part of the voyage at least. They and one or two other stewards felt that it was much safer being closer to the lifeboats than staying down below in the fo'c'sle.

Harry London reflected that there was no point in stacking the odds against himself for, if he had to abandon ship for a third time, he might not be so lucky.

"You know Dick, I enjoyed last night. Going to the flicks in Durban sure was different from back home!"

"Yes Harry I agree and what an amazing place that auditorium was. That ceiling certainly had me fooled." He was referring to the theatre where pinpricks of lights blinked on and off to give the impression that they were sitting out in the open.

Over the few weeks since leaving Avonmouth the two youths had become firm friends. They had gone ashore together, not to get drunk or find a whore as the others in the boy's peak had professed their intentions to be but to see a little of the town, have a meal and a drink and get away from the reality of their ship. They, of course, knew nothing of the drama that had such a dire effect on the third officer. Indeed no one should have known but Captain Spencer did, and that was by chance.

On their second day in Durban Spencer had visited the S.N.O. The man who had been in that position for the last three voyages was no longer there. In his place was someone he had not seen since leaving the Navy. They had been on a gunnery course together and in their spare time had played a few rounds of golf. It was arranged, therefore, that Spencer should dine with the S.N.O. During the meal the S.N.O, in strict confidence, had remarked what bad luck it had been for David Giles to become embroiled in the Kruger affair. Since Spencer had to admit knowing nothing about it, Commander Jackson reminded his companion that he would still be under the official secrets act from his navy days and then told him what he knew of the affair.

They discussed the sinking of the Bellevue, concluding that it had probably been caused by a mine. However, intelligence reports pointed to the possibility that U-boats might now be operating in the area with the help of the Japs. It was on the cards that air surveillance would be enhanced by the arrival of a few Catalina flying boats on loan from the Yanks. In the meanwhile he gave Spencer a course which would take the Patriarch a few hours to the east before turning south.

The following day the Patriarch's captain had visited the officers' saloon before lunch and there, armed with a bottle of Gin and another of Scotch, passed on the information given him by the S.N.O, except for the Giles' problem. All shore leave had now been stopped and he requested McTavish to lay off the necessary courses to pass through the co-ordinates of 35 degrees South, 30East, to 40S, 20E. Then, as much as the weather would allow, to run their westing down at 40 degrees until they were almost off the South American coast at 55W. That would keep them well clear of the South African coast and, hopefully, the trouble they had run into on the way up. Believing that there would be less likelihood of being sighted by any lurking U-boat he wished to approach the River Plate estuary from the south rather than by the more direct course almost due west from the Cape.

The second steward had been asked to provide two men during daylight hours to act as extra lookout from the after end of the boat deck while the DEMS gunners would provide two from the 4 inch gun platform. With luck no one would see anything until the end of the passage but just in case all were to keep on their toes. If the Patriarch did run into trouble, they would be a very long way from help.

"And now Gentlemen I give you a toast," he concluded. "Our ship and all in her. May God bless us all!"

During the forenoon the chief officer and bosun had satisfied themselves that all hatches were properly battened down; three tarpaulins on each with the oldest on first and all the wooden wedges hammered well home so that nothing could come adrift. Next, on the outboard side, they had one lifeboat on the after castle, alternate ones on the boat deck and then the accident-boat swung out and secured. Four boats would be enough for the whole crew but it had been known for lifeboats, when hoisted outboard, to be damaged beyond use when a torpedo stuck directly beneath them. Those boats on the shore side of the Patriarch would have to wait until they had sailed.

Boulton, having reported to the captain that the ship was ready for sea, then stood all the deck crew down, telling them to disappear to their bunks until sailing time. The gangway was hoisted a few feet above the wharf so that it could not be used and would be lowered only for the pilot.

Wentle was not `stood down'. He was told by Akker that as the only passengers aboard were the trooping commandant and his aide only the captain's table would be laid for afternoon tea.

The second steward and Akker had discussed Wentle's immediate future and decided that since he was now doing quite well in the job he should remain as steward for the senior officers. He would not, therefore, be required to join the other assistant-stewards in the general clean up of the passenger accommodation and the dismantling of the extra bunks in some of the cabins.

The fact that there were no passengers made no difference to the work of the officer's mess-boy but it did mean that he and Wentle were able to spend an hour together between lunch and afternoon tea. In those hours they were to learn a lot about each other and their aspirations for the future. Without realizing it Harry London was to play a major part in shaping his friend's plans.

Helping to look after the radio officers and listening to their conversations in the officers' saloon it had appeared to London that he might do worse than to become a `sparks'. He'd had several talks with Mr.Moore, the chief R/O, who was more than pleased to offer advice and the loan of a book or two; for all the officers liked their diminutive mess-boy. Harry had done his sums and it was likely that, if he kept his spending to a minimum, three more trips would see enough in his Post Office Savings to cover the fees at a radio college for nine months.

The two youths had discussed these plans while ashore the previous night and it seemed to Wentle that perhaps the nine month course would be preferable to the four year apprenticeship required to become an engineer. But for now, despite the attraction of the shore lights, sleep called and going into the canteen they settled down behind the bar on cushions borrowed from the settees.

At midnight the Patriarch was turned towards the south. When the captain was satisfied that the second officer understood the night orders for the middle watch he lay down on the bunk in the pilot's cabin. In the radio-room the second sparks relieved the third while down in the engine-room the junior second took over. Those going off watch took to their bunks and were lulled to sleep by the steady throbbing of the distant engines and the rattles and groans so essential to their lives.

Wentle stirred on his makeshift bed in the canteen. He had slept well, untroubled by dreams of the war but of pleasant ones about his girl friend back in Bristol. Yawning he opened his eyes and sat up with a jolt. It was broad daylight! He looked at his watch, it was ten to seven. "Oh Lord! Old Akker will be having kittens!" Since nobody on board risked undressing at night he had only to pull on his shoes, shake Harry and, grabbing his life jacket, fled along the deck towards the first class saloon.

"And just where might you have been for the last half hour, Mr.Bloody Admiral!" growled the saloon steward as Wentle hastily started sweeping under his table. "I've been looking all over the flamin' ship for you!"

"Sorry Sir. I overslept and had forgotten to tell the night watchman where I was."

"And just where were you?"

"In the after canteen."

"But I bloody well looked there for Christ's sake!"

"We were down behind the bar out of the way of the others, Sir."

"You'll be in the family way if you don't get your finger out! Leave the sweeping and get that bloody table laid. God help me!"

Table laid Wentle dashed off to the boy's peak for his toilet gear. In the bathroom he encountered the tiger.

"Not shaving today Toff?"

"Oh shut up, Perkins!" At sixteen the saloon-boy needed only to scrape the fair hairs from his chin once a week whereas the tiger shaved daily whether it was necessary or not. This action he fondly imagined proved him more a man.

Now he loudly proclaimed "I 'eard Mr. God help me Akker was looking for you. When I was a boy rating, an' I was adrift, I got me arse kicked or a thump round the ear 'ole. I notice that don't 'appen to you." He gathered up his gear and from the doorway said, "You know what, Toff, I reckons you must be showing Akker where the golden rivet is, 'e always did like little boys!"

For nearly two days the Patriarch sailed south and then southwest until they reached latitude forty south, where they turned westwards towards South America. On the afternoon of the third day old Jim Baines sat on number three hatch pulling on his pipe as he told London and Wentle what it had been like to be going in the opposite direction in a sailing ship, farther south in the `Roaring Forties'.

Down there the wind blew almost perpetually from the west and as it did so the seas became mountainous with white tormented crests that chased each other almost right around the world unimpeded by any land. Sometimes the wind let up and only blew strongly but mostly it blew a full gale, speeding the clipper ships along under double reefed tops'ls or bare poles at fourteen knots on their way to Australia as they ran their easting down. Or gales which could hold up a sailing ship for weeks at a time as she struggled to get around the Horn on her way to Valparaiso.

Those were the days when seamen spent days on end in wet clothes amongst the `Greybeards' of the southern ocean and thought nothing of loosing finger nails as they fought with ice hard canvas a hundred feet above a sea-washed deck. Then the ships were alive with a different spirit from the power vessels of today. Theirs was an exacting spirit which demanded total obedience. If a sailor stopped to tend his own needs, he would surely be thrown from the swaying yards to disappear from sight in the grey, tumultuous seas below.

The crew were slaves to the spirit of the ship which kept her alive and enabled her to surface after gigantic seas had swept her decks and left only her masts above water, or made her come back upright after she had been on her beam ends with the lower yards touching the rushing sea.

A spirit which enabled her to fight her battle with the relentless elements that gave no quarter.

Handmaidens to the spirit were the captain and his mates who drove the seaman with oaths, knuckles and belaying pins past and well beyond what in the steamships of today would be considered the limits of a fair day's work and physical capabilities.

"Yes," the quartermaster agreed, "the Patriarch has such a spirit but, as I said, it were different to a sailing ship." To another question he replied: "No I doubt we'll go down amongst the ghosts of such ships for there'd be no point, it'd slow us up too much and anyway, I doubt's we'll meet any ships or submarines where we are. With this light wind more than likely we'll see some fog."

The following morning, just as `Father Neptune' had depicted, the Patriarch found herself in dense fog. Normally seaman feared fog above all else, particularly thick fog such as this when the watch on the bridge could hardly see the man in the bows, when speed would be reduced to a crawl. However, since they were so far south and clear of all other shipping, the captain kept the Patriarch racing through the water at seventeen knots without zigzagging. It was an eerie experience and although the men told themselves that the captain was right and there was no need to slow down they nevertheless felt ill at ease. It was not natural for a ship to go fast in fog!

As they went about their duties their mood was subdued by the damp, grey murk that swirled around them and their voices became hushed, speaking only when they had to. From the engine room, where fog made no difference since their only connection with the outside world was the engine telegraph, came the steady throbbing of the engines. From ahead, accentuated by the fog, came the swish, swish of the bow wave as it came aft from the stem until it tumbled over itself.

Ronald Spencer sat hunched on his chair staring with unseeing eyes into the grey wall outside the wheelhouse. There was really no need for him to be on the bridge. The watch officer, young Giles, was perfectly capable of handling the ship under these conditions and no other ships in the area to worry about. Spencer could well have been in the pilot's cabin or even down in his day room. He had caught up with sleep in Durban for although he had dined with the agent as well as the S.N.O. he had gone back aboard early both nights. It was only habit which had taken him to his chair in the wheel-house.

His thoughts were on his home in Romford. A large Edwardian house which was really too big for them and with John away at sea it seemed silly to keep on living there but Jean had been left it, together with an old Morris Oxford car, by an uncle and she liked it.

The neighbours in Junction Road were mostly professional people. One of them, a doctor, had a tennis court and that suited Jean who loved the game. The tennis court had led to a job as the doctor's receptionist and then to his bed, or their own bed because the damn man was married. At first, after she had admitted to him that she'd taken a lover some four years after they were married, he'd been left to assume it had been the doctor. But for a couple of leaves, until the man had moved from the district, Spencer had a suspicion that there was something between the two.

As the years passed Spencer found himself brooding more and more on the fact that making love to Jean had become a passionless, unemotional affair. Perhaps he wasn't much good at making love? He didn't know because there had only been a couple of one time trysts in his youth and the girls had been just as inexperienced.

He could understand how these things happened for there had been times when he'd been tempted, but he found himself unable to forget and did not know if he forgave. Jean had seemed genuinely contrite about the affair but there were times when he wondered whether he was being unreasonable to expect her not to have an occasional fling with him being away so much. He was now not sure if he even knew the meaning of love. Did the passion of youth eventually just become a `comfortableness' between two people who stayed together over the years? Certainly he and Jean still seemed to enjoy doing a number of things together and there was laughter and plenty of smiles during those brief leaves. He wondered what still held them together or was it just a game of charades they were playing, or simply pining for his youth?

Third Officer Giles, who had the watch, stood with hands thrust deep in the pockets of his duffle coat. More often than was required he glanced at the gyro-compass repeater to check the course and then back to the fog casting little beads of moisture on the wheel-house windows. He felt jittery and ill at ease, so to relieve the silent tension he commented to the captain:

"Doesn't seem to be getting any thinner, Sir. Hope it clears before midday or we shan't be able to check the latitude. Going along in this makes me feel disoriented."

Giles' words jolted Spencer out of his thoughts. "Pardon Giles? Sorry, I was miles away."

The third repeated his remark, thinking that the `Old Man' must be trusting him with the ship more than he realized.

"No, you're right Mr.Giles. I'm surprised that the warmth of the sun hasn't dispersed the fog by now."

It is a peculiarity of the semi-arctic fog that it hangs low over the sea so that those on the bridge could see the dim brightness of the sun above them. The mast-head lookout was actually in sunlight above the fog and yet could not be seen by others on the deck. For the lookout in the crow's nest, a small bucket like perch accessible only by climbing up sixty iron rungs welded to the mast, it felt as if he was flying just above the clouds. His only communication with those below was by telephone to the bridge, which every now and then disturbed his solitude with its tinkling bell. He would repeat to the officer that he could see nothing but sunshine above, the forestay ahead and the mizzen-mast following on behind like a dog on a leash!

The four to eight watch had gone below, had their breakfast and were now asleep in their bunks. The second hour of the forenoon watch was just ending, the quartermaster on the wheel was handing over to old Jim Baines and the A.B. going below for tea and biscuits when the inconceivable happened.

"Sir, do you hear something?" The starboard lookout reported in a tone that was almost apologetic for he thought he must be imagining things.

Spencer and his officers just had time to take the few paces out on to the bridge wing when there was a scream from the invisible man in the bows: "Submarine hard alongside starboard!"

For a moment all on board, from the captain downwards, stood with mouths open in astonishment as a U-boat with several men out on deck, seemingly bound by ethereal wisps of fog, passed them not ten yards off going in the opposite direction! So close was she that the Patriarch's bow wave lifted her up and rolled her so that two men lost their balance on the narrow deck and were thrown into the sea. Spencer's mind recorded the picture of an officer, clinging to the side of the conning tower, eyes wide in astonishment, looking straight up at him from the U-boat's minute bridge. He wondered if he were the skipper. If so, then surely this must be one of the strangest meetings ever recorded between two enemy captains. A meeting which lasted but a brief four seconds as the two men came into each other's view before being swallowed again by the fog!

"Christ Almighty!" Young Stickland was the first to speak, followed a second later by the captain.

"Starboard twenty! Sound action stations!"

Strickland moved quickly back to the wheelhouse and pressed the alarm button. The shrill clanging of the bells caught all aboard, save for those on the bridge, by surprise and galvanized them into frantic action! Those who did not have an action station sat up and rubbed the sleep from their eyes, in total disbelief that the bells should be ringing while they were so far south.

"Third, keep the plot until the second arrives. I have the ship." In the navy the navigating officer would automatically keep track of the ship's movements but Giles was not navy trained and had never found himself in such a position before and Spencer knew this. For a moment the young man was not sure of himself. `Keep the plot'? Then he realised and grabbed the signal slate off its hook, looked at his watch and entered the time, then stood waiting to note the new course as and when the captain decided on it. At the end of this almost unbelievable happening someone, probably the second, would be expected to compute their position from his notes.

Spencer's mind moved swiftly as it had been trained to do those years ago in the anti-submarine practice area off Portland. The normal reaction of any sailor in such a close quarters situation would have been to sheer away from the submarine by going to port. He hoped that the German would expect him to do just that and by going the other way he would outwit the U-boat's skipper whom, he felt sure, fog or no fog, would come looking for them after he had recovered his men from the sea.

Just when they wanted the fog to get thicker and hide them it started to thin. The bows were slowly becoming visible. Spencer visualized the Patriarch's wake, an arc quarter of a mile long, curving away from their meeting place with the submarine. A chance meeting for which the mathematical computation was almost beyond comprehension. After two minutes the wheel was put amidships so that now they went off at a tangent to the arc.

The 'phone rang and the chief officer, bleary eyed and half asleep, answered it. "Gun crew closed up Captain."

For those who had been below decks and not seen the unwelcome invasion of their solitude, the captain had the sparks use the tannoy to put everyone in the picture. Now men from all departments who were not on watch and had been trained to use the Hotchkiss machine guns, were racing for the boat deck and the lockers situated at each end and on both sides of it. Once again the bridge look-outs brought out the lethal looking guns which smelt of fine oil and gun-metal, secured them in their mountings and clipped on the ammunition pans. Not until they were given the order to load would they draw back the bolt as the final act before firing. Should the German re-appear at close quarters they would be ready.

Spencer took up the 'phone to the crow's nest. "Lookout, Captain here. What's it like up there? Can you see anything of the U-boat?"

"It's Green 'ere, Sir 'an you knows me better than that; if I could I'd 'ave told you, Sir. But the fog 's thinning 'cause I can see the funnel 'an I couldn't when I got 'ere."

"O.K. Green and I'm sorry; I didn't know you had taken over. Watch from either beam to aft for she must come up from astern."

That Green was up in what would be a most vital position was good and Spencer did not mind the mild rebuke. Green was a permanent member of the crew and in line for a quartermaster's job when a vacancy occurred. The Jim Baines' of this world were a dying breed and as characters would be sorely missed. Their replacements, men like Green, would be just as good in their modern ways. Green at sea, once his hangover had cleared, was first class and had one of the sharpest pair of eyes aboard. It was just a pity that the man liked his drink and a good fight. The captain thought that he had probably logged Green more times than any other man.

"Sighting report, sir?" queried the chief radio officer.

"No, we'll wait a bit, David. She may not find us again and even if we do send a warning to the Admiralty there is not much they can do for us at the moment. Anyway, ten to one that Jerry operator is sitting on his D.F. set right now just hoping we'll open up so that he can get a bearing. You have our estimated position in case we change our minds?"

"Yes Sir, I've just taken it off the chart. I'll make up the message now."

"Sir?" It was Stickland the fourth officer, who spoke now. "Did you notice anything peculiar about that sub? She looked as if there were long crates lashed on her decks."

"Come to think of it you're right, Mr.Strickland. I wonder what the devil she's doing down here. If she was after our scalp surely she would have been far nearer to the coast? There is no way she could have known we were on this course. No. I think that, like us, she was trying to hide before going into the Indian Ocean. If so perhaps we should let their Lordships know; but we'll wait a little longer."

For seven long minutes they steamed on through the thinning fog with all on the bridge straining their eyes and ears.

Down in the galley the chief baker used his initiative when he heard what was happening and sent his two assistants off with the days baking and told them to wait in the first class lounge. If the ship got into serious trouble and had to be abandoned a few extra rations would not be out of place. In the meanwhile he and the chef might as well bring their pre-lunch drink forward a bit for they had, in accordance with the requirements of `action stations', closed down the galley stoves.

Once again it seemed that lunch might be spoilt and that was something which made the chef very cross for he and his cooks took great pride in their culinary responsibilities. Given half a chance, the chef told the baker, he would happily use one of his garlic crushers on the balls of the U-boat commander!

Aft, on the four inch gun platform, Sergeant Bill Howell and his crew were wondering if today would be their day. Up to now, the only target they had fired at had been old oil drums thrown over the side and then only for half a dozen rounds each time.

The back-up crew under the third officer, who had now been relieved on the bridge by the second, also hoped that if there was to be a scrap the DEMS gunners would not keep all the shooting to themselves.

When the Patriarch did steam out of the fog and the submarine became visible the two ships were too far apart for Bill Howell to open fire. She was just a speck on the horizon on the starboard quarter.

The U-boat was, at that moment, steaming slowly to the south west on what appeared to be a circular course turning to port. Although the large merchantman must have been clearly visible she made no attempt to follow them, disappearing into a bank of fog which was stretching northwards towards the Patriarch's course. The Patriarch's helm was put over so that they were steaming directly away from her and she rapidly dropped further astern before disappearing once again into the thinning fog.

From what Spencer had learnt about German submarines this one was probably a type VII with a surface maximum speed similar to the Patriarch's and therefore now had little chance of catching them. What Spencer did not know was that the boat's commander was under orders not to hazard his vessel unduly by engaging the enemy. She had on board twenty one extra torpedos and other technical spares for the new base in Penang, and the delivery of these items was paramount. Later she would take up a patrol area off the South African coast.

Spencer also did not know that both Germans and Japanese were using these lower latitudes for the very same reasons that the Patriarch was, trying to keep clear of the enemy! (Eighteen months later the large ex-Italian submarine UIT-22, being used at the time as a transport, would be sunk by the South African Air Force in almost the same position as the Patriarch's present one.)

There was another major factor to which Spencer was not privy. Before the fog had closed in during the night, two axis vessels, one German and one Japanese, had made a rendezvous and lain alongside each other until only a short while before the Patriarch and the U-boat had so nearly collided.

The meeting was primarily to hand over the latest charts and recognition codes for entering the U-boat bases in France. (I 30 arrived at Lorient on the 5th of August). However the German commander still had a few bottles of beer and the Jap some Saki so that in the more spacious Imperial submarine they had drunk a few toasts to the Emperor and the Fuehrer! Now, as all eyes on the Patriarch were watching the disappearing German, a shell exploded in the sea on their port quarter and about half a mile from them!

"Jesus Christ! What the bloody hell!" The chief officer, like every one else on the bridge looked, and for the second time that hour, unbelieving at the fountain of water erupting from the otherwise placid blue sea. Through their glasses they had seen that the U-boat's gun was not manned. So who on earth had fired at them?

"Another ship come out t'fog for'd t'port beam!" an A.B shouted, the words almost falling over themselves in his haste to report. He used the word `ship' because he had no idea that a submarine of such large proportions could exist; in fact other than the U-boat just now, it was the first of any kind he had seen.

The hanger for the spotter seaplane for'ard of the bridge and the long gun emplacement casing aft of the conning-tower, made the normal Jerry subs look midgets by comparison. The vessel had just cleared that peninsular of fog which was stretching northwards and was three or four miles from them. She was steering a course about nor'west to that of the Patriarch's more westerly one but now started to alter directly for them. At the moment she cleared the fog the Patriarch must have presented an almost perfect beam on target for a torpedo attack.

"Fucking hell!" muttered Jones the apprentice who's action station was on the bridge ready to run any errands for the captain.

"Hard a starboard! Emergency speed! Charles inform the engineers what is happening." Spencer's reaction was immediate as soon as he saw the new adversary. The Patriarch began to heel sharply outward as she came round at full speed showing her stern and hopefully avoiding any torpedoes which might be fired at her.

In the officers' saloon, as with the table that Wentle had laid, crockery slid to the deck and smashed to pieces but no one noticed because most were now above decks trying to see what was happening. The distant sound of the gun and exploding shell jolted the chef and baker from their laissez-faire attitude of `if our number's on it, we'll cop it' and as one they gulped down the last of the contents in their glasses. As the ship heeled the baker snatched for, but missed, the opened bottle as it slid from the minute table.

"Bloody Hell, Alf, what a waste!" grunted the chef as it shattered on the deck. Grabbing their life-jackets from a corner they made for the boat deck.

"Midships. Steady as she goes." Once again the Patriarch's captain was facing aft keeping an eye on the enemy sub as the ship's stern came around.

DEMS Sergeant Gunner Bill Howell swore, something he did not often do and then spoke to his trainer in the right hand seat of the gun. "Jim as soon as we get back to an even keel get on the bastard and stay on 'im." Then to the man on the left. "Corp, give 'er six thousand yards elevation, I doubt we'll 'it 'er but by Christ we'll 'ave a bloody good try!"

"That's right Sarge. Give the fucker a bit of 'is own back. Christ 'e nearly made me shit meself!" said the number one of the gun crew standing by the breech.

Slowly the Patriarch came back to an even keel but with the extra revolutions the trainer's telescope was vibrating so much he was having difficulty focusing. Finally the crossed wires held the Jap and he called out "On!"

"Six thousand. On!" called the corporal now shaking with excitement as the adrenaline started to pump in his veins.

"Fire!" Bill Howell shouted.

Down went the corporal's right foot on the firing pedal moving the rod, which went back to the breech and released the striking pin. The pin hit the percussion cap in the base of the shell case and the gun went off with a roar and a flash!

To the gun's crew that first shot was always the loudest and most startling. As it recoiled the smoke was blown away by the wind created by the ships speed. Ears sang as all became partially deafened by the explosion of the propelling charge. The number one of the gun grabbed the breech lever pulling it back so that the breech swung open ejecting the empty brass case, which fell noisily to the deck. The number three of the crew swung into action and pushed a live shell into the smoking hole. With padded knuckles he punched it hard home. The breech clanged shut and locked as the number one worked his lever.

Momentarily they were encompassed by the smell of burnt cordite. Standing to one side of the gun the sergeant screwed up his eyes, trying to spot the fall of the projectile so that he could make any necessary adjustments to the range.

"Dear God!" exclaimed Third Officer Giles, seeing a fountain of water rise up almost dead ahead of but well short of the target, "That was bloody good laying!"

Up on the bridge the captain thought so too. The fact that he had given no order to open fire did not worry him for he was, despite various naval courses, no gunnery expert.

"Note the time in the log please," he said to no one in particular.

"Excuse me, Captain but I think that we might now be justified in breaking radio silence?" David Moore the chief R/O was standing in the wheelhouse doorway head on one side and a grin on his face.

"Good lord, the sighting report. Thank you Mr.Moore, I had forgotten. Please make it `Two' subs. Let's hope someone hears you."

In the radio-room the third sparks had already run up the emergency spark transmitter and took the amended message from his chief. Back on the bridge they could hear the coarse note of the transmitter as the spark jumped the gap; its acrid smell heavy in the nostrils of the men in the radio-room. On the high frequency set the chief made his call...`S..S..S de.GKAS..' S S S being used to tell anyone listening that they were being attacked by a submarine. With years of operating behind him the chief made it in a clear perfectly spaced twenty five words to the minute and then repeated it at a slower twenty. Now was not the time to have a shaky hand or stiff wrist for upon their expertise as operators might rest the lives of the ship's crew.

Message sent both men automatically leaned nearer to their receiving sets as if willing the static noise to be broken by some distant transmitter responding to their call for help. With the fingers of the left hand caressing the tuning knob and the right clutching their pencils over message pads, the seconds seemed like minutes and then the minute like an hour before David Moore started to adjust the beat frequency oscillator and clarify the note that held their call sign.

The spark transmitter was designed to obliterate any normal transmitter's signal on the distress frequency but its range was limited and there were no other ships near enough to hear it. Nearly four thousand miles away a bored operator on the Falkland Island suddenly came to life when he heard the S.S.S. call on his H.F. receiver. Another on Ascension listened intently as the Patriarch's signal was acknowledged. Both stations then changed frequency and, since conditions in the ether just happened to be right, within an hour the Admiralty knew what was happening deep down in the South Atlantic. In the operations room a wren crossing to plot the Patriarch's position on the map dropped the several pins she was carrying. As she bent to retrieve them her knees were just far enough apart for the duty P.O. telegraphist to see that she was not wearing the regulation bloomers. The message in their eyes as they exchanged glances made it clear what would happen when they went off duty.

On the Patriarch they had no idea that their plight would serve as the catalyst for a sordid one night stand in a deserted Anderson bomb shelter. The captain thought only of keeping their stern to the sub, wondering how long the engineers would be able to sustain the increased speed before something overheated.

On the gun deck aft Howell told his lads to relax for there was no sense in firing off their none too plentiful ammunition with little chance of success.

"Jones, go and find the chief steward and tell him to issue a bottle of rum for the gun crew and when you have it take it to Sergeant Howell and tell him not to knock it back all at once. Got that?"

"Yes sir."

"Good, and Jones, tell the chief steward to put it down to the doctor; for medicinal purposes of course!" There was a ripple of laughter from those in earshot on the bridge. `Good,' he thought. 'weak but might help to relax taut nerves.' He was well aware how fast word traveled aboard ship. By the time the gun's crew received the rum all aboard would be fully acquainted with, and in some cases embellished by the vernacular, his thumbing his nose at company regulations.

"Jones," the captain called yet again "Tell him to see that everyone gets something to eat!" The apprentice, who had slid down the ladders in the same way that the tiger had done all those weeks before, was already on the accident-boat deck and waved a hand in casual acknowledgement.

"Cheeky whelp," the second officer said in a tone which boded ill for Jones.

"Let it ride, Mr.McTavish, let it ride. We're all a bit uptight." The captain looked hard and long at their pursuer. Was the distance between them increasing or not?

CHAPTER ELEVEN

Quarry and pursuer were now heading nor'nor'east, the advantage being slightly with themselves Spencer thought. He had racked his brains to identify their pursuer and realized that the vessel must be a Jap for they had built a number of subs before the war which could house a spotting seaplane. In fact, some had been used in the attack on Pearl Harbour.

In brilliant sunshine but cold crisp air, the Patriarch ran on across the almost mirror-like sea rolling only slightly to the undulating swell. On the bridge there was silence except for the sounds of sandwiches being munched and mugs being replaced on hard surfaces. It was twenty minutes before the engine-room telephone broke the silence.

"For you Sir, it's the chief." McTavish's voice was slightly strained.

It had been a greaser who called the attention of the fifth engineer to the excessive heating of the starboard thrust-block who in turn reported it to his boss.

The telephone made the chief engineer's comments sound tinny and distant. "Sorry captain but things are getting a bit warm down here. I'll have to drop the revs down a few notches or the starboard shaft might seize. I'll give you the extra again as soon as I can." The line went dead.

The chief engineer was only too aware what his few words portended. For the time being he and his men were more important than the captain and his bridge crew. Those extra few revolutions which made the Patriarch vibrate almost to the point of discomfort but kept them out of gun range of their pursuer, now died away. In the galley the pots and pans stopped their rattling as they hung from their hooks and those on the stove stayed where the cooks had put them.

Spencer, silhouetted against the sunlight streaming in through the front bridge windows, replaced the 'phone on its hook and turned towards the others.

"Well Gentlemen," he said to officers and seamen alike. "The chief can no longer hold the revs. Things are getting hot down below which means that soon they'll be up here as well. Malcom, work out the best course for the Cape and have young Jones pass it to the officers in charge of the boats. Put it on paper and tell them to stick together for surely a rescue vessel will come out to meet them. And Jones, my compliments to the chief steward once again and if it's not already done extra blankets and rations for all boats."

McTavish disappeared into the chart-room and made a cross on the chart where he estimated their position to be. Then he laid off with his parallel rulers a line from the cross to Cape Town. Carefully he moved the rulers to the nearest compass rose and allowing for the variation, noted the course of nor'nor'east. Then with the dividers he took a distance reading and made it about four hundred miles. Hastily he tore a page from the scrap working book and wrote the necessary notes with a further one for the radio-room which gave their updated position and added `survivors heading nor'nor'east'. Might as well do it now and be ready for the worst! He returned to the wheelhouse and sent Jones aft again.

Sergeant Howell and his gunners had stayed closed up and been brought sandwiches by the men in the stand-by crew. One of the loaders nipped down the ladder into their mess and re-appeared with their tin mugs which were soon holding a liberal tot of rum.

"Here's how lads!" the master gunner had said when he took the first swig, holding his breath as the fiery liquid went down his gullet. Sipping the rum and eating their sandwiches they talked about anything that came into their heads, as did all men waiting to go into action not knowing if they would live or die. Some talked of the good fucks they'd had with whores or one night stands. Others thought only to themselves of how they and their wives made love. One, the number four, went through his repertoire of poor jokes, which brought a few forced laughs even if all had heard them before. Anything to keep their nerves steady and thoughts from what might happen to them.

When they noticed the decrease in speed the stomach of more than one tied itself into knots.

"Right lads, reckon we might be having another go soon. Jack put that bottle down in the mess, there's at least another tot all round when this shemozzle is over." Sergeant Howell had been a battery sergeant in France during the last war and knew what it was like to hear a hundred guns open fire at once. Now he felt that the fight they were about to have was, by comparison, going to be quiet and peaceful; like in a shoot-out between two gunmen walking towards each other down a deserted street in some old western, aware that one of them would end up on `Boot Hill'. It was a new experience, in no way belittled by the last war ribbons on his battle dress.

Howell had suggested to David Giles that he take the stand-by gun crew to the shelter of the after-castle, since `If a shell comes a bit close and one of my blokes cops it like as not one of yourn would too and there's no point in that. I can always beckon to you if we need help.'

Giles admitted to himself that Howell's suggestion made sense. As the ship's gunnery officer he was in nominal charge, but having a piece of paper to prove that he had passed the requisite course at that holy of holiest naval gunnery establishment, Whale Island, in no way matched the old soldier's expertise gained in battles long gone by. Taking shelter meant that he would not have direct contact with the bridge from the gun platform, but then he remembered the hospital 'phone and stationed a greaser there after telling the captain where he was. Next he realised that he could not see the submarine from the main deck and climbed the stairway to the after-castle boat deck.

From his new vantage point the third officer trained his binoculars on the strange looking vessel following them. Although he had seen pictures of German U-boats and learnt their various types while on the gunnery course he had not studied the Japanese boats. The one following them looked very menacing indeed but, in fact, was not as big as some presently building. What mattered most about it was the fact that its speed was now a knot and a half faster than the Patriarch's. It would take only half an hour for it to get within range and fire.

That agonising half hour was one of the longest ever spent by those on the merchant ship. Everyone knew that for them there was no way out. When the next shell landed it was ahead and some two hundred yards to port of them. The submarine was beam on to what little swell there was which caused her to roll just enough to make it difficult for her gunners to aim. But the target was a big one compared to that offered to Bill Howell and his men who, on the other hand, were hardly affected by the swell.

On the bridge Spencer crossed to the 'phone and spoke to the sergeant gunner.

"Hold your fire ,Sergeant," and then to the quartermaster, "Starboard five." By bringing the Patriarch round he would be exposing more of the vessel as a target but he guessed that the gun layer on the sub would now be trying to correct his aim by training right. Hopefully a sheer away from the fall of the shot might mean the next one would still be off target. It was all a gamble but Spencer felt that the target was still a difficult one for his own gunner to hit.

After half a cable the merchantman was brought back to her original course and the sea erupted just to the port of where they would have been.

Spencer spoke again to the gun platform. "What do you feel Sergeant? Do you think you can get near her if I hold a steady course?"

"Dodge two more and then 'old her steady Captain. We might take a knock but our chances should improve." And so the wheel was put hard over to port this time and once more the ship heeled.

In the lounge, where all crew not on duty had been ordered to take cover, furniture which was not secured or being sat in slid across the carpet. One of the men closing a deadlight over a window, cursed as he lost his balance and fell across a chair. The deadlight swung back against the bulkhead with a loud clang and more than one man jumped at the noise. The deadlights had to be secured because if a shell shattered the plate glass it would have as devastating an effect as the splinters did from the wooden decks in the old battleships of Nelson's time.

The next shot did fall short but on the third try Spencer guessed wrong and a shell penetrated number five hold just below main deck level. The explosion caused the bosun's nice tight canvas to be rent asunder as three of the heavy wooden hatch covers were blown upwards, before crashing down onto the hatch coamings where they set fire to the torn canvas.

"Fuck it!" exclaimed the bosun's mate who was in charge of the after fire party. "That top cover was brand new!" He started giving orders to deal with the fire.

Hoses were run out from the fire hydrants situated either side of the after castle. Each nozzle was held tight by a seaman closely backed up by another taking the weight whilst two other men hauled the hose aft taking care not to put a kink in it. With all the canvas off the reels the red painted wheels on the hydrants were turned quickly to the maximum `open' position and the previously flat grey hose was transformed from an inanimate object to a hard round one which made the big brass nozzle buck wildly.

None of the fire fighters had ever actually fought a fire before. It had all been done in what was scathingly called `Board of Trade sports' which happened, by regulation, once a week together with boat drill. Now, as the water surged through the hose, one of the nozzle holders did not have the right grip so the water streamed out and upward with considerable force, drenching the four inch gun crew who let out a stream of invective. The water was extremely cold and the force was enough to knock a man off balance.

"Steady as you go, Quartermaster, and I mean steady. It's up to you to give Sergeant Howell the best chance he can have!" Spencer gave his orders clearly and concisely and then to the chief officer, "Charles you'd best nip aft and see what can be done? Take the for'ard fire party with you. Chief Sparks, tell anyone who can still hear you that we're under fire again and damaged but not mortally!" Adding under his breath, `at least not yet'. "Mr.Baines," who was no longer on the wheel, "Don't you think that we should have our colours up since we're in sight of another ship? The biggest and best please." It was an old naval custom that ships going into action flew their large battle ensigns. The Patriarch did not have such flags aboard but at least she could show her colours.

"The biggest and best it is Captain." Crossing to the flag locker the old man selected a Red Ensign and took it to one of the A.B's telling him to nip aft and hoist it at the gaff. There was no way that he, the senior quartermaster, was going to leave the bridge. Robertson on the wheel was fairly competent but one never knew when the captain might need him.

To the sixty odd men seated or standing around in the first class lounge the sound of the shell exploding in number five hold was like a clap of thunder as the noise vibrated round the empty space. To those still down in the engine room it was far worse. The greaser bent double checking the plumber blocks in the port shaft tunnel, was totally deafened. There were various exclamations of profanity as the lucky ones in the lounge came to realize that their ship had been hit. Akker went out onto the boat deck to find out what had happened. Lewis, sitting near Wentle and Harry London with their backs to the small stage, rose and took the few paces to the piano and removed its dust sheet. Seating himself he started to play. He was not a very good pianist but they all recognised the tune. `There'll always be an England' and took up the words with him. `and England shall be free as long as...'

Wentle had a lump in his throat as the tune conjured up memories of the last time he had heard it. His girl friend Mary was a good pianist and played in a concert party back in Bristol. Only the night before he had joined the Patriarch he had been with her at Horfield Barracks. The tune had been one of the last to be played and the troops had sung as lustily as the men around him were now doing. He had looked around at the soldiers singing there and had thought how no doubt they would soon be fighting the real war. Now he was being shot at, and out there on the sea there was someone who wished him and all those around him dead. He had little realised back in Horfield barracks that he too, would soon be part of the real war. Suddenly he knew that he had to go out on deck, if only for a moment, and see who was trying to kill him. He got up and hurried to the door leading out to the boat-deck.

"Where do you think y're going Wentle?" Mr.Boyd enquired. The tiger, sprawled in one of the lounge chairs with a leg over one of its arms, was about to say `Going to piss himself with fright I'spect' but wisely thought better of it. Now, perhaps, was not the best time to bait the Toff.

"Back in a jiffy, Sir." Before anyone could stop him Wentle was out on deck and caught a brief glimpse of the Japanese submarine fine on the port quarter about a mile away. As he looked there was a flash and a puff of smoke from its gun and the saloon-boy found himself back inside the lounge.

"Another time young man you obey orders and stay put. Understand?"

"Yes Sir."

`The Empire to, we can depend on you', the tune went on and he gulped as his throat tightened. Mary! She was three years older than Wentle and was secretary to one of his aunts. They had met only a few months earlier and, still very naïve where girls were concerned, it had taken a long time for him to summon up the courage to ask her for a date. During the last few school holidays he had been too taken up with his duties as a police messenger to date girls and he had been totally unprepared for the feelings which had been aroused in him when he kissed Mary that last night ashore.

The army truck that had taken them back to the city centre left them just as the air-raid sirens started their mournful warbling. Hand in hand they had walked with some difficulty because of the blackout, the last mile to Mary's home. As he plucked up the courage to kiss her good night the anti-aircraft guns had opened up with the crump, crump of their exploding shells clearly heard high above the young couple.

He was convinced that he was head over heels in love with Mary and had desperately wanted to touch her breasts but was afraid to do so, when he realised that the close contact of their bodies had given him an erection. He had drawn away from her not knowing how to cope. Whether Mary had known what she was doing to him he did not know for he had only just begun to understand it himself. As he mounted his bicycle to ride the seven miles home he had muttered `I love you' but had not heard her reply, if any, because the guns went off again.

Akker came back into the lounge and made good use of his voice to tell everyone what had happened and to say that the bosun could use more help on the fire hoses. Half a dozen stewards and a couple of greasers got up and left. Another greaser, in none too clean overalls, was about to sit in one of the empty chintz covered chairs when Mr.Boyd balled him out.

"Not in those dirty clothes you don't."
Obviously the second steward was of the opinion that the first class lounge might well be used again for its rightful purpose and he could see no sense in having to have the chair cleaned unnecessarily.

Lewis started another tune but stopped for a moment as the four inch gun aft went off with a bang.

With no range finder at his disposal Bill Howell could only use his own judgement as to the distance between gun and target and that was not easy. The shot went over and slightly to port of the Jap sub. "Down one hundred," he ordered. He was surprised to find that he was fully in control of himself just as he had been after that first day of the barrage back in Mons.

When they had initially moved the guns up the line many of the gunners had been sick just from the smell of the rotting horse carcasses, their own animals baulking and screaming and had to be whipped to get the guns with their limbers into position. Then the Hun howitzers had got their range and the battery officer had been knocked out and he, Howell, had suddenly found he was in charge. Fear had left him then and for his bravery under fire over the next two days he had been mentioned in dispatches.

"Down one hundred," echoed the gun layer and then "On!"

"On," called the trainer and the firing pedal went down again.

This time the water erupted just in front of the enemy who replied with a shell off the Patriarch's port quarter sending spray aboard.

For his next shot Howell made no alteration to the range, judging that the difference in the two vessels' speed would bring them that bit nearer. This firing at a moving target was new to him as was the need to judge the range. It was that judgement which saved the Patriarch.

The shell from her old four inch gun went through the upper casing right for'ard and exploded on the far side, causing minor damage to the pressure hull. Had the submarine's quartermaster not let her head wander off course so that the shell went in at a slight angle, the damage would have been far greater. Two seconds before being hit the Japanese gunners had also fired so that the two shells passed each other in the air - with the one from the submarine causing the greater damage. It hit and exploded just to starboard of the gun on the nine inch sill which ran round the gun deck. A piece of shrapnel detonated a round of ammunition being carried in the arms of a loading number and in that instant all of the gun's crew died.

They died quickly and without knowing it. Except for the sergeant they had fired only those four shots in anger. They fired them because someone was firing at them, the cause or reason why only vaguely understood. King and country? For wives and sweethearts? A country called Poland? Two of those who had just died had been glad of the war because it at least gave them regular meals and clothes to wear even if the pay was paltry, for they had always been out of work. The others had resented the war for they were the lucky ones with reasonable jobs and homes to live in.

The third officer had seen the hit on the enemy just before the blast of the explosion on the gun platform sixty feet away sent him reeling backwards. He tripped on a stag-horn bollard, cracking his head on the hospital bulkhead and collapsing to the deck.

On the bridge they too had seen the fall of the Patriarch's shot and then ducked as a sheet of flame appeared over the after-castle, followed by a pall of smoke. Their ears sang from the noise but not as badly as those who were by number five hatch. The fire parties had just managed to put the flames out in the hold when the gun deck erupted in a sheet of flame and became a twisted wreck. A seaman who had been tending a hose over the hatch coaming was flung to one side as Sergeant Howell's body came hurtling down from above. In death the gunner had shielded the other from a possible similar fate.

"How does she steer Quartermaster?" The captain guessed at what must have happened aft. The answer from the man at the wheel would be vital for beneath the gun platform and the gunners mess was the steering flat with its hydraulic motor and other paraphernalia needed to turn the rudder!

The quartermaster put ten degrees of wheel on and waited for the ship's head to pay off before applying opposite rudder. "She seems O.K. Captain."

"Sir, the sub is altering course away from us," reported Strickland.

Only superficially damaged the boat's captain, who like the U-boat was on a special mission carrying amongst other items much needed wolfram for the German armaments production, decided that enough was enough and that he still had a very long way to go. Men could be seen going up to the bow and a signal lamp flashed from the bridge. As one, the officers and Quartermaster Baines read the stilted Morse.
U...F.I.G.H.T...O.N.R.A.B.L...O.O.D...L.U.K

"U fight onrabl ood luk," McTavish repeated, reading the letters he had written on the bottom of the signal slate without at first comprehending their garbled meaning.

"Dear God!" Spencer exclaimed, momentarily stunned as he realized what the Jap had meant to say. He picked up the 'phone to the hospital.

"Whoever that is go and dip the ensign, and be quick about it," he snapped. It was all he could think of as an appropriate answer for he felt that to reply with the lamp might not be understood. Apart from which there were more important things to see to on the Patriarch.

At that moment the chief engineer increased the revolutions again so that the smoke was wafted astern from the gunners funeral pyre.

The Patriarch's first mate had been at the for'ard end of the main deck on his way back to the bridge when the ship was hit for the second time. He turned on his heel and ran, his footsteps echoing around the deserted deck. He half slid down the stairs to the well-deck, passed under the after-castle and came to an abrupt halt by number five hatch.

The fire in the hold and on the hatch had been extinguished, that he knew, but it was now replaced by smoke coming from two shattered portholes in the gunners' quarters and from charred remains around the gun platform.

The scene on the gun platform was not pleasant. The gun itself was pointing over the port quarter and leaning at an angle of about fifteen degrees where the explosion had wrenched it from some of its retaining bolts. The corporal gunner's lower body was still partially seated but the upper right half of him had disappeared over the side along with the shell which should have gone into the gun instead of exploding in the loader's arms. That loader, thrown backwards, now lay impaled on a stanchion with the shell case fused to his charred body. A second loader lay face down by the ready use ammunition locker, his back split wide open. On the right seat of the gun the man was still in his position but with his head half impaled on his telescope and his clothes smoldering. Of the last loader there was no sign.

Apprentice Bentley, who was a member of a fire-party and unhurt, vomited violently at the sight of the gunners' bodies.

"Bentley pull yourself together and get a hose on to the ready-use ammo locker before it gets too hot!" Boulton's orders were given in a staccato rasp but speed was now of the essence. "You fellows there, get a hose into each of those portholes and bosun's mate, another on the main ammo locker. Get bloody moving for Christ's sake!" his voice rising to a crescendo.

"Steady, Charles." The doctor was now at his side along with Brightman carrying a first-aid case and momentarily Boulton was surprised to note that their breath did not smell of drink. Seated with the other officers in the lounge neither doctor nor purser thought it would be right for them to be drinking while the crew could not. "What can I do?"

"Damn all at the moment Doc. That lot up there look to be beyond your help. Check the fire parties?" He raised his voice to a shout. "Anyone else hurt?"

A voice replied. "Yeah, the third don't look too good, 'e's up there by the boat!"

Someone else with a heavy west country accent chimed in. "Langley bisn't be too good neither!" Fortunately for those men around the stern end of number five hold the stench of the charred bodies, burnt cordite and paint was being carried away from them so that they only had the visual impact to cope with. Of noise there was surprisingly little. A hiss from inside the gunner's cabin as the flames came in contact with the water from the fire hoses and the greater hiss as the water left the hose nozzles.

The fire parties aft were lucky for soon the smoke from the gunners' quarters diminished and they were able to cautiously open a door and put the fire right out. Opening up the small hatch which lead down into the magazine they were more than relieved to find little heating there but just in case a hose was put on `spray' and played over the ammunition. Satisfied that there was no risk of any further explosion Boulton made his way up to the hospital 'phone and reported to the captain before setting about the grisly task of extricating the bodies from the gun seats and laying them with the other corpses on the blackened deck.

Sergeant Howell's corpse, miraculously almost untouched outwardly, was covered with a piece of canvas hastily cut from the torn new hatch cover.

* * *

Captain Ronald Spencer, D.S.C, along with those of his officers who were not on watch, wore his shore going uniform. Those of the crew who did not have a uniform were, without exception, clad in the best clothes they happened to have on board. At the feet of each lay a life-jacket for there did not seem much point in wearing your best clothes only to cover them with a bulbous blue garment.

Although the sun still shone it was cold and most wore a top coat of some description; one and all were bare headed, the officers with their caps tucked under their arms.

It was two o'clock in the afternoon watch and they were gathered around number five hatch. A collection of sixty men from almost every strata of life who made up the crew of the M.V. Patriarch. Most were there as professional seamen in whatever branch they worked. Not more than a dozen were there because of the war and had chosen to be in the Merchant Navy rather than one of the armed services or down a coal mine. Now they stood, all with the same thoughts, waiting to pay homage to the soldiers who had died so that they could go on living.

The captain looked at his watch and then towards the bridge wing where Second Officer McTavish stood waiting and watching for the nod he now received. He called to Bentley, already by the engine telegraphs, who moved the gleaming polished indicator handle to `Stop'. In the silence which followed they all heard the telegraph bells answer from deep down in the belly of the vessel.

Slowly the way came off the ship and Spencer started the burial service, glancing every now and then over the side to see if they had stopped yet. For a moment he was silent and then he concluded... `and so we commit their bodies to the deep.'

Together the bosun and his mate, the carpenter with his mate and Able Seaman Green lifted the inboard end of the planks so that the remains of the five soldiers slid out from under the flags which covered them. Weighted with used boiler bricks they started their journey into the deep as Lewis began to sing in crystal clear notes the Twenty Third Psalm. `The Lord is my Shepherd, I shall not want...'

Again the captain looked up to his bridge and nodded. Once more the ship, their home, throbbed to her engines and gathered speed. The A.B stationed by the ensign halyard dipped the flag from its half mast position, then hauled it to the peak before slowly lowering it right down. The officers put on their caps and saluted.

Whether by coincidence or for whatever reason, a lone albatross appeared and took station over their wake.

By eight bells that afternoon the gun platform had been well hosed down so that there was no sign of the gore which had been there only a few hours before. Boulton's quick action had undoubtedly saved more lives for had the ammunition lockers got too hot and their contents exploded....!

The gunners' mess was well gutted and the remaining two men, who had been up on the after boat deck with their machine guns, were given a second class cabin and told to join the seamens' mess. There the crew had a whip around for spare clothing since the soldiers had only the battle-dress they wore. If they were to go ashore in the Argentine in uniform they would immediately be interned. Fleetingly both wondered if that might not be a bad idea before their `number came up'.

David Giles and Langley the greaser were both in the sick-bay. The latter had looked worse than he really was since the blood on his clothes had come mostly from the gunnery sergeant. Other than a deep cut on his arm he had but a couple of cracked ribs and been winded, but now he reveled in making Brightman work for a change. He called for water every few minutes or moaned loudly so that the doctor's assistant had to keep coming to look at him.

David Giles was not so lucky. Doctor Hargraves diagnosed a bad skull fracture and was very concerned when by evening the man had not regained consciousness. Other than to take meals he stayed in the vicinity of the hospital the whole time. Ted Good the purser, came aft with a bottle just before dinner but was sent away almost immediately. In the years they had sailed together for the doc not to take a drink all day was almost unheard of.

The truth of the matter was that in his thirty years of doctoring, including two and half years of war, Hargraves had never been called upon to deal with the things he'd had to do this day. There had been the odd case of exposure when twice the ship had picked up survivors; clinical maladies he could deal with. The extent of his doctoring had been at worst having to deal with syphilis and set a few bones; once he had even amputated a couple of crushed toes. On rare occasions in peacetime a passenger, generally old, had died on board and it had not been difficult to sign a death certificate without having to do a post-mortem. But now his nice quiet shipboard routine had been rudely shattered and he realised with great clarity that, at its best his medical expertise was inadequate. Even during his days as an intern in the casualty ward at St. Bartholomew's he had not seen such mutilation.

He thought of the young army doctors who had so recently shared his surgery and wondered if they knew what they would be in for when they too joined battle. He had even baulked at having to take the `dog tags' from the dead men and made Brightman do it.

Back on the bridge the captain sat on the bunk in the pilot's cabin and started the melancholy task of dictating his account of the action to the assistant purser, who took it down in shorthand. When typed up and signed it would join the soldier's identity discs in the purser's safe ready to be forwarded to the Brigadier commanding the division of DEMS Gunners. Apart from anything else the disappearance of five gunners had to be accounted for and the books `squared away' upon the ship's return to England. He added a personal note to the effect that, without doubt, the ship and all in her owed their lives to the gunners who had died so valiantly.

That done he lay down on the bunk but could not sleep. With his third officer out of commission he would have to keep a close eye on young Strickland during the eight to twelve watch. He felt that the boy might panic if things went wrong. At least they did not have to worry about being in convoy, when he would have had to take over the watch completely. The changing of courses for the zigzag was quite straight forward. Time would tell.

In the first class saloon Wentle poured tea for the trooping colonel and his aide and set a tray for the doctor, which Brightman took aft. The purser, it seemed, was still asleep.

As they stood at the pantry servery drinking their tea together Akker said nothing as the youth chewed dolefully on a doughnut. `Why shouldn't the boy have a cake' he contemplated, `Christ, its a bloody miracle that they were not now all in a bloody lifeboat' and then out loud "You all right Wentle?"

"Yes Mr.Akker, Sir. But" and he hesitated, "But being fired at like we were this morning, was a bit different from being bombed ashore. When my father lost one of the shops in the city centre we accepted it as a bit of bad luck. The Jerry was undoubtedly aiming for Bristol Bridge and our place and a lot of others were just too close. This morning though, well, it seemed almost personal."

"Yes, I know what you mean, seeing as it was the first time for me too. However, worse things can happen at sea, as the saying goes."

"But we were at sea Mr.Akker?"

"Yes but we still have our ship and are not heaving our guts out in some bloody lifeboat. God help me!" the big man shuddered at the thought and noisily slurped his tea.

"Yes Mr.Akker. I must admit I don't fancy doing time in a boat. Although he doesn't talk about it I believe Harry London had a pretty tough time of it?" He took another bite of his doughnut.

"Yes he did. If Green hadn't spotted them the doc reckoned they wouldn't have lasted more than a few days. He's a good lad an' I wanted him down here but he says he's okay where he is for another trip and then he talks of becoming a sparks. But then seeing as how you'r fairly chummy with him I suppose you know all that?"

"Yes. I'm thinking of something on those lines myself."

"Well I think you're daft because I'll guarantee that I make more than the chief sparks does. With your education in a few years you'd be one of the bosses." And then, as if he suddenly saw his own job threatened, the saloon steward's expansive mood changed and he reverted to the hard faced petty officer he wished to be known as.

Wentle sensed the change. "I'd best go and see if old colonel Blimp is O.K," he said. "I don't think he likes me very much."

"Well don't let it worry you. You'll always have someone at your table who likes to bitch."

"I try not to but it annoys me. You see my father rose to become a Colonel and command his regiment in the last war but I'm sure he was never like this one." With that the conversation ended.

Subdued in spirit, scarred but not mortally wounded, the Patriarch steamed on across the South Atlantic with only the twisted gun aft and the two crew men up in the hospital to remind her crew of what had happened. A series of fronts came through their area and the weather deteriorated rapidly. The seas got up and the fiddles had to be put in place on the mess tables.

After two days of buffeting the Patriarch altered course from west to nor'west and hoped for calmer seas. Her crew slept and ate and then went on watch or about their daily jobs.

Whenever possible the men in the radio-room would keep them in touch with what was happening in the world thousands of miles to the north. When the watches changed at midday they would try to get some sort of news bulletin onto the tannoy but mainly it was a case of having to copy down the Reuter reports sent out in Morse code. Then, when a clear copy had been made, pin it up on the notice boards, but even that was not always possible. With Rommel barely being held at Al Alamein and the Russians still in retreat perhaps it was just as well that the news was scant!

The Patriarch and her crew remained very much in a world of their own with only the daily sights when they were able to see sun or stars. For Wentle, as a new man aboard, two things broke the daily monotony.

Akker, as with each senior petty officer in the various departments, came around one morning and asked the saloon-boy what he wanted in his food box? The purser, who looked after the deductions from their pay, and the chief steward, who did the ordering, arranged for each member of the crew to take a box of food stuffs ashore on their return to England. Each man could order up to thirty pounds in weight and include a leg of ham. After docking the parcels would be delivered to Avonmouth station for collection. The thought that he would be able to take such a present to his parents was wonderful. However, this created a problem for him because his parents were divorced. To which of them should he take what?

"Would it be possible to have two boxes, or split one in the packing?" he enquired.

"No it bloody well isn't," roared Akker. "It's a bloody miracle that the chief gets his finger out to do this much for us. God help me! You'll want the usual sugar, butter and tea I expect? Anyway fill in this form and let me have it back by this evening. And use more Goddards than that or I'll lose that bloody form!" Wentle was cleaning the cruet set and suppressed a grin for he knew that Akker did not mean what he said.

The second item was having his photograph taken for the Argentinean `seaman's identity card'. `And make sure that you carry it at all times when ashore for the police are not all that friendly', said the assistant purser whose job it was to look after such things.

On the ninth day after their encounter with the submarines Third Officer Giles died without regaining consciousness.

`Died from wounds received in action,' said the entry in the log. And so, once more, the M.V. Patriarch stopped her engines in mid ocean and buried one of her own.

When Harry London had helped push the bodies from the raft last year he had not been able to cry. His senses were numbed and his body incapable of producing tears. Now, as Mr.Giles' body slid from view, his tears silently flowed; not only for the officer he had so recently enjoyed serving but also for those others who had gone on the raft. And he cried again for his father. The constriction in his throat threatened to choke him and there was a terrible ache in his chest. He felt he wanted to scream and scream until he was utterly exhausted so that he could fall into a sleep from which he would never wake.

Even amongst the hard case sailors David Giles had been popular and respected. He never ordered a man to do something he could or would not do himself. More than one of those `hard case' men sniffed or blew his nose loudly.

Spencer found this second burial service charged with emotion. When they had buried the DEMS gunners it had been sad. They had been a part of his crew for some while and Sergeant Bill Howell had been widely liked and respected; but Giles? Well this seemed different.

Each day while at sea there had been almost eight hours or more when he was in personal contact with the young man. Now it felt almost as if he were burying his own son. Until now this had been, despite all the ships he had seen go down, a remote war as far as death was concerned. It had always been `the other fellow' who `bought it'. Unlike Harry London he'd not had to endure the privations of being torpedoed and touched by death almost daily. Now this trip had changed that. Suddenly it was as bad as it had been at Gallipoli or in the Dover Patrol. He longed for it all to end!

The captain later wrote in the letter of condolence to the parents - `The Third Officer will be sorely missed and the Merchant Navy will be worse off for his loss.' He knew that such banal sentiments, although most sincerely meant, would bring little comfort to grieving parents, but it was all he had to offer.

CHAPTER TWELVE

It was their thirteenth day out from Durban and an hour before Wentle had to go and make the afternoon tea. He and Harry London were leaning on the bulwark at the end of the passageway from the well deck to the galley taking what had become `their usual bit of fresh air'. A thin `scotch mist' type of rain made them seek the cover of the alleyway. There was no sunlight to lend colour to the dark blue trousers and patrol jackets and the lighter hue of the life jackets they wore. All around them was the drab dark grey paint of a merchant ship at war. Only when they looked overboard was there a different hue, for the water was now a muddy light brown broken a few yards out by the white creaming bow wave.

Later, no doubt, Mr.Baines the senior quartermaster would join them as he had done for most of the last week. A time which both boys had come to look forward to as they listened to his tales of the past.

Despite their close friendship and because it was a subject he felt was a personal thing, Wentle was hesitant as he asked London if he had ever made love.

Harry did not reply immediately, but only because he was recalling his leave last spring when he and Deborah had done just that amongst the bluebells up in Friars' Wood. "Why Dick?"

"Well I expect you know I haven't and I wondered if it would be the same with a whore as it might be with our girl friends?"

"I suppose if all you're thinking about is `coming your lot' it would be the same. I don't really know because I've only done it with Debbie and that wasn't 'til we'd been out several times and both felt we wanted to before I went back to sea. We're sort of unofficially engaged you see." Harry London was only a year older than Dick Wentle but his experiences over the last twenty four months had given him a philosophical outlook that belied his youth.

"I'd been on two ships that went down and nearly bought it last time and who's to say that if it happens again I won't be so lucky? We talked about it and felt that when this war's over we'll definitely get married. We thought that if we made love it would sort of cement our feelings for each other 'cause neither of us had done it with anyone else." Again he hesitated not sure whether to go on. then deciding that it would be good to tell someone of how he and Deborah felt for each other.

"Dick, like your Mary, Deb is a bit older than me, in fact she should be taking her final nursing exams about now, so because of how we felt we did it and I'm sure it wouldn't feel the same if you did it with any girl, particularly a whore! When you've learnt how, and believe me it's not all plain sailing the first couple of times, the feeling is something you can't describe. What it must be like when you're married and do it deliberately to make a kid, well, it... it must be about the most wonderful feeling in the world!"

For a while they were silent. The ever present swish, swish of the breaking bow wave as it tumbled over itself and the throb of the engines under their feet were the only audible sounds and even those seemed muted and in harmony. Their minds were thousands of miles from the estuary of the River Plate. London thought of that moment when he first entered Debbie and Wentle wondered if he would ever do it with his Mary.

"Afternoon y' two. An' 'ow are y' today?" Old Father Neptune appeared puffing on his pipe leaving wisps of blue smoke to mingle with the damp air.

"Good afternoon, Mr.Baines," the two lads replied in unison, returning the sailor's warm smile.

"Shall I make us a cup of tea, Sir?" Despite the previous admonishments from the quartermaster Wentle still found it difficult not to address the old man in the way he'd been brought up to respect age.

"Now that be a good idea, lad." He pulled extra long on his pipe as Wentle took the few steps into the galley to the waiting hot water urn. Baines enjoyed talking to youngsters who showed a willingness to learn, and these two certainly did. He would not be able to continue at sea much longer. His arthritic hands gave him considerable pain when on the wheel, so the more he could pass on to those who would follow the better it would be.

"When will we be picking up the pilot, Mr.Baines?" Harry asked. "The water's pretty brown so I guess we can't be far from land?"

"Y'ud be surprised how far out from the shore the mud carries when it's raining up on the Pampas. The estuary be more'n two hundred miles across at its mouth. We should be near the pilot station soon but 'cause of this cloud they didn't make no sights this morning an' 'ave run on dead reckoning since last nights fix. Could be that we 'ave to search around a bit to find the cutter."

Wentle appeared with three mugs of tea. Generally he preferred cocoa, particularly if, when Akker was not looking, he could make it with condensed milk, thick and sweet!

"Thank y' lad." The old man removed his pipe with one hand and sipped from his mug using the other. "I remembers once we tacked for a week before getting' in. Was in the MacAndrew Line's `Scotland'. A ship of a thousand tons, she were, an' carried skys'ls. No sooner we'd be aloft and get 'er down to tops'ls when the Pamperos came, than we'd 'ave to put it all back ag'in as the squalls passed. 'Still that were the way it were in those days; per'aps we're better off now with these big donkeys down below. Certain it be that I shan't stand a trick on an open wheel no more and keep one eye on the compass an' t'other on the sails.

Other times y' steered by the feel o' the wind on y'r face or in y'r ear!" His eyes seemed to glaze over as his mind went back many years while all three sipped their tea in silence.

"Mr.Baines, are we, ah...safe now do you think? Would the U-boats operate here so close to land?" Wentle asked, hearing again the cries of the men from the Alcavia. After the burial of the third officer he'd had several nightmares about being left to drown; only to wake as the last breath exploded from him and his lungs started to fill with water. As the sweat of fear dried on him he would wonder if he'd ever get used to the way things were. During the day he went about his tasks without thought of what might happen, but at night the dreams came to haunt him.

"Safe, lad? Well who knows what Jerry might be up to but I didn't yet 'ear about too many ships going down around this way. Talk is that they 'ave an unofficial pact with the Argees to leave the area in peace in return fer refueling facilities, but who knows? Anyways, thanks fer the tea an' I'll be off now." The quartermaster drained his mug and handed it to the saloon-boy, his black oilskin coat glistening in the damp atmosphere as he left the alleyway.

"Well, suppose I'd better lay up the tea table before Old Blimp starts yelling his head off!"

"Yep Dick, I'd best do the same for those that want it. Glad I don't have a Blimp; my lot are pretty decent really except, perhaps, for the third sparkie." The two boys went their separate ways.

The Patriarch arrived at where they thought the pilot station should be just as the evening sun started to break through the clouds. The slanting rays coming low over the sea turned the brown water to a vivid gold, making it difficult for those looking to the west. Wentle, now serving dinner, marveled again at how nature could change its moods.

Up on the bridge binoculars were being used to search for the pilot cutter which should have been in sight but was not.

Entering the chart-room the captain again studied the chart of the River Plate Estuary and then took down the appropriate volume of the Admiralty Sailing instructions. Perhaps they had not allowed quite enough for the tidal set?

Returning to the wheel-house he was about to order an alteration of course to the north when the mast-head 'phone rang.

Green, the best eyes in the ship, had been up there for the past hour even though it was not his watch. Now, with the extra height above the bridge, he could see what they could not.

"Small vessel three points on our starboard bow, Sir. Just hull up she is. Could be the cutter."

"Steer nor'nor'west, Quartermaster. Charles have the A.B make the pilot ladder ready on the starboard side please." After four thousand odd miles, the last twenty hours without a sight and more or less in tidal waters, Spencer mused that their navigation had been pretty good to be only about a dozen miles out. "Mr.Baines light up the ship if you please." The quartermaster and the fourth officer had come to the bridge well before they were due to take over the watch. The sighting of the pilot cutter was an important moment.

Since the death of the third officer an A.B from the bosun's day men had made up the numbers on the eight to twelve watch and Spencer had the senior quartermaster in a quasi `second officer of the watch' position. If Baines had been able to take a sight he would have liked to have made him `fourth' but doubted if the old salt would have accepted it. In his mind Spencer could hear Baines; `Me an officer Sir? Bless you but no. I can keep an eye on the young gentlemen better as I am.' Having Baines there ex-officio helped take some of the strain from the captain and Spencer was grateful. Now he looked deep into the old man's eyes and knew, such was the empathy between them, that he did not have to say `thank you.'

Baines moved to the back of the wheel-house and to the outline diagram of the ship showing the various lights and their appropriate switches. First the navigation lights and then the after decks were illuminated. Below it meant that portholes could be opened and blackout curtains hooked back. But above all it meant that tonight there would be no need for Wentle, London and the other stewards to sleep in the canteen. They would no longer need their life jackets with them at all times and for the next three weeks they would be able to forget the war.

An hour later they came up to the pilot cutter, hailed their name and requested a pilot to Buenos Aires. Although those on the cutter must have heard quite plainly, Stickland was asked to repeat the ship's name. When he had done so a number of men came out on deck, looked hard at the Patriarch and began a conversation, in the Latin way accompanied by much gesticulation, some pointing aft to the wreckage of the four inch gun.

The pilot cutter was beautifully kept and looked, under her floodlights, like a private yacht with four small varnished launches hung from davits. She sheered off and dropped one of the launches, which soon covered the cable of calm sea between the two vessels. While a pilot climbed up the ladder to the well deck a seaman hoisted up his bag on the end of a heaving line. Once aboard the fourth officer showed him the way to the bridge where the captain waited.

"Captain, we did not expect to see you again," the pilot exclaimed as they shook hands. "We understood that you had been sunk. Yes, definitely sunk. How is it that you are here? We see that you have scars on the ship so you have had some trouble, yes? You have fought a battle perhaps?"

"Yes, Pilot we have had some trouble as you put it." Spencer sighed. Over the many years that he had been on the South American run he had become indifferent to the Argentineans as a race. He knew that he was probably being unreasonable but the pilot's manner now grated on him. Perhaps it was the way the man referred to their battle and the way it brought back the memories of those for whom he had so recently read the burial service. "Is there a berth for us?" he asked.

"A berth Captain? I don't know. I expect yours was cancelled when we heard you were sunk. No, I do not think so. You must call the coast station and tell them of your arrival, so that your agent can arrange one by the time we arrive at `Intercencion' and the river pilot takes over. Now please, if possible, I would like to see more closely your scars and know how it all happened!"

Boulton, who was still on the bridge despite having handed over the watch to Strickland, muttered, `Morbid sod'. He knew only too well that there were some amongst these people who were well disposed to the Third Reich and would report everything they heard or saw to the German Embassy. It seemed that German propaganda had succeeded in getting the Patriarch's berth cancelled. `Oh well, he thought, it might at least give them a few extra days in port!'

Spencer took Stickland by the arm, walking him to the bridge wing. "Show him Mr.Strickland but tell him nothing except that we gave a good account of ourselves. Understand? I'll take the watch until you get back"

The pilot gave the course to steer and followed Strickland from the bridge, whilst the third sparks sent a message through the coast station to their agent. While that was being done the Patriarch started on the ninety seven mile voyage up the estuary to the next pilot, most of it done at a reduced speed due to the mud banks either side of the fairway. With the reduced speed the ship became much quieter and the crew not on watch could sleep soundly for the first time since leaving Durban.

Satisfied that young Strickland knew what was required of him while the pilot was aboard, Spencer went below and took a long shower, free of fear of being caught naked by the alarm bells. He had heard of one master who arrived on his bridge still dripping with only a towel draped round him, which had fallen to the deck when he grasped the proffered binoculars with both hands!

Shower over, Perkins provided hot soup and cold cuts. Spencer felt no compunction at breaking his self-imposed wartime requirement of not drinking at sea and ordered a bottle of cold larger.

When McTavish took over the watch at midnight Spencer turned-in in his own bed, wearing pyjamas for the first time in two weeks. He fell into a deep sleep until, in accordance with his night order book, he was called ten minutes before the Patriarch arrived at the second pilot station.

During the night those on the bridge occasionally saw other ships whose lights, like their own, shone brightly. Then there were the winking bouys. Not small, hard-to-see pin pricks of light like those back in the Bristol Channel, but big definite blobs of red or green with now and then a white one to mark a wreck; caused by nature or some careless pilot, not the war.

As they made their way up river the loom of town lights could be seen on both sides, and just before dawn two large moths fluttered past the night watchman as he made his way along the promenade deck. The Patriarch was indeed almost at the end of her long journey and her crew would soon be in a city at peace, with its bright lights, riches and squalor. A city that offered dark skinned girls whose swaying hips would tantalize them until the price had been agreed and, for some, give Brightman, the doctor's assistant, an excuse to jab them hard with a needle when the `dose' started to take effect.

For Wentle it would be the epitome of a run ashore crystallized by the fact that only a few of its inhabitants understood English and he would need to buy a Spanish dictionary. Truly it was that `port in far off places' dreamed about by so many before they knew what lay in between!

"One day, Wentle," breathed Mr.Akker into the boy's ear. "One day, you will do a day's work without my having to chase you. Now get a bloody move on! Damned if I know why we ever signed you on. God help me!" The saloon-boy was laying the table for breakfast and had paused by the open window to watch the land come nearer, sniffing at its scent, made especially sweet by the happenings over the last fourteen days. As Wentle placed the last knife and fork on the clean white table cloth he remembered how `Father Neptune' had told him that coastal skippers in the old sailing ships knew where they were just by the scent off the land. He could believe, now, how that might be true.

Captain `The Padre' Spencer had never been heard, at least since his Navy days, to blaspheme but very occasionally he was heard to swear and that he did now. The clouds of yesterday had given way to weak sunshine but the more pleasant weather did nothing to assuage his anger. He was livid at the way the tug skippers were handling his ship. As if the stern did not have enough scars to mark the passage of war it now had a large dent in it where the tug had used far too much power and slammed the ship hard against the wharf right where there were no fenders to absorb the shock!

"Hell and damnation!" He said it loud enough for the pilot to hear but not loud enough for him to complain about. Spencer knew that some of the tug skippers took `kick backs' from the German Consulate for such deliberate actions and more than one British master had complained, of course to no avail. On the other hand there were those who covertly helped the Allies in many ways but still, this sort of thing was infuriating.

The night had passed well enough, except for the constant smoking by the pilot of cheap cheroots. Despite the open doors the wheel-house still reeked of the pungent smoke. Although both pilots had been competent enough at their job they were not exactly the dashing Latin American portrayed by Caesar Romero of film fame. The river pilot now docking them was scruffily dressed with breath that stank of garlic, if you were unfortunate enough to get too close.

Green, up on the fo'c'sle waiting with his second heaving line also swore. "Bloody Dagos!" as he watched the water surge forward between wharf and ship due to the rapid movement of the stern. The pressure sent the bow outwards so that the for'ard spring, an eight inch manila rope, which had just been made fast around the bits, began to hum dangerously as it grew bar taught. The for'ard tug which should have slipped its tow rope and been pushing the bow in now, whether in collusion with the one aft or not, put tension on its rope and actually helped the bow to swing outwards!

Later the tug skipper was to say that at the crucial moment he had a coughing fit and misunderstood the pilot's orders!

Spencer was not sure that Strickland was competent enough on his own to moor the ship aft, so Boulton was in the eye of the fo'c'sle. He saw the danger and yelled. "Clear the starboard side! Watch out for that hawser!"

The men scrambled clear of the danger side just as the rope parted with a report like a small cannon going off. The inboard end, short though it was, whipped back and fouled itself around the anchor cable. The outboard piece snaked shorewards with a loud hiss and caught one of the dockers across the chest. With a cry the man was hurled backwards five yards and landed in a heap against the leg of a crane.

"Poor bastard," the bosun said to no-one in particular. "Bloody good job for 'im it weren't a wire rope or it 'ud 'ave cut 'im in two!"

On the bridge the pilot grimaced and shrugged his shoulders as Spencer's eyes bored into his. "These things happen, Captain," he said with an air of total indifference.

Spencer turned away before he lost his temper completely. They had endured this sort of thing before and he knew he was powerless to do anything about it. The pilot yelled at the dockers who had crowded round their injured colleague and all but two returned to the wharf edge where Green had already sent another heaving line ashore. With the for'ard tug now pushing the bow gently against the wharf the Patriarch lay dormant until all the lines were properly secured and hauled tight.

An ambulance arrived with loudly clanging bell and took the injured man away. As the bosun and his crew lowered the gangway several cars and vans arrived alongside disgorging officials clad in various uniforms.

Wentle, along with Harry London, was watching from the well deck and, up to now having seen only the drab blues or browns of British uniforms was fascinated by them all and remarked. "The hosts of the Philistines. What on earth are all the uniforms for?"

"Search me, Dick," replied his companion who had been to Buenos Aires before. "Never have been able to find out but it seems that every official here just has to have a gaudy uniform! Some of 'em at the top can hardly walk for the weight of their gold braid and decorations. What's more, they're everywhere. You've gotta have a watchman for this and a watchman for that and then another to watch over the others and all the while they're likely to be pinching anything they can lay their hands on! Still for all these tin soldiers, as I've said before, it's a good place for a run ashore. If you thought Durban was just the job wait until you see this lot. The grub is cheap and first rate, and there are dozens of picture houses, all lights and polished chrome! The shops are full of everything you can imagine." He paused to watch the first of the officials climb the gangway. "Anyway, it's time we got back to work. Akker will be chasing around like the proverbial blue-arsed fly looking for you if you don't!"

*   *   *

"There seems only one way to tackle it James, and that's to hang a scaffold over the side, cut away the ragged plates and weld new ones across the space. It's lucky that the shell passed between the two frames and exploded inboard." The chief engineer and his opposite number from the company's shore office were assessing the damage to number five hold and how best to repair it. Because the company traded many of its ships to this port they had one of their ex-seagoing chiefs permanently based in the port precinct. It would now fall to him to organise the repair work.

"Another foot higher and it would have exploded on the double plating of the sheer strake and that would have been more difficult to deal with, although there might not have been so much damage inside the hold. Swings and roundabouts I suppose!"

James Harley was a fine engineer and when the agent had 'phoned him with the news of the Patriarch's imminent arrival he, along with others from the office, had been on the dockside as she tied up. He had gone directly to the chief's office and they had not even stopped for a coffee but went straight down aft.

"Do you have much to do below. Brian?"

"The usual couple of cylinders to draw and one of the gennies needs looking at but we'll cope with that if you can see to this lot? Will you be able to sort out the damaged freezer pipes without much trouble?"

For the next hour the two engineers and the engineer's writer, a sort of clerk who did most of the paper work and looked after the engine room stores, climbed around number five hold and made copious notes as to what would be required.

Elsewhere on the ship, once the customs, health and immigration formalities had been dealt with and the required number of `bottles and packets of cigarettes' handed over to keep the shore officials happy, normal routine took over. The purser asked for the passenger list but was told that he would have to wait. Due to the fact it was thought the ship was at the bottom of the Atlantic some had been re-allocated to other ships. A new list would be ready in a couple of days.

The doctor passed on his list of requirements and the chief steward was ensconced in his cabin with a ships' chandler on whom he knew he could rely to produce all the provisions that would be required, and at a price which would leave both men well satisfied.

With his ship now firmly alongside, the only sound that could be heard from the engine room was the hum of the generators and the occasional clatter of a dropped spanner. In the cabins the forced-draft gave its soft, soporific hiss while Spencer changed into his shore going uniform. Although still looking tired he was once again the handsome and immaculate officer who had been admired by the wren cox'n all those miles ago in Belfast Lough. He took another cup of coffee and prepared for the onslaught ashore.

With the ship roughly on a south-west heading there was no direct sunshine through the long windows but nevertheless it was still a pleasant enough place to be in. Perkins had worked hard with the polish so that the mahogany furniture shone and there was not a mark to be seen on the dark red carpet. Spencer noted that his tiger had procured two more foot mats so that there was one both outside and inside the door into the alleyway as well as the open, and hooked back, door to the day cabin. Before long the agent would arrive with the usual bunch of fresh cut flowers that he knew Spencer would appreciate and which would add to the atmosphere of the cabin.

The outlook over the wharf was one of drabness. The dull looking buildings were a slaughter house and meat processing factory in one. Live, loudly protesting, cattle were herded over from the railway siding yards and into those at the farthest point from the ship. Sent into the crush just inside the building they were pole-axed and then the processing began. Eventually they would arrive, quartered and frozen, on a balcony over the wharf where they were put into a cargo net and hoisted aboard by the shore cranes.

Perkins, who had been leaning over the rail on the small deck leading to the alleyway, watched the smartly dressed man carrying a bulging briefcase and a bunch of carnations mount the ladder towards him. Ascertaining that he was the agent the tiger lead the way to the day-cabin, knocked on the door and announced him, although there was no need to for the two men were old acquaintances.

The agent was the first of several callers. He stayed only a short while, collecting the ship's register, load line certificate and other documents necessary to enable the port dues to be paid. Every ship in every port had to pay for the use of port facilities. In some cases charges were extortionate and little given in return, but here they were reasonable and even as the agent was speaking with the captain, two men were connecting up the fresh water hose under supervision from the carpenter. In the next three weeks the agent would be a familiar face aboard to see either the captain or one of the heads of department and always working in close liaison with company officials.

The arrival of the Patriarch, considered back from the dead, had caused quite a stir in the city. Although they had been tied up for only three hours and it was not yet past noon there had been an almost continuous stream of people coming aboard. Many had no reason to be there other than morbid curiosity and Spencer had issued orders to the gangway officer that no reporters were allowed aboard. Disgruntled, they had climbed a nearby crane, taken their photographs and gone off to concoct their own story as to how the Patriarch had received those scars aft. Not since the Graff Spee incident had there been such a news story.

One shore official, a young naval officer whose job it was to ensure that the four inch gun aft was disabled, normally achieved by the removal of the firing pin, had made the chief officer very angry by insisting that the pin be removed in accordance with his written instructions. In the end Boulton had taken him to the wrecked gun and told him to 'Take the bloody thing out yourself if you can!' (The anti-aircraft machine guns had all been stowed away out of sight!)

Another, who had no real reason to come aboard was now with the captain. If there was something which required the attention of the British Consulate one of the vice-consuls or a clerk would come down to the ship but now the consul himself had turned up and would see no one less than the captain.

"What will you have to drink, Sir?" Spencer crossed to the cocktail cabinet having told his tiger to wait outside lest the consul wanted a word in private. Apart from which Spencer had forgotten to ask if Perkins knew anything about mixing drinks.

"Pink gin, please Captain." The man settled himself comfortably into the armchair as if the walk aft to inspect the damage had tired his large frame. Apprentice Jones, who was acting as the captain's messenger, had told the consul no more than had been told to the pilot yesterday. Like Spencer, Jones did not like the man's pompous attitude and had enjoyed being devious in his replies. As Spencer handed over the drink the consul wriggled his ample bottom farther into the chair.

"Ah, thank you, that's fine. Must say that when we heard from home you'd got entangled in sole combat with a U-boat we did not expect to see you again. Don't know how the news got out but it did after a few days and there was quite a bit in the papers about how the Patriarch called here over the past years. You know, all the usual tripe that papers write. Yes. Must say you had a damned lucky escape!" And he downed a large swig of gin.

Spencer, glass in hand perched himself on the desk. "Oh, I don't know about luck. I'd say it was damned fine shooting by the gunner and his crew, poor devils."

"Umm, perhaps. Anyway, you got away but there is a point that I must raise, Spencer." He made it sound as if he was addressing some wayward schoolboy and not a senior officer responsible for the lives of nearly a hundred men and a million pounds worth of ship. "It would have made things a lot easier for us here if you had let someone know that you were safe. I mean to say we really did have a frightful time with those press fellas and all that sort of thing!"

`Ye Gods!' thought Spencer `How the hell did you ever get to where you are?' and then out loud and doing his best to hide the annoyance in his voice. "I suppose I could have sent a signal immediately after the fight but I was pretty sure that those two subs must have been where they were to re-fuel from a supply ship or a raider. If that were so then whichever it was might have got a D.F. bearing on me and it could have meant curtains! No, I considered that it was best to let my owners and their Lordships suffer in silence rather than jeopardise my ship."

"Uhmm, yes, quite so, quite so. No doubt you're right, but still it was an inconvenience not to know what was happening."

Spencer left his perch on the desk and turned to face the open window, trying to control his rising anger. "Hell and damnation!" he muttered louder than he meant to so that he was sure the other man must have heard. "I'd like to know what you would have done in my place?" He heard the ice tinkle in the gin glass behind him, his own drink forgotten on the desk.

"There's another thing, Spencer that my vice-consul happened to mention and I think he has a point. It's about your seamen getting into trouble here. One in particular caused a lot of hassle for my chap to bail him out last trip. A fellow, what was his name, some colour or other. Green, yes Green that was it. Anyway he really is the end, fight after fight according to our records. Damned riffraff some of these seamen. Should be left to rot in jail! See to it like a good chap that he's kept on board or something." He held out his now empty glass towards the captain. "Wouldn't mind another old boy."

Spencer froze, speechless, with one hand poised above the other as he was about to place them on the window sill. If he had been annoyed a few moments ago he was now passionately angry. Slowly and deliberately he lowered his now shaking hands, the wrist of one still in an elastic bandage. Then, least he should be tempted to hit this person who had dared to call one of his best men 'riffraff', thrust them into his jacket pockets. He turned and lent forward until his face was within two feet of the other's. With an edge to his voice, so sharp that Perkins and Jones, supposedly out of ear shot in the pantry, hardly recognized it as their captain's.

"Don't you, Sir, ever again call any of my men riffraff! Do you know what it's like to spend three or four weeks at a time out there knowing that you could die at any moment or, worse still, perhaps spend weeks dying slowly in some lifeboat? Have you, Sir, ever seen any action?" Spencer was almost beside himself with anger. "No I'll bet you haven't! Too young for the last lot and no doubt been sitting on your fat bum in some nice, safe office all through this one. Dear God! You don't have the first conception of what war is like and why men, if they are lucky enough to make port, need to get drunk or fight or whore around! You'd like another drink? Not ever again on my ship!" In one movement he withdrew his left hand from its pocket and side swiped the glass from the flabbergasted consul's grip.

Controlling himself with difficulty he called out, "Jones! Escort this man to the gangway, and tell the officer there not to let him back aboard!" He stood quivering with rage as the startled consul pushed himself from the chair and made for the door, the shattered gin glass crunching underfoot as an equally startled Jones appeared in the doorway.

"You've not heard the end of this, Spencer. Not by a long chalk!" the consul spluttered, and then almost ran the last three steps from the cabin as the captain moved towards him.

Spencer unhooked the door and, seeing Perkins staring at him across the alleyway, told his tiger that he was not to be disturbed for a while. After closing the door he downed his almost untouched gin in one gulp, spilling some over his beard, then slumped into an arm chair and closed his eyes.

Slowly the anger subsided and he knew that he had been very wrong to lose his temper. Maybe he was losing his grip and should ask the doc for something to soothe his nerves before he went round the bend. Then, despite the racket from the quayside and the shouts of the dockers as they began cleaning out the holds and the clanking of a moving crane, he fell into a deep exhausted sleep.

CHAPTER 13

"For Pete's sake, Dick, how d'you stop this crazy thing," shouted Harry London clinging desperately to the saddle horn as his horse broke into a gallop. The afternoon was drawing to a close and was not particularly warm but the sweat started to pour from the mess-boy's brow. His tie streaming out behind him, he bumped up and down as a stirrup, from which his foot had lost its hold, slammed into the piebald's flank urging it to greater speed.

"Had enough?" Wentle enquired bringing his own horse alongside the other and, leaning outwards, grasped the right rein of his friend's animal whilst reining in his own. As the two horses slowed to a walk the dust they had created caught up with and enveloped them. London managed to put his foot back in the loose stirrup, coughed and moved wearily in his saddle.

"Lord, Dick is it always like that? Beats me how you just sit there like it were a piece of cake! I feel as if I mightn't ever be able to walk again let alone sit. God, my backside!"

The two youngsters, like everyone else on the Patriarch, were spending as much time ashore as they could. London and the officer's steward, as with Lewis and Wentle, were able to have a run ashore after serving luncheon on alternate days and from after dinner on the other days.

For the first few days the two youths spent umpteen pesos in milk bars, where the milk was not watered down, like at home, and there were far more flavours to choose from. They whiled away hours looking at brilliantly lit shop windows in the various plazas, wondering what presents they could take back for their girls and families.

The further they walked away from the docks along the Passe Corientez the more opulent became their surroundings. They had gorged themselves each evening in one of the cheap cafes, which generally smelt of garlic while Latin music blared forth, or done themselves proud with thick steaks topped with fried eggs and heavily oiled side salads at the Seaman's Mission or Toch-H.

It was at the Toc-H canteen that Wentle had asked a girl to dance. He explained that he only had a very rough idea how to do a waltz, learned when he had dutifully danced with his mother during `Parent's Weekend' at school, whilst secretly longing to dance with the rather smashing sister of a fellow prefect.

In general conversation afterwards he had discovered that her grandfather, a Scotsman, had a riding stable some twelve miles inland. If Wentle could really ride, and she emphasized that point because many said they could sit a horse and promptly fell off, then she would arrange for him to go out there. There would be no cost as the old man felt it was his little bit towards the war effort.

This was Richard's second time at the stables. Despite the fact that the young lady had written down the bus numbers and how to get to the bus centre, he had taken a couple of wrong turnings before boarding the final bus. He had shown his directions to the driver and made him understand that he wanted to get out at the `El Vapour' inn. Now he and Harry, who had said he would `give it a go', were out on the pampas riding in western saddles in best cowboy fashion. Richard was thoroughly enjoying himself. Harry was not quite so sure!

Richard had learnt to ride several years earlier at an aunt's farm in South Wales. The last time he had been in the saddle back home was the previous autumn when he and his sister, a staff sergeant in the army, had ridden across Clifton Downs. He grinned to himself as he remembered how her horse had also taken off and he had come to her rescue!

While her crew enjoyed the pleasures ashore the Patriarch's holds were having their final clean out. They had to be spotless since the sides of beef were wrapped only in muslin. Then the freezer pipes were re-fitted ready for the loading, which was slightly delayed because of the work patching up number five hold.

The purser, who now had his passenger list, advised the second steward how many cabins would be required for the passage back to England. These were then given an extra cleaning and the beds made up. The saloon-boy found that with so many people coming and going, the deck around the offices in the entrance lobby required a lot more scrubbing each morning. Indeed, as he had been made to do in his early days aboard, which now seemed a very long time ago, Mr. Akker had made him do it twice on their third day alongside.

Slowly the gloom and despondency of their last passage left the ship and was replaced with an almost peacetime atmosphere. Her crew worked hard and also played hard.

Some, like London and Wentle played quietly and without trouble. Some found trouble because they could not hold their liquor; whilst others found it because trouble seemed to be looking for them! However, two weeks passed before any of the Patriarch's crew fell foul of the law. When it happened it was not Able Seaman Green but two middle aged greasers. Calloused and hardened from many years shoveling coal into insatiable boilers, they had visited ports all over the world before changing to the much easier work-load of a diesel engined ship.

The fourth engineer, who knew what it was like to spend a night in the local calaboose and with whom the greasers were supposed to be working on the diesel motor for the second generator, managed to cover for the missing two until just before `smoke-o' time. The gangway 'phone rang and the third sparks, who was gangway officer, answered it. Had Jim Baines, quartermaster of the watch, got to the 'phone first he and the donkeyman senior greaser could have kept officialdom at bay. The officious third R/O, however, wrote their names in the gangway note book and 'phoned the chief engineer's office.

The lieutenant on duty at the police station had dealt with many drunken seamen in his long career and had come to realise years ago that it was worthwhile to have fines paid in cash, and not through a magistrate via the offending man's consulate or ship's captain. A quick `whip round' in the fo'c'sle (to be paid back later) would be beneficial to everyone concerned! But now the gangway officer had set bureaucracy in motion and although the consulate had not been informed it did mean that the two men would be duly logged and, over-all, loose a weeks pay. An amount far in excess of what they would have paid the woman who had unwittingly been the cause of their trouble.

The two men had gone ashore early the previous evening; had a meal and started on a round of the bars nearest to the docks. By their very location those bars and the whores in them were there to extract the maximum number of pesos from the crews of the visiting merchant ships.

`El Diablo' was either the fourth or fifth bar, they couldn't make up their minds, that the two greasers entered. They plopped themselves unsteadily down on a bench seat against one of the white-washed walls; at least they had once been white but like the rest of the place were now dull and dirty. Cigarette butts littered the floor along with spilt beer, and where the two met the dog-ends split and disgorged soggy dark tobacco. In one corner a trio, playing on drums, guitar and a tinny sounding cornet, blared out the inevitable tangoes and rhumbas to which several couples gyrated on a space in the middle of the room.

Three bored looking waiters wearing soiled aprons went from table to bar and back with beer and what passed for spirits. The air was heavy with smoke despite a couple of slowly revolving fans. The two men from the Patriarch ordered beers and leered at a group of women sitting at a nearby table. Sensing new customers two came over and joined the men. One, about eighteen years old and quite attractive with firm breasts and large nipples that almost thrust through the flimsy dress she wore, pushed herself between the two sailors. The other, tending towards the plump side and whose age was difficult to discern under her heavy make-up, drew up a chair and pressed her knee against that of the nearest male.

The waiter brought the beers and the older woman ordered two drinks for themselves, naturally to be paid for by their clients. On the bar each 'hostess' had her own coloured abacus, the barman moving a bead for every drink ordered. When the right number was obtained the Patron would let them go upstairs to the bleak cubicles containing creaking beds and a metal bowl of water. The latter made available in the mistaken belief that washing 'it' would prevent catching a 'dose'.

When the younger women sat down she had drawn her dress half way up her thighs and when two hands, one from either side, caressed her knees she opened her legs to make access easier. As the two hands reached her pubic hairs they collided. In that dismal bar she saw the funny side of things and laughed! Had she not done so the two men might not have come to blows.

"Fuck orf out'a it George," grunted the man on her right. "This be my bit o' twat! Yours be t'other." He tried to push the other hand away and in doing so caught some of the ample black hair. The girl's laugh became a squeal as she tried to get to her feet.

"Ya bloody git!" exclaimed George, and both men stood up, their fly buttons ready to burst open under the strain. Over went the table, beer and glass tumbling to the floor. The second woman tried to get out of the way as both men swung half hearted punches but her chair went over backwards and she with it, sprawling on the floor with one pendulous breast escaping from its scant cover. The musicians fled through a nearby door and the barman lowered a heavy grill which hung over his counter for moments such as this.

As so often happens when men are in their cups in places such as `El Diablo' one fight started another and soon it became a free for all until the Vigilantes arrived.

Thus it was that the second engineer and the assistant purser duly went to the police station with a large wad of notes and bailed out the two greasers. When the lieutenant complained that the money was not enough, `Ass-Pee' did as his boss, who knew the ropes of old, had told him and said that was all they had on board. If more was required then it would have to go through consular channels etc. The policeman shrugged and grabbed the money before officialdom took over and his `cut' became a figment of the imagination!

Earlier, on the Patriarch's second day in port, the naval attache from the embassy, a captain, and someone who passed as a third secretary but in reality was the naval control shipping officer, came aboard to debrief her master and mate on their fight with the submarine. They, like Spencer, came to the conclusion that the two boats must have been there to rendezvous with a supply ship. The fact that a Japanese boat might be operating in the South Atlantic was disturbing. This information was quickly passed, via the secret radio which NCSOs in each of the main ports of the eastern coast of South America now possessed, to the C-in-C South Atlantic in Freetown. In turn the C-in-C advised the two cruisers that had the almost impossible task of patrolling that vast area.

Allied merchant ships sailing from South American ports were given precise courses to follow by the NCSOs which, eventually, were also advised to the patrolling men-of-war. Because there were not enough ships in such a vast area to sail as convoys the vessels with their precious cargos of wheat and meat had to sail singly. The cruisers, hopefully, were there to keep enemy raiders at bay: a case of `cat and mouse' or `hide and seek' depending on how you looked at it.

For the naval crews it meant long boring periods at sea with little action. The boredom occasionally relieved by a brief visit to a neutral port for fresh provisions and fuel. The time being strictly limited by international law to twenty four hours and not more than one visit a month. At other times there were, as with the German vessels, clandestine meetings with supply ships in remote bays and anchorages. The use of Walrus seaplanes, affectionately know as `Ding-bats', greatly increased the patrol or search area. Even so, for the cruisers, it was like searching for a needle in a hay stack.

The local papers had published their lurid and somewhat conflicting reports of the Patriarch's fight for survival, with the result that the English Society made her captain guest of honour at a dinner. After which he, and John Beverley, the company's manager in Buenos Aires and an old friend of Spencer's, sat on the veranda of Beverley's yacht club. The dinner, although a good one, had finished early and the two decided that a night-cap would be in order.

"How's the loading going Ronald?" Beverley eyed his companion speculatively across the small table. Before Spencer had been promoted captain the two men had sailed together as chief officer and purser and Beverley had come to like and respect the officer who, even then, was known as `The Padre'. As purser he had never heard of Spencer losing his temper at sea; now he wondered at the kind of pressure that had caused the captain to have a consul shown the gangway!   The consul, perhaps wisely, had made no official complaint but let it be known that he was far from happy over his treatment aboard the Patriarch.

Spencer, immaculately dressed in full peace time mess- kit, the lights shining on the gold braid and twinkling back from the silver of the miniature medals, cupped his brandy glass and swirled its contents around, gazing into the amber liquid as he did so. It was some time before he answered his companion's question. When he did, his voice, despite nearly three weeks in port, once again sounded desperately tired, as if the short speech of thanks and, within the bounds of security, account of the battle, had drained his last reserves of strength. That speech had been delivered in Spencer's usual precise and coherent tones but now he sounded as he had done upon the ship's arrival in Buenos Aires.

Beverley assumed that having to re-live the fight with its aftermath was no doubt the cause of The Padre's present dejection; or was it from the letters of condolence he had so recently left at the office for onward transmission to Giles' parents and the DEMS brigadier?

"Loading? Should be finished on Wednesday afternoon. Shift berth Thursday as arranged and sail Friday morning. I know it's the thirteenth but barring the unforeseen I can't find any excuse for altering it. Passengers aboard by eighteen hundred on Thursday and the usual farewell party." Spencer paused to sip the brandy and Beverley thought he saw an almost imperceptible tremor in the strong, well manicured hand. He beckoned to a waiter and ordered two more brandies during the ensuing silence, wondering whether the thought of a return to the conflict was the cause of Spencer's behaviour.

It was cool and pleasant on the patio with the water lapping gently at the piles below. In the distance could be heard the slap-slap of halyards beating on a myriad of yacht masts. Several couples danced to a band playing in strict ballroom tempo. The music finished with a flourish and the couples, all dressed in evening clothes, returned to their tables. Here, to most of them the war did not seem to exist. It was remote; a part of another world; something talked of vaguely; sometimes something heroic but to Spencer there was nothing heroic about it.

"I wonder how many of them," he said sweeping an arm in the general direction of the room, "realise what is happening on the other side of the Atlantic. Here they are with no apparent cares, plenty of food and no blitz while we are really part of another world. I wonder what they would do if I put them down in the middle of an air raid with no taxis and only saccharine for their ersatz coffee?"

"You forget, Ronald, that some of them are going to find out when they board your ship. Most are going of their own free will, the same as many before them," Beverley replied, referring to the English contingent who made up a considerable part of the club membership. "You know, the locals are not really as bad as you think. They're just lucky that's all. It costs no lives for them to live like this and they have the meat and wheat which we need. If they put the price up a bit well, who can blame them? We'd do the same! Look at me, I live like a lord while you poor devils sweat it out with the U-boats at sea."

Spencer sighed. "Perhaps you're right John, but at least you tried to get back to sea and anyway we need you here. Someone who knows our problems. God knows what we would have done without you and James; he certainly worked wonders getting that damage repaired." He took a long sip of the second brandy and as he returned his glass to the table his eyes met those of his friend. Slowly he smiled; "Sorry John, I'm getting morbid. Perhaps it's the drink. Or maybe I should see the doc and get a pep pill!"

"What you need, old chap, is a break ashore, away from it all for a while. Get Head Office to give you a trip off. Soon put you right!"

"No, no." Spencer's voice again sounded vexed, "Holidays are no good for you. They merely soften you up and you spend most of the time wondering what the hell the next trip is going to be like. It's best to keep on until the whole damn thing is finished and done with. Why, what we go through is nothing compared to what the poor devils on the close escorts have to put up with. They really have it tough. They get in, refuel and are out again almost before we have the hatches open!"

Beverley flicked a moth from the sleeve of his dinner jacket. "Perhaps so but at least they are not generally the targets and can hit back."

"I'll give you that point, it's certainly better to have something to do. The chaps I really feel sorry for are the ones down in the engine room. With their chances of getting out alive much less than ours on the bridge. I'm damned if I know how their nerves stand it!"

"How do any of you stand it? I'm sure that had you asked a psychiatrist pre-war, what was the mental breaking point of a man he would have told you that it was half what you people are going through in this thing called total war! War or total war, what's the difference? The idea in both is surely to kill the other chap before he kills you!"

The shore man raised his own glass to his lips realising that he, too, was getting morbid.

"Yes, I suppose you're right really," Spencer replied. "Kill or be killed, it's the law of the jungle. Damn it, if that Jap had attacked us with torpedoes I wouldn't be here now and why he gave up shelling us the Lord only knows because we didn't think we damaged him all that much. 'Struth, John it was a bloody close thing!" Spencer found himself sweating at the thought of what might have been. The five piece dance band was playing a slow fox-trot selection and now started on `You'd be so nice to come home to.' He wondered, as he had done on so many voyages, if he would get home after this one. Why couldn't he just stay here and drink himself into oblivion?

"Tell me, Ronald. There have been rumours that some Jerry skippers have been machine-gunning survivors in the lifeboats. Is it true or just propaganda?"

"Yes, I've heard it too and I believe it could happen. I mean, logically it's the thing to do in a war, but I doubt whether I could do it. It's one thing to kill an armed man who's trying to kill you, and God forgive me I had to do that in the last lot, but an unarmed one?" He paused, remembering that awful moment when he had run his cutlass through the German skipper and how the man had dropped his empty Luger, clutched the blade with both hands and sunk to his knees. Those eyes which had stared straight back into Spencer's in the light from the deck fires. What message had they contained in that moment before they had glazed over? Not hate, Spencer was sure of that. More of wonder, or stupefaction that two men of the same age doing the same job should try to kill each other at such close quarters. That look was something Spencer would carry with him to his own grave. "Logical? Yes, logical. Look at it this way. You sink a destroyer and her crew take to the life rafts. They might be rescued and form the crew of a new destroyer. That new ship comes and drops a depth charge and sinks your submarine. Well then, the obvious thing to do is to make sure those men in the water don't get the chance to sink you later! `No quarter given!" Isn't that what it was called at one time."

John Beverley did not reply, instead he took out a cigar case from his inside pocket and offered one to his companion.

As Spencer prepared the end he said: "Fortunately the law of the jungle does not always apply. You remember old Ken Trafford who had the Blantyre? Well I bumped into him last leave. He'd been sunk by a sub in the Caribbean. The skipper surfaced and offered medical help for the wounded, and there were several, and made sure they had the course to the nearest land. No James, war is a crazy thing with neither rhyme nor reason. As the bible says `there will always be wars and rumour of wars'."

While their captain took his after dinner brandy at the yacht club the two cabin-boys hesitated at the half height double swing doors of the `Bristol Bar'. Wentle had been ashore for the afternoon and had met London in the Plaza Inglese. The latter had, in order to keep in with his immediate boss, agreed to swap duties with the officer's steward and could not get ashore until after serving tea. Wentle, on the other hand, was about to go from the sublime to the ridiculous.

He had taken afternoon tea at Harrods amongst well dressed women and a few older men; presumably the younger ones were hard at work making the money for their ladies to spend. He had felt he wanted to shed his present menial status and return, however briefly, to the sort of life he had been more used to. Anyway the large cream puffs in the window had looked as if they were filled with fresh cream!

After the youths met up the two had devoured giant sized Spanish omelettes washed down with beer. Wentle was not sure that he really liked the beer in a bar off the Passe Corrientes. From there they had walked a while until they came to the `Bristol'.

"You know Dick, I've been told that there's hardly a major port in the world that doesn't have a bar called the Bristol."

"Well," replied Wentle peering into the smoke laden atmosphere. "Bristol was a port before London. The Romans started it all at Seamills."

"Maybe, but the Romans didn't start what goes on in these places. You sure you want to go in here, Dick?"

"Certainly. According to Akker this is probably our last night ashore and anyway it's my birthday. Can't come to a place like B.A. and not see a dance hall or two, particularly after what the other chaps in the cabin say about them. Must see for myself, God help me!" he finished in a more strident tone.

"O.K. then, but as Akker would say, `don't blame me if you catch a dose'!"

"Good Lord, of course not, I .... I just want to have a look that's all!"

The youths passed through the doors and once inside, hesitated a moment before Harry lead the way to a vacant table not too far from the doors. The place was not unlike the `El Diablo' nearer to the docks but differed in that it was considerably cleaner and the grill over the bar was festooned with variously shaped and coloured bottles. This caught Wentle's eye and London explained its use.

"Do they have fights here very often then?" Looking round at the other men in the place there seemed to be quite a few well on in their cups.

"Well, I don't know how often but you heard what happened to the two greasers from our ship, so that's why we're sitting near the door. If trouble does start we quietly nick off."

A waiter threaded his way to their table and two women, one of them old enough to be their mother, sidled up.

"You buy us coffee, Johnny?" she asked.

"No, not now," London replied and then ordered two beers from the waiter. The women pouted and moved sulkily away. "We'd best stick to beer, Dick it's safer."

At that moment the now seventeen year old saloon-boy caught sight of Perkins the captain's tiger. He was in a corner seat a couple of tables from them and was hunched up over the table. A hostess sat tight against him with one arm under the table and her hand, Wentle could just see, was moving rapidly up and down in the tiger's lap.

"Bloody Hell, Harry! There's the tiger and she's giving him a wank! 'Struth he's coming his lot all over the floor!" Flabbergasted Wentle could only stare as the tiger, somewhat glassy eyed, pulled out a handkerchief and wiped his prick.

"You wanted to come in here, Dick! Look at it this way. It's a lot cheaper having a rub-off than going to bed with the woman and there's not much chance of catching a dose either. Definitely a lot safer!"

"Oh!" was the only reply Wentle could muster.

"Christ, Dick, don't tell me you've never had a wank?"

"Well of course I have, but not in public like this. Occasionally in the school bog that's all."

At that moment a voice hailed them from the doorway. It was Jones the senior apprentice. Like the two at the table he was dressed in civilian clothes but his looked as if he had been rolling in the gutter.

"What cheer, my merry ship mates, having yourselves a good time eh? Going to get some of that dirty water off your chest then?" His speech was slurred and Wentle realised that the apprentice must have already had quite a bit to drink.

Again Wentle could only raise a feeble "Oh!"

Here was a situation about which he was not at all sure. Aboard, the apprentices did not have much to do with the other boys on the ship, for other than the officer's mess-boy, none of them normally went on the bridge. To Wentle he was a junior officer. London, however, was a little wiser and he knew that there was nothing `stuck up' about Jones. In fact, when other officers were not present mess-boy and apprentice often indulged in light hearted banter for they came from similar backgrounds.

"No, not enough cash left for that. Just came in for a last drink. I hear we're shifting berth tomorrow morning so that'll be the end of shore going for Dick here."

Jones had, until then, had a semi-serious look on his boyish features, but now he grinned broadly and chanted the opening line of a current ribald song. "Dead-eyed Dick and his mighty prick went down to the Rio Grandee!" and after a guffaw, "You dipped yours here yet, Dick? Anyway, that's utter balls, London. Not enough cash? You stewards make a dam sight more than I do with all your tips an' what not. Don't try and fool me! Hell it's hot in here." The apprentice wiped his forehead with the back of a hand.

"You blokes got no women? To hell with that! Must have a woman! Hey, senorita, come 'ere." Jones gestured to some hostesses sat on their own looking bored.

Seeing him wave three detached themselves from the group and, wearing false smiles, came across to the table. Without being asked two sat down on vacant chairs. Jones grabbed the third with one hand and pinched her bottom with the other, making her squeal

"Gotta make sure there's plenty to catch hold of when you're on top." He laughed as he swung her onto his lap, sliding a hand up her skirt. "Jesus! that feels damn good." Then, seeing the other two making no move to follow his example. "Oh come on you two, don't sit there doing nothing. Anyone would think you didn't know what it was for! Hell you behave like a couple of greenhorns!"

"That's just what he is! A bloody greenhorn what's never had it in yet!" interjected Perkins now recovered from his orgasm and well able to hear Jones' loud voice.

"What of it Perkins? You were a first tripper once!" Harry London had no time for the tiger even if he had astonished one and all on the bridge by the exemplary way he was looking after the captain.

"You fucking shut up, London. Just 'cause you've been torpedoed a couple of times don't make you a know all!"

Jones, bent on having a good time, and at that moment particularly enjoying the sensations at his finger tips and caring little about differences of opinion between a steward and the boys, said: "A first tripper eh? That explains it! Wentle, you need educating and that's what you'll get, starting from right now. Mozo! Trez whiskey y pronto!" he almost trilled the order to a waiter, his Spanish spoken with a decidedly Welsh accent. "And you, Dick, can pay for them as part of your school fees! Hey-ho and a life on the ocean wave!" He kissed the girl hard on the lips as Wentle looked enquringly at London.

"You wanted to have a look mate!" said the diminutive mess-boy with a grin, removing a female hand from his crotch.

"Yes but..."

"That's what comes of arse 'ole creeping with officers," Perkins broke in, but Wentle refused to be drawn; he was far too worried about what three whiskies would cost in a place like this and what it would taste like. He wondered, also, what other things would be like... as Jones had said, he needed educating.

CHAPTER 14

"Hey Dick, for God's sake get out'a your pit! Akker 'll do his nut if you're adrift today of all days. And you can't blame the night watchman, he called us at six as usual." The officer's mess-boy stripped the bedding from his friend's recumbent form and shook him violently.

"Oh God, Harry I feel lousy," Wentle replied as he swung down from his bunk.

"Akker won't give a bugger about that and anyway you didn't have that much to drink last night. I'm off up topsides before I get in the rattle as well!"

Sleeping, as all the others did when in port, in vest and underpants it took Wentle only a moment to pull on his work trousers, grab a towel from his locker and fly to the bathroom, where he found Porky Bates and the others taking their time over a morning wash.

"Here comes Sleeping Beauty. You dip y'r wick last night then Toff?" asked Ginger with mock seriousness.

"Don't be bloody daft, Ginge. He wouldn't know 'ow. He'd need 'is ma to hold it for 'im!" guffawed Bert Hitchcock in his heavy Liverpool accent.

Wentle ignored them, doused his face with cold water and ran back to the peak, chucked the towel in his locker and snatched up his patrol jacket, not bothering to put it on as the morning seemed quite warm. Making his way around the open number one hatch and up the stairs he came out by number two and noted that since he had gone ashore yesterday it had been closed and the tarpaulins put back on.

Struth! I didn't notice that when we came back last night. Hell I wasn't really drunk was I? he mused as he went into the saloon and gathered up his gear for scrubbing down his portion of the office flat. He found Lewis and the other assistant-stewards already started. Dropping to his knees he slopped water on the deck planks, dipped the brush in the bucket, ran the soap over it and, using two hands, started scrubbing for all he was worth. Fortunately there was no sign of Mr. Akker.

The office flat completed Wentle went down the stairs to the saloon and started scrubbing under his table. He was about to dry the last square yard when he noticed out the corner of his eye a pair of shiny black shoes over which hung dark blue trousers with knife edge creases. The shoes, Wentle knew, belonged to Mr. Akker. They were made of very soft leather on the lines of dancing pumps. Akker had once said to Wentle that in this job you should always look after your feet if you didn't want to end up with varicose veins. From the nimbleness of Akker's large frame when serving drinks Wentle was sure that those shoes must play an important part.

"Finish what you're doing, then I want a word while you're laying up for breakfast," boomed the stentorian voice of the shoes' owner.

"Yes sir!" Wentle replied sensing words of some import were to follow. He wrung out his cloth, got up and emptied the dirty water into the slops sink in the pantry and returned the scrubbing gear to the locker under the stairs. After wiping his hands on the sides of his trousers he shook out a clean white table cloth and commenced laying the table.

"Mr.Boyd and I, Wentle, have once again discussed your future. This afternoon we shall be taking our passengers aboard and although there will not be enough to have all the dining tables occupied and therefore there will be four stewards spare, it has been decided that you will remain serving the captain's table. The chief officer will continue to preside in the captain's place while at sea but the other senior ship's officers will revert to their own tables. Do you understand?"

"Er, yes Sir. Does that mean I'll still have `Old Blimp'?"

"Yes it does mean you will still have the Colonel and his aide." Despite the implied rebuke Akker grinned slightly. "Don't you let me down Wentle. God help me!"

"No Mr.Akker I'll try not to."

Breakfast over, the Patriarch was moved without incident to the passenger berth. An air of expectancy settled over her deck and catering crew. The men on gangway watch, including the assistant purser with his passenger list and several stewards ready to carry baggage, were all conspicuous by their clean, freshly pressed, uniforms. The quartermasters wore white polo necked sweaters and the seamen in dark blue, the ship's name emblazoned across their chests in red.

There was no need to hide the ship's identity in this port for the German Embassy already knew all about them, even to their time of sailing. The Patriarch even had the `Blue Peter', denoting she was under sailing orders, flying from the yard arm.

The usual peacetime atmosphere as the passengers boarded was absent, spoiled by the dull grey paint and lack of dressing the ship over-all with flags.

Wentle was ordered to lay two of the middle tables for afternoon tea, for some of the passengers would no doubt wish to partake of refreshments after they had been shown to their cabins. During the afternoon the passengers started to arrive. Some in large opulent cars, others in less conspicuous ones or an occasional taxi. Some had friends come aboard to see where they would be spending their time on the voyage.

In the cabins to be occupied by ladies, small bunches of carnations had been placed in the vases secured to the bulkhead. Small posies were delivered to the saloon for the eight tables which would be occupied from breakfast the next day. They would not last more than a couple of days but it was the `custom', the bright colours helping to dull the pangs of parting. In fact, thought Wentle after he had set them on the tables in specially weighted short vases, the saloon really did look quite pleasant with the lacquered mahogany panels and shining brass work of the windows and, under foot, the scrubbed deck boards. The weather was still being kind to them and rays of the afternoon sun slanted their way in through the port windows, adding warmth to the place.

Up for'ard the lower 'tween-deck of number one hold was packed full with knocked down trooping bunks. In the upper 'tween-deck, the bosun and fourth officer checked in those passengers' cases and trunks which were too big for the cabins. They were swung over the ship's side and lowered into the hold by a crane, which made a racket that prevented those of the crew who were off watch from sleeping. Waiting seamen positioned the articles in alphabetical order of their owners' name and then secured them under cargo nets, but in a way that they were easily accessible should they be required during the voyage.

By tea time all items designated for the hold had been stowed, according to the paper work and number one hatch closed and made ready for sea. The bosun was the last up the steps and out through the door leading into the catering accommodation. Placing a heavy padlock through the eye of the hasp and staple he snapped it shut and gave the key to young Strickland for onward transfer, together with the check list, to the purser.

Seamen were stretching the last canvas cover across the hatch when there was a shout from the promenade deck that there was one more large trunk to be stowed. The crane driver had already knocked off and the bosun was damned if he was going to re-open the hatch for anybody! Cursing the silly bugger who had not read his boarding instructions properly, which clearly stated that all heavy baggage should be alongside by sixteen hundred hours, four seamen had to man-handle the offending item along the decks and down the narrow stairs to the hold. The owner, when he realised the trouble he was causing, at least had the decency to pass a few pesos to the disgruntled men.

The bosun double checked around the hatch-coaming that all the toms were hammered properly home and then made his way to the chief officer's small office in the bridge accommodation. He now reported, as he had done on so many voyages before, that one more job had been finished. All hatches were safely secured and the decks of the Patriarch ready for sea. In the morning, once under way, the two men directly responsible for the vessel's hull and decks would make one more round just to make sure.

Earlier in the day the carpenter and second mate had checked that all water tanks had been properly topped up and tasted for any contamination. Down below the chief engineer and his right hand man had been through their department and made sure all was ready for the long journey home. Yesterday the bunker barge had pumped in fuel oil until it was impossible for the Patriarch to carry any more.

Of all the engine room staff the three refrigeration specialists had become lynch-pins. Since the day before loading had commenced they had been hard at work checking the re-installation of the holds' refrigeration pipes. With those holds now firmly battened down they adjusted a valve here and increased pressure there, scrutinising every little movement of the quivering temperature repeaters. Even if the chief kept the propellers turning, and assuming those on the bridge did not get the ship lost, it would have been a fruitless journey if, when the holds were opened, the meat was found to be full of maggots! Those three men were of vital importance to thousands of people who would be queueing for their meat ration; no doubt without a single thought as to where it came from or how it reached them.

Since the demolition of the DEMS gunner's mess, Brightman, in his small cabin adjacent to the hospital, lived farther aft than anyone else. He had scrubbed and re-scrubbed the hospital until the odour of death had been replaced by that of carbolic disinfectant. He was odd man out by the standards of the rest of the crew. He took his meals in the engineers' mess and, apart from surgery time, had little to do except read, which he enjoyed doing. He had, with the doctor, received and entered into the hospital register the replacement drugs and bandages and now awaited whatever the future would bring. Certain it was that there would be at least a couple of cases of the `pox' to be dealt with in about ten days time, or perhaps sooner.

Up on the monkey island Mr.Moore had checked that the emergency wireless batteries were fully charged and last night Malcom McTavish had started the gyro-compass so that it would have plenty of time to settle down. Charts for the trip down the Canal Punt Indio and thence to the last pilot station were on the chart table. In the ready use drawer the Atlantic charts lay waiting to be brought forward and the courses northwards marked in. Those courses would be given to the captain at the very last moment by the NCSO and not passed to the Patriarch's navigating officer until the last pilot had left them. It was not that the navigator could not be trusted but rather a case of the least number of people who knew the better the security.

As the passengers came aboard it was the purser and his assistant who were making up for their dearth of work on the previous passages as far as Buenos Aries. They now had their hands full making sure that the right people went to the right cabins. Last trip a young lady with a male sounding Christian name, whose father had obviously wanted a boy when she was born, ended up in a cabin with an eligible bachelor. Of course the error had been corrected but rumour had it that it might as well have been left as it was! Slowly the paper work was sorted out and the final ship's manifest signed and the copy given to the agent.

Up in his office Boulton signed the mate's copies of the bills of lading for the cargo and also passed the appropriate ones back to the agent.

The chief steward in his diminutive office within the sound of Wentle laying up the tables for tea, shared a late after-lunch coffee and suitable `chaser' with the second. The large store rooms, both cold and otherwise, were full to the brim and the last delivery of fresh produce, milk, had just come aboard; not that it would last more than three or four days.

From the passenger list `Secundus' had made out his table seating plan, a large copy of which now stood at the bottom of the stairs on a stand made for the purpose. Of course there would be any number of alterations as friends or relatives wished to sit together but one had to start somewhere!

Yesterday the chief steward and chef had decided on this evening's cold buffet menu, which would be served in the lounge for the benefit of the passengers with friends or family who would be seeing them off.

At seventeen hundred hours both catering officers would be in the lounge ensuring the tables were properly set and the food passed up, a slow business because the lift at the back of the galley had been made too small. The chef and his assistants must be able to display their culinary arts in the best possible way. The bar was fully stocked and Akker and his wine stewards looked forward to a profitable evening!

Slowly the Patriarch was once more exchanging the lethargy of being tied to the shore for her sea going spirit. Whilst the heads of departments ensured that everything went according to plan her captain told his tiger that he would take `forty winks' and to call him at three o'clock.

Later, when he had finished his afternoon tea, with freshly made cinnamon doughnuts sent up by the chief baker, shared with his chief officer, Spencer spent several minutes on the bridge wing watching the passengers come aboard before he wandered down to the purser's office.

How different it was from a real peace time sailing; the hustle and bustle were there but the chatter and laughter did not have the usual air of gaiety. The purser advised him that there were only thirty five men, three women and a young family which included two children, one of three and the other seven years old. With the exception of the mother and her children all were going home to `do their bit'. The wife with the two kiddies had apparently decided to endure the bombing so that when her husband came home on leave he would be able to see his children. `Very laudable,' Spencer had remarked but he would have preferred it if they'd not decided to travel on his ship.

"There's one gentleman whose reasons for returning to the `Old Country' are not known;

however his presence on the passenger list is of importance, even though it is no doubt regrettable and he is none other," said Tom Good with a flourish and mock bow "than Mr.Broughton!"

This gentleman was on the company's board of directors and had traveled to the Argentine on the Patriarch's last year. It seemed that he had now decided to return with them.

Spencer grimaced. "Oh Lord. Thank goodness I shan't have to sit at table with him. I pity Charles!" On the trip last year the man had been an absolute pest. It was rumoured that he was only on the board of directors because he had been left a large number of the company's shares which he seemed to believe entitled him to tell all aboard how they should run their ship!

Tom Good also mentioned that because they were thought to have been sunk the Brisbane Star, which sailed the day before the Patriarch's arrival, had taken most of their passengers, a detail that Spencer already knew.

A short passenger list was to Spencer's liking. Whilst he was sorry for the company's loss in revenue he was only too aware of the dangers the Patriarch faced on her homeward journey. Her two sister ships had already gone to the bottom.

Jones arrived to inform him that the NCSO was waiting in the captain's day cabin. Despite the onset of acne and the ravages of the previous night ashore, he looked very spick and span in his best shore going uniform with three buttons on each sleeve and thin gold tabs on the lapels denoting his rank.

Wentle was having a cuppa and a cake when Akker came to give him more orders. "You will not bother to lay up for dinner as all your officers will be attending the cocktail party this evening. I shall require you at half past six in the lounge. You will be immaculate in your turn out. Your job will be to clear empty plates and send them down in the lift, nothing else. You will not converse with the passengers and if you're asked a question by one you will refer them to your superiors. Do you understand Wentle?"

"Yes, Mr.Akker." Wentle was now used to his boss's intimidating manner of speech.

"Good. You will be privileged to witness an almost peacetime farewell party in the best traditions of this company. Don't let me down. God help me!" He turned away, missing the lad's smile at Akker's pompous oration.

Wentle wished he'd been a passenger when he reported to the lounge at half past six. The amount and variety of food spread out on the tables was worthy of a special function buffet at the Savoy Hotel in the Strand - had he seen one and been able to make a comparison. Here and there small vases of flowers added colour to the artistic arrangements on the plates. He had seen the galley staff putting up the plates during the afternoon but now that it was all spread out it looked sumptuous and even surpassed fond memories of the birthday party teas his grandmother used to provide. As a small boy the full sized billiard table, fitted with special plywood covers for such an occasion, had looked huge, with his favourite sweet of chocolate blancmange surrounded by whipped cream as the centrepiece. Looking at the spread before him with saliva forming around his taste buds, he hoped that some would be left over.

`Hells Bells, what a feed,' he muttered as Akker showed him where to stand by the lift hatch. The chef, chief baker and butcher appeared in spotless white with stiffly starched hats; the chef's being just a little taller than the others to show his status. Taking up their positions behind the tables, the butcher ceremoniously applied his carving knife to the steel as he prepared to carve the baron of beef and a large ham. At the top of the stairs stood old Gobbledyguts and Mr.Boyd. Their heavy zigzag stripes of gold braid catching the light when they moved their arms.

Wentle noted the doctor and purser by the door to the starboard boat deck, the one he had dodged out of to catch a glimpse of the Jap sub some five weeks ago. Could that have really occurred? Did Lewis really sing `There'll always be an England' as the shell which had killed the gunners exploded? It just didn't seem possible and the present scene like something out of a dream. Yet there was Lewis quietly standing with three other stewards whilst Mr.Akker gave them some instruction or other.

Wentle shook his head as if to shake himself awake from the dream.

"You all right boy?" The chef had seen the head shake.

"Yes Sir, Mr.Mathews. I was just thinking back."

"Yes boy, I understand." For the first time that Wentle could remember he actually saw the chef smile. A paternal encouraging smile such as his father might have given him.

The passengers started to enter the lounge and as they did so Mr.Boyd directed them to a table upon which stood a large bowl of punch, provided by the company and, so said the regulations, there should be enough for at least two glasses each before passengers would have to start buying their own drinks.

The chief and second engineers appeared, the purple between their gold braid marking them as different from the scarlet of the doctor or white of the purser. It would not take long for those passengers who did not already understand the ranking of the merchant service, to learn who was who on the Patriarch.

The party lacked some of the glamour of the yacht club where long dresses and black ties had been the order of the day, but it was designated a `cocktail' party and therefore slacks and blazers were in order, especially for a ship in wartime.

When the captain and his chief officer arrived fifteen minutes later the passengers were mostly engaged in animated conversation, interrupted only as they started to tackle the buffet. James Harley, the marine superintendent, and the office manager, John Beverley, had of course been invited and since they knew some of those going back to the U.K, helped to keep things going and suppress the pangs of having to say good bye to family and friends.

When the first course was finished and the sweets began to look depleted Spencer caught Akker's eye as he weaved his way back to the bar.

"Sir?" he queried balancing the silver tray of empty glasses above his shoulder on the palm of his hand. Even the captain was impressed by the man's nimbleness.

"Do you think you could call for a little `hush' please?"

Akker's face broke into a broad grin. "Of course Captain." He took a deep breath. "Ladies and Gentlemen, may I have your attention please!" There were times, other than for balling out his subordinates, when `Bull Horn' Akker's vocal powers came in useful. "Quiet for the Captain please."

Slowly the babble died. "Good evening, Ladies and Gentlemen. Welcome to the Motor Vessel Patriarch. My name is Spencer, although I am also known by some as `The Padre'. Unfortunately, due to the pressures of a wartime captain's duties, I shall be unable to bore you with my Sunday sermons." A ripple of laughter went through the assembly. "Once we sail I shall not leave the bridge, but I know that Mr.Good, my purser whom most of you have already met, will look after you very competently. I must add that I have never known anyone complain, and indeed the buffet we are having this evening proves the point, of the service given by Mr.Brown our chief steward." The captain turned to indicate the egg shaped man in question, "and all the men in his department. I assure you that there is never a need for anyone to go hungry!" He paused as some clapped and others called out `here, here'. "Thank you and I hope you all enjoy the voyage. Now if you would see your glasses are charged I would give you a toast." He paused again as one or two people sought the punch bowl. Then raising his glass, and it would be his last drink until they were in sight of their destination. "I give you the Patriarch and all who sail in her. May God Bless us one and all!" As glasses were tipped he caught sight of Broughton pushing through the crowd towards him.

Fortunately Charles Boulton was nearby and Spencer took a step towards him and whispered. "I'll need rescuing in a couple of minutes, Charles."

"Captain. A word if I may!" Broughton called imperiously.

*   *   *

Friday the thirteenth dawned with overcast skies and light drizzle; far different from the beautiful spring morning when the Patriarch had hove up her anchor and left Belfast Lough. At 0600 hours she started to single up her lines. Once again Charles Boulton was on the bridge and the `fourth' up for'ard. Despite his doubts about the man's reliability he'd decided that the `fourth' could not do much harm since, apart from taking on the tug's tow rope, all there was to do was to retrieve the shore lines. Anyway, master and mate were sure that the assistant bosun would soon put young Strickland right if there was any danger of a `cock-up'.

By 0630 hours the ship was clear of the wharf and the tugs swung her bows in the right direction. "Slow ahead both," and as the Patriarch once again came alive. "Let go the tugs."

Neither the hour or the weather was conducive to seeing people off and from the shore came the sound of only three or four car horns. In reply the grey ship sounded her deep throated siren in a long blast which echoed around the wharfs and beneath the low clouds. In the shelter of the promenade deck a number of the passengers waved a farewell to the people and the shore they might never see again.

As he had been ordered Wentle picked up the five barred xylophone and went up the stairs and into the port side accommodation passage. Stopping for a moment he studied his watch until the minute hand came clear into the opening of the silver guard exactly above the nine. He raised the small stick with its over large head and smote the first bar of the instrument. Walking down the passage he started to play what he fondly believed was a rendering of `Come to the cook house door'.

At his preparatory school the very young Wentle had, during music lessons, occasionally been required to bang a small steel rod against a triangle suspended from his left hand. The precise moment at which that should have happened did not always coincide with the requirements of the tune being played. So much so that, in exasperation, the Maestro in charge gave him a snare drum to play, and since there were several of these noisy instruments his errors were not so apparent. Anyway, he considered playing the triangle to be very much a job for a sissy! If he had felt a sissy then, he now felt an utter twit.

"Tradition, Wentle, tradition. The company does not want us to lose all sense of the way it's passenger ships are run just because there's a war!"

A week before they had sailed Akker had suddenly remembered he had not told the saloon-boy about his roll in summoning passengers to meals. When Wentle had protested that he didn't know how to play a xylophone, no matter how small, the saloon steward had said that he would just have to learn and that he would be the first saloon-boy who had failed in this particular duty if he did not!

"What tunes do I play Sir?"

"Tunes? Any bloody thing!" Akker replied angrily. "Christ, Wentle you make life unbearable at times. The one that goes with, `They found his bollocks on a rusty nail', is a catchy one but don't sing the words! God help me!"

Wentle had decided that if the object of the game was to summon people then he had, when attending a cadet junior N.C.O.s' course at the Dawlish army camp, got to know the various bugle calls which dominated life there. He hummed to himself the `Reveille, Cook house and Fall in' and tried each on the xylophone. He practised each day so that when he came to play the first tune in earnest the passengers may not have immediately recognised it but it did have some sort of melody.

At the end of the passageway a cabin door opened and a young woman asked what all the noise was for? Wentle blushed and said that breakfast was about to be served.

"Oh. Thank you." She smiled at him making him feel not quite such a twit after all. `By the end of the three week trip they would get to know what the noise was for. God help me!' he muttered to himself.

The chief engineer, purser and doctor came down for breakfast more or less on time and took up positions at the head of their respective tables. Amongst the passengers, as expected, there was some confusion as they studied the seating plan with a few asking there and then if they could sit with this or that person. Smiling profusely the second steward did his best to placate one and all.

One by one the three passengers allocated to the captain's table came over from the stairway and Wentle bade them good morning. The first to arrive was the young woman who had accosted him by her cabin. She was about the age of his sister he thought. Again she smiled at him and asked where she should sit. The colonel and his aide had already seated themselves on the settle in the space vacated by the purser and doctor and they half rose, as manners dictated, from behind the table.

Wentle had given no thought as to where the passengers were going to sit. "Er, perhaps you might like the end of the settle Miss. It might be a little more comfortable than a chair." He also had no idea how he should address the lady. At that moment an authoritative voice behind him pronounced.

"No, that's my place. I always sit facing the captain's chair." Almost as an afterthought it added "If you don't mind young lady." Mr. Broughton slid into the seat in question. He was slightly built, with a hollow face accentuated by high cheek bones and a balding pate. Wentle was reminded of an unpopular housemaster who went by the name of `Pea Nut'.

"Oh. In that case, Miss perhaps you would like to sit next to the chief officer. He takes the captain's place at lunch times and occasionally breakfast but is on watch in the evenings." He pulled out the chair next to the chief officer's seat, then passed a menu to the young lady and a second to the colonel, deliberately ignoring the objectionable 'Pea Nut'.

"Steward, a menu for me please and look lively!"

"Sir, there are only two per table and the colonel was here before you." Wentle had never heard the term `dumb insolence'. Had he done so he would undoubtedly have couched his words differently.

At that moment the saloon steward arrived with another gentleman for the captain's table.

"Ah. It's Akker, if I remember rightly. See that there are three menus on this table in future."

"As you wish Mr.Broughton." The saloon steward replied subserviently but under his breath added `You obnoxious bastard!' deciding that, as there were no drinks to serve, he had better keep a close eye on Wentle.

As the Patriarch sailed on towards the open sea the drizzle diminished. When `boat stations' were sounded and passengers advised what to do over the tannoy, the boat deck smelt fresh and clean as they mustered. Despite the instructions on the back of the cabin doors there were some who still did not understand where they had to go.

It was half past ten and the passengers started to mill around the boat deck, having had enough time to digest their breakfast and get to know each other a little. The crew had finished swinging out the boats with the last of the gripes secured, preventing the boats swinging from their davit heads.

The mate had divided the forty odd extra people now aboard amongst eight lifeboats so that there would be no crowding should the unthinkable happen. At each muster point an officer lectured the passengers on the utmost importance of the ship being totally blacked out and that under no circumstances was smoking on deck allowed after the sun went down. Infringement of this order could mean the difference between life and death for all of them!

They must learn by heart the quickest way from cabin to the boat deck and at all times carry life belts with them. The officers apologised for belabouring the various points but everything they had said really must be fully understood. Whilst still in sheltered waters there would be another boat drill after luncheon. And, as the troops before them had been told, the boat drill would continue daily for the time being.

The lectures at boat stations had, for most, a sobering effect. For many it brought home the fact that the war would start immediately after the pilot had been dropped that evening and not wait until they joined whichever service they had volunteered for.

Most of them were paying their own fares. One or two had been able to `sign up' at the embassy because of special qualifications such as the aircraft owner who had twin engine and instrument flying experience. Another gentleman at Wentle's table had resigned his commission from the Hussars after a rather stupid prank had misfired in the mess. They were on board 'all found'.

If there was some gloom and despondency because of the lectures it was not apparent over the luncheon table where conversation once more flowed with vigour and Akker and his `side-kick' were kept busy with drink orders.

Serving lunch was not an auspicious occasion for Wentle who fell foul of Mr.Broughton again. There were now three menus. Akker had an extra one printed after a word with Mr.Boyd and he had warned Wentle that the company director was a tartar, so the youth had made sure the table was laid with absolute precision and the table cloth and napkins were all in pristine condition. It was the impetuosity of youth which landed him in trouble this time.

The conversation between the chief officer, Hussar officer and the young lady, who laughed easily, was light hearted and seemed to give the table an air of jollity.

Wentle had noticed that the badge on the blazer worn by Mr.Broughton was that of his last school. Although he realised that the man must have been a pupil there before Wentle was even born, he could not resist the temptation to remark: "It seems Sir, that we went to the same school." as he removed the finished avocado pear from in front of Broughton.

The remark had been made because the boy had been genuinely pleased, as well as surprised, to see his old school badge. He had forgotten, however, that it was unusual for a public school boy to be found serving at table.

"Tripe boy you couldn't possibly have gone to the same school as I did!" was the cutting reply in a tone which caught the chief officer's ear.

At the rebuke Wentle's face coloured and then Boulton, sensing possible trouble, interjected with a request for more water. `Why, oh why,' thought Wentle `did I ever decide to come to sea this way. I must be stark staring mad. God help me!'?

And so the voyage home began. As the sun disappeared below the western horizon and the burnished copper of the muddy waters gave way to a dull brown, the Patriarch dropped her sea pilot and went her lonely way. The captain and navigating officer plotted the courses given them by the NCSO, while the bosun and his men went around the decks ensuring that the blackout was complete. The all important sea routine once again establishing how they would all spend the next three weeks.

CHAPTER 15

The Patriarch had been at sea for just over six days during which time the south east trade winds had been kind to her. She had sailed over placid blue waters with only the slightest trace of pitching. Her bow wave tumbled outward in an unceasing sparkling cascade. To keep it tumbling her crew once again worked around the clock, whilst the passengers lazed away their time reading, playing deck tennis or taking a dip in the small canvas swimming pool which the carpenter had erected on the well deck by number three hatch. Their only interruption to these pursuits being the morning boat stations.

The four stewards who were not serving in the dining room, waited on the passengers' every whim. Save for the irritating necessity to carry their life belts everywhere they went, the war seemed non-existent; even some of the crew became lulled into a false sense of security. It was only the radio officers, sitting hunched over their sets in the shack abaft the chartroom, who heard the cries for help as the U-boats went about their deadly harvest. There seemed to be no stopping the horrendous losses allied shipping was suffering. Men who had spent their lives at sea and knew that it took a couple of years to build an average sized ship in peacetime could not see how the shipyards could possibly keep pace with it. Most of them had not yet seen the mass-produced all welded

'Liberty' ships which had begun to roll out of the vast American shipyards; only heard rumours that they were floating coffins.

To those who had seen half a convoy wiped out in a matter of days there appeared but one logical conclusion. Sooner or later their turn was bound to come and they would not be around to see the defeat of the allies, caused by the strangulation of Britain's life line across the seas. Yet, if they reasoned thus they said the opposite.

An occasional passenger might ask what would happen if.... to be told that the Patriarch was a lucky ship and that she would carry them all home to 'Blighty'. So she sailed on towards that far land with her passengers in ignorance of the sinkings heard by the men on the radio. But on that sixth day all aboard were brought back to the reality of war.

Why the mast-head or for'ard look-outs had not seen it no one could say, although certainly it was difficult to see. It was the first day that the trade winds blew enough to cause an occasional white horse to disturb the blue surface of the sea. Just when it was not wanted the faded grey paint of the boat made a fair camouflage in such conditions.

"Lifeboat on the port beam!"

It was one of the remaining DEMS gunners on the after port side of the boat deck who made the dramatic cry. For the umpteenth time he had swept his arc of surveillance from the beam to aft and back again. Then he would rest for a moment before repeating it again and again until the eyes grew weary and began to smart and, if one was not careful, the eye pieces of the heavy binoculars would leave bruises on the cheek bones.

The gunner lowered the glasses, wiped his eyes with the back of his hand and looked again. Was he imagining things? He handed the glasses to a nearby passenger.

"'Scuse me Sur, but can 'ee see a boat out there?" and he indicated the bearing with a wave of a hand.

Unfortunately the passenger happened to be Broughton, unable to pass up any opportunity to denigrate. He took the binoculars and raised them to his eyes saying to anyone in earshot.

"Trouble with you people these days is most of you don't know how to look properly! A boat you say? If it's there I'll find it mark my words. Hm, lousy focussing on these things, can't see..." his voice trailed off as he studied the far off sea and then exclaimed "Yes by God! Told you I'd see it if it were there, deuced small though."

McTavish, two hours into the afternoon watch, heard the cry and the confirmation from the bridge look-out that there was a boat. "Port fifteen, Quartermaster. Bentley call the captain!"

Ponderously the Patriarch came around towards the lifeboat. The second officer was concerned that if he turned the vessel too fast they might lose sight of so small a craft.

"Ease to ten port."

"Ease to ten port Sir.....Ten of port wheel on Sir."

The captain had already swung his feet off the bunk in the pilot's cabin before Bentley called him. The change in the ship's motion was more than it would have been for an ordinary zig or zag alteration and that change was enough to tell him that something unusual was happening. He arrived in the wheel-house to hear the order: "Half ahead both." Sensing the captain had arrived and without taking his glasses off the lifeboat, McTavish said.

"Lifeboat, Sir. I took the liberty of changing course without waiting for you, Sir. I was worried we might lose her if we carried on even for a moment."

"Quite right, Second." He raised his glasses in the direction the second officer indicated. "Yes, I see it. Right, I have the con. You see to the usual drill; cargo net port side number three hatch please...Wheel amidships....meet her." With Spencer's years of experience orders flowed automatically as he calculated or pondered on the required manoeuvres.

"Mr.Bentley, please tell Sparks to use the tannoy and pipe `all departments stand by to receive survivors.'" Spencer's standing orders were clear and well understood. Blankets from the linen locker, stretchers ready to take those unable to walk to the hospital or free cabins. The doctor and Brightman ready to give immediate attention to any who needed it. The bosun and his party rigging the cargo net for those who might be able climb it and, an innovation of the bosun's, a peculiar `sling' for those who needed to be hoisted aboard. Seamen standing by ready to throw heaving lines for those in the lifeboat to secure and draw it alongside.

Down in the engine-room the chief and his men would know that engine manoeuvres were likely and that the compressed air bottles would be needed. Even the saloon-boy had a job to do, making sure that the water in the urn was boiling for cups of tea.

While preparation for taking on survivors went on the Patriarch approached the 'boat at 'dead slow' until it was clear to the naked eye. The little boat was bobbing up and down in the small waves. Passengers and crew alike watched in silence. Clearly from the bridge came the captain's voice: "Quartermaster. You see that boat out there? I want this ship to pass her ten yards on our port side. No more, no less!"

"Aye, aye Sir," came the laconic reply.

"Stop both!"

"Stop both," replied Apprentice Bentley by the engine telegraph. From below came the answering tinkle of the telegraph bells. As the Patriarch's forward momentum slowed the quartermaster, Powell whose brother was on the Nelson, sucked his teeth. This was the first time he'd had to steer the ship by eye on a single object. It was one thing to follow the orders of the officer of the watch or steer on leading marks but quite another to have to judge the distance himself. If he came too close he could swamp the small boat or, worse still, he might hit it and cut it in two. If he was too far away they would have to come around for a second try or even have to stop and launch one of their own boats. He shuddered involuntarily as he shifted the wheel two spokes to bring her head round a fraction.

"Sound the whistle!" Spencer's order had been heard by those on the for'ard end of the boat deck but still they jumped when the siren, high on the for'ard funnel, shattered the silence.

As the deep throated roar of the siren rolled across the water there was no sign of movement in the boat and nothing showed above its gun'le. One cable's length to go, half a cable and then only fifty yards. Now the Patriarch glided past at two knots and the heaving lines snaked out and landed fair and square in the boat. From up on the boat deck it looked so terribly small to be all alone out there in the middle of the ocean. Powell had done his job well and the bow wave, such that it was, lifted the boat so that the watchers from above could see into it quite plainly.

As if from one throat, a groan went up from those on the ship's decks ... the boat was empty, save for a broken oar and a lone orange life-belt.

"Starboard twenty. Full ahead both!" The captain's voice rang out from the bridge wing.

"Starboard twenty. Full ahead both," came the answering cry from the wheel-house.

The engine telegraphs rang once more and the throb of the engines rose urging the Patriarch to greater speed. Then the men on the well deck were galvanized into action. Each had been nursing his own thoughts as to what might have befallen the men who had been in that boat, when Able Seaman Green broke into their musing.

"My lines caught," he cried as the heaving line began to run out through his hands. Quickly he took a turn around a staghead bollard normally used to secure a derrick's guy rope. The knot at the end of the line, a tight tarred `monkey's fist' put there to give more impetus when thrown, had caught under the gun'le of the boat and now dragged the craft towards the Patriarch's side, hitting it with a thump.

"Let it go, Green," ordered the second officer but the bosun moved like lightening; his knife flashed and the line was cut near the bollard.

"No sense losing it all," he remarked.

Green stood looking at the ugly red weals across the palms of his hands, as if he had grasped a red hot poker. In the fraction of time that the rope had slid through his hands it had almost burnt the flesh from them.

"Better get that seen to by the Quack, Green," said the bosun who, catching the eye of an offended doctor, added hastily. "I mean the doctor."

"I reckon I 'ad at that, Bose." He turned his hands to the medico.

After a cursory glance Hargraves told the seaman to go aft with his assistant who would dress the wounds with aquaflavine.

Back on course again the lookouts swept the horizon with renewed vigilance and passengers, unasked, who had their own binoculars became extra pairs of eyes. All knew that there might be other boats out there or, though most tried not to think of it, there might be the cause of whatever had sent the lifeboat's parent ship to the bottom of the sea.

The boat had passed by too quickly for anyone to be able to read the carved but paint covered name of that ship.

On the passenger decks the chatter had been replaced by subdued voices. Everyone had their life belts near at hand; even those who had brazenly condemned the carrying of them everywhere as a blasted nuisance, surreptitiously sneaked off to their cabins to get them. In the crew more than one had noticed that the life belt in the boat, which now lay bobbing far astern, had looked fresh and clean and not parched and faded as it would have done if it had been exposed to the tropical sun for any length of time. One or two also noticed and thought it peculiar that there were no oars, other than the broken one. None, however, voiced what was uppermost in their thoughts. They went about their duties waiting for what they all hoped would never happen.

*   *   *

Kapitan zur SEE Eric Von Sprieckles braced his legs against the gentle rolling of his ship and trained the powerful telescope on the bearing indicated by the look-out. His own binoculars had not been strong enough to pick up the two pin sized topmasts that were just visible above the horizon off the starboard bow.

In the sky to the east and behind the masts, low clouds of a threatening rain squall gave a darkening back ground so that the mast-head look-out could have been forgiven if he had not seen those tell-tale masts. But he had and now a decision was required from the Norden's captain. He turned to his first lieutenant.

"What do you think, Carl?"

Carl Schmit took the telescope and studied the two, almost microscopic, masts for half a minute before giving his opinion.

"They are some way apart so I would say she could be a fairly large vessel and almost on the same course as us, Herr Kapitan." He moved back and gave the glass to the starboard bridge lookout. "Don't loose them Webber whatever you do!"

"A merchantman, Carl?"

"I would think so. Difficult to say but they do not look heavy enough to be those of a warship."

"Thank you. That is what I think. Steer one point to starboard. Increase to maximum revolutions. Distance Carl? What do you think, thirty kilometres perhaps? If it is an allied merchantman it would be a good end to our commission if we could take her!"

"Distance between masts is decreasing, Kapitan." This from lookout Webber.

"She's come to port then. Zigzagging. That means she must be an allied ship! A neutral like ourselves," and he grinned at his first officer, "would keep a straight course. Do you not think so, Carl?"

The Norden was steaming due north from a midday position, just taken, of latitude 5°S longitude 20°30'W. To the west, some 750 nautical miles away, was the coast of Brazil while in the opposite direction lay the coast of Africa but at nearly three times the distance.

Launched from a yard in Cuxhaven in 1937 as a cargo liner destined for the banana trade between the West Indies and Hamburg, she displaced a modest 8,000 tons. Her double pressure turbines gave a designed cruising speed of 20 knots and with steam provided by oil-fired boilers she was a clean ship. On her first voyage she had set a record for the run between St.Johns, Antigua, and the Elbe 1 buoy and in doing so sealed her fate.

Commandeered by the Kriegsmarine to become an armed merchant raider, her lower holds were falsified to contain extra fuel tanks. Her promenade deck was lengthened so that a six inch gun could be mounted at either end and on both sides thus giving a clear field of fire from a point abaft the bow to a point for'ard of the stern. Each was cleverly disguised with side plates which could be quickly raised so that from a distance she looked like any other merchant ship. Her passenger accommodation provided ample room for her large crew, many of whom would form prize crews.

Painted in her company's colours she had sailed in the June before the outbreak of war loaded with U-boat spares and munitions to act as both raider and supply ship in the South Atlantic.

The outbreak of hostilities found her in the small harbour of Puerto Deseado in Patagonia. Like the Altmarc, the supply ship for the battle-cruiser Admiral Graff Spee, she was deployed to this strategic position well before the declaration of war, making a mockery of Hitler's professed peaceful intentions. Now, after nearly three years without dry-docking, her hull was festooned with weed and her boilers and turbines desperately needed a major over-haul.

As one of the last raiders operating in the South Atlantic she was on her way to Bordeaux. With a large Spanish flag painted on her sides and the name San Jose and `Barcelona' as her port of registry clearly visible on her stern, they were hoping to make the run unhindered by Allied air or naval patrols.

Von Spreckles's career had many similarities to that of his opposite number on the Patriarch and, indeed, they were not dissimilar in looks, although the German was a little older with more angular cheeks. He had been a lieutenant while serving in the battle-cruiser Seydlitzÿand. Badly wounded at the battle of Jutland he walked with a pronounced limp. When the victorious allies insisted that the German fleet be scuttled he had returned to the family estate near Flensburgh just in time for his father's funeral. As the reparations of the Treaty of Versailles added to Germany's already desperate economic woes he watched the estate decline until he was forced to look for another source of income. With some influence from friend's of his late father he managed to return to sea in the merchant marine and eventually gained command of the Norden.

He was not enamoured with some of the Nazi party's ways of doing things but he nevertheless admired the fact that Hitler was improving the lot of the average German and willingly agreed to once again don the uniform of the Kriegsmarine.

Under Von Sprieckles command the Norden had been only reasonably successful as a raider; a fact that had nothing to do with his ability as a captain but rather to the luck of the draw in sighting allied ships. As a supply ship she had kept her rendezvous with several U-boats with meticulous precision thus saving them the long haul back to France. She replenished her supplies from the ships she sunk or captured as well as an occasional visit to the Argentine, where she even acquired some of the Graff Spee's crew who were supposedly interned there. She was, however, short of fuel oil for the boilers and was therefore proceeding at only ten knots. Thus it was that the Patriarch had unknowingly overhauled her.

At the time she sighted the Patriarch's topmasts there were a hundred and thirty one prisoners aboard. Her last victim, sunk only four days ago, had supplied forty two of those. That ship had been an old coal-burner and bound for Rio de Janeiro in ballast. Her master had surrendered without using his radio so that the Norden had been able to search her at will while her crew rowed their lifeboat over to their captor. The only thing they took from the victim had been the oars from the boat. The Norden's `bootsman' had noticed they were new and it seemed a pity to waste them. A broken one was left in the boat.

As the revolutions increased so did the vibrations, making the prisoners wonder what it might portend. Another allied casualty or could it, just possibly, be that one of the patrolling British cruisers had sighted them and rescue might be at hand?

The increased revolutions took the Norden's speed up to eighteen and a half knots, her dirty bottom would not let her do more, and she started slowly to overhaul the Patriarch which was zigzagging at her seventeen knots blithely unaware of the vessel coming up on her port quarter. It was not until those on the German's bridge could clearly see the two funnels appear between the masts ahead of them that the same gunner who had sighted the lifeboat two days previously, now reported an apparent over-taking vessel to the Patriarch's bridge.

Once again young Bentley called his captain from the pilot's cabin but this time Spencer had been asleep. Out on the wing of the bridge master and second mate studied the two masts with a single funnel between them and decided that, like their own vessel, she was a merchantman and travelling a bit faster than themselves. As she did not appear to be zigzagging they concluded that she must be a neutral.

At a quarter to four Wentle, together with Lewis and Brown, who served the doctor's table, started to pour tea for those passengers wishing to imbibe. While Mr. Akker's back was momentarily turned he had managed to hide a doughnut in his dumbwaiter just in case they were all gone by his own tea time.

In the chartroom Perkins placed a tea tray with its shining silver teapot and cakes on a locker ready for his captain who stood listening to Mctavish hand over the watch to Boulton.

Down in the officer's saloon Harry London poured tea for the assistant purser and the junior radio officer. Far below in the engine room the watch was also changing while on the boat deck the gunner and the other lookouts passed over their glasses. From the crow's nest high up the foremast the lookout descended the iron rungs.

Throughout the ship at this time of day there was activity. The two apprentices were quietly talking by the flag locker and in a few minutes the A.Bs and quartermasters would be relieved by their opposite numbers.

Spencer took the proffered cup from his tiger and told him he could go for his own tea. Then, sipping from the cup, he watched as the two officers went out onto the port wing to study the ship which was now about six or seven miles on their port quarter. The clouds from the rain squall were well to the west having passed to the north of the Patriarch taking the white horses from the wind with them. The sun shone on both vessels as McTavish told his chief that he estimated the following ship would pass clear of them at about two miles, allowing for the fact that their own vessel was at the moment on a port `zig' from the mean course. As the distant vessel did not appear to be zigzagging McTavish assumed her to be neutral. Anyway, as the over-taking vessel it was her duty to keep clear.

On the Norden the watches were also changing, only the atmosphere in her was totally different from that of her quarry. The crew moved with well drilled precision as they checked the starboard guns and made sure that all was ready the moment the order was received to open the gun ports.

Armed with machine-pistols the boarding crew, with polished leather pouches and belts shining in the light, well turned out despite their long time at sea and slightly frayed tropical uniforms, lounged in the vicinity of their launch.

Excitement was rife as all aboard the raider contemplated what was to come. This was the type of war for which they had been trained and why they had endured the lonely years far from home.

Not for them the war of the U-boat who had, perforce, to shoot first and ask questions after. Not for them the frightful conditions which the U-boat men endured. Instead they lived, by comparison, a life of luxury, all be it that at one stage they had been a year without going ashore.

They did not have to endure the terror of being depth charged, indeed they had not even heard a shot fired in anger against them. Up to now it was they who had done the firing. First there would be the challenge and possibly a shot across the enemy's bow. If she did not heave-to then, and only then, despite how some of the men felt, would they be at liberty to blast the merchantman to pieces.

In the meanwhile word had gone around that it would be another hour or so before they were in a position to go into action so there was time for another cigarette.

Under the Norden's bridge in the splendour of a very comfortable day cabin Kapitan Von Sprieckles took his tea. He had two competent officers in each watch and felt that there was no reason why he should not take his tea as usual. His steward, properly turned out in the uniform of the Kriegsmarine placed a tray on the table, clicked his heels and retired to his pantry. The Norden's first lieutenant poured the dark tea and added a slice of lemon and together the two officers contemplated what the ship out there might bring them. Certainly they should be able to replenish their bunkers and, if she had come from South America, as seemed likely from her course, there might be some interesting wine aboard!

As far as the Kapitan was concerned there would be only one drawback to sinking the enemy ship and that was if it meant more prisoners to look after. On the other hand he might be able to make it a prize and transfer the present prisoners to her. Then he would give her command to Carl Schmit with the hope that he would follow in the Altmark's footsteps and make Norway. There were still plenty of men aboard to form a prize crew as well as guard prisoners. Yes, that is what he might well do and it would be an even better end to their commission. In the meanwhile he would have another piece of freshly baked Kirsche Kuchen' which was one of his favourites.

Spencer had snatched two hours sleep after lunch and would take another after dinner before sitting in his chair in the wheelhouse while young Stickland did the eight to twelve watch. He had told the tiger to bring his dinner forward to six o'clock while on this passage so that he could take that extra hour. When they got farther north and more liable to attack, he might not be so lucky. Now, afternoon tea finished, he wandered out onto the bridge wing where every now and then Boulton took a look at the ship coming up from astern.

It was quite pleasant out there and he spent some time, in between Boulton's carrying out the changes of course, chatting to the chief officer. By half past five the overtaking vessel was about three or four miles away with the large Spanish flag on her side now visible through the glasses. The sun was getting low in the west and occasionally dodged behind long streaks of cloud which had formed on the horizon. Clouds which, with the sun behind them, took on a dark hue with silver edges that were slowly changing to gold. In the east it looked as if another shower might eventuate, however, the barometer was steady and portended another calm night.

Down in the fo'c'sle Wentle had a quick shower. It was nice not to have any water restrictions and have to wash in salt water. He then decided to sit on number three hatch until the necessity of serving dinner would call him back to the saloon. He doubled up his life jacket to make a soft seat and also because someone had told him that if he sat on the sun warmed canvas for too long he would get piles. A few minutes later Harry London joined him. From where they sat on the fore end of the hatch they could just see the vessel coming up astern but then the Patriarch altered course to starboard on her eternal zigzagging. At 1745 she came back to port to steer her base course for a while before making the next zig to port. Now the vessel was almost on her beam and considerably nearer.

Just after 1700hrs the first lieutenant of the Norden had pointed out to his captain that the merchantman they were closing on had no gun on her stern, something that for an allied ship was most unusual. Could it possibly be that the British had a `Q' ship, the term used in that earlier war to describe ships like theirs, and that if they got too near her might she also suddenly produce guns ready to do battle? It was a disquieting thought, which decided Von Sprieckles to stay six thousand metres off their quarry so that he had plenty of sea room in which to manoeuvre should the unthinkable happen. The seat up on the monkey bridge which hid their telescopic range finder was folded down and the instrument raised so they could gauge the distance exactly and the guns could be set. It was highly unlikely that the instrument would be seen by the enemy.

At 1755 Wentle looked at his watch and thought it was nearly time for him to go. With the sun now sinking rapidly to the westward horizon it was only when it was behind a cloud and the boys not blinded by it, that they were able to look at the ship out on their beam. Without glasses they could not clearly see when the Norden uncovered her starboard six inch guns, swung them outboard and then trained them on the Patriarch. What Wentle did see and clearly read, was the slowly winking light. Sent slowly because the German signaller was aware that many allied merchantmen were not able to read a fast signal lamp.

Wentle read out loud, thanking his days in the school cadet corps. `Stop your ship, do not use your radio' and to lend emphasis to the message, as he read the word `use', there was a deep sounding crack followed by the whine of a shell as it passed slightly ahead of the Patriarch.

Up on the bridge Jones was watching the clock as the minutes crept on towards the next alteration of course so he knew that it was precisely 1757 hours when the gun went off and without exception all on the bridge jumped in alarm. The port lookout had just noticed that the other ship was signalling and was about to report the fact when he heard the shell and ducked. In fact the first two words of the message had passed unseen and by the time officers and lookouts had recovered from the shock of once again being fired at, the message had gone un-read except by the saloon-boy. Now as it was being repeated an ensign was broken out from the Norden's gaff; red with a black cross etched in white and in the middle a large dark swastika on a white circle.

For perhaps five seconds all on the Patriarch's bridge stared in disbelief as the Norden made clear her identity. The chief officer, who with the captain had been facing for'ard and therefore had not seen the signal lamp, raised his voice and shouted at the lookout, although the man was only a few feet from him.

"What the hell did he say, Cartwright?" forgetting that the A.B could not read a lamp and that the second quartermaster was on the starboard wing.

Wentle, somewhat stupefied by what had happened and rooted to the deck, heard the raised voice and automatically called up; "Stop your ship do not use your radio!"

"Good God. The saloon-boy!" Spencer said in amazement, looking down to the hatch and noting who had called the message.

In the wheel-house Jones, who had not ducked at the sound of the gun or the whine of the shell, clutched the hand rail in front of him and started to shake, his thoughts racing. `Not again. This was not possible; to be shelled twice in one voyage? Definitely not. He was dreaming and someone would wake him in a minute to tell him it was time to go on watch!' The chief officer's raised voice brought him back to reality. Although no one had given him an order he moved his hand a few inches across to the alarm bell button and pressed it for `action stations'. It seemed the right thing to do and also he must remember the time, that was most important; later he was bound to be asked to fill in the log-book!

For a further five seconds Spencer just stared at the Norden and then, as had happened only a few weeks earlier, subconsciously his Naval training came to the fore. 'When caught with your pants down and your guns won't bear give the enemy the smallest target!'

"Hard a starboard. Emergency speed!" The order was given without thought. Despite the three weeks of peace in the port they had so recently left Spencer was still tired and despondent. Now, faced with this new situation, nearly three years of war took their toll. His brain was numb and he felt physically sick, as if his body was shrinking from within.

The quartermaster on the wheel started to spin it; round and round it went and slowly the rudder indicator moved across the green arch until it registered thirty.

"Thirty of wheel on Sir." Years of training motivated the report despite the quartermaster's stomach tying itself in knots.

Automatically Jones had moved to the engine telegraph and sent the pre-arranged signal. The crash of the gun and whine of the shell had gone but the alarm bells were screaming their message and it seemed that the ship was in bedlam!

In the saloon there was once again the sound of knives and forks tinkling to the deck backed up by the noise of breaking crockery. On the galley stoves saucepans slid to the end of the hob while the cooks tried to stay on their feet. Some passengers, not used to adapting their stance to quick movements of the ship like the crew, fell over. In the shade of the starboard boat deck one of the two children gave a screech as she was rolled over and only just saved herself from going overboard.

Wentle had one foot on the first rung up the emergency ladder to the boat deck and had to stop climbing as gravity tried to dislodge him.

"What are we going to do, Sir?" As the ship heeled Boulton gripped the hand rail and looked at his captain.

"Do Charles?"

Boulton was horrified to see the vacant look on Spencer's face. He seemed to be staring with unseeing eyes at the chief officer, oblivious to the Patriarch as she turned eastwards. At that moment both the Norden's guns belched smoke and two pillars of water erupted well clear ahead and to port of the Patriarch.

The sound of the two heavy guns going off almost together jolted Spencer's mind back to reality. Much to Boulton's relief the vacant look disappeared.

"First I think we had better go to boat stations. Even if we had a gun I doubt we could fight that damned ship, so change that alarm." Then he gave steering orders until they were heading at right angles away from the German. Ahead lay darkness but would they be able to reach it in time? It was unlikely. They would be overtaken well before the night could hide them. He was needlessly hazarding the lives of all on board if the shelling continued for there would be no escape this time.

"Port twenty. Stop both!" But before they completed the turn and their drop in speed became apparent a shell came aboard. The mizzen mast slowly collapsed to starboard as, one by one, the shrouds broke. Brightman had left the hospital only moments before and escaped death by a hair's breadth.

Spencer was distraught, realising that this was the end for his ship. Assuming that the German raider would take them aboard internment lay ahead for them all for God know's how many years. But he knew he had made a very wrong decision by turning away from their aggressor. He must stop the shelling.

"Jones, the lamp. Tell him that we are surrendering!" but Charles Boulton took up the Aldis and sent the signal himself not trusting the youngster to get it right. Clickety-clack went the shutter at a speed which surprised the German signalman, who replied `I am sending a boarding party'. Of course they would. Then it occurred to Spencer how he might be able to fight on. The German had played it dirty by coming up under Spanish colours, so why shouldn't he use subterfuge ?

"Charles!" The Chief Officer put the Aldis back in its bracket, turned and looked quizzically at his captain, glad to see a more positive attitude even if the voice was strained and weary.

"Get everyone away in the port boats as quickly as you can and then somehow delay their boat but don't endanger life. As soon as you're clear I shall get under way again but it's vital that the Germans must not be able to board us. No `ifs or buts' just do it. Please! Jones, all of you, go to your boats. No, Mr.Moore." He stretched out a hand towards his chief radio officer who was standing halfway in the short passage to the radio-room. "Not you. Tell your chaps to throw the code books overboard and if possible I would like one of you to stay aboard although I must warn that it could be rather uncomfortable."

"Jones!" Charles Boulton's voice quivered slightly. "You heard the Captain's orders. As fast as you can make it to the boat deck and let everyone know!" For the last time the apprentice slid down the ladders but without the sang-froid so apparent before.

Boulton let the others on the bridge precede him to the ladders and took a step towards Spencer looking into the man's eyes. In them he saw that this would be a last farewell and as he took the outstretched hand, a lump blocked his throat.

"Good luck, Charles and thank you. God go with you." Then for a moment Spencer was alone on the bridge.

The engine room! Damn, he should have acted sooner; would he be too late? He had ordered `Stop Engines' and not `Finished' so they should be idling. Quickly he crossed to the engine room 'phone and cranked the handle. A moment's delay and the chief's voice was on the other end.

"Chief we're going to abandon ship. Has word got down to you?...It has?" Spencer was now quite calm and in control of himself. "Damned amazing how quickly the grape vine functions. Listen Brian, as soon as everyone is clear I'm going to get underway. Can one person get those toys of yours going and then leave them at as many revs as possible?...Fine, but it may not be too healthy for whoever stays. Once we're under way it will be a case of a quick retreat and jump off the ass end! And Brian, please open all the sea cocks you can right now. Jerry musn't get a damned thing from the Old Girl! Thanks." Then he hung up.

`Old Girl'. The term used by Jim Baines back in Avonmouth and Durban, now he had used it while deliberately setting in motion her sinking. He felt that he was almost committing murder by ordering the engineers to open the sea-cocks to hasten her death. He wondered where Baines was now? He would have liked to have been able to say goodbye to the old sea dog for he knew that there was little likelihood of them meeting again.

CHAPTER 16

Jim Baines, senior quartermaster of the Patriarch, was by number two starboard boat when Apprentice Jones came out from the lounge yelling that everyone was to get into the port boats and shear off damn quickly. Baines realized that the end was near for their ship unless the Germans put a prize crew aboard but whatever happened it looked as if there was no alternative to a prison camp. At his age he didn't like the idea at all; rather take his chances with the sea. He took Wentle's arm in his gnarled hand.

" Y' fancy being a prisoner young Dick?"

"Not really," replied the saloon-boy still not fully understanding the situation.

"Neither do I, lad so I'm goin' ta sail the accident-boat away from this lot! She's light an' should move easier than these big 'uns. Y' with me boy?"

Wentle was suddenly reminded of the cabin boy `Jim' in `Treasure Island' when asked that question by `Long John Silver'.

"I'm with you, Sir!" Somehow Wentle felt that he would be safe with Old Father Neptune. At that moment the second officer, with the girl from the captain's table, came past on their way to the port side and Baines quickly told him what was in his mind.

"May I come too please. I have a fiance waiting for me in London."

"It'll be hard miss, make no mistake!"

"I can take it. Saw all sorts of nasty things as a nurse. Please?" and she smiled one of those easy smiles that Wentle had seen so often over the past few days.

"Second, y' with us?"

A brief thought of Fiona growing up without a father or mother made his decision for him. "Let's go!"

The four broke into a run, through the lounge and down the two flights of stairs, through the shambles that was the saloon, through the galley where Wentle slipped on spilt soup and crashed against the baker's oven, out past number three hatch and up the ladder to the starboard accident boat. Baines went to the winch brake and freed the becket whilst Wentle helped the woman into the boat and McTavish knocked off the gripes so that the boat swung free of the ships side.

Before he had forgotten it but not now. "The bung, God help me! This boat must have one so where was it?" he mused out loud.

Spencer heard the sound of running feet on the welldeck and then voices from the accident boat deck. What the blazes was happening? He walked from the port wing to starboard and looked down.

"What the devil is going on, Second!" he demanded. "I ordered that everyone should use the port boats!"

"Sorry, Capt'n but I'm making a run for it. Bugger being a prisoner!" It was Baines who answered. "Begging y'r pardon, Sir. You com'ng?"

For a brief moment Spencer hesitated. Here was his chance to live. He need only go down a short flight of stairs and he would be in the boat before they lowered it. He could let the enemy have the Patriarch's oil and stores. He'd ordered the sea cocks to be opened and if the Germans got aboard before they were past shutting again he had at least done his duty and no-one would blame him.

"Lower away, Jim and for God's sake get a move on. Good luck!" The die was cast and time was running out.

To keep her guns bearing on the target the Norden had followed the Patriarch only partly on her turn. Von Sprieckles was still not sure if his quarry might turn on him, and that running away from them was just a ploy while the British sailors rushed to clear their guns. Keeping his distance just made Spencer's idea possible. At about two miles off the Norden glided almost to a stop slipping her launch while still making a couple of knots.

From the Patriarch's boat deck came the sounds of her boats being lowered to the water. Wire falls slid over squeaking blocks as winch brakes were taken off and in a higgledy piggledy line five boats dropped down the ship's side. Two went in a jerky motion because the men on the winches were not sure of themselves and applied too little or too much brake so the first boat hit the sea with such force that water came up both sides of it, wetting its occupants and jarring their backs. Then the seaman who had lowered it jumped out and caught a life line. Desperate not to be left behind he went down to the waiting boat hand over hand with legs free and kicked a seated passenger in the face as he landed with a thump.

To the uninitiated it all seemed out of control but Spencer noted that there was no confusion and little talking amongst the passengers. Earlier he had heard one of the children cry out but she had stopped when her mother made a joke out of what was happening to them.

When Spencer had finished on the telephone to the engine room Mr.Moore asked for orders because, since it was his watch, he would be staying behind. He assured the captain that the emergency aerial to the for'ard funnel would work on the H.F transmitter and that it would only take less than half a minute to tune it up before he could start sending. He had then gone to the chart and taken off their position and made out his message form before pre-setting the aerial matching tuner for the emergency aerial. That done he descended to the captain's quarters and took the briefcase from the desk cupboard, catching its chain on the door handle as he left the day-room. Out on the small piece of deck which was the master's special preserve, he threw the case overboard.

Back on the bridge Mr Moore waited quietly with the man who had virtually signed his death warrant.

Together the two men on the Patriarch's bridge watched as the last boat pulled away from the ship. From the starboard side came the call `All clear, Sir' and the sound of a motor starting up.

One of the lifeboats was fitted with an engine and Spencer watched as Boulton steered straight for the launch, now only about half a mile away.

"O.K David, stand-by but don't tune up until I call; those guns will be trained right at us." So saying Spencer crossed to the engine-room 'phone, cranked the handle and immediately a voice the other end growled.

"All right mon, I can hear ye; ye dinna have to blast ma ears off!"

"Who the devil's that?" Spencer snapped beginning to panic as the voice the other end was not the one he had expected.

"McIntosh, your second engineer, who else d'ye think?"

"Where the blazes is the chief?" Surely things had not gone wrong down below at this late stage!

"I sent him awa'. Ye dinna think I'd let a wee laddie like him tak ma engines on their last run, did ye?"

McIntosh! Of course. He should have known! The man had been with the ship since she was in the builder's yard and was more than a little sore when the company had sent Brian Tingle, a much younger man with a B.Sc in engineering, to take over as chief. A dour Scot, McIntosh loved his engines more than his wife and was often heard talking to them in caressing tones! Of course he would be the one to stay behind.

"All right Mac, start 'em up and give her all you can. Then come up and jump for it! Good luck!"

"Oche aye, as ye say Captain." The phone went dead.

Spencer moved over to the wheel and turned it until the indicator showed twenty of port. As soon as he felt the engines start to come to life he called out: "O.K Sparks start transmitting. We're on our own now!"

Walking out to the port wing he saw that Boulton had his boat across the bow of the German launch and that the others were catching up to him. `Good for you, Charles' he thought and then saw the German push the Patriarch's boat aside and plunge forward towards the boats behind where it ploughed straight through the starboard oars of one smashing them to pieces. The chase was on!

Slowly the big merchantman gathered way and perceptibly the position of the German raider started to alter as the Patriarch answered her helm. To Spencer it seemed an age before the speed became appreciable and he was sure that the launch would catch him and German seamen would come swarming up the trailing life-lines now hanging forlornly down to the water.

Spencer moved into the wheel-house and took up a position behind the wheel. God knows how many years it was since he had actually steered a ship. He wondered if he still had the `feel' for it. Perhaps he should have asked Jim Baines to stay behind as well? From the radio-room he heard the tapping of a Morse key as David Moore let the world know what was happening. Then, inexplicably, there was another sound but from right aft on the boat deck. A machine gun stuttered into life.

When they had gone to boat stations, Harry London had heard the chief officer loudly telling those in charge of the boats what was required of them. Looking at the advancing German launch he thought how vulnerable it seemed from here on the boat deck. Its crew were a mass of white who, when it got closer, would become individuals and would be the first Germans he had seen. A German pilot had killed his father for no other reason than the red van made a nice vulnerable target. Suddenly London was filled with hatred. Gone were any thoughts of his mother and family, even Debbie faded to nothing as he realized that here was his chance to even things for his father.

Quietly he backed off into the lounge and then ran the length of the starboard boat deck to the locker where the machine-guns had been replaced after leaving B.A. Like many others of the crew he had been instructed in the use of these weapons against aircraft and at action stations he was the loader for one of them. Now he wrenched open the locker and took out the heavy gun, carrying it round to the sun-lounge shelter on the port side, making sure he was not seen by the few crew still near the boats. Running back to the locker he took out two pans of ammunition and then stood waiting until the last man had slid down the life lines and the deck became empty and silent.

Left momentarily with nothing to do he felt like he had just run a tremendously fast race, his heart thundered inside him leaving him panting. He clenched and unclenched his fists repeatedly trying to ease the pain. Beneath his feet he felt the deck quiver as the Patriarch's engines were connected to the propeller shafts and once again she started to move ahead.

Picking up the gun he struggled to place it on its mounting, his lack of height making it difficult but finally it was there and he pushed in the locking pin. Doubling back to the sun lounge he picked up the ammunition pans, clicking one in position on the gun and dropping the other to the deck.

He watched the boats and saw that one seemed to be up to the launch while the others were being rowed after it, with oars out of time and hitting each other. Then the launch started to come clear of the boat across its bows. Once again he had to wait.

The Norden's launch was covering the water at about seven knots and was throwing some spray back from her bows. A light breeze had come up and there were a few white-caps to be seen on the blue and darkening sea. Still London waited until he guessed that his target was about a quarter of a mile away and well clear of the lifeboats. He cocked the gun and then, raising himself onto the balls of his feet in order to depress the gun and get the Germans in his sights, he opened fire.

The ammunition had been loaded `one in five tracer' so that in the fading light the path of the bullets became quite visible as they sped towards the target; or they should have. The recoil from the machine gun was more than London had expected for he had not actually fired one before. Now he altered his stance and gripped tighter as he brought the stream of bullets down and into the water alongside the Germans. He tried to shift slightly right but the gun took over again and the bullets went harmlessly into the air.

He had once used a friend's four-ten shot-gun up in Friar's wood and thought the kick from that was bad enough but it was child's play compared to this. He stopped firing and moved his feet farther apart.

Taking a deep breath he fired again and this time saw a sailor rise up and fall back. Suddenly he was like a demon possessed. "Die you bastards. Bloody well die!" he screamed as the coxswain fell dead and the launch slewed sideways presenting a better target while more and more bullets tore into it until the gun stopped firing when there were none left. Sobbing he knocked off the empty pan and replaced it. Totally bereft of all feeling other than the hatred and pain inside him he resumed shooting; but he could not get his aim again for the Patriarch had gathered speed and the launch was now well astern.

Muttering "Dad, Dad," again and again he sank exhausted to his knees and then slowly crumpled over in a heap to the deck. And so he died. His young body made old before its time by those weeks on the raft and his mind so full of anguish that he just gave up. The sleep he had craved at the burial of Mr.Giles finally encompassed him.

Momentarily Spencer had left the wheel to see who was firing. The diminutive figure of the messboy had been clearly identifiable from the bridge and once again he was amazed that two of the boys aboard his ship could have acted with such distinction. He had, of course, no idea why London had acted as he did but now there was no way the boarding party could catch him. Then the first shell since getting under way landed on the fo'c'sle sending the anchor winch into the air to come crashing down on number one hatch. As the noise subsided and despite the singing in his ears caused by the exploding shell he was still able to hear the tapping of the Morse key.

Under his feet he felt the increasing vibration as the engines gathered momentum after being clutched in to the propeller shafts.

As soon as he realised that the Patriarch was moving again Von Sprieckles ordered his own ship to Voll veraus and got underway. Now he knew that the Englishman was no `Q ship', particularly when only a machine gun began firing. Furious at the sight of his men dying in their launch he came further to starboard and crossed the oncoming Patriarch's bow ordering his gunnery officer to fire at will.

Spencer saw the Norden altering course and tried to follow her round for his idea was to ram her if he could. Again there was the belch of smoke as the guns fired. Had Spencer not altered course when he did the two shells would probably have landed on the boat deck or around the funnels. Instead one came straight into the wheel house sending flying glass to decapitate the Patriarch's captain, granting his wish that, when his time came, he would go quickly.

The shell entered and exploded in the chartroom against the after bulkhead, behind which the chief radio officer had just heard Freetown naval station acknowledge his Mayday message. Unlike his captain he was not killed instantly but thrown heavily backwards into his auxiliary charging board to lie with broken back and punctured lung in frightful agony as he watched flames erupt above him. Just before they reached him the pain mercifully brought unconsciousness.

With no one on the wheel the pressure from the rising speed forced the rudder back amidships and as if a ghost were there, the spokes of the wheel moved around on their own as the Patriarch began to die. Aft the hospital flat was now ablaze. The flames there and on the bridge were the only living things aboard for two shells had pierced the engine room and killed the lone engineer as his engines vibrated almost to the point of parting with their huge beds. Slowly the sea water rose higher and higher bringing with it the dirty, oily bilge water, which was now sullying the unseeing McIntosh's almost pristine engine room.

The Norden's captain continued to circle the now flaming ship until he was able to cross her stern in a figure of eight and give his port side gunners callous practice. With all eyes on the blazing vessel no one noticed that they almost ran down a small boat heading into the darkness of the approaching night.

For those in that boat it was a macabre sight to behold the end of their ship. Her tormentor pumping shell after shell into the grey hull until a flare called the Norden's attention to her sinking launch.

Like a modern `Marie Celeste' the Patriarch steamed unattended to the northwest sinking by the head with smoke coming from two large black holes in the side of the engine room and her upper works an inferno.

For several minutes the four in the boat watched the funeral pyre, stark against the black streaky clouds, thinking of the four gallant men who had died so unashamedly just to deny the enemy what he wanted.

As if she knew what was happening to her the Patriarch stayed afloat just long enough to cock a snoot at those who would have raped her. Finally her engines stopped and she came to a weary halt, pausing for a few moments to let her soul depart and then disappeared beneath the sea as the last rays of the sun sank over the horizon.

As the water quenched the flames Baines removed his sailor's hat and Wentle remembered those words of the old quartermaster back at that first boat drill. `So many fine ships; and men too.' The woman shed a silent tear, sensitive to the two men's grief. For the ship's second officer there was no feeling, he had already suffered too much in this war.

EPILOGUE
DECEMBER 1944
BRISTOL

Len Wentle was snoring gently in his winged arm chair. With slippered feet on a dumpty and his head resting to one side he gave the appearance of being at peace with his world. In the hearth, behind the fireguard, a coal fire glowed giving the small lounge a gentle warmth which kept at bay the dismal weather outside.

As was his custom after closing the bars at two thirty he was taking `forty winks'. On the side table an empty plate held a few crumbs from the meagre sandwich of plain bread, the butter ration was finished yesterday, and tomato pickle which had been his lunch. Over the last eighteen months, ever since he had known his son was missing, food had lost any interest for him. Had it not been for the fact that he still had a daughter somewhere in the army he would have given up living.

It had been a friend in the Pilot service who had told him that the Patriarch was now well overdue and must be presumed sunk with no news of any survivors and that, no doubt, an official letter would be forthcoming in due course.

When her berth in Avonmouth had been cancelled after a two week wait the friend had made a few discreet enquiries that she had not been diverted to Liverpool. An acquaintance in the owner's office confirmed that they had just been officially advised of her loss. Of course the loss of a vessel did not necessarily also mean the loss of her crew. They could well be in their lifeboats or have been picked up by a foreign ship or their attackers and on their way to goodness knows where, so there was still hope.

Although he had felt great foreboding Len had kept alive the hope that his son would still come home. Then almost a year ago the official letter from the company had arrived and he had gone to pieces for a day. His chest had felt as if he had been kicked by a mule and his stomach was in continual cramp. The anguish in him knew no bounds. A distant cousin, who had been helping since his wife had left, opened the pub on her own.

The brewery traveler, who had called that day, sympathised with him, for he too had felt the pain as he held his own brother in his arms as he died long ago on the beach at Gallipoli.

Slowly the numbness had diminished. In front of the customers he put on a facade of pride that his boy had done his duty, but he questioned the sense of it. Why, after he and his generation had gone to war, was it happening all over again?

The worst time was at night after the customers had gone and he was alone. Then the darkness brought back memories of the battles he had fought and he would often scream himself awake as his men were shot to pieces around him, only the nearest was always his son and it got to the point that sleep became a horror for him. Strangely he did not dream while taking his afternoon nap and for that he was grateful, but now the front door bell wakened him and for a moment he was not sure what was happening .... then came that faint hope... 'Could it be Richard?'

He stumbled across the room and down the short hall, his heart racing as he turned the latch and opened the door.

"Rich..." he started to say but the word died in his throat for the man in the blue navy Burbery and cap was not his son.

"Captain Wentle, Sir? I'm John Spencer. Could you spare me a few minutes?"

Len Wentle was mystified, he had not been addressed by rank since the last regimental reunion in '38. "Yes of course, come in. Hang your coat here. You look pretty wet."

"I wasn't sure where to get off the bus so walked a bit further than I need have". As he hung up his Burbery the older man was able to see his visitor wore the insignia of a lieutenant in the naval reserve.

Seated in the lounge the navy man said, "Sir, did you have a son, Richard who was aboard the motor vessel Patriarch?" Receiving a dumb nod from his listener he continued. "Did this watch belong to him?"

Len Wentle took the proffered timepiece and unstoppable tears welled up in his eyes as he answered in an almost inaudible voice. "Yes it was his. The guard was mine in the last war and I thought it might bring him good luck. How did you get it?"

"I thought it looked old and the inscription inside bore your name and the date."

"Oh God!" the now distraught father muttered as the picture of him giving it to the boy came back. "Yes I had that put in when we were on leave in Katmandu before being sent to Mesopotamia. My son," and now he could not contain the sob in his voice, "my son is dead Lieutenant?"

"Yes Sir, I am afraid so." He produced a signet ring with the initials R O W on it. "This was his as well, Sir?"

"Yes, but how…?" he tailed off, looking pleadingly into the younger man's eyes.

"Captain.Wentle, my father was captain of the Patriarch when she was attacked by a raider and, presumably, since no more was heard from her, sunk. Naturally when we were detached from a convoy to investigate a lifeboat and found it bore the name Patriarch I was more than interested. The boat contained what was left of four bodies, three of which were wearing sailors' gear; the fourth was that of a woman.

When preparing the bodies for burial our doctor noticed the watch and ring and our captain allowed me to keep them. During my next leave, thanks to Dad's company, I was able to see a copy of the crew list of her last voyage and from it gleaned this address for I was sure that the saloon-boy must have been your son.

The company offered to see you got these items but I wanted to bring them myself. I'm sure that's what my father would have wished. I would have been to see you sooner only we were sent for a refit in Norfolk, Virginia, and then various other places."

While the young man had been speaking the one time commander of a regiment had composed himself. He realised that they both had lost something which could never be replaced. He also realised that the young man was handling this meeting far better than he was.

"Sir, it may be of some comfort for you to know that, according to the doctor, all in the boat had died instantly from a shot to the head. A U-boat with a skipper of the worst kind probably came across them."

"Your father?"

"No news of him or any of the others."

"I see, I'm sorry."

There followed a short silence. "Lieutenant, would you keep this watch for me and when this damned war is over bring it back?" He stood up, shoulders no longer bowed with grief, and held out his hand.

Tonight he knew that at last he would be able to sleep.

* * * * * *

They shall not grow old, as we that are left
grow old
Age shall not weary them, nor the years condemn.
At the going down of the sun and in the morning
We will remember them.

Laurence Binyon